the
'idiot spy'
(the series)
book three of ten

marco, marco, marco polo

c. benjamin lattimore

marco, marco, marco polo
Published: September 2020
Printed in the United States of America
ISBN: 978-1-7334945-2-6

This book was published with the assistance of Writer's Relief.

Cover design by Writer's Relief

a lattidreamer™ publication
© C. Benjamin Lattimore, 2020

To my wife, Marisa,
my number 1 editor,
words cannot express my appreciation
for the many hours of competent, intuitive
suggestions and corrections
that you offered for book # 3.
Lucky me!

ACKNOWLEDGEMENTS

To my wonderful and smart children, Christopher, Monica, and Courtney, as well as my grandchildren, Isaiah and Desmond, for just being special. A unique and heartfelt expression of love to my sister Mary E. and my brother Darryl A. Venerate regards to Maurice Cheeks and Reggie Wilkes.

A special shout out to Marisa, Dawn Marie and Nikki; their contributions were priceless. A very special thank you to Writers Relief—Jill.

Lots of love ethereally to my mother, Mary Alice, my father, Walthro M., my little sister, Barbara Ann, and my brother, Walter Eugene, and to two special friends, Gordon Gant, a longtime friend, and to my witty brother from another mother—Joseph Bongiavanni II.

CHAPTER ONE

A kiss is defined as: a touch with the lips as a sign of reverence, greeting, love, or sexual desire. In the case of Zanthius Beckmire De Lombardo, the significance of a kiss took that meaning to a new level when he touched lips with a spy who inserted a capsule in his mouth and made him swallow, quite the opposite of today's macho man's mantra. The moniker for Zanthius, is the 'idiot spy', a term that has a double meaning. To his friends and family, as well as admirers, it was a sign of respect for the manner in which he, his family, and a few loyal friends outsmarted the competition. To his foes, it was their impertinent way of discounting him and making excuses for a non-spy that could avoid capture, annihilate hundreds of highly trained mercs, and still be alive and in possession of the actual or fictional blueprints for the Carbon Factor a new dirty bomb.

As the world began to realize and agree on the negative facts and impacts of carbon on humans, as well as the environment, nations signed on to the Paris Treaty. This global alliance was formed to reduce individual country's footprints from the use of carbon on the environment and, was dedicated to the premise of exploring alternative fuel sources to energize the homes, plants, businesses, and governments of the world. Russia, which has a substantial reliance upon carbon-based fuels, was one of those nations signing the treaty. However, in the case of Russia, there was a dual purpose for agreeing to reduce its utilization of carbon. First, it made sense. Second, it had discovered a way to harness and dispel the by-products of expended carbon-based fuels. By using the virtual reality technology of Facebook, a Russian scientist discovered a way to mix and match key scientific elements and inadvertently developed a new miniaturized dirty bomb that was carbon-based, and exportable in tiny containers. Of course, the Russians signed on to the treaty not planning to adhere to it and, with the intent of regaining its prominence as a global superpower.

The 'idiot spy' and his band of "has-beens" were about to make the playing field equal for their side, the United States of America, and the rest of the free world. Not only would that be made possible as a result of a simple kiss as defined earlier, a touch with the lips and the passing of information, but also because of the placement of a condom and a card from a strip club in the wallet of the 'idiot spy', both made in Mother Russia. Yes, the question remains whether the formula is fact or fiction. It is the 'idiot spy', his family and their friends who control the answer. There is one constant in this equation, and that is, a lot of people will die, and many will be tortured. The few will conquer the many because they are the benefic, frequently the wretched, and occasionally, the despicable.

CHAPTER TWO

As the three planes landed in Wyoming, the group was met by Clyde in his shiny new school bus. He welcomed the group and was told that the pilots needed at least eight hours of uninterrupted sleep before they could embark on dispersing group members to places near and far. Bernstein, Brown, Jilkes, and John Lee were scheduled on flights back East, but Brown could sense a change in Bernstein's behavior. He deduced it involved the issue of making Yvett whole, on so many fronts, which provided a complex scenario for Bernstein. Brown suggested to Bernstein that he take this valuable time to secure, or unsecure, his relationship with Yvett and not make the trip back East. Bernstein wanted to get back East to check on his properties, and an old girlfriend/lover that he was not committed to.

John Lee said to Jilkes, "You know I don't think I be making that trip back home. As a matter of fact, I'm going to ask Asiram to look at my plans and give me some ideas for my new house. I don't think I be ready to go back to that place where that wench, Scottie, hung my woman, cut her inners out and placed them in my refrigerator like she be some animal or something. I also sure as hell don't want to go back there knowing that my favorite pig is buried right outside of my front door. No sir, I think I just be staying here to get my head right. I will say that I will miss your black ass, but I'll be alright. How about you?"

Jilkes looked at John Lee and replied, "What about that property you wanted me to look at? Don't you still think it's a good idea?"

"I don't think your woman be liking that kind of living where people are slow and don't give a shit about rushing for any reason," John Lee replied.

Though the two men knew each other so well that they could complete each other's thoughts, Jilkes finally confessed, "My woman and I ain't slept in the same bed in two years. She found religion, and the preacher found her purse, and she gives him and his church a shit load of my money. I don't know if I told you, but she gave him $500k for his building fund, and I know the two of them are building more than a church. In other words, he's doing her and she's liking it. I don't have a problem with it. I don't want to be with her, but I don't want her spending my money on that new age Elmer Gantry, you know, stealing in the name of the Lord. So, I had my lawyer draw up some papers just in case I didn't survive this shit. I left a shit load of money to her, but the bulk of my funds to you with the proviso that you develop schools and help people with it."

John Lee stared at Jilkes and broke out into a hysterical crying episode and finally between sniffles and blowing his nose said, "I left my entire estate to you, with that thing you called a proviso, to take care of my current family on my farm."

"Listen, you don't have to make shit up as we go along, unless it is for our safety." John Lee reached into his wallet and pulled out a raggedy piece of paper. He showed it to Jilkes who broke into tears and said, "At least with you, I don't have to worry about you cheating on me. I love you, Man." The two men hugged and expressed their undying affection for one another.

The Sarge walked up on them and deadpanned, "Who is the pitcher and who is the catcher?"

John Lee said, "We don't do that pitching or that there catching shit. What we be doing is making sure that we all live to see another day, and in the middle of that, help out some people who don't have what we have." Beckmire's smile turned to a smirk that turned into blurry eyes.

Beckmire quietly said, "I hope you will never tell any of the others, but you two people are the reasons why we are still alive today. You guys are my spirits, you keep us focused and you watch our backs. I made light of your embrace, but I want to tell you that I, or rather we, owe you guys our lives. What's more important is, that it is not only about us. It's about us helping people help themselves. I love you and would take two bullets for your asses, but keep in mind, my limit is two."

Everyone laughed and Jilkes said, "Old Country, I can handle my shit by phone. All I need to do is call my lawyer and the deal is done. Why don't we go into town and see if there are any architects who can render us some drawings of potential palatial homes? Oh, and if my place isn't next to yours then the deal is off."

John Lee grabbed him and said, "I hopes you not be competing with my new favorite pig, but I like that idea and we can, like, talk about starting some programs where people learn to be self-indulging."

"I think you mean self-sufficient, but it's okay, don't worry, I'm going to teach your country ass to speak English before I die," Jilkes teased.

"And I'm going to teach you to speak human," John Lee retorted solemnly.

Beckmire interjected, "I understand you both, though I'm not sure I understand the meaning of what you say most times unless it's critical to our survival. I love you guys and if you can stay, I would feel so much better about surviving this shit."

Jilkes said, "He can't go home because he's stupid. I can't go home because my wife loves my preacher, so there you have it. We ain't going nowhere. Is that right, Big Country?"

"You should know because you replaced my favorite pig and where you go, I be going," John Lee stated.

The Sarge saluted them and walked away.

Jilkes said, "He has never done that before. What the hell does that mean?"

John Lee hesitated, but finally exclaimed, "Now, that be some strange mess to me! I ain't never seen him salute anyone including them there messed up generals and that asshole captain that we wanted to kill when we were in the Nam. I guess we be having to ask him to give us the 811 on that one."

"Damn, son, can't you get anything right? It would be called the 411 not 811." Jilkes stated.

"Yo black ass understood what I was saying, didn't you?"

As Beckmire entered his room, his phone rang. It was Walter who said, "Fate must want you people to be involved in this high intensified drama. I had the damn thing in my hand and gave it back to you. Now, how crazy is that?"

"Walter, stop the horseshit. You and your people didn't know what you had and it was up to a bunch of senior citizens to figure out the meaning of a condom and a card from a strip joint in Russia. Are you in training to be a spy or are you attempting to graduate from the freshmen class to the next phase of where stupid people go?" Beckmire inquired.

"Can you stop being so condescending to me? I got those two planes attached to your non-profit. Cousin, everyone agrees those are some expensive aircraft that would be best served in the hands of people who do wet-work for our government," Walter announced.

"Wait a minute." Beckmire interrupted. "I said that we would entertain the notion of conducting some missions, if the work is based upon ethical factors, things that you clearly lack an understanding of, but that are particularly important to me and my boys. I will not allow you to arbitrarily assign work to us. Any involvement on our part will be after a vote by my men to make sure that morally and spiritually, it is something the team feels need to be done. Are you following me?"

Walter continued, "I also took the liberty of getting you four pilots and two attendants. That should count for something, don't you think?"

"Don't want your pilots and don't need attendants. We got our own and they are a part of our brotherhood and not part of some agency that can commandeer expensive planes and order people terminated. I really think you should retire from that crazy shit and come and hang out with people who have a real mission in life. By the way, when can I expect you?"

Walter hesitated and then asked, "How about brunch later?"

Beckmire answered, "Call one hour before you land so that I can clear you and your plane through the locals. They are genuinely concerned about who lands at their airport. They had a few problems with some New York carpetbaggers and they tend to be, let's just say, cautious. See you in a few hours."

Walter inquired, "Is it possible to ask the 'idiot spy' and his new bride to attend, and if so, I would also like to request that they bring the card and the condom."

"Whoa! That stuff is in a safe place that once again only the, as you call him, the 'idiot spy' knows where they are. We dropped him at a FedEx office and he posted the package to somewhere and to someone that I do not have a clue about. His bride doesn't know and I sure as hell don't have a clue. I suggest that when you come to this table, you be prepared to offer a boat load of benefits to him, his bride, his family, and his friends. Bring your check book, Cousin, because it is now going to cost a tad bit more than a couple of planes. See you later."

Beckmire immediately went to Zanthius's room and banged on the door. When Asiram opened the door, Beckmire muttered, "By the looks of that outfit, I can see that you guys are busy. Please have my son call me when he is conscious again." He turned and walked away with a huge smile on his face. When he entered his room, Courtney asked, "What's that smile about?"

"I want to make love to my wife and I'm so happy that I have the time to do that without someone trying to shoot me." Courtney pushed him up against the door and began to kiss his lips and breathe heavily into his ears. Beckmire began to clumsily attack her blouse and finally decided to be macho and rip it apart. He fondled her voluptuous breasts, kissed her lips, and searched the inner most depths of her mouth with his tongue. He lifted her off the floor and into his arms and made his way to the bed, all the while searching her mouth with his tongue. He laid her down and said, "I love you more than life." As the two started to disrobe, there was a knock at the door. He looked at her and they both broke into laughter. Beckmire went to the door and it was Zanthius and Asiram.

Asiram said, "By the looks of things, you might want to call us once you have regained consciousness."

#

An hour later, Beckmire called Zanthius and said, "I need to see you and Asiram as soon as possible. Can we meet in your room in ten minutes?" The timetable was agreed upon.

Beckmire entered their room and said, "I hope I'm not disturbing you as you disturbed me."

Zanthius smiled and exclaimed, "Whatever!"

"There is an urgency for this meeting because of the card and the condom. I think you need to do the same thing that you did with the capsule and that is send it to a mail stop and get it out of your hands. I also think that, as before, you should be the only one who knows where you send it and what protocols are needed to access it. When the word gets out that the capsule was a ruse and the real information with coordinates and codes was instead encoded on a condom and a card from a Russian strip joint, the entire world is going to be hunting for us in a fashion that I can't imagine. What are your thoughts?"

Zanthius replied, "Pops, you are not going to believe this, but Asiram and I were just having the same discussion. We want to rid ourselves of the information as soon as possible. I mean why don't we just give it to Walter and be done with it?"

Beckmire asked, "Do you remember when Walter had that conversation with the horse? He said that no one is going to believe that you accidentally stumbled upon this information, and coincidentally, hired your father and his ex-military buddies to provide security. We have come into a ton of money and still have the essential information for the product. Even I agree with the horse, who the hell is going to believe it? This is all conjured and distorted truths."

Asiram acknowledged, "It becomes more incredulous since we happen to have a holographic card from a Russian strip club and a condom made in Russia with precise coordinates that were given to us by an agent of the government. I'm with you Daddy-in-Law, it's just too hard to believe that this is coincidental. Now, to broaden that theory, look at the body count that we have amassed and the money that we have transferred to offshore bank accounts."

Quietly, Zanthius considered the information and the input from his father and his wife. He asked his father, "How many of your guys are leaving for home this afternoon?"

"If I'm not mistaken, I think that five are leaving and six are staying."

"Is my brother staying as well?"

"Yes, Larry is going to stay and help protect us."

"Don't I qualify as protection as well?"

"No need to feel that way, Son. Larry and I have done a lot of things together and you and I are just starting to get a handle on how we each roll. You are my blood and I know you saw all that you needed to see when we were in the outback. Realize your strengths and don't get caught up in how I deploy my friends and family."

"Sorry, Pops, I really didn't mean it that way. My reason for asking is quite simple. I would like to transfer the onus of this to Larry, who is a complete enigma. It could provide the cover that we all need. What if they catch me? I sure as hell wouldn't know who Larry sent the product to or what his pseudonym or proclivities for passwords are. Do you people see where I am going with this? I am the focus and it's going to be on me, yet, Larry will be the one who has the information and the details. If you think about it, he has been a silent partner other than that post office mess."

Beckmire raised a finger in the air, walked away from Zanthius and Asiram and then circled back. He looked at them and began to have a conversation with himself.

Finally, he looked at Zanthius, smiled, and then at Asiram and said, "Now, that is some brilliant thinking. This 'idiot spy' has once again found a way to outsmart the other side. Asiram, what are your thoughts?"

Asiram appeared to be cogitating about the options and their outcomes and finally said, "My husband, Zanthius Beckmire De Lombardo, is one smart-ass 'idiot spy'. It's brilliant! Keep the focus on Zanthius while Larry walks about freely and unconcerned, with the full knowledge of where the documents will land. My husband is simply brilliant. I can't say it enough. My husband is the smartest 'idiot spy' that I have ever met and I love him to death; well, not literally. What I should have said is I will love him throughout eternity."

Beckmire hugged his son and whispered in his ear, "I won't let her hurt you."

Both men broke out laughing and Asiram asked, "What was that about?"

Zanthius answered her mockingly, "Must you know everything that a father and son talk about?"

CHAPTER THREE

Jong, McArthur, Chakes, Montomie, Whitmore, and Gladstone were outside of the main ranch house discussing the key aspects and impact of the Carbon Factor situation.

The Sarge came outside and without inquiring about the nature of their meeting, hugged each man and told them individually how much he loved them, respected them, and honored their commitment to each other. It was a tearful goodbye for him. Jong was the last man in the que and the Sarge mumbled, "I can't tell you how much you mean to me, the guys, and my family. I know you have to go and make sure that things are good on the home front and like the rest of the guys, you have been away too damn long. So, I bid you farewell and hope that I don't have to make another call for your help, anytime soon."

Jong looked at the Sarge, then at Whitmore and said, "Unfortunately this thing isn't over. If you need us, give us a call and we will be here. It's been exciting and I think I speak for the rest of the guys in saying that we enjoyed the stimulation and anxiety that this challenge presented. However, my liege, our conversation was simply an inquiry relative to the need to secure family members, if at all. If I can speak frankly without being insubordinate, you must be crazy to think that we're going to leave at a time like this. We were talking about whether or not there was a need to retrieve any family members. So Sarge, if you disappear, I will continue our discussion."

The Sarge walked back into the house and Asiram said, "If our government were as loyal to its people as your friends are to you, our Constitution would have a different interpretation. Your people are some of the finest human beings that I have ever encountered. You, Mr. Beckmire, aka, Daddy-in-Law, should be extremely proud of what you have been able to accomplish with mere mortals." She hugged him and gave him a kiss on the cheek.

Zanthius said, "I agree with my wife. I so very much want to do something special for each and every one of those guys."

As they thought about the people who had saved their lives, Larry walked by and said, "Hey guys, nice to see you. I think I'm going to take a run around the ranch."

Zanthius vehemently announced, "Larry, that's not a good idea. I went for a run by myself the last time we were here and the damn wolves chased my ass."

Larry asked, "Wow, why would you run without someone following you? My wife is going to accompany me in one of the ATVs that will be loaded with a few weapons. Do you want to come along?"

"Larry, Pops, Asiram, and I would like to meet with you a little later. We have a couple of ideas that we would like to discuss, after you have had your run."

Larry raised his thumb and said, "See you when I get back."

#

Clyde's people at the airport called him and told him that six suits had just gotten off a private plane and were carrying a few big bags. Clyde, in turn, called Beckmire who told him that he would circle back to him in a few minutes.

Next, Beckmire called Walter and asked, "Where are you?" Walter responded that he and a few of his guys had just landed and were being watched by everyone in the airport. Beckmire told him he would clear them and that he would meet him in town in an hour. In the meantime, Beckmire called Clyde and told him that they were good guys.

# # #

After Larry finished his run, he saw Zanthius and Asiram near the barn and ran over to them. Asiram called Beckmire and told him that Larry was in the barn and that they needed him there as well.

When Beckmire arrived, he jumped right into the proposed scenario. He gave Larry the details and asked him if he felt comfortable being the unknown factor. Larry told the trio that it was a no brainer and that he would gladly help in any way possible.

The Sarge asked, "Do you have a post office box like your brother had, where women can write to you if they are interested in an affair or some other kinky behavior?"

Asiram gently slapped Zanthius upside the head and uttered, "I'm sure Larry doesn't dabble in the risqué."

Larry replied, "Absolutely not. However, I still have a box from when me and pops used to carry out certain functions, if you know what I mean."

The Sarge exclaimed, "Wow, what's with you youngins? I think the less we know the better it is for everyone. You guys agree?"

Zanthius and Asiram completely agreed with that sentiment and Zanthius inquired, "When would you like to do a handoff?"

"I'm meeting Walter in town for brunch and that might be a great time to make this happen. Larry, are you sure the box is still available to you?"

"Sarge, I still have some items in the box and I pay the fee on an annual basis. It's still operational."

The Sarge said, "I'm leaving here in thirty minutes or so. Larry, I need you to follow me into town. A few of my guys will be watching your back from afar and I need you to head to the post office and send the material to wherever it is you have the box. Zanthius, can you secure the items and meet us in twenty minutes?"

Zanthius responded, "This sounds like a plan and no one will know what this mess is or where it goes from here."

Beckmire called Clyde and asked him if he could give him a ride into town. He added that he needed some of his people for surveillance work. Clyde found this request stimulating and told him the town will forever be on alert and people will never again just stand-by and watch a bunch of bad guys waltz into their town.

CHAPTER FOUR

In town, Beckmire met Walter and said, "So, I hear you have now earned the title of 'idiot spy' number 2! How goes it?"

Walter answered, "You're really trying to piss me off, Cousin, after all that I've done for you and your people. Oh, before I forget about it, how is Yvett doing?"

Beckmire looked at him and wondered what card he was trying to play and announced, "She's doing very well and my people are keeping a close eye on her. As a matter of fact, I think she is at the local hospital having a series of tests conducted and perhaps you might be able to meet her. How do you know about Yvett?"

Walter answered, "Her second cousin called me and asked me to inquire about her health. I'm not trying to play you on this one because we both want only the best for her."

As the two men ordered Coors Lights, they saluted each other and got down to business. Walter began the conversation by saying, "I'm going to give you something, and then I expect, a thing of equal or greater value, in return. Does that sound like a game we can play, here and now?"

"I'm not sure we can play any games because I don't have my people with me who are part of the decision-making process, but why don't we start and see how we progress."

"I have two G5s for you with clear titles for ownership in this little envelope. Would you like those two planes?"

Beckmire corrected him, "The planes are not part of the deal. We have already settled on the planes."

Walter stared at Beckmire for a few seconds and said, "You're probably correct. Okay, I'm going to take those off the table and pass you the titles to the aircrafts. I have strong intel about the whereabouts of the person that placed the C-4 under your vehicles."

Beckmire's body came to attention, a fierce look took over his face and he demanded, "Tell me where I can find him!"

"How soon you forget the rules. I give you something and then you give me something."

Beckmire's patience was wearing thin as he demanded, "What the hell do you want? The card and the condom?"

"Hell no, cousin! I don't want to be on the world's hit list," Walter replied.

"I don't understand. Why don't you want what everybody else has killed and died for?" Beckmire inquired.

"Cousin, it is simple. I cannot get my work done while looking over my shoulder for the next attack; that's your job. In three days after tomorrow, I want you to take that C-4 and place it strategically around a certain house that sits on a secure hill and blow it up with a certain former high-ranking official in it. Please do this before he has a chance to use his dual citizenship and escape without prejudice."

"I believe that we have the motivation to accept this assignment, but my question is what are you up to, Walter? What is it you really want me to sign on to?"

"Remember the rules of the game. I give you something, and you reciprocate, I have given you two jets and the location of a person that wants you very dead. Now, you must give me something in return and that something is going to cause you a lot of grief." Walter took a swig of his beer and afterwards blurted out, "I need you to turn Asiram over to me. I know the senator took care of a lot of her issues, but we need to debrief her."

Beckmire abruptly stood up and asserted, "Nice to see you again. From now on, don't show up or call me. Save yourself some time and expenses. Goodbye." As Beckmire turned to leave, Walter pressed, "Ben, I need her to testify against a former rogue agent. One that you had the opportunity to meet."

Beckmire asked, "Are you talking about Harold? You placed a bullet in the back of his head."

"That would be the same person."

Beckmire looked at him and said, "If you can't do it by video conferencing then it can't be done. Besides, she doesn't know a thing about Harold. Harold is your problem, not hers."

"That is exactly what I am talking about. It's my problem and the weapon that was used was mine, a real problem for me," Walter stated.

"Asiram is not going anywhere with you. If you want to see a recording of your work then I will gladly send you a copy. My suggestion to you is that you concoct a story using one of the mercs we captured. Create a story about how a merc got loose and shot your partner while you were tied up. Say it was because he was giving information about who his clients were and talked about the crazy-money they paid him towards his retirement for that information. Asiram or anybody else, is not going anywhere with you."

The two men sat back down and drank their beers staring at each other. Walter finally asked, "Do you really have me on film?"

"You can bet your sweet ass, we do. I mean from the discussions with the horse to that dastardly deed you committed to your partner," Beckmire responded.

"So, what's the solution. Is there any way you can help me?" Walter asked.

"Any help you need I will render to you, but Asiram is not going anywhere nor is anyone else in my clan. It wouldn't be so bad if you didn't speak at times with a forked tongue, but you know you are still on our credibility watch list. What is the information out there about the event? How on earth do you think Asiram can help you?"

"Listen I have to go to the john. I'll be right back."

# # #

Meanwhile, Larry was accompanied into town by Jilkes and John Lee. Jong arranged a meeting with the local architect for the design of John Lee's new house and a rendering of a possible new place for Jilkes. Due to this distraction, no one saw Larry slip away and go to the post office to send the package he received from Zanthius. As he exited the post office, he saw Jilkes looking at him and he gave him the okay sign.

Larry walked to the nearby restaurant where the Sarge was sitting close to a window by himself. Larry walked in and reported, "It's done and I'm going over to the architect's place to watch these guys try to out build each other."

The Sarge got up, hugged him, and asked, "Do you have a weapon on you?" Larry smiled at him, turned, and walked away.

When Walter returned from the restroom, Beckmire could see that Walter's eyes were bloodshot and he asked him, "What happened in the john? Your eyes are red as if you have been crying."

"Naw, no tears, just allergies." He ordered himself a vodka martini and asked the Sarge if he would join him for a real drink.

After being served the drinks, the two men toasted each other, Walter's eyes began to water and, he started to cry.

Beckmire said, "Okay, Cousin, tell me the real story and leave out the horse shit." Walter knew that he had two men stationed outside of the restaurant and waved them on.

He then said, "Let's enjoy this drink first, Ben, and then I will try to reconcile my sins."

"Before I do that, I need to know if any of my people are in immediate danger?" Beckmire inquired.

Walter looked at him and said, "Fortunately, the answer to that one, is no. No imminent threat that I am aware of. This is all about me, Ben."

After several huge gulps of his martini, Walter said, "Ben, please don't judge me. I am a happily married man with two wonderful and beautiful daughters, but somewhere deep inside of me there is this need for something else and that something else was exploited by Harold. Ben, in terms used at home, I am a "poofter". Do you know what that means?"

"In all honesty, I don't, but it doesn't sound like something that is life threatening," Beckmire replied.

Walter smiled and said, "Ben, on two occasions while on assignment, Harold and I got pissed, another word for drunk, and I wound up in his bed. Not only that, he had sex with me, ergo the term poofter, what we call homosexual. He filmed us while we were engaged in sex, and I will not lie and say that I didn't enjoy it. Then he blackmailed me to gain contacts and made those illicit deals to have you and your family murdered, for what I would consider, a handsome fee. I had dreams and extremely unpleasant visions from home and that is when I realized that you and I were related. I thought it was a mistake and just knew that there couldn't be a clan member involved in this overpriced bounty hunt. I was distraught and when you gave me the opportunity to face my demons, I didn't hesitate to conclude him and my nightmares. The reason I didn't want you guys to get into his safety deposit boxes is because that is where he kept the film. I'm ashamed on all fronts. I knew that one day all of my hiding and scheming would come to an end."

"Walter, I'm not going to judge you because I had visions of a two-headed clan member and it was you. I didn't know what it meant but there was a good head and a bad head connected to one body. My only emphatic statement to you is that my daughter-in-law, as well as the others, are hands off!" Beckmire exclaimed.

After a significant pause, Walter announced, "Asiram, can be made up to look like Harold's wife, who is an acid head with dementia and has a huge cocaine problem. I need Asiram and others to enter banks, with bona fide credentials, and empty Harold's safety deposit boxes at the three branches. Mike has agreed to be the lead on this one for me and he understands the importance of this mission. I just need you and a few of your guys to come along and make this thing happen. All I want is the film. Whatever else is in those boxes, that are not personal, such as, diamonds and other jewels, are up for grabs. I know you are disappointed in me, but I am who I am. I fight my problems every moment I am home."

Beckmire reached across the table, grabbed his hand, and said, "We're family Walter. You have done some good things for us and you have also gotten us into some rotten situations, but as I balance the equation, you are still family. If I convince her to do this, I must have your word that there are no other known obstacles that you may have inadvertently forgotten to share with me."

"Ben, I promise on the lives of my children and my wife that what I am telling you is accurate and true. The only thing that I wish is that this conversation, and all of its hidden meanings, remain between the two of us and not be used to have some levity or leverage at my expense."

Beckmire put his hand out and said, "We have an accord subject to the approval of Asiram and Zanthius. Is that agreeable to you?"

"We have an accord drawn in ancient blood from the righteous. This is why I am out here, Ben, to cover my ass with the help of a family member. Thanks for being here and listening to me without making any judgement or snide remarks."

"So, how long will you and your boys be out here?" Beckmire asked.

"We're out of here once I receive a response from you about that matter, I shared with you. We have already concluded the C-4 issue. I just need personal assistance on that other matter." Walter stood up and extended his hand to Ben and in the process passed him a note. He said, "Some notes are better read in private. Catch you later and let me know what Asiram and the 'idiot spy' say. Oh, I almost forgot to give you this fob, it works on one of the planes and I can only guess what it might open."

CHAPTER FIVE

Jong, McArthur, Asiram, and Zanthius were at the airport discussing the credentials of the possible pilot candidates for the two new jets with the pilots of their three jets when Beckmire called Jong and asked, "Can you guys wait until I get there before you board those two planes?"

Jong replied, "Your wish is my command. See you when you get here."

The woman candidate had piloted big Hercules transporters and was extremely up to date on the avionics of the new planes. She was an astronaut candidate but was disqualified after breaking her leg in a motorcycle accident. Jong asked her about her ability to handle the controls of the plane given the fact that she was disqualified as an astronaut candidate. She responded, "Unless you're planning a trip to the moon in one of these planes, then I'm not impacted by the leg break that I suffered. Matter tends to expand and contract in space at an exponentially higher rate than in the normal atmosphere of an operating jet. I can fly this plane and push it to the limits of its capabilities. You can watch me and tell me if I have a problem with my leg. This can be done without the use of autopilot."

Jong said, "We have four other candidates and we will let you know our decision once we have interviewed everyone."

The young lady got out of the chair, went to a near wall and raised her leg as high as her head and said, "Sorry about that, I just like to stretch whenever I can."

McArthur said, "I'm in love; hire her ass right now."

# # #

Clyde drove Beckmire to the airport. When he arrived at the terminal, he asked, "How are we doing?"

Jong answered, "I know for a fact that we want to hire the two mechanics on some kind of basis. I think that the young lady has a lot of stuff with her and might be an asset, but I'm also looking for people who can pull the trigger."

Beckmire said, "I need you guys to take a walk with me and let the pilots interview the rest of the group."

Beckmire entered the first plane with Jong, Asiram, Zanthius, and McArthur and said, "There is something on one of these planes that we need to have a look at." He started in the cockpit and moved throughout the plane pressing the button on the fob, but nothing happened.

He said, "Let's go to the other plane and see if we can make this thing work." The group went to the other plane. He pressed the fob and the lights came on and the steps automatically lowered.

He exclaimed, "Damn, now that's some crazy technology." They entered the jet and everything seemed to be in order. He hit the fob again and the lights went out.

Jong stated, "Let me have that for a moment." He clicked it twice in succession and a rumbling sound occurred in the belly of the plane. The four men opened the hatch to the belly and descended into what could be considered the baggage compartment. Everything seemed normal. Jong struggled to climb into the belly of the plane and when he did, he clicked the fob twice in succession and another compartment opened on the plane which was loaded with weapons.

He yelled, "Sarge, you need to get over here. There are some crazy ass weapons on this thing."

Beckmire said, "Wait a minute, I need to read a note that Walter passed to me." He reached into his pocket and pulled out the piece of paper and read it to himself. It was titled *Bagman,* and it looked like an article from Barons. It read: "$1 million worth of $20 bills weigh 110 pounds and fills four briefcases. The same amount in $100 bills fit into one." Beckmire pondered the note and wondered why Walter gave it to him as he looked around in the belly of the plane.

Zanthius asked, "Jong, can I see that thing?"

Jong, who was excited about the weapons, handed the fob to Zanthius and never saw him press the unit three times in succession. Lo and behold a panel slid open and three cases popped out as if they were from a vending machine.

Jong looked at each case and said, "You might want to leave while I open this thing." No one left. When he opened the first case it was loaded with $100 bills as was the second and the third case.

Beckmire proclaimed, "Well, I'll be damned! My cousin is an honorable man, after all. Look at all this money. You know when this shit is over, we're going to take on the government's secret organizations and investigate the off-budget funds they don't account for. This is some incredible shit. Oh, Asiram and Zanthius, I must have a serious conversation with you guys about another matter that involves Walter. McArthur, you're in control of this money. This shit gets crazier by the minute."

## CHAPTER SIX

Back at the ranch, the Sarge asked Asiram and Zanthius to take a short walk with him. As they walked in the fields, he asked, "Do you people trust me?"

Zanthius replied, "What is it you need, Pops?"

The Sarge looked at Asiram and said, "I need you to do me a favor which in turn is a favor for a family member."

Asiram asked, "What on earth is this mumbo jumbo you're talking about? What is it you need me to do?"

The Sarge replied, "I need you to impersonate Harold's wife and retrieve the contents of his safety deposit boxes. I suspect that there will be several million dollars in the boxes, but that is not what I'm looking for. I will have real government types, with the necessary paperwork and ID, to escort you, and of course, a few of our own, really close by. Will you do that for me?"

Asiram walked up to him and whispered in his ear, "Daddy-in-Law, as long as you got my back, then I'll do whatever you need me to do. Love you!"

The Sarge said, "I knew I could count on you. I will get back to you with specific details once I have all of the information we need. I love you as well."

#

Jong in the meantime met with the potential pilot candidates, along with his four existing crew, and told them that they would have to give him a show in the air. He asked the mechanics about the functioning of the planes and he was given an excellent rating on each plane. He called the Sarge and told him that he and McArthur were going to take a couple of plane rides with the existing crew, as well as the potential new hires. All candidates had extensive flying experience from their days in Afghanistan and had been trained on large and small jets.

After speaking with Jong, Beckmire called Walter and told him that Asiram had agreed to play the part. He added that he wanted to know all of the details in terms of exactly what they needed to do. Beckmire reminded him that Harold had said that the three different boxes were within the same bank chain but at different locations.

Walter told Beckmire that he had talked to the senator and was told that the capsule, with all of the drama and death associated with it, was a complete ruse. It only contained two numbers and a degree sign.

The Sarge dismissed his conversation and said, "By the way, the locals are preparing a feast for us tonight, and if you and your boys want to join us, you are perfectly welcome."

Walter responded, "Thank you, I think we'll be there. I do want to confirm one thing--I need that film from the boxes in three days. The person that sent you the C-4 is out of here in three days. I promised the senator that I would have the formula in her hands by then. Is all of these tasks, possible to achieve?"

Beckmire vehemently exclaimed, "You need to stop promising things that are completely beyond your control! If you give me and my guys complete information and surveillance of the house on the hill, as well as what to expect when trying to access those boxes, then I would say that we can accomplish all three things. I will meet with my people and give them the skinny on the situation. I expect you to provide us with badges, IDs and anything else we might need to pull off the bank ruse, and explicit information concerning ending my row with the sender of that C-4."

Walter stated, "Insofar as the boxes are concerned, I need to make sure that the film is immediately handed over to me. Is that good with you?"

"Absolutely, and more importantly, my people don't ask what or why, they just place their faith and trust in the man setting up this 'OP'. That person would be me, Walter, and believe me, I need all of the details or your house may be the next place that comes tumbling down. I hate to mention this, but with all of the people in it."

"You play hardball, Ben."

"Naw, you haven't seen me play hardball, Walter. You might not like how we play that game, so I suggest that every conceivable detail be provided to us for review. Let me be clear--if you place any of my people in harm's way as a result of not providing us with all of the details, I will personally walk on Dreamtime exposing you and your ways. Don't screw with me and endanger my people."

Walter ignored the threat and meekly replied, "I will see you later at dinner, and thanks for the invitation."

# # #

John Lee, Jilkes, and Larry returned from town and were met by the Sarge who said, "We have three missions in three days. Do you think we can make them happen?"

Jilkes asked, "Are we all involved or is it a limited strategic strike force?"

Beckmire replied, "I just wanted to take your mind off your farm and your houses. The locals have prepared a feast for us. I expect you gentlemen to be there. I'm expecting Walter and his crew and when we have finished eating, or perhaps before, I would like to discuss the details of our next missions. By the way, how did things go with the architect?"

Jilkes answered, "This country bumpkin has requested some interesting design features that will make what I had in mind look like a dump. I'm going to wait until he approves his design and then step up my game without his knowledge."

Beckmire asked, "Why don't you two just move in together and call it a night?"

John Lee responded, "No way on this side of earth he be moving in with me. I love him but he ain't moving in my house. He can come and visit for a year at a time but then he has to take his black ass to a motel for 24 hours and then he can come back for another year."

"Wow, so it be like that?" Jilkes asked jokingly.

# # #

Beckmire, looked around the huge dining room and tapped on his glass to get everyone's attention. He asked the group to be mindful of the fact that they were guests and that the people providing them with this scrumptious meal were neighbors, and not hired hands. He also took the liberty to say a prayer for forgiveness, peace, and love. He introduced Walter and his crew. As he looked around the room he proclaimed, "My goodness, where is Jong and McArthur?"

Clyde replied, "I think they're at the airport interviewing some people for jobs or something."

Beckmire replied, "Oh, yeah. I forgot about that."

CHAPTER SEVEN

The Sarge asked Asiram, Zanthius, and his guys to huddle with him because he needed to get their buy-in on three distinct missions that were being proposed by Walter. As the group met in the barn, Walter and his crew entered. Walter said, "If you guys don't mind, I want to have Mike here with me to make sure that I cover all aspects of the proposals." He asked his other guys to form a twenty yard perimeter around the barn area.

The Sarge exclaimed, "Our government needs our services once again! You guys all know Walter and Mike. Walter is here because he screwed up big time when he returned Zanthius's wallet that was found in St. Moritz that contained, what is believed to be, the real information about the Carbon Factor. Just for our safety, the condom and the card have been posted to an unknown mail stop and only one person in this room knows its whereabouts.

"The first thing that Walter wants us to take care of is, the pseudo high ranking government official, who is about to go missing. However, prior to Mr. Government leaving his post, he was kind enough to send us those C-4 packages.

"The second thing that my cousin Walter needs us to do is secure the contents of safety deposit boxes from three bank branches. Now, guys, Walter has been extremely generous, by providing us clear titles to the two G5s at the airport. As of early this afternoon, those aircrafts became the official properties of our foundation and for that we should give Walter, my cousin, a hand," the group clapped faintly.

The third thing that my cousin needs us to do, is to surrender the gateway materials to the senator, on the Carbon Factor."

The Sarge further stated, "I don't want to forget any details, but my Cousin, Walter, needs all three things accomplished in three days," In response to the seemingly impossible timeline, the group booed.

The Sarge concluded, "Now, that I have given you people an overview of my cousin's requests, I will yield to him and let him fill us in on the details and I do mean all of the minutia about when, where and especially the how."

Walter said, "Thanks for the boos and the applause. I think that the person who planted that C-4 in your vehicles with your families in them should have his products returned to him before he flees the country in three days. He has a house that sits on a hill that is protected by approximately fourteen mercs. He has allegedly agreed to turn himself in to the authorities, but I have precise information from a foreign operative, that he is planning to flee the country. I think that it is only fitting that you send him off with a bang. The details of his whereabouts will be handled by Mike. We can circle back to any questions you might have later or tomorrow."

Walter looked around the room before continuing and said, "The second issue relates to some sensitive files in a few safety deposits boxes. The capsule appears to be a ruse, the only information it contained were two numbers and the symbol for degrees. The real product, possibly, with the critical information, was in my hands. My people failed to conduct due diligence with the wallet belonging to the 'idiot spy', and we missed the information on the condom and the card from a strip joint in Russia. Now, your fearless leader, also my cousin, has indicated to me that once again you people have posted the information by mail to protect yourselves.

"Once it's leaked that you are still in control of the information, all hell is going to break loose. To assist in that process, I know that one of your newly acquired aircraft has a ton of new weapons and ammunitions on it. Until you get rid of the condom and the card, you and your people are sure as hell, going to need those weapons and munitions."

Asiram asked Walter to pause a moment and beckoned the Sarge and Zanthius to escort her outside for a minute.

Once outside, she said, "I have pictures of what was on the card and the writings on the condom."

Beckmire whispered, "Hush, girl! I don't want anybody else to know about that until it's time to once again bargain with these government types and make sure we get those 'get-out-of-jail-free' cards for every living soul, here."

"Daddy-in-Law, you are the best and the brightest. No wonder my husband is so smart and cute."

As the trio reentered the barn, Walter asked, "Was that conversation about something that we all could benefit from?"

Asiram responded, "If that were the case, we wouldn't have left the room. Please continue with your briefing."

John Lee looked at Jilkes and said, "She be some kind of firestorm, ain't she? She don't be taking no sass from nobody."

Walter said, "I would like to meet privately with my cousin, his son and his wife to discuss the details of transferring that information to the senator.

"Now, the third issue that I'm requesting your assistance on is a little more delicate and entails the retrieval of sensitive information. I could say some dumb stuff like its classified, but that don't mean a damn thing to you people. Nevertheless, the information concerns an ongoing blackmail plot." Walter looked at Mike and said, "I'm sorry Mike, can you leave the barn for a minute?"

After Mike was out of listening range, Walter continued, "Some of you are aware that I blew the back of my partner's head off after he confessed to setting you people up and to having three safety deposit boxes in different branches of the same bank. He also had money in an offshore account that was mysteriously depleted prior to his death. What I'm looking for is a fob, floppy disk or any other device that can record and store information. I have asked my cousin if you, Mrs. De Lombardo, would ride point on this one and assume the role of my dearly departed partner's wife. Once again, this has an expiration date of three days, because on the fourth day, the Department of Justice will have the option of confiscating the contents. Are there any questions of me, so far?"

Mallory inquired, "Do you have an aerial shot of the SOB's place who sent us those packages?"

"Mike has topographical and aerial shots of his hideout including where his power lines emanate from, as well as, his sewer drainpipes."

Mallory asked, "What's your take on the mercs that are providing protection? I mean, do you want them incapacitated or permanently removed from future equations?"

"I believe, that's your call. I mean, it's not like they're marching on this ranch, they just happen to have the job of providing security for a real asshole," Walter replied.

The Sarge said, "I think if we can give a quarter without jeopardizing any of us, then so be it. I just don't want to kill people who simply have the unfortunate assignment of protecting a jerk."

John Lee said, "Now, I likes that one. We spare a life where possible, but we put such a hurting on their asses so that they won't want to come up against us again, even if it be on Mars."

Walter stated, "I have left the planning of this event to Mike, because it is apparent that I can't, or we can't, be anywhere near where this action takes place. Circling back to the Carbon Factor, I think the only way to end this mess is that you people obtain, secure, and deliver the actual information to the senator. I don't mean coordinates and other treasure hunting leads, but the actual documents that can be captured on TV by all the major and minor networks.

"You people remember my story as ratified by the horse, about believability, conjured and distorted truths? Well, anyway, let me give you the skinny on that one again. No one in their right mind is going to believe that this kiss passing capsule shit was random; nor are they going to believe that a rogue spy just happened to throw her career away for a complete stranger. I can also assure you that it is hard to believe that twelve 'ole heads from Vietnam just by chance, came to the rescue of and is providing protection for the 'idiot spy'. And it is especially hard to believe that they inured to their benefit, hundreds of millions of dollars for providing that protection.

"Now, if you happen to have a clear path to the Pope, then I suggest you communicate with him and perhaps he can summon Jesus to earth to champion your cause. Otherwise, you people are now on a radar screen that is bigger than it was for Bin Laden, ISIS, and the whole lot of other nuts who do bad stuff in the name of some cause. Your fate and mine are tied together on all three of these matters. My cousin knows my predicament and I trust he will protect our discussion based on the primitive laws of our forefathers. Nevertheless, let me be crystal clear-- since you have not obtained, secured and delivered that damn

Carbon Factor to the senator, your next visit may possibly be from people sporting leather vests that you will clearly recognize as hired guns by the government of the United States of America."

Beckmire said, "Damn, Walter, if you wanted to strike fear in us, then I believe you have accomplished your task. Mallory, I would like to meet with you, Chakes, Montomie, and Mike to layout the strategy for returning the gift. Then I would like to meet with my son, daughter-in-law, and you Walter, to discuss how we make entry into the three banks. Finally, at 2200 hours, I want to meet with my entire team including Larry, Zanthius, and Asiram. Are there any questions? Let's go to work people."

"Wait, wait one minute. Walter, you're one slick ass, dude. Let me be extremely clear, and precise. In three days, you would like us to accomplish the tasks that you have laid out. We will let you know our decision within the next two hours if we will participate in your wicked schemes. Prior to that decision being made, Walter, my Cousin, you are not to call, text, write, or send carrier pigeons to me or any member of my team, unless there is some national security emergency. In that case, we will only accept calls from the President of the United States; is that agreeable?" Walter hesitated and turned to Mike who had reentered the room. Walter whispered something to Mike who whispered something back to him that they both seemingly agreed upon.

Walter said, "You have my word."

Beckmire proclaimed, "Second, Cousin, I need 'get-out-of jail-free' cards for everyone here, including Asiram and legal confirmation that during any of our OPs, we are not responsible for any collateral damage! Thus, I am stressing our need for those go free cards. Can you make that happen?"

Walter whispered something else to Mike who said, "You've got to give that to them."

Walter said, "I'll have those documents ready for you prior to your departures for the agreed upon tasks. This has been a fruitful meeting and I want to thank each of you and wish you the blessing of Pigeon and other warriors that have come before you."

As Walter was walking away, he turned and asked the Sarge, "By the way, was there anything else on that plane?"

The Sarge looked at him and responded, "Like what? Is this another mystery that I have to figure out, Walter, or what?"

"No, just asking because the previous owner had extracted an enormous amount of money from our system prior to heading this way." Both men knew that the treasure hunting note was passed.

"Did you happen to lose more of those hard-earned taxpayers' dollars?"

Walter looked at him and answered, "I think we have more important things to attend to right now, and besides, my signature is not on a single document."

On the hour, meetings were held about strategies for accomplishing the three tasks that were laid out by Walter. Beckmire in the first meeting proclaimed, "I want to blow that motherfucker to Hades! I want to give him back his gift and surround that place with enough dynamite to cause an earthquake. Asiram, will you ask Clyde if he knows where we can acquire some explosives?"

"Daddy-in-Law, I can take care of that one. Somewhere in the field out there is some really bad mess that fell off a truck as I was passing by."

Beckmire said, "I like your timing, dear. You always seem to come along as stuff falls off trucks."

## CHAPTER EIGHT

The Sarge and his team met with Mike and reviewed the aerial pictures of the place, as well as, the surrounding countryside. Mallory said, "This seems too easy to me. Therefore, I need a second opinion on this one."

Zanthius, who was staring at the pictures with intensity, said, "I see exactly what you mean. This becomes a turkey shoot for them as our energy is exerted trying to get up the hills. In my opinion, we become sitting ducks. If this guy has land security, such as laser beams, then I know we are in for an ass whupping. If I were running this OP, I would do a power blackout in the entire area for a couple of minutes. When the power comes back on, the beams should come back online and realign themselves. Does that make sense?"

John Lee responded, "I be liking it, except that we don't have any night goggles."

Jong, who along with McArthur, had arrived late to the meeting, said, "We found about a dozen head sets in the belly of one of the new planes. We just have to pair and share."

Mallory asked Zanthius, "Since you and Larry are the fastest people here, how long do you think it will take you to scale that hill and establish a command post for us?"

Zanthius looked at Larry who replied, "The perimeter of the place looks like it is a solid mile in circumference and I can do a mile on flat land in a little under five minutes, but going uphill I would have to add another two or three minutes max.

However, it looks like there is less of a slope in this area of the map. If I were on protection duty, this is where I would concentrate my effort. What are your thoughts, Zanthius?"

Zanthius replied, "If your calculations are correct, then I would be two minutes, maybe more, behind you."

The Sarge looked at Mallory and asked, "May I confer with you for a minute?"

The two men walked outside of the barn and the Sarge said, "I don't know if I like using both of my boys for this, but I understand the need for speed and agility."

"Unless there are land mines, they will be well protected by Jilkes, John Lee, Chakes and Montomie. We will also have their backs with long guns scoping the place out held by, me, Jong, Brown, and Bernstein. To draw fire on the other side, I would use Whitmore, Gladstone, and McArthur. Before you interrupt me, let me finish my analysis. If you want to hold one back, then you make the choice."

"It's okay, I just had that fatherly pang for a moment and felt sorry for my ass. They are a part of the deal! They are the youngest, and the fastest. I like your plan."

Mallory paused and said, "Sarge, let me rethink the deployment, and I'll get back to you."

"No, sir. This is the plan. I like it, and they gave input, so let it be. I would like to get this one done tomorrow night if Walter gives me the intel that the SOB is at home."

As they reentered the barn, John Lee said, "I think we have a plan, and your boys be the designers of it. They go first, then Brown, Bernstein, then Jilkes, and me. Then, you old farts come up with the birthday gift, and place the candles on that feller's cake."

Mallory inquired, "Mike, you, and your boys will not be around, is that accurate?"

"You are correct. We will be in Washington at a birthday party. However, I'll have someone get their communications channel and relay it to you before we depart."

Beckmire mumbled, "I wish we could dip arrows in some sort of solution, and just incapacitate the guards, as opposed to killing them."

John Lee replied, "You still going to leave a wound no matter what you shoot them with, bullets or arrows. If'n you want to make them pass out in a hurry I can make up some shit that I used on my pigs to catch their asses when they be horny."

Beckmire asked, "What kind of shit?"

"Well, it be a little of this, and a little of that, plus some of the other."

"Can you make some of that whatever from stuff here on the ranch?"

"Well, hell yeah. I don't want to give away my secret because I am going to get a, ah, ah, you know what I mean, one of them there property protection devices. What's it called?"

Jilkes looked at him and answered, "Do you mean a patent or a trademark?"

"That there be the thing I be getting one day."

Jilkes suggested, "How about we flatten the arrow tips and attach darts to the housing of the arrows so that they operate like those self-medicating pens for different illnesses?"

John Lee looked at him and said, "You be one smart African American. That be a good idea, but the only problem there, is that if we hit them fellows in the vests or somewhere with protection, then we better be ready to place rounds in their heads.

With Walter and Mike in attendance, Beckmire finished the plan for attacking the house on the hill and began strategizing with his group.

Walter said, "I need two of your guys to escort Asiram into each bank branch, flash their badges, and guns with two others stationed at the door to make it look really official and important. They will have to wear suits, ties and be clean shaven. They not only need to play the part, but they must also look the part. Who do you have in mind?"

Beckmire, momentarily looked around and yelled, "Brown, Bernstein, Larry, and Chakes--a Wasp, a Jew, an African American, and a Hispanic. How diverse!"

Walter laughed and asked, "Is there any place we can go to get them outfitted tonight?"

Beckmire stepped away from the group, called Clyde and said, "I need suits and ties for four of my guys. Where can we get such things tonight?"

Clyde replied, "Well, hell, I'll just drive them down to Target. They can find suits there and the ladies around here can make them look tailored. You be needing shoes as well, I suspect."

A few minutes later, Beckmire told his people, "I am going to have Clyde drive you guys downtown, so you can get suits and whatever else you'll need to look like honest or dishonest government agents. Oh, and don't forget to get those space age looking sunglasses. We have the communication devices that will allow you to talk into your wrist. Walter, how about making a call to each branch prior to our arrival and give them the fake ID information. That would legitimize the whole ruse?"

Walter looked at Mike who said, "I can make that happen. I'm going to need Mrs. De Lombardo to sit in a makeup chair for about an hour."

Beckmire looked at Asiram and announced, "Now, that ain't going to happen."

Larry asked, "Do you have a picture of the lady she is supposed to look like?"

Mike answered, "Affirmative."

Larry said, "If you give it to me, I can prepare Asiram. I'm sure she would rather have a person she knows work on her."

Beckmire said, "Good thinking, Larry. We don't want any of our people out of our sight on any of these missions. Is that clear, Cousin?"

Walter responded, "That is crystal clear, Cousin. By the way, who was the woman you used in that post office maneuver?"

Everyone broke out laughing and the Sarge responded, "Oh, she's our secret agent."

Walter said, "Obviously, because we tried that facial recognition software and got nowhere."

Beckmire was still laughing at the notion when he said, "I have to call Clyde and get you guys down to Target. Walter, we are going to need four bullet proof vehicles at the airport when we go to do the first job. I want four of the same when we go to do the bank thing. We are going to need four of the same here at the residence, as well. Is that a problem for you?"

Walter looked at Mike who said, "I will place the order from South America, and make it look like Texas."

Mallory asked, "What the hell does that mean?"

"It means that I'm not going to order those vehicles in Wyoming for jobs that are going to take place in this country. No sir, I am going to reserve them from Argentina or somewhere and pick them up where the work has to be done. I want no direct connection, that's all. It's a government process that would take me a while to explain."

###

Larry looked at Asiram and said, "I understand the fact that you don't want just anyone messing with your beautiful face. I believe I can make the necessary adjustments to your liking, I hope, as long as she isn't drop dead ugly," they laughed.

Larry then added, "Oh, hell, we need a copy of her signature as well, so we can work on duplicating it."

Walter exclaimed, "I must admit, a slight oversight on our part! We'll get on that immediately."

Beckmire looked at him with a jaundiced eye, and Walter knew he had screwed up. Walter attempted to assuage him by saying, "I will handle it." Beckmire continued to look at him skeptically and finally said, "In our business and line of work, a slight oversight is the difference between life and death. If you want our help, you had better become anal about the details or you can kiss our asses' goodbye." He stormed out of the barn. Zanthius, Larry, and Asiram, followed him. Asiram grabbed his arm and said, "Daddy-in-Law, calm down. It's going to be alright."

The Sarge looked at her, hugged her and said, "I know, Baby Girl. That was just for show. I want his ass to sweat the details when it comes to any assignment that we may consider. There is no room for cavalier attitudes, here. We need precise information if I'm going to place any of you in harm's way. Just for show, I'm fine."

When the Sarge and the group walked back into the main area of the barn, Mike was having his ass chewed out by Walter.

Walter calmly turned around and said, "This lack of attention to details, and minutia, is not who we are or what we represent. We will strive to be more thorough, and account for every aspect of any OP that we commission to you people. Once again, I apologize."

Beckmire looked at him with what one might consider the evil eye, and proclaimed, "Don't compromise my people or you, and I, will dance with the devil!"

Walter said, "I would rather have a crash course on how we deal with the condom and the card once we have completed the aforementioned missions. I need to make sure that all of my planning is complete so, therefore, I am not going to express any opinions on how I think we should proceed on the final plan at this time."

The Sarge said, "If it is agreeable to you and your people, we will deliver the birthday package, the C-4 that is, and then we access the boxes at the banks. The first two missions can be conducted and concluded within the next twelve hours, which will give us forty-eight hours to exercise and discuss all options for retrieving, securing, and delivering the factual or fictional formula for the Carbon Factor. Are there any questions or concerns?"

Zanthius replied, "I have one question about the bank mission. Do we leave the contents of the boxes as they are and just scrounge around for recording devices?"

Walter answered, "Now, that is an excellent question, because I believe there is a considerable amount of money in each box, and if I know his widow, she will spend it on smoke, and dust in a matter of weeks. I am not suggesting that you help yourselves to the contents, but I don't know what the contents are, therefore, if you want to extract a service charge from the boxes, so be it. I would leave at least a quarter of the money in the final box, just so she can smoke or dust herself into rehab. I believe what you people can do with a fortune in the outback and other places, deserves more consideration than Harold's widow smoking, blowing drugs up her nose, and the nose of her lovers. I'm just saying. It's your call."

Zanthius asked, "What makes his boxes so important to the government?"

Beckmire recognized how this question could be interpreted terribly wrong, and interjected, "Let me just say, that we are protecting the good guys for a change, who have not taken a rotten dime, nor have they tried to exploit us. I would ask all of you to trust my judgement on this one and have faith in the fact that I serve only you and our families, but I am partial to helping people and institutions who are being blackmailed."

John Lee said, "Enough of this pigshit. We follow the Sarge. We know he is an honorable man. I don't need to know who screwed whose sheep or what horse screwed my cow--I just want to make sure that there be justice for all, and forgiveness for the weak."

###

Asiram pulled Larry aside and inquired, "Where did you learn to do make up and disguises?"

Larry smiled and replied, "The Sarge has a friend on the West Coast who taught me how to look like or be anything that I could imagine. I spent a summer watching him, and I began transforming people and myself into their minds' creations. I never lost the knack for it. As pretty and health conscious as you are, you're going to ask me about the chemicals and stuff, right?"

"Larry, I'm not going to ask you a damn thing. If you muff this face up, oh well, I guess Marisa will have to raise the twins on her own."

They laughed, and Larry said, "I will only use natural ingredients and as my sister-in-law, I have to make sure that you are as beautiful as can be because we are family, and I reserve all bragging rights."

Later that night, the plans were ratified, and the details were studied by those who would execute them. The outfits were purchased, tailored, and refined. In addition, replicas of the official badges, and credentials were obtained. Everything was in play. Jilkes, John Lee, and a few others, found ways to be contentious towards each other, and keep the flames of horseshit lit. Those who had mates, made the most of their private time together—the sounds of love were in the air, and the poets of love, lust, sex, and fulfillment were writing new sonnets because the ranch was moonstruck, by the moon's fullness. The old saying is, 'you either go crazy, or fall in love under the spell of a full moon, or you're already in love, and beyond crazy--a double entendre if ever there was one.

Asiram asked the question about historical lovers, and Zanthius told her about a woman he loved so dearly that, at one point in time, he would have jumped off the pyramids for her. Yet he assured Asiram, that was nothing, for he would jump from the earth to the moon, because she satisfied his need for existing. He told Asiram that he would throughout eternity, honor their love. She in turn, cried in his arms and never said a word because she had never felt such love before, and was learning what love could do, and provide. She was secure; pregnant, healthy, happy, and horny. All 3 "H" s, plus a "P", were in synch.

## CHAPTER NINE

While sitting high on top of a hill overlooking the nearby mountains in Poughkeepsie, New York, with a view of the old Culinary Institute of America, the once famous breeding ground for would-be chefs, the person who sent the packages to the Beckmire group was resting, and planning his escape. His house was partially supported by stilts and had a spectacular view of the area and its lush forestation. His double, a corpse, was prepared for a fiery after death experience. The corpse would sport rings, a watch, two twin gold bracelets and a fine gold necklace that belonged to the perp.

Since the target preferred partial plates to invasive implants, this too was accommodated for the corpse. Explosive chemicals in the paint shed, plus a leak in his gas line, would provide the cause for the explosion that he thought would allow him to escape, board a private plane, and head to Jacksonville, Florida, where he would board another jet for his ride across the big pond. It was an immaculate plan that included a call to the gas company to complain about the faint smell of gas, which would require a visit by two technicians to search the premises for a possible gas leak. Unfortunately, a call to the 'idiot spy' and his family would have made better sense for the purpose of begging for forgiveness for placing C-4 in the vehicles their families rode in.

The team thought they would be able to operate without a lot of civilians around, but Asiram would not tolerate being separated from her man and insisted that she fly with them or she would bring Ava, Courtney, Rashida, Monica, Yvett, Marisa, and all of the children. She was chosen to represent the women and, therefore, was on the plane with the guys.

As the groups' two planes continued on the descent pattern, final review and minor modifications were being made to the plan. Asiram looked at the map and said, "Two guys running up a hill at a fast pace will deplete themselves of energy in an accelerated timeframe. Why not use a leapfrog strategy? Listen, by the time two people get from point A to point B, they will be tired. Why not send a fast person and a slow person and replace them at quarter mile intervals until everyone is in place? If there is a problem, you won't have people totally expended of energy and making poor decisions from a lack of oxygen to their brains, especially at these altitudes."

Beckmire looked at Larry, and then Zanthius, and asked Asiram, "How do you figure into this equation?"

She smiled and responded as she pointed to a map, "Daddy-in-Law, you are so smart. Okay, I am going to be the second tier with Jilkes and John Lee. That is where we will stay and provide cover from these three locations."

Mallory looked at Beckmire, shrugged his shoulders, and said, "You will not advance any farther than this point, Ms. Asiram, and you will provide cover for some people moving downhill fast once those charges are set. Do we have an accord?"

Asiram threw out her hand, and replied, "Indeed, we do. What is the spacing going to be between Jilkes, John Lee, and me?"

Mallory answered, "You will follow John Lee on that one, and if he tells you to put your head in a hole, then do it. Don't waste time trying to figure out why, just do it."

"Yes, sir!" Asiram dutifully replied.

As the wheels of the plane that Beckmire was riding in touched down, he received a call from Walter who said, "I see you guys made it safe and sound. There are four vehicles waiting for you at the airport. A young black guy is going to ask you a couple of questions and if he is satisfied with your answers, he will give you the keys. I have people from my place monitoring those vehicles and there are no bugs or explosives in them. There are also two scanners in the lead vehicle and you and yours can scan the SUVs yourselves. Please accept the vehicles as gifts from your cousin."

Beckmire asked, "Can you confirm that the target is in place and awaiting his gifts?"

"Affirmative," Walter replied.

"See you tomorrow for that other business," Beckmire stated.

As the caravan of SUVs left the airport, a black sedan pulled out behind them and continued in such a proximity that suggested it was following the group. Gladstone called the Sarge and reported, "We have a tail on us. I'm going to pull over and see what they do and if they continue, I will fall in behind them."

"Roger that. Is that vehicle alone or did it come with company?"

Gladstone replied, "As far as I can tell, it appears to be a loner."

The Sarge said, "We're going to pull off at the next exit, and go to that SunWay Gas Station, then we'll decide what to do next. We'll pull over, see what they do and try to get a head count."

Asiram said, "I would like to try out this gadget I have. This little gizmo shuts down a car's electrical system and kills any communication devices, quickly and permanently."

Zanthius exclaimed, "Wow, and you just happen to have that with you!"

"Sweetheart, it has been with me since we first met. Look, at first glance you think this is a compact powder case and mirror for attending to my beauty. At second glance, you see that it can convert into a metal attaching device with an electrical impulse that will shock the car and kill all electronics in it."

The Sarge said, "Before we disable that vehicle, I think we should make sure that they're not friendly."

As the caravan pulled off at the exit where the SunWay Gas Station was, the vehicle continued on its journey. Thirty minutes out from where the target lived, the Sarge got out of his SUV and walked to each truck and said, "Weapons check and from here, we offer a quarter where possible. Our mission is to eliminate any person who tries to hurt us. We will be at the site in thirty minutes."

At the vehicle that Whitmore, Gladstone, Mallory, and Jong were riding in the Sarge said, "I need you guys to take the lead. In five minutes, pull off the road and allow us to catch up with you; we're going to switch the order because of the vehicle that may have been following us. Asiram has a toy that she says can disable that car and all of its electronics if it is a threat to our mission."

The caravan proceeded towards its target and there was no sign of the vehicle. As they passed another exit, a black sedan pulled onto the highway and began to stalk the convoy. Beckmire asked Asiram, "How close do you need to be to that car in order to engage your toy?"

"I just need to throw it on the vehicle and in a matter of seconds, it will be disabled."

The Sarge announced, "Okay, get ready because we are going to pull off the road in a hurry and then immediately get back on to give you the opportunity to make the throw. Get ready, here we go."

The Sarge made an abrupt move to the shoulder of the highway, giving the trailing vehicle just enough time to catch up and pass them. He floored the gas pedal, came back on the road, and got close enough for Asiram to throw her device out of the window and onto the roof of the sedan. Beckmire called ahead to the lead car and told them to pull off once the sedan, hopefully, begins to have operational issues. Like magic, the car started to sputter, sparks began to fly, and the vehicle pulled off the road. John Lee and Jilkes were first on the scene with handguns pointed at the driver. As they covered both sides of the vehicle, Jilkes said, "Well, I'll be damned. What are you doing here?"

The Sarge approached the vehicle and Walter said, "Hi, Cousin, I wanted to tag along and develop some new tactics. Hope I didn't cause you any concern."

The Sarge looked at him and asked, "Can we take a walk? I have a horse I want you to talk to." After giving a lot of reasons why he didn't want Walter on the actual scene, they both agreed that he could watch from the position of the third leapfrog.

###

At the access road to the target's house, the team performed a radio check and then embarked on foot up the hill. True to form, the leapfrog campaign worked well, allowing the leaders to catch their breath and rest, as opposed to trying to run completely up the small mountain and exhausting all their energy.

As two guards leisurely smoked cigarettes, John Lee opened a jar containing his concoction and dipped two darts in it. He carefully handed one to Jilkes and suggested that they aim for the legs or the arms. Considering his concoction had not been tested prior to this engagement, Jilkes asked, "Are you sure this shit is going to work?"

John Lee answered, "I don't know, but it's better than just killing those boys. Now, you know if this here stuff don't work, we have only seconds to gather our weapons and give them there guys a shot to the head."

Asiram said, "I got that. Are you firing your arrows at the same time?"

Jilkes announced, "On 3-2-1 and then we fire."

He began the countdown, and both men fired the arrows together striking each man in the leg. The concoction that John Lee developed, on impact, created a burning sensation. It resulted in the men immediately feeling disoriented. Seconds later, both men simultaneously, fell down gasping for air.

Team members approached their positions, stripped them of their armor, and assumed their positions. Each man was bound, loosely gagged, and placed out of harm's way.

Mallory asked the Sarge, "I wonder if they would give us the same consideration that we are giving them? This process is too cumbersome and time consuming."

The Sarge said, "You're absolutely right, but I personally don't feel like killing anyone tonight except the asshole that sent us those packages." Mallory gave him the thumbs up and they patiently watched as other individuals succumbed to John Lee's potion.

The Sarge said to Mallory, "The benefit of this time-consuming operation is that Jong can safely plant that C-4 and those other ordnances that we borrowed from Asiram. I think this is working out to our advantage."

Mallory indicated, "It's time-consuming, but lifesaving. I am buying into this process. I think the next time we have a lull the in action, we need to figure out a more effective way to administer this stuff."

"I agree. We will ask our new chemist about his concoction. I mean, you have to admit, it knocked those guys out in a hurry."

Jong and McArthur placed three of the five bars of C-4, along with a significant amount of dynamite, to make sure that the structure would be annihilated. Jong was smart enough to place the heaviest concentration of explosives on the opposite side of the house from where his team was operating. As they reached the area where the fourth set of C-4 and dynamite were to be placed, they literally walked up on two guys lounging near, what appeared to be, a garage. McArthur pointed his weapon at them, smiled and said, "I know what you're thinking! You are thinking that you can retrieve your weapons and shoot us before we shoot you, right? Let me tell you something, you are as dead as can be unless you follow my instructions to the letter. You on the right, ease that pistol like it was a baby out of that holster and place it on the ground." There was full compliance by the first guy. McArthur looked at the second guy, whose head Jong had his weapon pointed at and said, "Follow those instructions and you will live to see another day." The second guy turned his body away from McArthur and reached for his weapon. Jong fired a conclusive round into his head.

Jong said to the first guy, "He must have had a death wish. I was pointing my weapon at his fucking-head. What's wrong with people?" Jong then asked the first guy, "How many people are in the house and how many are out here, supposedly, guarding the perimeter?"

The guy replied, "The owner and his young girlfriend are in there along with a maid and his personal attendant."

Jong inquired, "What the hell is a personal attendant?"

The guy answered, "The owner likes to watch and be involved, but mostly watch and throw dust on them, like in one of the movies."

"Would you characterize those people as good people or bad?" Jong asked.

The guy responded, "Good people don't need to hire this many people to keep them safe. Do they?"

McArthur called the Sarge and reported, "We have one down and we're sending one down the hill with his hands bound behind his back."

Jong looked at the guy and said, "We have six of your people down the hill in various states of injury, but they're alive. When you walk down that hill, don't be a hero or think that you can outrun a bullet. We have this entire place covered, and all we want is that SOB in there who sent us a birthday present that we didn't want or appreciate."

Mallory called McArthur and asked, "Was it necessary to put one down?"

McArthur reported, "Jong made that decision and I affirm it. The guy was simply stupid. He tried to draw his gun against the odds."

Mallory proclaimed, "Roger that!" Jong looked at the captured guy and inquired, "How do you people communicate?"

The guy answered, "We have the same stuff you have."

"Do you call for relief?" Jong asked.

"Yes, when we rotate or head to the kitchen, two will come to replace us."

"Make the call." McArthur handed him his weapon minus the chambered round, but with an empty clip, of course. Jong then added, "Let's see how many lives we can save tonight."

Approximately three minutes later, two men with their weapons slung around their necks walked right into an ambush. McArthur said, "We're on a crusade tonight and we don't want to kill anyone else. Please, gently remove those pistols and place them gently on the ground, one at a time. Don't be like the guy over there with the hole in his head who thought that he could out draw two people with weapons pointed at this head.

"Now, remove those assault rifles and place them slowly on the ground. You on the right first, then you on the left. Now, you on the right, ease that knife out of your boot and if you have any other weapons, now would be the time to rid yourself of them. Now, you on the left, do the same damn thing. If my people find a weapon on you, then you will have a hole blown in your head." Both men complied, their hands were bound, and they were told to walk down the hill and to remember that they were being covered and not to try to outrun long guns. McArthur turned to Jong and said, "I'm starting to like this new 'MO' where we don't kill everyone who comes up against us. How about you?"

Jong replied, "I didn't want to shoot that guy. He must have been crazy. I mean, I was pointing a gun at his head. Did he think he was a new Jessie James? That was crazy and a true sign of a death wish that was honored."

The two men continued to place the ordnances around the perimeter of the structure. On the other side of the building, Brown and Bernstein were instructing Zanthius and Larry on the most propitious manner to handle explosives. Larry said to Bernstein, "So, I guess you really like Yvett?"

Bernstein said, "Larry, when you're handling explosives, the only thing you think about is not blowing yourself, or those around you up. Now, if you want to continue to talk about Yvett, that would be at the risk of all of us."

Larry exclaimed, "Shut the hell up and let's get out of here! I don't like this stuff, and I sure as hell don't know a damn thing about it."

Larry looked at Zanthius, and asked, "What's wrong with you?"

Zanthius responded, "I have never been this scared in my life."

Brown noticed the sweat dripping off Zanthius's face and calmly said, "You have a detonator and a bar of C-4 in your hands. I want you to take your left hand and place the detonator on the ground, slowly, and now." Zanthius complied.

Brown continued to give directions and said, "I'm going to hold out my hand and you're going to slowly place that bar in my hand." Zanthius placed the bar in his hand.

Brown said, "I'm just messing with you. This stuff is harmless until they have been connected and timed."

Zanthius breathed a sigh of relief, and whispered, "I knew you were messing with me, but that snake behind you is for real. Don't move, I beg you, don't move."

Brown slowly moved his head and Zanthius said, "I was just fooling with you, that snake is harmless until he bites your ass."

Brown said, "Touché, 'idiot spy', touché!"

Meanwhile, on the other side of the structure, John Lee said to Asiram, "Now, I be wanting you to do exactly as I say or we might have to shoot those guys on the other side. I be needing you to put your tiny feet into the same place that Jilkes here puts his big feet. Now, don't be getting cute on us, just be putting your feet where he places his big feet, and we'll be good."

For about fifty yards, Asiram followed instructions to the letter. When they were within sixty yards of two targets, John Lee slowly descended to his knees. He pulled two darts out of a container and dipped them generously in his concoction. He signaled to Asiram to focus on the guy on the left because he seemed to be active and engaged.

The arrows with dart tips, whizzed through the air, hit their targets, and rendered them immediately unconscious. Asiram asked, "What the hell is in that shit?"

John Lee replied, "I put a little of that, a little of this, added some of the other stuff, shook it, and then added some of something else, that's all."

She looked at Jilkes and inquired, "How long have you known him?"

Jilkes responded, "All of my life and I still don't understand a damn thing he says."

The Sarge said to Mallory, "Damn, I like this approach. We only terminated one person."

Mallory astutely said, "Perhaps it's because we're now chasing them, and not protecting our turf. What are your thoughts on that?"

The Sarge answered, "You might have something there, except in the Nam, we were always the aggressor. Now, that we have seemingly captured the perimeter, do you want to save the lives of those inside, minus the target?"

Mallory replied, "My feelings are the same as yours on this one, we only want the target."

The Sarge opened the channel up and said, "We're going in. I'm lead, and Mallory is my chaser. I want Chakes, Montomie, Whitmore, and Gladstone, as my backup. I want my retreat covered by Jilkes, John Lee, Asiram, Zanthius, and Larry. I want the front covered by Jong, and McArthur. Brown and Bernstein, I want you at the bottom of the hill with the captives, and ready to implode this damn place. Walter, when you see Brown and Bernstein waltzing prisoners by you, head behind them. Okay people, let's get prepared to watch the gift giving celebration."

As the two men entered the palatial house, they could hear sounds of music coming from upstairs. The Sarge motioned to Mallory to scour the downstairs area. As he entered the kitchen, he saw a lone woman placing dishes, in the dish washer. He pointed his weapon at her, placed a finger over his mouth and pointed to the door. He placed the weapon at her throat, and asked, "How many people are in this house?"

She responded, "There are three upstairs in the master bedroom."

He said, "If you're lying to me, I will kill you."

The lady made the sign of the cross, and mumbled, "Three people in the bedroom." Mallory led her to Chakes and told him to get her to safety.

Walter decided that he wanted to personally say goodbye to the target, entered the house against the wishes of McArthur who radioed the Sarge, and told him that the government type had entered the front door. The Sarge told him to let him in. As Walter scaled the steps, Mallory was there to greet him and said, "Don't compromise this mission or I will personally blow your fucking head off. Are you crazy? You can't show up in the middle of an Op as though its natural. We're here to kill this guy."

The Sarge saw Walter and raised his hands as if asking, 'what the fuck'? The Sarge then listened for sounds other than music emanating from the room, pointed to Mallory to cover the left, and he would cover the right side of the room. He indicated to Walter to cover all action straight ahead of them. As Beckmire turned the doorknob gently to open the door, the three men were amazed at the admixture of sexual activity that was in progress. The Sarge lowered his weapon. The three men watched for the better part of a minute as the target moved from one woman to the other. He was dominant in every manner, and the women were clearly under the influence of the white powder.

Mallory stated, "Yelled, enough of this voyeurism. Ladies put your clothes on and move slowly. Any quick movements will result in your death."

The target asked, "What do you want? Why are you here? Who sent you?"

The Sarge retorted, "We decided to give you back the gifts you placed in five vehicles that our families were riding in." A quiet came over the room, and the target inquired, "How much will it cost me to have you guys just go away?"

The Sarge aggressively stated, "Approximately $1 billion dollars."

The target asked, "Suppose I offer you half of that, will you accept it?"

The Sarge replied, "Naw, we're good. We just want your ass, and not your money."

Mallory tore the top sheet off the bed and wrapped the target in it, led him downstairs, and placed him in a chair that seemed to be a product of the Victorian Age. They strapped his hands and feet to the chair and wrapped him in duct tape. The Sarge vociferously exclaimed, "We take it personally that you came after me, and my family! We will meet you again in Hades, and hope you enjoy your trip."

The target yelled, "I can offer you $10 million right now, promise you another $20 million, if you let me go. I can get another $50 million if you turn over the information that the whole world is seeking."

The Sarge looked at Walter and inquired, "What's your take on this? Can we trust him?"

Walter asked, "How did you come into this kind of money?"

The target winked at Walter, and responded, "I work for the U.S. government as well as other governments. I have access to untold amounts of money. Now, if you are smart, I can set you guys up for life, and we will call that matter of the C-4, the cost of doing business."

Walter huddled with the Sarge, and Mallory, and said, "You know another $10 million could help a lot of people." The Sarge told him to play devil's advocate and make it appear as though they had reached an accord with one member, abstaining. Mallory said to the target, "This is your lucky day, two agreed to your terms and one abstained. Where is the money?"

The target answered, "I'm not stupid and I wasn't born yesterday. What guarantees do I have that you won't take the money, and run?"

Mallory replied, "We have principles, unlike you. We just don't randomly attempt to kill innocent people for a questionable item that has yet to be proven. Nor, do we seek revenge because a nefarious person has been caught, and sentenced for peddling drugs."

After a brief pause, the target announced, "Listen, the word on the street is that you people have access to the Carbon Factor, a subject worth discussing in principle, and in terms of monetary enrichment."

Beckmire said, "You know what, we're out of here, negotiations are over."

Walter winked at the target and asked, "So, who is your main contact?"

The target said, "That's way above your pay grade. Now, if you want to make a deal and release me, I'll fill you in on all kinds of interesting intel that might just save the lives of you people."

Walter looked at the Sarge, and said, "I just have a few more questions for this guy, please indulge me for a minute."

Walter then looked at the target and said, "You know your ass is pretty much cooked. It sure wasn't too smart of you to act as if you were carrying on negotiations with those fellows from Asia while your son was in another part of the hotel conducting a drug deal, all while the people you were meeting with were offering you their product for information on the Carbon Factor. Were those two really from China and Japan? When did they begin a drug smuggling business, and develop détente as well? If you want to make sure your son doesn't leave prison wearing a skirt, then I think you need to make some choices here."

The target looked at Walter and then the Sarge, and said, "First, your people like that product; it's cheap, and it's a quick high. It can be cut a thousand times and make money for everyone involved. That product was developed for the blacks because we know you people have an addictive gene. The Chinese, and Japanese fellows are diplomats, but they're looking for an early retirement.

We started our meeting talking about some piss-ass little island in the Pacific, but once the room was scanned to everyone's satisfaction, the conversation turned into a bidding war for information on the Carbon Factor. The drug deal was a distraction, that had been confirmed, and agreed upon, earlier.

"The notion that a high-level diplomatic meeting was taking place gave it security, distance from the police, and the press. You people showed up and screwed up both deals. We were at the threshold of a billion-dollar deal with the drugs as an income factor and distributed only in the black neighborhoods. The Carbon Factor became a three-way deal between two industrious Asian gentlemen, and me. Now, if you want to know who is, or are the person or persons who pull my strings, then you have got to reach a deal with me and release me. Otherwise, I will die with my secrets."

Beckmire muttered, "Hold that thought, a minute." He called Jong and Asiram and asked them to make their way into the house. He was informed by Asiram that Zanthius had to come as well. The Sarge, directed Gladstone, and Whitmore to take their places alongside Brown, and Bernstein.

As Jong, Zanthius, and Asiram entered the house, the target exclaimed, "Well, I'll be damned. Alive, and in person; it's the 'idiot spy'! I have heard a lot about you, your woman and I am hoping you're a bit more compassionate than this Vietnam vet. Is he related to you?"

Zanthius smiled, and replied, "That woman is my wife, and that Vietnam vet, is my father. We have gone through extraordinary challenges to meet and send you on your way."

The Sarge motioned for them to huddle outside of the captive's hearing range. Once they were away from the captive, the Sarge told Jong, Zanthius, and Asiram to go to the master bedroom and check for safes or lock boxes. He told them that he was especially interested in this guy's phone book.

Asiram, with her keen nose and eyes for distractions envisioned what she would do if she wanted to hide something in her own place. She knocked on the walls of the room, entered a closet and recognized a significant difference in the sound of the walls in the bedroom as opposed to those in the closet. The answer became simple to her because the design of the shoe rack was identical to one that was proposed to her by her in-wall safe builders. It was the same in that the third shoe in the rack was the opening mechanism for the sliding wall, which gave full view of the wall safe. She called Jong in and reported, "Here is the safe and it's locked."

A few minutes later, and prior to descending the steps, Zanthius proclaimed, "Honey, I got this one. Lend me your knife."

Zanthius walked down the steps and saw the target smiling. He smiled back and announced, "We located your safe, but it's locked. So, before I ask you how to open it, I'm going to bleed you." He walked to where the target was strapped in, and slowly but methodically, penetrated his leg enough to allow for blood to gush from the wound. Walter was about to say something when Beckmire grabbed him, and whispered, "If this is too much for your stomach, then wait outside."

Zanthius said, "I know that hurts. Now, my next move is going to make you piss your pants." Zanthius moved to the targets other leg, penetrated it lightly, and knew that the deeper he dug the knife into the target's leg, the quicker the flow of information would follow. Zanthius said, "Now, I'm going to ask you a couple of questions. At this point, it really doesn't matter to me what you say because you were going to kill everyone that matters to me. So, here is question number one. What is the combination to the safe?"

The target yelled, "Go screw, yourself." Zanthius began to dig the knife deeper into the target's leg and his screams turned into a cacophony of distress sounds. Zanthius highlighted the target's sounds with his own variation on the theme by making unintelligible sounds.   As the target screamed for mercy, Zanthius screamed at the top of his lungs, "Hell man, ain't no mercy here! You want mercy, call Marvin Gaye."

As if playing a game, Zanthius withdrew the blade from the man's leg, wiped it on the garment he was wrapped in, threw the blade towards the target's right foot and the blade entered the floor.

Zanthius shouted, "Keep the combination! I'm just going to enjoy cutting your ass to pieces. By the way, I hate people who call me the 'idiot spy'."

The target screamed, "04 right, 14 left, 24 right and 44 left." While Jong was heading up the steps, Zanthius pulled out a roll of duct tape and aggressively taped the target's two leg wounds.

Meanwhile once Jong was upstairs, he looked at the dial and realized that the number four, or any combinations of fours, were considered unlucky in the Asian culture, and they certainly would not end that sequence with the number forty-four, the sign of death in Asia. He walked downstairs and screamed, "That asshole has the safe wired. It was made in China. Numbers that end in four are a sure sign of treachery, especially with the annotation of the number forty-four as the last digit, a sure sign of death. I think there is another combination. Why don't we make him open it with the numbers he gave you?"

Asiram called down to Jong and asked him to come up to the room a minute. When he arrived, she showed him three large duffle bags. Jong looked at the bags individually and said, "Doesn't feel like clothes to me. Let's take them downstairs and watch his reaction."

Jong carried two bags, and Asiram carried the third. They dropped them in front of the target. He smiled, and said, "That, my dear, represents a part of the deal I'm willing to make with these guys. It will prove that I am playing straight now by making amends on my reckless actions of placing C-4 in your vehicles. To me, this is my way of saying, I'm sorry. All I need from you guys is some indication that we have a truce, that the past is truly prologue, and that you'll get me to the hospital."

Zanthius inquired, "So, if I empty these bags on the floor, nothing is going to explode or bite us, right?"

The target responded, "Unless money bites, then I think you'll find that I'm a man of my word."

Jong asked, "If a snake is frozen and then thawed, what does that make it?"

The target replied, "It will always be a snake." Jong carefully opened the first bag and gently poured the contents on the floor. It was a shit load of money. Zanthius gathered the spoils and placed them back into the bag. As he felt inside one of the inner pockets, he found a small bar of C-4. He gently pulled it out and said, "Once a snake, always a snake." He left what money he had replaced in the bag. He placed the C-4 into the bag and shoved it near the right leg of the target.

Zanthius waltzed into the kitchen area and looked in the utility closet and found a box of industrial strength trash bags. He came out of the kitchen whistling, 'She Be Coming Around the Mountain When She Comes." The target said, "Obviously I couldn't disclose everything until I was certain that we had a deal; do you fault me?"

The Sarge replied, "I understand completely what you've done. It makes for good business when doing business with strangers." He then asked, Jong, "Can you and Asiram escort those bags out to our guys, so we can wrap up this matter?"

He then looked at Walter and said, "The vote is two to one in favor of us letting him go. Now, the question I need him to answer before I ratify that vote is, what is the true combination of the safe? Don't play games because I will rig that shit at your feet and blow the bottom parts of your legs off. Again, I warn you, don't play games!"

The target answered, "There is nothing of value in that safe that will assist you or your people in this matter. It's mainly personal stuff and insurance policies."

"In that case, you won't mind if we confirm that to make sure you are trustworthy."

The target paused, and said, "12 left—18 right—27 left—38 right". Walter said, "I hope you're not playing a game with me because I'm going to go open that thing and hope I don't get blown away."

Beckmire asked, "You sure you want to trust him?"

Walter responded, "I think he knows we're the key to him getting out of the country."

Walter walked up the stairs, inadvertently made a left turn instead of a right, and ended up in another bedroom. In that room to his horror, he found a corpse that looked exactly like the target. He yelled, "Sarge, I need you up here."

When the Sarge reached the top of the stairs, Walter mumbled, "Come and have a look at this." Upon seeing the corpse, the Sarge did a double take and exclaimed, "Damn! So, that was his plan, to use this corpse, and implode the place himself. I think we need to forget that damn safe and get the hell out of this place. Let's walk out the front door, and not look back." The Sarge called his group and announced, "Exit in five minutes, people. Let's make it happen. Cover your faces when dealing with the captives."

###

At the base of the hill, some groggy people, and others who were happy to be alive were being given a stern warning. "If you come after us, we will take you, your families, and friends to a place of no return!" the Sarge warned. The Sarge then turned to Jong, and said, "Give each man a stack of money."

As they entered the SUVs, the Sarge looked at Jong, and asked, "Is everything ready?"

Jong replied, "Just waiting on your word."

The Sarge inquired, "Are we all present and accounted for?"

Asiram asked, "Where is Larry?" The Sarge took a head count, and Larry was missing. As they exited their SUVs, three individuals slowly walked towards the vehicles. Jilkes and John Lee assumed the low position and gave each other the go sign. One of the mercs announced, "We will blow his head off! Now, drop your weapons."

The Sarge said, "Here's the deal, I don't know what you expect to gain by endangering your lives, but I suggest you let our team member go and you walk away from this event alive."

The merc who was talking proclaimed, "We want our money, and if you don't give it to us, he's as good as dead."

The Sarge said, "Your money is at the feet of your boss. We didn't come here for money. Your boss placed C-4 in our cars, and we were just returning the favor. The money is in the house. Let our man go, and we will call it a draw."

The guy talking exclaimed, "Asshole, we make the terms, not you!"

The Sarge said, "Please, just let him go. We'll let you live like the rest of your people, and you will get to see another day."

"Shut the fuck up." Jilkes and John Lee then started their countdown and after they reached number one, two shots were fired, and two men forfeited their lives.

The Sarge said, "I gave them every opportunity to live. I guess that wasn't enough. What happened to you Larry, how did they catch you?"

Larry said, "I cold cocked one of them as he was walking by. I leaned up against a tree, and the next thing I knew, I'm falling down a shaft. The guy has tunnels all over the place. Must be a spy thing, I guess. Anyway, when I hit the ground, those two were standing over me with their weapons drawn."

"Walter, did you know about the tunnels?" the Sarge asked.

Walter responded, "I didn't know about tunnels, and therefore, no harm, no foul."

The Sarge was fuming as John Lee walked over to him, and inquired, "Why don't we just get out of here, and discuss this here problem somewhere later? I be knowing what you be thinking. It won't help this here cause, we need to vacate."

The Sarge said, "Jong, are we still hot, and if so, let it rain." Jong looked at the device, turned to Asiram and asked, "Would you mind doing the honors?" Asiram took the device, clicked the on button, and then pressed the hot button. The night sky lit up in a spectacular array of colors assisted by the explosives the target had placed to cover his escape. As the caravan started down the highway, it was obvious the Sarge was still upset. Asiram exclaimed, "Daddy-in-Law, that was pretty cool! I mean pushing a button and blowing up somebody else's house. Now, I understand the joy you got out of blowing my farmhouse to bits." She purposefully shifted the attention from Walter and defused the potential ass whupping that the Sarge was about to deliver to him.

The Sarge said, "Blowing up your house was not easy for me but was necessary. By the time, this thing is over, the footprint of your new place should be going up with those special windows, and a few tunnels for you as well, my love. I took the liberty to have them design a couple of exits. I hope you don't mind my interference."

Asiram looked at him and said, "This entire situation could not be orchestrated by one man alone. I can't believe that I saw the 'idiot spy' in the airport, fell in love, made love for the first time in my life, and joined this crazy/whacky organization by default. I have had the best time of my life, and I absolutely love all these guys. I really want to kiss you Jong, for giving me the opportunity to blow some shit up."

###

Moments, prior to the explosion, a figure emerged from a wall panel, freed the target from bondage, and helped him to a hidden elevator that led to an escape tunnel.

The target yelled, "Get the bag, get the bag."

Two minutes later, and thirty feet underground, the two individuals could hear and feel the tremendous roar from the explosion. The explosion and after shock rocked the foundation of the house, and those of nearby homes and businesses.

Walter's wink was an acknowledgement, that help was in the walls. Walter knew about the main tunnel and the huge safe that was in it. The bedroom safe was a ruse and was used as a pay out if things went south if he was ever compromised.

Prior to meeting Beckmire on the road, Walter escorted one of his trusted mercs, blindfolded, into the tunnel, and eventually, placed him in the wall space.

In the safe in the tunnel, Walter knew that there was at least forty million dollars in uncut diamonds, twenty million in bearer bonds, eighty pounds of $100 dollar bills, and more importantly, still photos and videos of himself doing what he likes to do best! There was also a disk that was satanic in nature featuring pagan rituals that were depressingly vial, wicked and inhumane! Walter knew exactly what was in the safe because it was his safe and the target was his puppet. Walter was indeed on a mission to clean up his history.

Outside of the safe in the tunnel, the target said, "Stay right there, I'm going to make us both rich."

He then entered the safe and began to look around. The merc acted as though he was not interested in what was in the safe but was sadly surprised when the target pulled the pin of a grenade, threw it into the tunnel and shut the door to the safe behind him.

Inside of the safe, the target piled bags with bonds, diamonds, and cash and placed them onto a cart, re-taped his bleeding legs, and ventured out of the tunnel and into a garage that included a shiny 500sl Benz.

As the car started without a hitch, he screamed out loud, "I fucked up once, while dealing with you people, the next time will be unfortunately, catastrophic for all who are in your compound."

## CHAPTER TEN

At the airport, the Sarge showed restraint and walked over to Walter and said, "That is exactly why we don't welcome uninvited guest to our operations. You could have gotten my son killed by not having complete intel on the target's house. Then you act cavalier about it, and say some dumb shit like 'no harm, no foul'. That was your last mission with us and if you ever provide me with incomplete intel and place one of mine in harm's way again, I will personally terminate you. Then you won't have to worry about your little secret."

Walter, looking extremely sad and uncomfortable said, "I have to admit, I'm not as good at this as you people are. I made a huge mistake and I promise you that I will never intervene in one of your Ops, unless requested by you. I'm so sorry, and that is all I can say."

Beckmire placed a call to Courtney and told her that the job was a success and that they captured, rather than killed, most of the enemy. She told him she was happy there were alternatives to killing, because she had sworn an oath to help to preserve life. Courtney indicated to Ben that she had experienced a mixed set of emotions when she was helping the sick and injured as he was killing people. Courtney advised, "Tell that Bernstein that he had better call Yvett or she won't be waiting here for him. She has been withdrawn all day, saying that he hasn't called her once to check on her."

As they were boarding the two jets, the Sarge yelled, "Hey, Bernstein, can I have a moment?" Bernstein walked over to him, and the Sarge asked, "Is there a problem with you and my niece?"

"No! I don't think so. Why are you asking?"

"Dude, you can't go off, and fight small wars without checking in. She is distraught about the fact that you haven't called to check on her."

"I wasn't sure she wanted me to do that. I mean we talk and all, and I have been extremely respectful. I just don't know what else to do to show her I am genuinely interested in her. I say things, and she seems to just to discount them."

"Can you imagine the amount of shit that she has heard from people she was forced to relate to? Dude press the issue on all fronts. Send some damn flowers, I hate the idea, but send them anyway, plus a box of chocolates. Now, if that don't get her going, then I'll ship her ass back to the outback," both men laughed.

Bernstein inquired, "What plane is Jong on? He knows how to contact those kinds of people."

The Sarge laughed and replied, "The same plane you're on, my brother."

As Larry settled into his seat, "Whitmore walked over to him and stated, "Glad you're okay, my brother. You know some of us had doubts about you, and the post office stuff, but you demonstrated you are truly a Beckmire--shoot first and ask questions later." They laughed and then engaged in a weird handshake.

The Sarge closed his eyes and entered a state of soliloquy. "He thought, I must be addicted to this kind of trauma, because frankly, I'm enjoying every minute. This is exciting and dangerous, but I love the adrenaline rush and my guys are looking younger by the day. Jilkes and John Lee move like snakes, shoot like guided missiles, roll in the dirt, and are as reliable as can be. Mallory keeps me grounded, cuts through the chase and manages our emotions. Then you take the almost crippled Jong with his contacts. He has abilities, and planning skills that are off the chart. Chakes, Montomie, Gladstone, McArthur, and Whitmore are as solid as a rock, and effective in any scenario you thrust them into. And, let me not even think about my all-around guys, Brown, and Bernstein; two odd but brilliant players who play for keeps. I am blessed to have met, trained, killed, and survived episode after episode with a group of guys who I would take a bullet for."

The planes roared into the night sky and everyone was sound asleep after the wheels left the ground, except Larry. Larry was wondering to himself how he fell into that tunnel. His eyes began to water when he thought that the Sarge might discount his abilities in the future. As he recalled the incident, he concluded that all he did was lean on a tree, the ground opened up below him, and that was all there was to it.

Mallory looked across the aisle, saw Larry apparently in a quandary, walked over to him and asked, "Who the hell knew that guy had built tunnels? He must be related to Asiram. Anyway, it could have happened to any of us, but you're going to say it didn't, and you're right; it happened to you. Larry, get over it and realize that this is a new kind of conflict for us, and one that you understand better than most of us--the war in the concrete jungle. We all learned from tonight and will keep learning until this mess is over. Insofar as we're concerned, we owe you one for that post office deal. In other words, we're even at this point. Think nothing about the incident because we always watch each other's backs. I, and the rest of the team members are not concerned; you proved yourself in D C, my brother."

One down, two to go, to satisfy Walter's three part play. While the others were sleeping, Larry took the opportunity to study the photo of Harold's wife. He envisioned what he would need to make Asiram look like her. His only concern was the signature. To make it look authentic, Asiram would have to dedicate time to perfecting the resemblance. He looked forward in the cabin and saw Asiram and Zanthius in a deep sleep. He decided to wake her, and start the preparations for the next job, if she was amenable to such a thing at this hour. He nudged Asiram, and whispered, "Sorry to wake you, but I need to have your input on this next project."

Asiram looked at him, and asked, "Can it wait? I'm tired as can be."

Larry answered, "It is at this level of mental fatigue that I need you to practice replicating the signature. Please trust me on this one."

Asiram got out of her seat. Larry showed her the signature and said, "Please follow my instructions. I don't want you to study the signature, I only want you to look at it and attempt to remember what it looks like. I want you to consciously write down what you think it looks like, and then I want you to write it down as you remember seeing it. Two different requests, that probably could be considered the same, but there is a difference. Don't ask me what the difference is until you have figured it out yourself."

Asiram said, "Larry, I used to like you. I'm now questioning, that decision."

Asiram wrote the signature as she first recalled it and realized that there were points of emphasis that she omitted. On her second attempt, she nailed it with the curves, flows, and articulation of her last name. She looked at Larry and inquired, "What were you, a forger in your last life?"

Larry smiled and replied, "Naw, nothing that sexy. I just have a knack for realizing that the first thing you see is not always a picture of the entire environment, something that the Sarge and I discovered years ago."

Asiram said, "That keeps haunting me. What exactly did you and the Sarge do?"

Larry smiled at her and responded, "It's much like what I suppose you did, things that you'd like to forget, but you remember the survival skills and other lessons that you learned while executing your mission."

"Touché. Perhaps one day, you and I can have a long discussion about yesteryear and learn to laugh about it as well."

"That would be nice, by the way, here is a photo of the person I'll transform you into tomorrow. I want you to do the same thing with the photo as you did with the signature, and together we will make you look convincingly like this person."

Zanthius had awakened and approached the two. He asked, "Can you replicate the signature?"

Asiram gave Larry a high five and said, "With his help, it was a piece of cake."

In another part of the plane, Mallory nudged the Sarge and muttered, "Man, stop calling those hogs."

The Sarge said, "That wasn't me, it was you. What's up?"

Mallory answered, "I have to tell you, I have a really good feeling about letting those guys live. Other than the main mission, it would have been poor judgement to just execute those guys who chose that line of work to earn a living; much like us not choosing Nam but having to do that kind of work. I really feel good about sparing those guys."

"You're absolutely correct. I mean we came after them this time, not like them coming after us, which gives a whole new meaning to engagement when your family and friends are at stake. I think whenever we get a chance to spare a life, we should do it. It makes us better human beings and lowers the number of souls that we have to dream about," the Sarge said.

"Have you had a chance to talk to Larry about his little incident? I'm asking because I know how much you mean to each other. I know that he only wants to impress you and make you feel proud of him. Hell, that could have happened to anyone of us. Luckily, it was a young guy who could land on his feet," Mallory stated.

The Sarge smiled at Mallory and said, "Larry knows the difference between a blunder, and an unexpected, or unarticulated trap. He shrugged it off, and therefore, I'm not going to mention it to him again but, I can guarantee you one thing, it won't happen again. My boy is sharp as a tack, and who the hell could have known that resting up against a tree would open up a portal to a tunnel. That was some wicked shit, a tree post that opens into a tunnel. Now that is paranoia at its best."

Mallory laughed and replied, "I think on this mission we needed those civilians because we were outmanned and outgunned. When we land, and after the third part of this mission, I think we all should find some salty blue water and just lay the hell in it, all day. Not sure if I want to head all the way back to Australia to do that, but maybe an all-inclusive stent on one of the islands would be nice. Think about it and let me know."

###

Forty-five minutes later, the captain engaged the fasten seat belt sign indicating they were starting their descent. In the rear of the cabin, Asiram, Zanthius, and Larry were having a heated discussion about photos that she had on her phone. Zanthius contended that the first photo of the condom gave directions to a particular place, and that the second photo of the card from the Russian strip joint gave the latitude and longitude of the place. Larry was telling the group that he thought there must be more to it than those simple coordinates because it was alleged that the capsule had two numbers, and the degree sign on it.

The Sarge and Mallory went to the back of the plane, and the Sarge asked, "What's going on?"

Larry responded, "We're trying to figure out the intel on the condom and the card. We have differing opinions as to what it means in light of the fact that two numbers and the degree sign were on the inside of the capsule."

Mallory smiled and asked, "Shouldn't we be preparing for tomorrow's challenge first?"

Asiram replied, "Larry, and I, got that one, unless it's a set up." The Sarge looked at Zanthius, and shrugged his shoulders as if to say, "you heard her; they got this one."

The captain came on the intercom system and announced, "We are approximately thirty minutes from landing, and I need everyone in their seats with their belts tight across their midsection. See you in a few."

Mallory asked the Sarge if they concluded the selection of pilots for the other two planes. The Sarge told him he didn't think the process was complete, but he would ask Jong as soon as they landed.

CHAPTER ELEVEN

As the teams disembarked, Beckmire saw Jong, and inquired, "Where is the dive that we're staying at tonight?"

Jong answered, "If I told you, would you know how to get there from here?"

The Sarge started to walk away and mumbled, "I love a smartass."

Jong yelled, "I heard that, Sergeant Beckmire."

As Larry, Zanthius, and Asiram were descending the steps, they were still discussing the card and the condom. The Sarge walked over and asked, "Are you people still debating the logistics about that card and condom?"

Asiram responded, "Seems to us, the sooner we get rid of that card and condom, the sooner we get rid of all of this mayhem." The Sarge turned and walked away without saying a word.

###

Later, as the groups entered their SUVs, the Sarge began to think about what Asiram had said relative to the Carbon Factor. The Sarge had an epiphany. In reality, a part of him was enjoying every aspect of this adventure; with him calling the shots once again, his team in place and efficient, and his family playing a part as well. Yes, in a way, he really was enjoying this adventure and didn't really want it to stop. Actually, the situation began to make him second guess his reasons for not wanting the matter to conclude anytime soon, because he was surely enjoying the brotherhood, and family bonding that was taking place in the interim. He thought about the emotions that he felt when Jilkes and Bernstein were injured, and more recently his emotional reaction to the capture of Larry. He slammed his hand against the dashboard and proclaimed, "We have got to end this shit! There are other ways that we can commune without endangering our lives and compromising the lives of other people." The other occupants of the vehicle became as quiet as church mice.

Asiram said, "Daddy-in-Law, I think you took my statement the wrong way."

"No, honey, I was beginning to enjoy this shit with you, my boys, Zanthius, and Larry, as well as, Carlos, and his guys, all playing a part. No, your words shocked me back to reality. I was thinking about how I felt when I heard that Bernstein and Jilkes were injured. My body went into shock because I thought, prematurely, that they were at the end of their days. Your words, and I thank you for them, are what I needed to hear. I have been so caught up in playing Sergeant Beckmire that I almost forgot the fact that I'm a family man with friends who have families, who really don't want to be doing the same shit that we did in the Nam. Jesus, I lost focus, and you brought me back to reality.

"At every venue, we have collected untold amounts of money, and not a single person has ever asked the question, 'what's my share'? It has not been about the money or our two new planes, but about the fact that I am with my family, and my lifelong friends. I screwed this up by enjoying my self-appointed superior status as the master of all decisions. Wow, Daughter-in-Law, I love you, and thank you, for bringing me back to reality. I was out there, looking to start my own private war for the simple pleasures of being important, and active again."

Zanthius said, "Pops, you need some rest. I will not, nor will anyone else, say or think that you did this for your own personal reasons when we all know that people were trying to kill us at every turn. No, what you did was man-up, and lead us to a place where we are secure, and a lot safer than we were when this mess first started. I mean, can you say you went to meet my mother at that restaurant because you knew that some nut was going to shoot the place up? Can you honestly say that because I kissed a woman, and was passed some mysterious capsule, that you were called to action to protect me when you didn't even know I existed? Maybe you knew in the spirit world of our ancestors, but not in the context of what we have been through. And by the way, can you tell me that you enjoyed watching me execute those fellas in the barn, especially knowing that I was truly from your seed? No, Dad, like the man said, "this is conjured and distorted truths."

Zanthius continued, "Now, if you can give me affirmative answers to that mess, then I will say that my father is a war monger and loves to live in the midst of chaos and destruction. There is no way I can say that and mean it. Let it go, but I will tell you one thing--I have absolutely loved the action. I mean, I love the whole gun thing, the torturing thing I learned from my new wife and discovering how to foil an ambush. This shit has gotten my adrenaline flowing big time and I do not want it to end. But I also realize that we have overcome superior numbers and survived, but can we continue to do so, is the question that lingers in my mind.

"I just know that I love my wife, my mothers, my father, his friends, their children, my brother Larry, and, oh, my sister, Rashida. To be completely honest with you, I was probably a day away from killing myself when my mother showed up at my door. Guys, I was in a bad place, and state of mind. I was deep into the booze and probably hadn't slept for over forty-eight hours. I was distraught, and completely suicidal because I had hurt people in search of pleasure. I had destroyed marriages, relationships, and was in the process of being divorced by my first wife. I was a mess, and yes, I love these adventures because they gave me you, Asiram, and you, Pops. I didn't quite know about Larry and Rashida, but I have come to really dig them. So, do I want this to end? Hell, no, because it keeps me and my family extremely close to one another. Can I accept the outcomes if this ends tomorrow? Hell, yes, because me, and my baby, are going to have a baby."

The Sarge and Asiram were crying their eyes out. Larry reached across the seat, and put pressure on the Sarge's neck, and said, "Man, you know I love you, and I don't have to prove it; you just know it. Just let it out and enjoy the fact that you can cry without being judged a weakling. I know you have got to love that."

As the Sarge looked over at Jong who was driving, he saw that he was crying. He asked, "What the hell are you crying about?"

Jong between deep breaths answered, "There is no bond stronger than the true love of friends and family. The Sarge already knows that I would take two bullets for him, but now I'll say that I'll take a half of a bullet for each of you." They all broke into laughter.

CHAPTER TWELVE

The motel they pulled into was truly a dive and the Sarge asked Jong, "How do you find these places?"

Jong looked at him and replied, "You want to be on, or under the radar?"

"Good point, my brother."

Larry told the Sarge that he needed to shop for supplies for tomorrow's transformation and that Asiram would have to accompany him. The Sarge told him to take his eyes and ears, John Lee, and Jilkes, with him.

###

It was obvious from the pictures they had of Harold's wife, that she was not a bargain basement shopper. They went to a nearby mall and Asiram picked out a blouse similar to the one in the picture. Larry looked at the photo and realized that Asiram's hair was brunette, while Harold's wife sported slightly darker red hair. Larry asked Asiram if she wanted a wig or preferred to color her hair. Asiram, without hesitating, told him that a wig would be preferable. Although Harold's wife was heavier than Asiram, Larry realized that the blouse color and loose fitting pants would provide the necessary façade. While walking through one of the higher end stores, Asiram said, "You have got to tell me how you learned all of this stuff."

Larry smiled and asked, "Do you like those pants? They are cut wide and will betray the true figure hidden beneath. They are what I suggest you try on; I'd rather you not query me about my taste in fashion and make up."

Asiram laughed and said, "You know Larry, if we are going to continue to work together, I suggest that you lighten up a little and share some trade secrets." Larry pointed to the pants and then to the dressing room.

Prior to sending her into the room, Jilkes had scouted out the area. He, and John Lee were strategically placed and aware of their surroundings. A salesperson came over to Asiram, and exclaimed, "Honey, you don't hardly need that cut!"

Larry snapped his fingers, waltzed over to where the salesperson was standing, and said, "Honey, if you don't know the party then you shouldn't bring the music." He pointed to the dressing room, and off Asiram went.

John Lee said to Jilkes, "Now, he be having a lot of personalities in that mind of his. He flipped that switch on a hog's ear."

Jilkes asked, "How do you flip a switch on a hog's ear?"

John Lee responded, "How the hell should I know? But you knew what I be talking about. Now, didn't you?"

Asiram came out of the dressing room and Larry took the liberty of checking her out.

Asiram asked, "Might I ask what you're feeling for?"

Feeling a little embarrassed, Larry replied, "A place with room enough, and ease of access to conceal and gather a weapon in case all goes south."

Asiram shrugged her shoulders and said, "Continue, Maestro, do what you must."

"My touch was not personal, but I should have advertised my movements and asked permission. However, I'm looking at you from the point of view of the tellers, security, and the cameras. This action is serious, and I must make sure that you act the part, look the part, and are prepared to be a tiger if necessary."

Jilkes said, "That dude is as serious as can be. I like how he prepares for things that I never would have thought about. Would you have thought about her appearance?"

John Lee replied, "I be a lot smarter than you, so the obvious answer, be yes."

Jilkes said, "I hope we're smarter than those two knuckleheads over there casing the joint."

Jilkes got Larry's attention, and motioned towards the door, meaning it was time to vacate. Asiram saw the change in expressions on Jilkes, and John Lee's faces, and realized that something was awry. Jilkes motioned to John Lee and the two men headed towards the register with the garments that they had picked out. As they placed the items on the counter, the smaller of the two men commanded, "Put your money on the counter, or I'll blow your damn head off."

John Lee said, "Okay!" He reached in his pocket and pulled out a roll of hundred dollar bills and sat it on the counter. The guy was stunned by the sight of so much money, and as he reached for the it, Larry was on him with his pistol placed in the guy's ear. He vehemently instructed the man to lay the gun on the counter. Jilkes, in the meantime, had slapped the other guy into next week after taking control of his pistol. Realizing that they were on camera, Asiram walked by and announced, "You have eyes on you."

The two men hustled the little crooks outside and Jilkes said, "If I ever see you two around here again, I'm gonna give you the whupping of a lifetime. Now get the hell out of here!"

As they entered the SUV, Asiram said, "That was pretty fast. You guys have a nose for stuff that's out of place, and Larry you keep surprising me. That was bold, conclusive and they didn't have a chance to react."

John Lee said, "I was going to give him the money and tell him to leave, but I didn't want them taking them guns with them."

Back at the motel, Beckmire was in the lounge and asked them how it went? He was told that it was business as usual. The good guys versus bad guys, and that there was a situation where there was no harm done and, therefore, no foul. Beckmire asked, "What the hell does that mean?"

Asiram answered, "Just a minor misunderstanding, but we handled it, no one was hurt, that's all."

Zanthius saw his bride, and said, "I missed you. How was your date with my brother?"

Asiram said, "Other than his fast hands, I think everything went okay."

Zanthius asked, "What about his fast hands?"

Asiram replied, "Honey, he was searching for a place for me to carry a weapon, that's all."

Larry looked at Zanthius, threw both hands in the air, and said, "Trust me, I didn't think it was out of bounds, but I guess I surprised her and that is what this is about. Absolutely nothing, other than her trying to get you upset at my expense. Oh, and by the way, I'm going to need that wig to style tonight. Catch you guys later."

As Zanthius and Asiram were walking towards their room, he stopped her and asked, "What the hell happened in that store?"

Asiram apparently surprised by the question, replied, "Zanthius what do you think happened? Where are you going with this? Listen, Larry, unlike you and me, plans his jobs. He picked out the pants in this bag and had me try them on. I went into the dressing room alone, and when I came out, he grabbed my waist, and pulled on the pants in the front and back."

"What the hell was he doing that for?"

"Sweetheart, he wants me to carry a weapon in case this job goes south, nothing more and just a ball breaker for you. Your brother is very respectful of you and me. Plus, he apparently sees things differently than you and me, do. Okay, he said, here is a blouse that looks like the one she's wearing, and the pants will give you a fullness like her. Then pulling on the pants he says, 'I need a place for you to conceal a weapon'. He is looking at me from a teller's point of view, security, and the cameras. He is covering all the angles."

Asiram noticed Zanthius still seemed concerned. She grabbed his hands and continued, "Baby, do you think I have a thing for your brother? If you do, then you had better sleep somewhere else tonight because I will break you apart. If you have issues, then we had better start seeking therapy and I mean in a hurry. I like Larry, yes, I like him, but he's your brother, and a real gentleman, and he doesn't seem to give a shit about what I think as long as he can get back to that wife of his, and the twins. Let this one go. Let it go. I am surprised by your jealousy, but I'm also flattered by it. Listen, you rescued me from an abyss. I'm hopefully pregnant with your child, and we're married. What the hell is going on in your head? I'm yours, and I will die being yours, and only, yours."

Asiram was about to say something when Zanthius placed a finger over her lips and said, "If you asked me to go in the room and shoot myself in the head, I would gladly do it. I just lost it when I heard about fast hands and thought about my good-looking brother. I mean, I just thought that he made a pass at you and, to some degree, it was acceptable to you."

Asiram quipped, "He came back with both of his hands, didn't he?"

Zanthius smiled and acknowledged, "I love you more than life. When I'm away from you, I miss you terribly. Please forgive my reaction, I love you so much." In the hallway he kissed her and began to search her mouth with his tongue while her tongue was seeking acknowledgment in his mouth. The kisses were beyond the notions of passion and led to the ultimate meaning of a kiss. They literally fell into their room. Asiram became the aggressor, seeking his hands, and searching his mouth while making sensuous sounds of pleasure and whispering in his ear, "take me, take me, take me now."

As the two fell onto the bed, Zanthius began to provide Asiram with pleasure by kissing and sucking her toes, an experience she had never had, and gently rubbing her inner thighs. He turned her on her stomach, began to kiss each leg, both sides of her voluptuous rear, and worked his way up to the nape of her neck, and then whispered continuously in her ear that she was the most magnificent person that he had ever met, and the best lover he had ever encountered. He turned her over and began to suckle her breast while rubbing his fingers close to that zone of craziness. Asiram became so excited that she had a massive orgasm just from his touches and kisses.

Zanthius continued his expose` and began to kiss her sides. He made his way to her navel. It was at that point that Asiram screamed for joy once again because her man had found various ways to satisfy her without the basic approach. As she panted and attempted to catch her breath, Zanthius whispered, "Don't take your eyes off me, don't close your eyes. Watch me make you explode once again." He began to kiss her stomach and slowly worked his way down to the center of her universe and began to give her untold pleasures. She watched her man provide delectation beyond anything she had ever experienced and with the sanctity of love and fidelity. Asiram had eruptions and explosions, one after the other. Zanthius exposed his wife to the creative ways love could manifest itself. After six massive, earth-shattering, cataclysmic eruptions, the volcano, named Asiram, fell into the world of dreams.

Zanthius exclaimed, "Hello? Hello? I'm still in the bed! Hello?"

## CHAPTER THIRTEEN

At 0700 hours, Zanthius woke up and said, "Hello, I'm still here. Can I get some attention?"

Asiram stirred and mumbled, "You are the best husband that a woman could possibly want. You are unselfish and accommodating and you aim to please without any consideration for yourself, I love you so much. I'm famished, can we get something to eat, my love?"

Zanthius looked at her and then his member and said, "Of course dear. My goal, and charge in life, is to apparently, make sure that all is good with you. I'll just jump in the shower, and hopefully we can shower together."

Asiram said, "No dear, you have it all to yourself, and I will take a long and invigorating shower after you finish. I can't tell you how much last night meant to me. I have never had such enjoyment and pleasure. All of this is so new to me, and I thank you for being so kind, considerate, and patient with me."

Zanthius mumbled, "Considerate, and kind, eh"?

At 0800 hours Larry, was in the lobby stretching when he saw John Lee and Jilkes and asked, "Are you two ever separated? Anyway, want to go for a long stroll through the hood?"

Jilkes replied, "We already did. I hope you have a little back up with you. Lots of people who are down and out and are hanging around looking for a millennial to come running by them so that they can mug his ass."

Larry retorted, "Then why don't you guys come with me and keep the bad people from mugging, my millennial ass?"

John Lee answered, "The way you handled them there people at that post office tells me that you got this, and don't need no old ass vets tagging behind you and slowing yo young ass down."

"Whatever! Catch you guys in thirty."

Later, while having coffee and debating who beat whose ass, John Lee said, "I don't feel right about him being out there by himself. You got the keys to that truck, let's go and scout it out and make sure he's safe."

Jilkes said, "I was thinking the same damn thing. Come on, let's go." As they were walking out of the front door, Jong appeared and asked, "Where are you going?"

John Lee said, "We got to go and protect one of those millennial types while he is running through the hood."

Jong stated, "I'm going with you because I need to ask you guys a question."

As they rode around the neighborhood looking for Larry, they saw a gathering of people and decided to check out what was happening. As sure as shit, and in the middle of it, Larry was doing his dance on three hoodlums. As sirens began to blare, John Lee announced, "We got to evacuate him out of there or the whole deal is going to go bad. The Sarge is going to be really mad as hell that we didn't go with him."

Jilkes replied, "I know. I thought about that. These youngins can sometimes push the wrong buttons, without even knowing it."

Jong said, "Stop thinking about what you should have done and get his ass out of that crowd before the law arrives. You know he's probably packing."

They hustled Larry into the truck and John Lee asked, "Now, what the hell was that all about? Why you beat up on three people from the neighborhood? Did you try to steal their money or something?"

Larry responded, "Incredulous. You are insane, John Lee, but you know what, I love you. I'm so happy you guys came looking for me."

Jilkes jumped in and said, "We were taking a ride and saw the commotion but didn't think that a millennial like you would be engaged in a street fight so early in the morning. No sir, we were just taking a ride."

Jong said, "Larry, that's pure and unadulterated horseshit. We came looking for you because you could put the entire mission in jeopardy. Now, that is some serious shit and the Sarge is going to have both sides of your ass when he finds out about this."

Larry sank in the seat and looked out of the window. It was obvious that he did not want to disappoint the Sarge by being involved in a street fight. Larry manned up and said, "Listen, I can't offer you guys money because you have more than you'll spend in a lifetime, however, how about I teach you guys how to do make up and I take you to dinner, if you don't tell the Sarge?"

Jilkes looked at John Lee who shrugged his shoulders, turned to Jong, and asked, "You be interested in learning how to put make up on your face?"

Jong replied, "Hell, no. How about you, Jilkes? You want to play with dolls and shit?"

Jilkes answered, "Absolutely, not."

Larry said, "There has to be something I can do for, or offer, you dinosaurs."

John Lee said, "Now, that there be the root of the problem. See we ain't no dinosaurs, like that Jurassic Park mess, we just be good old friends who do for each other and keep our brothers' back protected at all times. Also, you talk so funny. I don't even understand half the things you be saying. Now, if you were to come down to my farm and work with my people and teach them that there language you speak, then I think I could keep my mouth shut about your running into the hood and looking for poor people to beat up and rob. How about you, Jilkes?"

Larry, becoming extremely emotional pleaded, "Guys, please don't tell my father."

Jilkes advised, "Dude, we're just messing with you. I think we can keep this one to ourselves, right guys?" Everyone agreed.

John Lee said, "I must say though, I be glad you didn't just shoot them fellows like you did them fellows at the post office. I mean you executed them poor guys."

Larry relaxed and said, "They were trying to hurt me, my family and friends. A thing that, you will realize, eventually, I hold dear to my heart. The Sarge is everything to me, and one day I will tell you three guys exactly who I am and how I came to be."

John Lee took the opportunity to say, "Well, now, looks like we just got a bargaining chip."

Waiting on the foursome at the entrance to the motel, was none other than Sergeant Ben Beckmire. He inquired, "Where the hell have you people been?"

Jong answered, "Sarge, go and eat a Milky Way because your hair turns blue without your daily dose of sugar. We went for a ride while you people were sleeping."

"People, we have a mission today, and I don't like last minute surprises." He looked at Larry and asked, "What on earth happened to you?"

"I tripped on a branch outside and fell."

The Sarge exclaimed, "Horseshit! Did Marisa kick your ass again?"

"Honestly, ask your three mates and they will tell you I fell." The Sarge started to walk away and Jilkes poked Larry, and said, "Your ass belongs to us and don't forget it." Those words did not sit well, with Larry. In another life, he was called Larry the Wanderer aka Larry Holland.

## CHAPTER FOURTEEN

Larry was the product of the mean streets of Philadelphia and got caught up in the very business that he would later find antipathy for and resolve to personally end, if possible. He was arrested, and subsequently, befriended by none other than Sergeant Ben Beckmire. Larry was arrested for selling a controlled substance and was booked at the precinct where the Sarge worked. When he encountered Larry, the Sarge thought that he was a good-looking guy and was impressed by his command of the English language. The Sarge spent extra time in the booking process with Larry because he wanted to find out what and when things went wrong for him. Larry spent two days in a holding cell because the Sarge purposefully wanted to keep him in the precinct so that he could keep an eye on him. Larry's paperwork was, therefore, stalled and not filed, giving the Sarge an opportunity to evaluate and help Larry out of his current conundrum.

On the second day of Larry's incarceration, the Sarge came to work early, and on his way to the precinct, he stopped and picked up a couple of hoagies. He had a staff member retrieve Larry from his cell and bring him to his desk. The Sarge was interested in Larry, and after looking at the information that was gathered, found that Larry was just trying to survive and make ends meet.

He offered Larry a hoagie. Larry thanked him, but was curious about his generosity, as well as, his interest in him. The

Sarge wanted to know how this good-looking guy with obvious great communication skills and intelligence, could end up in this situation.

The Sarge spent an enormous amount of time listening to Larry, and at each turn, was perplexed by why he chose this life, when he could probably earn enough working legitimately, and without the constant danger that the drug trade brought with it.

In most cases, a person who is arrested is held for twenty-four to forty-eight hours and then presented to a magistrate by TV monitor who asks such questions as the person's income, ability to make bail, and reviews any prior convictions a person may have had. Larry was fortunate because the Sarge continued to hold his paperwork, against protocol, for an entire week. During that period, the Sarge learned a lot about Larry Holland.

Fast-forward to a month later, the Sarge wanted to test Larry's honor, and his loyalty. He told Larry that if he told him who his supplier was, he would in turn, find a way for Larry to escape prosecution and imprisonment. This conversation lasted for several days with Larry, unequivocally, stating that he would not give up his supplier to avoid jail time. The Sarge reminded Larry that he probably would not survive the exigencies of jail, and that he would probably "be sold" on the open market in prison for a pack or two, of cigarettes. The Sarge painted a dire, dark, and life changing picture of incarceration, but Larry would not yield to the notion of betraying the worthless scum bag that supplied him with the substance because he provided him with an employment opportunity. For days, the Sarge pleaded with Larry to divulge who his supplier was, and for days, Larry held true to some artificial code of honor.

The Sarge finally had to submit Larry's paperwork, and off he went to one of the worst prisons in the Philadelphia area— Curran-Fromhold Correctional Facility, better known as CFCF.

Through his connections with the prison system, the Sarge was able to get Larry stationed in an environment that he thought was slightly less stressful and demanding than the general prison population. Larry would find his new quarters filthy, confining, morally and spiritually, bankrupting. His roommate was the chef of the prison and was categorized as a nonthreat to Larry. He was also characterized as schizophrenic and psychotic but, otherwise, was considered no threat to himself or anyone else.

Upon entering the general population, Larry became, the property of a gang leader, from the bidding process. A warning was issued by the gang leader to anyone who might approach his property.

As a schizophrenic and psychotic cook, Larry's cellmate could give a hoot about such things as warning, as he admired Larry while he was sleeping. For hours, he would lay awake, and imagine himself having consensual sex with Larry.

After two nights of fantasizing about Larry, on the third night he slid out of his bunk, onto the floor, as if he were a snake or some other stealthy animal, positioned himself for an attack on his prey. He knew how to administer a submission hold. He pounced on Larry, gained control of his neck, and placed a sleeper hold on Larry, until he was unconscious. The rest is history of sorts. Larry was violated. When Larry was finally conscious, he found a part of his anatomy in disrepair.

As the cook was being released from his cell to prepare for breakfast, Larry awakened, realized what had happened to him, and screamed for all to hear that he was going to kill his cellmate.

The prison population screamed that another cherry had been popped. It was not good news for the gang leader who would have to exact revenge on the chef for violating his property.

Needless to say, the cook was shanked, and murdered on the same day. Larry was exonerated because he was still in his cell. So, the notion of 'your ass belongs to us, and don't forget it', was full of unintended meanings and consequences, that no one but Larry, and the Sarge could know.

Chapter Fifteen

In the room that Zanthius and his wife shared, Larry proceeded to transform Asiram into the likeness of Harold's wife. He was methodical and precise and included every visible detail on her face. As he stood back and admired his work, he said, "I guess there is only one other thing we need to attend to and for this project, Zanthius, I'm going to need your help."

Zanthius inquired, "What do you need me to do?"

Larry said, "I need you to carefully strap Asiram's weapon on her. Then turn her around so that I can see if the weapon is concealed, can be gotten to in a second, and more importantly, will not fall out and down her pant leg. I wish we had a smaller weapon like that new Ruger that's hand size, but we don't, so this Smith and Wesson will have to do."

Asiram asked, "Do you really think I'm going to need a gun in the bank?"

"I'm sure when those wolves were chasing your husband for a quick snack, I bet you he wished he had a weapon on him. What say you, Zanthius?"

"Yeah, I did wish I had a weapon, but I outran their asses."

"No, you didn't. Your father and I shot a few of them and they turned and ran off," Asiram professed.

Zanthius said, "That is all a matter of interpretation as to what I was doing during the actual incident. What the hell does any of that have to do with you carrying a weapon into a bank?

Anyway, I think if she places it straight on, there won't be a problem."

"I think I agree. Asiram, slowly turn sideways and then fully around," Larry requested.

Walter provided the Sarge with bogus IDs, as well as the box numbers, and keys. Everything was in place and everyone was aware of their roles. As the team loaded into the SUVs, Larry said to Asiram, "Hey, sign your assumed name on this piece of paper." She grabbed the paper and pen and with precision and accuracy, signed Harold's wife's name perfectly.

As Jong drove past the bank, Larry, John Lee, Jilkes and Zanthius began to take mental notes of the area. Larry turned around, looked at Asiram, and saw that her earpiece was visible. He called the Sarge and commanded, "We have to abort until I can attend to a minor detail in Asiram's appearance."

"What's the problem?" the Sarge demanded.

Larry responded by saying, "Her earpiece is visible. I think she moved her wig a little bit and it's out of order. Just give me ten minutes or so to correct the issue and then we can continue with the mission."

"Roger that," the Sarge said.

Jong drove the group approximately a mile away from the bank. Larry exchanged seats with Zanthius and began to make minor modifications to Asiram's appearance. Zanthius noted, "You seem to like working on my wife."

"Not as much as I like working on my own. I wish you could do this. That way I wouldn't have to worry about what you're thinking when I'm trying to make sure that your wife does not get arrested for committing a felony. What are your thoughts on that one, my brother?" Larry inquired.

"I think that I'm glad it's you and not one of these other guys like Jong, or John Lee, and definitely not Jilkes." Everyone laughed except Asiram who inquired, "Honey, is there a problem?"

"No dear. I'm just amazed at Larry's attention to detail, but, more importantly, I just look at you in utter fascination and say, "that's my beautiful wife and I love her." Asiram's eyes began to water and Larry exclaimed, "Please, you're wrecking my masterpiece!"

Larry, carrying two large briefcases, entered the bank with Asiram who went to a teller and told him that she wanted access to her safety deposit box. Asiram produced her ID, a pouch with a key in it, and was asked to sign the private registry for her box. She nailed the signature. The teller led her into the vault and asked her for her key.

After retrieving the box, she and Larry were led to a private room. As she opened the large box, she was astonished at the amount of cash in it. It was not the box that Walter was looking for because this box only contained neat stacks of $100 bills, taking up every square inch of space in the box.

Larry opened the briefcases and began to stack the money in one of them. After emptying the box, he made sure that there were no recording devices, fobs, CDs, or any other storage devices, in it. Larry reached in the other briefcase and pulled out stacks of $1 bills that had been soaking in water in a plastic bag to put in the box. He thought that the weight was approximately the same as the bills he removed and motioned to

Asiram to finish up. Larry walked out of the private viewing area first and waited for Asiram. She asked the teller for help with the box and watched him place it in its slot, secure it, lock it, and return her key. She thanked him and motioned to Larry to follow her.

Once they were in the SUV, the Sarge called and inquired, "Did everything go as planned?"

Asiram responded, "No, it didn't, but thankfully Larry counterweighted the box with wet $1 bills. That made it seem normal enough, so it didn't appear as though a complete evacuation of the box had occurred and draw suspicion."

"What do you mean a box full of wet $1 bills?" Beckmire asked.

Asiram said, "Talk to Larry."

Larry got on the phone and said, "At the last minute, I figured it might look suspicious if the box, when returned, was completely empty, so I decided to get a bunch of one dollar bills and soak them in water to compensate for some of the weight."

The Sarge said, "Excellent thinking. Do you have enough to do the same at the next branch, and by the way, were there any recording devices in that box?"

"There were no recording devices in that box. The only thing in it was a boat load of $100 bills. It was stuffed to the brim and I do have enough wet one dollar bills to handle the next two boxes."

The Sarge said, "Wow, what on earth are we going to do with all of this money we keep getting?"

Larry said, "Not to worry, I have some new ideas about how to support people for the long term as opposed to short term interventions."

"Thanks, Son. Is there anything different that you guys will do at the next bank?"

Larry looked at Asiram and asked, "Do you think we have to modify our actions for the next branch or do you think it went well?"

"Let's keep it simple. It worked, so let's not fix a tire that's not flat."

Larry said to the Sarge, "Naw. We're good."

On the other side of town, and at the second bank branch, Larry and Asiram exited the SUV and entered the bank. The attention to detail for security was more extensive at this branch starting with verification of Asiram's IDs, including her driver's license, as well as, her passport. The guard on duty had the audacity to ask Larry what was in the briefcases, a question that got him a stern warning from Asiram.

Asiram watched as the box was retrieved and taken into a private room by the bank's assistant manager. Asiram asked Larry, "Are you going to stand there or are you coming in?"

Larry answered, "I'll be right in, something is wrong with this place." Larry entered the room and was not surprised to find a box full of cash.

Asiram inquired, "How on earth do people steal this much money and get away with it?"

"When your soul is for sale, all kinds of opportunities avail themselves to it. However, and contrary to your thinking, Harold didn't get away with shit. He forfeited his life," Larry reminded her.

"Larry, you're so dramatic. Load the cases and let's get out of here."

While Asiram and Larry were loading the cases with cash, Jilkes and John Lee were in the process of watching people suspiciously stake out the bank as if they were planning to rob it.

John Lee said to Jilkes, "Them there fellas be up to no good. Call the Sarge and tell him to back us up."

Jilkes called the Sarge and told him that John Lee smelled a dead fish.

Jilkes said to John Lee, "We had better get them before they go in the bank and create a problem for Asiram and Larry." The two men got out of the SUV and told Jong to look out for a get-away car.

The two would be bank robbers paraded past the entrance twice and took their time scouting out the place from afar. John Lee walked one way and Jilkes the other and then turned around and came upon the two unlikely robbers. Aware that cameras were watching their every move, the two men intercepted the would-be robbers approximately fifty yards away from each other and dealt with them. Jilkes displayed his weapon and told the guy to take a walk with him and to keep his hands in view. John Lee on the other hand, went ballistic on his catch and slapped the guy around a little. The guy attempted to pull his weapon and John Lee yelled, "Now, that's going to get you a real ass whupping!"

He snatched the weapon from the guy and kicked it into the street and began to slap the life out of the kid. He told him, "This here stuff, will get you sentenced to life in prison, and this here ass-whupping is going to get you back in school."

As John Lee led his guy towards Jilkes, Jong got out of the SUV and retrieved the weapon but first put a towel around it. Jilkes looked at both guys and said, "We're probably saving your dumb ass lives. We heard every word you said about how you were going to pull this bank job off. We are giving you fair warning that your pictures are in our files and we'll be watching you every minute of the day. Get your dumb asses out of here and don't show up on our radar or our next encounter will be fatal."

As Larry and Asiram were preparing to return the box, Larry whispered, "Be prepared to use your weapon when we come out of the vault. Something is not right out there."

"What's the matter? Have we been set up?"

"No, nothing like that. I think people are trying to rob the place, that's all. Not sure about that, but that's a feeling I have."

"Okay, now I'm concerned," Asiram responded.

"Don't be concerned, just be prepared if something goes down."

As they exited the vault area, everything seemed normal. When they exited the bank, they saw John Lee and Jilkes walking up the street and Jilkes gave Larry the all clear sign. Once in the SUV, Larry asked, "What were you two doing out of the truck?"

Jilkes said, "We were saving your ass, that's all."

"And just how were you able to do that?" Asiram asked.

"There be two guys who were trying to figure out how to rob that there bank you guys were in," John Lee stated.

Asiram looked at Larry and he said, "I think there might be two others in there doing the actual robbing. I guess the guys you caught were the look-outs. Get in the truck, call the Sarge, and ask him what he wants us to do.

Jilkes explained the situation to the Sarge who was watching all of the interactions and said, "I want Jong at the door, Jilkes to the left, and John Lee to the right of the door. Mallory and I will enter straight on and try to avoid being filmed. Larry get Zanthius and casually place yourselves behind the vehicles just in case they get the best of us."

"Okay, Sarge," Larry responded.

Asiram announced, "Larry, if you wonder where I am, I'm going to be with Zanthius."

"I apologize, Missy. You cover us, along with your husband, and make sure that we don't encounter any issues on the way out."

As the Sarge and Mallory entered the bank, it was obvious who was doing the robbing. The bank manager appeared stressed out. The Sarge asked, "Do you have any savings deposit forms around?

"On the counter to your left," a bank employee responded.

John Lee said, "We would like to open another account for our business, who do me and my mate see?"

"Take a seat over there and we'll be right with you." Jilkes nudged John Lee and motioned for him to walk towards the vault.

John Lee asked, "Is this here bank safe? I mean there be a lot of banks being robbed in this neighborhood and we don't want to walk in on any bad deals."

"Sir, I can assure you that this bank is safe and that your money will be protected by the FDIC."

"What's the FDIC, some kind of fire and safety protection group?"

"No sir, the Federal Deposit Insurance Corporation, or FDIC, underwrites most private bank deposits and protects your money, which means that your money is safe."

"Do they underwrite my money when I give it to you. I mean we have hundreds of thousands of dollars that we make every day from our company. Do that there FDIC insure our money too?"

"Yes sir, they will insure every dollar that you put in our bank."

John Lee said, "Jilkes, go fetch those briefcases that we have with all that cash in them."

"Yes sir, boss. I'm on it."

It was as if lightening had struck when the Sarge pointed a .45 automatic weapon at the decoy teller and John Lee and Mallory pointed weapons at the other would be robber.

The Sarge proclaimed, "You people must be the dumbest damn bank robbers in the world. Keep your hands high and come from behind that counter."

"He has a bomb strapped to his body," a teller yelled.

Beckmire said, "Good, then he won't feel this bullet go through his empty head." As the guy came from behind the counter, Jong walked over to him and opened his jacket and reported, "Sarge, this is just clay."

The Sarge said to the bank manager, "Take that gun and give us four minutes to leave. We are on a mission and can't be caught up in local police matters." The Sarge flashed his credentials and the team was out of there and on their way in two minutes.

Beckmire called the car that Asiram was riding in and asked, "What was in the box?"

"Cold hard cash. We didn't see any recording devices, just cash and a few bonds and insurance policies."

"Did you leave those things behind?" the Sarge asked.

"Absolutely! We emptied the box of cash, but we probably left $20 or $30 thousand because it wouldn't fit in the case," Asiram replied.

"How much do you think was in that box?" the Sarge asked.

"I would say that it was at least a third more than the first box. What are we going to do with all of this cash?" Asiram inquired.

"I have no damn idea at this point, I just want to get to the third box and be done with banking for a few days. I can't believe that we stopped a robbery," the Sarge announced.

Asiram mentioned, "Larry told me to keep my weapon hot because something wasn't right in the bank. Boy he's good. You guys must tell the team what you people used to do back in the day. The things that I'm seeing from you two is not the kind of things that happen on a basketball court late at night. Are you sure you two didn't do spy shit, or something like that?"

Larry responded, "You and your husband are the only spies that I know. I must say, I too, am impressed with how you two, think on your feet. Come on now, what makes for a perfect marriage? Two spies, who live together, eat together, love together, play together and, more importantly, spy together. A perfect combination for people who are in your business."

"You're full of it, Larry," Zanthius replied.

Larry looked at Asiram and said, "Your wig is lopsided and you have lost some of the base color around your neck. Have you been rubbing your neck?"

"Larry, I don't remember everything that I have done since we went into those banks. Can you repair it?"

"Yes, but we need to stop so that I don't have to worry about bumps and quick stops and making a mess of your face. In a few, we will have you looking like the lady in the picture again."

"Do you have a copy of her picture with you?"

"I do, but I can't share it with you because it is a mental picture."

"Oh my; a genius is amongst us."

Jong stopped the vehicle and the rest of the caravan proceeded to the last bank to do surveillance work. Larry made the minor adjustments to Asiram's façade and acknowledged, "That's it, you look just like her once again."

Chapter Sixteen

As the Sarge drove by the bank, he saw a familiar person and yelled, "What the fuck!"

The person waved at him and kept walking. The Sarge pulled out his phone and tried to call the person, but to no avail. He cursed the person vehemently and a few minutes later, Walter called and said, "Hey Cousin, nice to see you around these parts."

"What are you doing here?" the Sarge asked.

"I'm here because this is the bank where Harold put that information. I wanted you to have the money that was in the other boxes as a kind of apology for my last incursion and screw up. I knew there was only money in those boxes because he told me so. I surely didn't want his wife or the government to take advantage of those funds, so I decided to make a gift to you and your people with the hope that you use the booty to help with the problems back home."

"You're a person who cannot be trusted, Walter. I don't like the way you operate. Why didn't you say this shit up front, rather than show up at a gig to profess your sorrow and give us a gift? Why can't you go down the right road, Man? You keep deviating from your heritage and will never be able to walk amongst your people on Dreamtime and Walkabout. Your entire history is subject to be erased."

"Cousin, I have done some really bad and dumb shit. I know I can't buy my way back to the right road, but I can sure as hell help my people and perhaps be forgiven for the obtuse things that I have done. I just can't have my immediate family know what I did and how much I liked what I did. It probably won't happen again, but I did it, and I can't erase that shit. However, once again, I feel that I can help with a significant problem that exists back home and deep down in my heart, I'm looking for salvation."

"I'm not authorized to provide salvation, but if you keep screwing with me and my team, I will provide you with the answer to your suicidal behavior. I will place a weapon to your head and end your life, if you compromise me or any of my people. Ask God for salvation. Go back home and plead with the elders for salvation, but if you screw with me and my people again, Cousin, I will blow your damn head off. Stay out of our OPs. Is that clear?" Beckmire screamed.

"Cousin, it is crystal clear and I promise you I will not show up on your jobs unless I'm asking you for the salvation that I need," Walter replied.

"Walter, stay away or do it yourself. Don't get me wrong, I'm not going to be your private executioner unless you provide a real and present danger to me and mine. Walter, I will lose all of my faith and execute you like a common dingo. Give me the OPs and stay the hell away from our missions,"

"Cousin, I need help and you are the only person who I can share my heavy burden with. You know when we first met there was a connection. You also knew that when I first told you about your heritage, it caught your attention. I have no one else here. You are it and you have the responsibility to help me according to ancient codes. Don't forget, Ben Beckmire, you are part Aborigine and you are from a royal clan. So, my salvation is tied to your ability to carry out those precious rituals that most people don't understand, or believe in."

"You're absolutely correct, but I will not help you escape your past mistakes by providing you with a way out of your misery. Listen, I am not passing judgement, and, I am not a saint, but if it becomes a choice between you, me, or mine, then you are dead. We're going to abort this mission because you're compromising my people. Goodbye, Walter, and good luck."

Beckmire hung up the phone but Walter called him right back. He repeatedly dialed the number, but Beckmire didn't respond. Walter walked over to the vehicle and said, "I need to talk to you privately."

Beckmire got out of the SUV. As Jong was driving towards the bank he asked, "What on earth is he doing here?"

Zanthius said, "Keep driving. We may have been compromised."

"That's not how we operate. I'm slowing this damn thing down to look for a hand signal from the Sarge."

Sure, as can be, the Sarge placed two fingers behind his back and waved them on.

"I'm going to turn this thing around at the corner and place us in an offensive position," Jong said.

"Good idea, I'm not sure what the hell is going on at this point, but if we see anything out of order then, Jong, you drive up there and we grab the Sarge and shoot anybody that even looks our way," Jilkes stated.

"I'm on it. People cover the side of the vehicle you're on. Shoot first and we'll ask questions and for forgiveness later," Jong said.

In front of a hardware store, Walter stridently addressed the Sarge and pointed a finger in his face several times. The team knew if you wanted to piss Sergeant Ben Beckmire off, then point a finger at him. The Sarge seemed nonchalant during

Walter's tirade, but finally grabbed him by the neck and lifted him off the ground.

John Lee said, "Goodness be! He's pissed and is going to throw that there fellow through that window." As Jilkes started to exit the vehicle, John Lee yelled, "Jilkes, no wait, Mallory is on his way." The members of the SUV watched the interaction with mixed emotions because they did not know if Walter was alone or had his team with him. John Lee said, "Jilkes, you and I had better go over and handle the Sarge. Mallory can't control him when he has gone to that there other side."

The two men got out of the SUV and Asiram said to Zanthius, "I think we had better go rescue your father and my daddy-in-law."

Jong advised, "Wait a minute and let's see what happens."

Zanthius said, "It's already happening. He might just relate differently to me and Asiram."

Asiram watched as Jilkes, John Lee, and Mallory attempted to restrain the Sarge and then she decided to intervene on her own. She walked up to the Sarge and said, "Your grandchild is concerned about your ballistic behavior. I, rather we, need you to calm down and get control of your emotions. We are outside of the establishment that you want me to rob. Do you want them to call the police and place Larry and me in a compromising position?"

The Sarge looked at her and answered, "Baby Girl, I have this under control. My cousin and I were attempting to best each other and I guess I won. Now that this is over, I want you to return to your position and prepare to end the second phase of our operation. Can you do this successfully for me?"

"We got this, but you have got to realize that there are cameras everywhere."

"What you saw was staged. We have another team watching us and Walter is not privy to who the hell they are. I am under control, but I'm not sure about the identity of the people in the window on the third floor of that building directly across from us. I told my cousin that if he compromised any of us, I would put a bullet in his head. I knew that the team knew that I would go ballistic if someone pointed their finger in my face and yelled at me at the same time. I need you and Larry to go into that bank and be suspicious of everyone who is in there. There is something terribly amiss here, even my crazy ass cousin is perplexed."

Asiram stroked her eyebrow and briefly threw her left hand with three fingers in the air and all eyes followed the direction of it. John Lee said, "We got to get into that there building from the rear and get to the third floor. That there Asiram just gave us a signal, and I believe that we have to be there to watch their backs."

"I saw that as well. We're going to need you, Zanthius, to cover our retreat if this thing goes south. Get one of those assault rifles and that canister. It's gonna fire at least a hundred rounds. Try not to shoot any friendlies," Jilkes said.

John Lee and Jilkes made their way to the rear of the building and were momentarily delayed by a locked door. John Lee saw another door on a loading dock, climbed the steps and discovered the door was open. The two men made their way to the third floor and approximated the distance to the office where people had eyes on them. Their first attempt to gain access to where the people were watching them was slightly off as they entered an office which was full of storage items. As they entered the next office, they heard a commotion, drew their weapons, and quietly entered the room. To their surprise and amazement, they found a man and a woman in the midst of having an aerobic sexual experience. Jilkes said, "Don't mind us." He walked to the window and confirmed that it was the office that the team felt held suspicious people who were watching them. As the individuals tried to gather their things, Jilkes said, "Wait a minute, stay like you are. Were you people watching the activity outside of the bank a few minutes ago?"

The woman replied, "We're on assignment."

John Lee said, "I bet you be on assignment. Why you need guns for your so called assignment and no clothes?"

"Listen mister, we're local law enforcement and that bank has been robbed three times in the last month. Look at our credentials," the man said. John Lee passed them over to Jilkes who verified them as locals. Jilkes asked, "Where's your camera equipment?"

"In the next room," the guy said.

Jilkes walked through the breezeway and saw a camera mounted on a tripod and retrieved it. He took out his cell phone, took a photo of the couple, and removed the sim card from the camera. Jilkes said, "Please get dressed. I took those pictures because we are on assignment also. I must admit, not as enjoyable as yours, but yet, we are on assignment. I must take this sim card and keep your picture. I hope that we never meet again. We will forget what we saw, if you forget who you saw, and we'll call it a day. No harm, no foul."

"Do you have ID on you?" the woman asked.

Jilkes flashed his phony ID that Walter had given them and replied, "You're really not in a position to request anything. Now, here is how this is going to play out. We're going to cuff you guys and when our people finish extracting a certain matter from a box, we'll come back to free you. Now, if you think that you're smart and can pick cuffs, then go right ahead. The next thing you will hear is that window shattering from a high powered bullet tearing into your head. Stay calm and relax, and we'll be back in ten minutes to free you." Jilkes then called the Sarge, told him that all was okay, and to proceed with the extraction. He added that he and John Lee would be in position in two minutes.

Asiram and Larry entered the bank and were suspiciously viewed by everyone who worked there. Larry said, "Doesn't feel like a friendly bank to me. How about you?"

"Feels as though we did something wrong. Perhaps they're curious because I'm a white woman and you're a man of color." The manager cautiously, welcomed them and said, "We are a little leery of strangers. We have had a series of robberies this month. How can we help you?"

After a few moments of discussion, Asiram and Larry entered the vault area and presented the key to the designated box. The box was retrieved and they were led into a private room. As they opened the box, Asiram whispered, "Damn, this is incredible."

"Incredible is not the word. It's insane! Larry began to load the briefcase with cash and in the bottom of the box, were two data disks. She placed them in her purse and closed the box leaving $15 to $20 thousand in it. They left the private area, returned the box to the manager who placed it in its slot and thanked them for coming to the bank.

Once they were outside of the bank, Zanthius, with the big gun on his lap, and Jong were waiting for them. They got into the SUV and drove off. Jilkes and John Lee made their way back to the building where the lovers were, freed them, and told them to continue on the journey they were on.

Asiram called the Sarge and said, "There were two data sticks in the box and I have them both. Do you want me to come to your truck and give them to you or do you want to play a little game with Walter?"

"I like that idea, but it might get us involved in other covert shit that we don't need to be in."

Everyone was on the same channel. Jong said, "I can plug them into my computer and copy them in a matter of seconds."

"Can you do that, and secure it so that I can make the determination about what we need to know and what we need to discard?"

"Give me the order, Sarge, and it's done," Jong said.

"Damn it, copy the shit, but make it quick. No one is to open any files. Is that crystal clear?" the Sarge asked.

The Sarge called Walter and said, "Meet me at that dive we're staying in so that we can give you what we have found. We can plan for tomorrow's retrieval of the card and the condom."

"I'll be there in one hour, and thanks a million, Cousin," Walter confirmed.

CHAPTER SEVENTEEN

As the team was driving to their dive, Jong called the Sarge and reported, "Mission accomplished."

"When we get to that joint you have us staying in, make sure your computer is not in sight. Sir Walter is meeting me there in an hour and I don't want to spook him or give him any reason to think that we have compromised his ass."

"10-4," Jong replied.

During the ride back to the motel, Asiram asked her husband, "Are you feeling okay. You're sweating an awful lot."

"I am, I just missed you and I still get jealous when you are with that good looking and smooth talking brother of mine." Asiram reached over to kiss Zanthius and exclaimed, "Oh my goodness, you're burning up! You have a fever!"

"Sweetheart, I'm fine."

"Yes, you are fine as can be and I'm the luckiest woman on this planet, but you're still running a fever." Larry reached over and felt Zanthius's forehead and looked in his eyes and said, "We need to get him to a hospital. He either has food poisoning or something a lot stronger than the flu. These symptoms are not natural, Zanthius. We need to get you to the hospital."

"People, I'm fine, I just need some rest." His next move was epic! Zanthius's head hit the back of the driver's seat and that was all she wrote. Asiram called the Sarge and said, "Zanthius just passed out and has a fever. We need to take him to the hospital."

"Shit, tell Jong to find the nearest hospital."

"He's on it and we're on our way. Don't know if we need the entire team there. What are your thoughts on that one?" Asiram inquired.

"We don't separate, that's how we stay alive," the Sarge replied.

At the hospital, Zanthius's vitals were checked and they were off the charts. His blood pressure was 205 over 150, stroke level, and his blood sugar was elevated to the diabetic stage. He showed signs of kidney failure, and more importantly, there was a lack of oxygen flowing to the brain. Zanthius was in critical condition and required a multitude of test to determine where treatment should begin.

The Sarge suggested that the team gather in the cafeteria. He pulled out his phone, dialed Walter, and told him that Zanthius was sick. He also informed Walter that they were at a hospital and that he would get back to him when they were leaving. Needless to say, Walter had the group followed.

As the team viewed the options for food in the hospital cafeteria, John Lee said, "I'm going to have me some of that there fried chicken with mashed potatoes and gravy." He stepped in line and ordered the fried chicken platter. As soon as it was served to him, he bit into a piece of chicken and said, "Now, this here be some damn good chicken."

Jilkes ordered the same thing and when he was served his, he bit into it and said, "Holy shit, this is the best damn fried chicken I have ever had. Who's the cook? I know it's a brother. Tell him to come out here and get his due."

The server smiled and said, "I'll be right back."

Moments later, she returned with a little old white lady. The server said, "These two think your chicken is the best they have ever had and they also thought that you were an African American."

John Lee pointed at Jilkes and said, "He said that, not me. He usually says dumb things all the time, so please forgive him. Fortunately, I'm the smart one in this group and I be complimenting you on great tasting chicken, fried just perfectly. Where you be from if I might ask?"

"I'm from Alabama and I been cooking chicken all my life."

"Well, honey, you be the best and you're one of the few people who I can understand. The rest of them there people talk really strange to me. Thanks for being here for some hungry people."

Asiram and the Sarge were waiting on news of Zanthius's condition and she was feeling a little out of sorts as well. The Sarge commented, "You look a little pale yourself, love. Did you and Zanthius eat anything at that dive we're staying in?"

"Honestly, I didn't, but I did see him feeding his face on some kind of sandwich that was dripping lots of juices."

"You didn't eat anything?"

"No, Daddy-in-Law, I did not eat anything from that filthy place."

"Good, because I am suspect of places like that."

The doctor came from behind the curtain and said, "We are lowering his blood pressure and we are hydrating him. We did a full body scan to see if he had picked up any parasites and we're waiting on his blood work to return. This is very perplexing to us because so many bodily functions are out-of-whack at the same time. There are no compensating factors from his immune system off-setting the responses to issues affecting his body. In English, some things should fight off other things, but they are not doing so. Therefore, we are as baffled, and as concerned as you are. Until we receive the blood work back, there is little I can tell you. We placed him in isolation because we don't know if he's carrying some new kind of virus.

The doctor paused to make sure Beckmire and Asiram understood before he continued and said, "It will be at least a couple of hours before we have the results back. I recommend that you people go down to our cafeteria, have something to eat or a cup of coffee and check back with me in a couple of hours."

Asiram was about to ask a question when the doctor interjected, "Please, I don't know a damn thing at this point in time. I need time to evaluate and study what's going on with his body. Give me the time and I will get you the answers to the questions that you're most likely going to ask me. By the way, has he been in the jungle or forest lately?"

"Not at all," Asiram replied.

"Thanks," the doctor said.

As the Sarge and Asiram entered the cafeteria, there was a commotion going on in one of the back corners. It was his guys. He walked over and asked, "Have you people lost your minds? What's all the noise about? Do you remember where we are? DUH! We're in a hospital. Keep the noise down."

Mallory stood up and inquired, "Sarge, may I have a private word with you?" The two men walked away from the group and Mallory asked, "What's wrong with you?"

"I just screwed up royally, didn't I?" the Sarge asked.

"You damn sure did! You need to go over there and apologize to each and every one of those guys who risk their lives for you and your family every day."

"I'll start with you, my oldest and best friend. I'm out of sorts because a child that I didn't know I had, is now fighting for his life. Please forgive me and remember that I'll take any bullet that comes your way. I am tired. I need to see my wife and ask for forgiveness for all the bad shit that we do."

"It's okay, my brother, but they need this opportunity to vent about bullshit. Go make a speech and pay for their damn meals."

After making a pitiful speech to the guys, the Sarge said, "At least I can buy your meals and when we get back to civilization, I'm going to buy you each breakfast at McDonald's."

John Lee said, "We know these be trying times but sometimes we just have to exhale because we be doing some bad things on this here adventure."

"I would really like to be back in Kansas with Dorothy trying to find the yellow brick road, if you know what I mean," Bernstein said.

"Okay, I know I messed up and I owe you all my life. It will never happen again. I'm just exhausted. You are the best friends that a man could ever have, and I guess, I'm worried because this shit ain't over. I know that Larry deposited the card and the condom in a place that only he knows, and in essence, we don't need Zanthius, but I'm not sure who is still out there stalking us. I will not split my forces. We are who we are.

When we are together, it's a bad dream for anyone on the wrong side of the play book. Anyway, I apologize to each one of you and promise to keep a Snickers in my pocket at all times."

"How about keeping a box of them in your pocket?" Whitmore asked.

"Funny guy, but if you insist, I will do that." Larry looked around for Asiram and saw her sitting alone at another table. He suggested to the Sarge that he bring her over to where they were.

The Sarge went over to where Asiram was sitting and said, "Team members sit together, no matter the issues."

"I guess I don't feel like a team member when my man is lying in a bed with some unknown ailment. I'm just kind of worried because it came on so sudden. I mean one minute he was fine, and the next he was sweating profusely and burning up with fever," Asiram replied.

"I know, Baby Girl. I, or rather we, are all concerned about him, that's why we are all here. It would help the guys if you would eat with them. They are worried about you as well."

"I don't feel much like being in a group right now. I'm just so distressed about Zanthius."

"I know, and so am I. I just yelled at the guys and had to apologize because I didn't see this one coming. Like you, when I last spoke to him, he was fine. Hopefully, the doctor will have some information in the next hour or so. Why don't you go and get some of that delicious chicken? At least have something in you in case we have to be here all night."

"I'll be alright. Why don't you and the guys go back to the place. I will keep you informed of his condition."

"Asiram, haven't you learned anything about us? That is not how we operate. As long as he's here, and until we know what's wrong with him, this is where we will be, as well, my dear."

"Thanks, Daddy-in-Law, you're the best. I think I will have a piece of chicken and a roll."

One hour later, Asiram and the Sarge went upstairs to confer with the doctor and found him and two other doctors sitting in his little office shaking their heads. The lead doctor said to them, "We have never seen anything like this before. We have searched the medical journals, and have made calls to pathologists, cryptologists, and linguists. I have been basically laughed at for the past few hours. What did he have to eat or drink? This condition is virtually unknown to science and is making us the laughingstock in the medical world. We have all seen the x-rays and we're stumped. I mean, we are literally baffled by what we see, and are more intrigued by how it was activated."

The lead doctor continued shaking his head and finally blurted out, "Your husband is a walking message board, but we don't have a clue about the meaning of any of what we have seen. Listen, your husband ingested some material that left a profound and obvious inscription in his body, and it was time released. Look at these x-rays of his lower intestinal wall. At 100%, you only see that there is something minor going on in his system. When you expand the x-ray to 200% this is what you get."

Asiram said, "I'll be damn! Daddy-in-Law, may I have a private word with you? Doctor, please excuse us for a moment."

Out of hearing range of the doctors, Asiram announced, "Helga was one smart cookie. She forced him to swallow the capsule knowing that the real information was ingested and the capsule was the method of transferring the information. The capsule was not the product, but a message board of sorts."

"I'm not following your line of thinking," Beckmire said.

"She coated the capsule with a microscopic message. She used the notion of the capsule to throw people off. I'm assuming this is the real Carbon Factor information and hints to its location. She sent everyone on a wild goose chase."

"So, that damn thing that all of those people died over was just a gimmick?" Beckmire asked.

"That's exactly what I'm thinking. I heard about this stuff when I was in Bulgaria, but I didn't think it was possible. Helga was into discovering different ways to send a message and she used my husband as a carrier on two levels. I can't wait to catch her in hell! I'm going to kick the shit out of her."

Asiram was about to ask the doctor something when Jong walked into the room and announced, "We have a situation that needs your attention."

The Sarge said, "Get the guys up here and quarantine this area. Doctors, you have a special patient in your hospital, and I need to know, other than you guys, who else has seen these images?"

"Who are you people?" the lead doctor asked.

"We are your best friends, or the last people you will see on earth." The Sarge flashed his credentials and said, "Our agency is at the top of the food chain, and we are without oversight. I will ask you once again, who has had access to the information you have seen?"

"We just discussed it with others from a hypothetical standpoint and did not share it outside of this room."

"What about the technicians who developed the film, or your comrades who laughed at you?"

"The technicians take general pictures of the patient's internals. They would not have consciously looked for any abnormalities because they are technicians, and not doctors. It was only when we enlarged the pictures to the 200 percentile that we began to understand that there were symbols illustrated on his anatomy."

Beckmire flashed his weapon as did Jong, Asiram, John Lee, and Jilkes. "I'm going to ask you one more time Doctor. I want you to believe me when I say that this is a matter of national security and that I have the right and the power to pull my weapon and blow your head off. Has anyone else seen this information?"

"I don't know who you people are, and we really don't want to know, but I'm telling you the truth. Unless the technicians are now scanning for internal inscriptions, then I'm telling you, just the three of us have seen it. I need to make a call to my superiors."

"If you're going to make a call, Doctor, I recommend you call your family and tell them that you won't be coming home tonight or ever again. You touch that phone and that tall guy over there will put a bullet in you. One more thing, Doctor, I will ask the questions, and you people answer. So, overall, what is his status? Is he in any danger, or will this pass like a virus or something, and when can he be moved?"

"His body is rejecting whatever it is he ingested. We think this is the final stage. He was dehydrated. His potassium level was significantly low, and he lacked vitamin D. That is being restored, so he will probably be well enough to be moved in the morning."

"It's important that you forget all that you have seen here because your lives depend upon it. In a year or so, if you want to write in one of those journals about this story, then so be it.

But until then, I caution you not to mention this situation to anyone. People, I hate to sound like a bad ass, but I need to move him now. What are the consequences of such a decision?"

"If we missed any details or misdiagnosed his condition, then his life is in your hands. We don't understand those symbols, but if they are time released, or on a GPS signaling system, then he is totally in your hands. We don't understand anything that is happening with his body but to move him could essentially kill him."

"We need you three doctors to stay for the balance of the night, increase the rate of hydration, as well as attend to those other deficiencies, you spoke about. Is that a problem? By the way, we're going to need your phones and addresses in case you think this is some kind of a game and you want to bet on the fact that your families will be healthy in the morning if you try to contact anyone. Think about 911 and the consequences. What we're dealing with is so much larger than that. We are talking about devices that can be placed in a milk carton and blow up most of a city. This is national security at its highest level. Asiram, Jilkes, and John Lee, you're up. You people have first watch."

The Sarge motioned to Jong to meet him in the hallway. Jong said, "I turned my computer on and a most disturbing video appeared."

"Was my cousin featured in it?"

"As a matter of fact, he was the star."

"Did anyone else see it?"

"Sarge, I'm the only one who had eyes on it."

"How embarrassing is it?"

"Sarge, he's playing a very precarious role, but he is enjoying every moment of it. He's also discussing millions of dollars while he is literally being nailed by the guy he shot in the back of the head."

"What the hell are you saying?" the Sarge asked.

"What I'm saying is that your cousin is bisexual, a thief, a multinational arms dealer, drug smuggler/dealer, and exporter of oil out of Iran. He was once in charge of a prostitution ring, as well as extracting oil out of Iran, and selling it below market price. Walter is the boss of all those things. However, he appears to be a patriot and was adamantly opposed to selling information about the Carbon Factor to any foreign government or group. That positioned him adversely against his partner Harold. He's a chameleon, Sarge, a dangerous one at that."

"Did you scan any of the other files on the data disk?"

"Absolutely not! That file of him and Harold, came up as if it were a pop-up document," Jong reiterated.

"Okay, once we have the attention of the entire group, I will divulge this information to everyone."

"Do you really think it's necessary to show him getting nailed?" Jong asked.

"I'll have to think about that one. I mean he has done right by us in a wrong kind of way. He also has protected and provided us with necessary equipment, not to mention two new G5s. I think that should at least count for something. Listen, I know we are greater than a fraternity and some things don't need to be exposed. I also believe that you should let sleeping dogs lie. However, the team does need to know about his other part-time activities. That protects us all."

###

Asiram took pictures of the x-rays of Zanthius's internal organs.

Beckmire asked, "Why are you taking pictures? I'm not leaving here without those large prints and we probably need to secure the negatives, if there are such things. Doctor, is this the only copy, or record of this matter?"

"The originals are stored on a digital system in our data bank."

"How do I retrieve, or erase them?"

"You have to go down to the X-ray Department and ask for the digital printout of the film."

"Why don't we escort him to wherever it is they keep the records and let him procure them?" Jilkes asked.

"You and John Lee take a walk with the good doctor and retrieve the originals of that film. Now, Doctor, in the interest of science, I will have those sent back to you as soon as we have accomplished our mission. Now, please, don't try to take advantage of us because there are too many of us."

"I just want you people out of the hospital. We hate guns around here because they're the source of most of our work. We see too many kids shooting each other over a corner they will never own."

"I understand exactly how you feel. However, I want you to imagine an event like 911 happening around you from a product that that can fit into a half gallon milk carton. So, in my estimation, two cases of that stuff set off in strategic locations would leave this city in ruins and the population annihilated. This is bigger than guns. What we are talking about; is an apocalypse!"

## CHAPTER EIGHTEEN

At exactly 0630 hours, Zanthius woke up from a much needed sleep. His body had been restored with fluids that had been depleted as a result of being dehydrated. He looked at a sleeping Asiram and reached over and grabbed her hand. She stirred, realized that he was awake, and said, "You scared the living crap out of all of us. You provided the doctors with a baffling set of details, and pictures about where the real Carbon Factor is located."

"Honey, slow down! What on earth are you talking about?"

"I'm talking about you and your kisses. Don't ever kiss another woman other than me, and swallow. Okay?"

A few minutes later, the Sarge walked into the room, and inquired, "How are you feeling, Son?"

"I'm feeling a helluva lot better than before. You stayed here all night with me?"

"Oh, my Son, the 'idiot spy'. Where the hell else was I going to be?"

"Excuse me. He is your son, right?" the doctor asked.

"Yes, he is. Why do you ask?"

"Is he a spy as well?"

"If I answered that truthfully, that big guy over there would have to shoot you, and, so far you have cooperated without a fault. No sense in getting killed now, right?"

"There is one thing that we didn't tell you about. I'm only going to tell you, if you promise to have him give us a call once you have completed all of this spy stuff you were talking about. Do I have your word?"

"Once we extract and deliver the information, I think it will be alright if my son, in the interest of science, have a long conversation with the three of you so that you can publish the remarkable findings. In other words, we will give you the unedited version, but on our timetable."

"Okay, I trust you, even though you're a spy. We copied the info on a data disk. I'll give it to you, with the hopes that you will return it and engage in a conversation about the findings."

"Doc, first, I'm not the spy here. My son and his wife are spies. Now, me and my boys, are like the Secret Service protecting our Commander-in-Chief. Listen, I know we may appear dangerous, with all of the weapons, but again, this is some scary stuff we're trying to keep away from the bad guys. You keep the disk but wait until we contact you before you start looking at things that will place you and your families in harm's way. The people we're dealing with will torture your kids in front of you until you confess to things that you haven't done or don't know anything about."

"In that case, you keep the damn thing. We hope that you will honor your word about having the conversation and returning the disk."

"I think we have an accord. So be it," the Sarge said.

Asiram was giving her man the attention he needed but was taking every opportunity to chide him on his kissing skills. Zanthius proclaimed, "What the hell are you talking about? I got rid of that thing in Europe!"

"You got rid of a decoy. The real information was somehow stored in your system and was time released, or GPS activated. We really don't know how, but I'm happy that my man is looking and feeling better."

"I'm still confused about my being here—by the way, where the hell am I, anyway?"

"You're in the hospital, darling. You passed out, and that good looking, smooth talking brother of yours, said that we should rush you to the hospital."

"Larry said that. I would have thought he would have abandoned me."

"Don't say that. Larry is your family. If you can't trust your kin, then who? Get over the stupid."

"Honey, I'm just kidding. I've grown to love and respect him, but really did he insist that I be brought here?"

"Honey trust me! It was Larry who said we had to get you to the hospital immediately."

"Wow! What happened to me? Was it something I ate?"

"No, 'idiot spy'. It was that person you kissed. My friend, and your girlfriend, who passed a capsule to you, as you well know. It was like a script to a movie. It was projected into your body. The capsule was a ruse and a big one at that. The capsule is of no consequence. Look at those pictures on that monitor. Those are x-rays of your internals. It was either time released, or GPS activated, but it was definitely the work of Helga. She wants you to suffer beyond her grave, Romeo."

"Whatever. Zanthius then turned to the doctor and asked, "When can I get out of here?"

The doctor said, "We are anxious for you and your hit team to leave. We drew blood from you three hours ago and are fast tracking the results. That will indicate to us if you are out of danger, or whether there are other time released, or GPS activated toxins, in your system. More importantly, we want to make sure there are no other hidden abnormalities in your body," the doctor said.

"I am never going to kiss another woman as long as I live."

"Then you had better plan your funeral because I need the passion of your kisses and the love that follows. Where do you want to be buried?" Zanthius, as well as everyone else in the room, laughed.

"So, Doctor, you have never seen markings like this before?" the Sarge asked.

"Frankly, I have not, but I think my Egyptian counterpart was intrigued by them. She swears that they are hieroglyphics, but can't be sure because she studied medicine, not linguistics. She did say some of the symbols are Asian based, as well. She was in the process of calling her cousin when you people barged in here flashing weapons and threatening our families. Why don't we ask her?"

Later, and with everyone in place, the Sarge stated, "Doctors, I apologize but this thing we're dealing with has, as I said before, catastrophic outcomes associated with it."

Asiram was half listening to Zanthius, as well as the dialogue, between the doctors and the Sarge. She was casually interested in their conversation. The Egyptian doctor was now in the room and the Sarge asked, "I'm repeating myself, but, Doctor, have you ever seen any marking like these?"

"Well, Clint Westwood, the first one is clearly the sign of the dead. 'Amenta' represents land of the dead. The second one is the 'Ankh', the symbol of eternal life that is usually pictured with the Gods, and the third one is the 'Was', this symbol represents power and dominion. The other symbols or words, I think, are written in an Asian dialect. I'm a doctor, not a linguist."

"Are you sure those first three are hieroglyphics?"

"I'm not sure of anything other than the fact that in my culture what I see is what I defined; land of the dead, eternal life, and power and dominion," the doctor answered.

Zanthius looked at Asiram and asked, "What the hell are they talking about?"

"I think that discussion is about the symbols and other characters that showed up on your x-ray. I haven't really been listening to them, but I think the Sarge got the beginnings of an explanation of a few of those characters. I need a kiss and a hug from the husband that scared me half to death."

"Open your mouth and let me examine it," Zanthius suggested.

"Are you out of your mind? I just want a kiss, not an oral exam!" Asiram exclaimed.

"I'm never kissing another woman until I examine her mouth first to see if she has some object in it that will make me glow when x-rayed," Zanthius declared.

"You know I told the admitting nurse that you have a living will. Buster if you don't pucker up and give it up, then it may be put to use."

"Honey, I was just kidding you. I love you and I don't know how, on earth, I would have survived any of this madness without you." He kissed her tenderly, then again and again until the doctor said, "I think you might be ready to leave here in a few minutes. Can you control yourself until I have a chance to check your vitals and the blood work that should be back soon?"

###

Beckmire was looking at the pictures and studying them when John Lee said, "I bet you a full-grown hog that what Larry sent to his site is another one of those, ah, deceptions. What's that word them there English people use when they be misdirecting you?"

Jilkes replied, "Ruse."

"That be the word. Now, I think that there girl that kissed him and made him swallow knew that the entire world was gonna be looking for his ass. She be done laid out a puzzle, and I be thinking that if we go to Larry's site, then we be toasted. I just be seeing a puzzle here. I don't know what you people be looking at."

Jilkes looked at the x-rays and asked himself, "Why make him swallow a capsule with coordinates on it? Why put a card from a strip joint in Russia and a condom with writing on it in his wallet unless you weren't sure about who you were giving it to, or their survival skills? Why load a guy full of artwork unless that was the real trick?" He said, "Sarge, I think that country ass, John Lee, has done it again. Think about it! They gave us a capsule that turns out to be a dud, a card and a condom that are probably duds. Why go through some elaborate process to make a guy sick and have x-rays that show his inners are full of crazy ass symbols? This is the direction we should be heading in, not following that card and condom."

"Oh shit! Remember the women in Nam used to give out cards and condoms for her whorehouse that a lot of guys used to escape active duty because the women were known carriers of everything that was considered venereal? John Lee, your country ass is smarter than that Einstein fellow. I'm thinking that woman knew that if Zanthius didn't get sick and have to be admitted to a hospital, then by all likelihood, he was probably dead, and anyone attempting to retrieve that package was going to have a surprise ending," Beckmire stated.

The doctor came back in the room and said to Zanthius, "All of your vitals are perfect. This thing was a hiccup. Now, I want you to get these prescriptions filled and buy yourself bottles of Vitamin C, D & E, all at the 1000IU plus levels. Water is your best friend and you should spend more time consuming it. I don't know if there will be any residual effects from the artwork, but in case there is, I want you to flush your system by obtaining a common enema product and inserting it in your rectum and drinking a laxative that any druggist can recommend. Not the best experience you'll have, but it is a very cathartic process. I'm going to have an orderly come up with a wheelchair, and then you, and Clint Westwood, and his gang, can leave our little family oriented hospital."

"Doctor, I promised you some groundbreaking information. Don't you think that at least deserves some gratitude?" the Sarge inquired.

"Clint, your character shoots first and never asks questions. We would like to study this information further, but we have to lay out the ground rules first, because we don't want you and your band of conspirators visiting us at home."

"You keep your word and give us time to complete this mission, and I'll give you the whole package and donate $1 million to your hospital for you and your fellow doctors to figure out how the hell this was possible. Do we have an accord?" the Sarge asked.

"Is your word your bond?" the doctor asked

"Ab-so-damn-lutely!" the Sarge exclaimed.

"Clint, then we have an accord! As a pirate would so profoundly, state."

## CHAPTER NINETEEN

In the SUV Zanthius was riding in, he said, "That was really some weird shit that I saw on that monitor and really can't believe that it was emanating from my body. How the hell could that slut Helga know of such things and know precisely when it was time to retrieve the card and the condom?"

"I want you to save all of your questions for your father. He and his guys were listening to the scientific discussions, while I was trying to figure out where to bury you since you were not going to kiss me ever again."

In the SUV the Sarge was riding in, he was thinking about the information that had been presented to him. He was keenly focused on what John Lee and Jilkes had added to the equation. He knew that he and his team had completed two of the three missions that were agreed upon but also realized that everything that related to the Carbon Factor was troubling, problematic, and deadly. He considered the information that Jong had passed on to him about Walter and was disappointed by the tremendous amount of deception Walter practiced. He was concerned about the potential residual effects of the product that Zanthius had ingested and wondered if there was more to the equation than the doctors could figure out. He knew that it was coming upon the hour when the card and the condom were to be retrieved and turned over to Walter. As he cogitated about the possible outcomes of the various scenarios, he had an epiphany. He smiled to himself as he thought to give Walter the data disk, the codes to Larry's secure box, and let him figure out its contents. He had no faith in Walter and thus wanted him to have to sort the whole mess out.

At the motel, the Sarge, Jilkes, and John Lee escorted Zanthius and Asiram to their room. Once settled in the bed, Zanthius inquired, "What was all that talk about life, death, and dominions?"

"What on earth are you talking about?" Asiram asked.

"The conversation that Pops had with that Egyptian doctor about land of the dead, eternal life and power."

"I wasn't really listening to his conversation," Asiram stated.

"Pops, so what was that doctor talking about?"

"Son, I have no hard facts to base this on, but I think that woman Helga gave you three tests. One was to secure the capsule and deliver it. The second was to understand the meaning of the condom and card from the Russian strip joint. The third was for you to realize that the whereabouts of the Carbon Factor was encoded in hieroglyphics and Asian writings inside of your anatomy. Now, how perplexing is that? I mean the doctor identified the symbols for the land of the dead, eternal life, and dominion; but it doesn't make sense. Until we find out what those symbols from Asia mean, we are still clueless." As the Sarge was talking to Zanthius, Asiram's brain kicked into overdrive and she yelled, "I need a moment of quiet."

"I'm sorry if we're disturbing your aura, but we have a timetable to make and I don't think now is the time for me to keep quiet," the Sarge said.

"No, wait, just wait. You said the doctor identified one of the symbols as a representation of the land of the dead. Is that correct?" Asiram asked.

"That's right," the Sarge stated.

"The other symbol that was identified represented, if I'm not putting words in your mouth, eternal life. Is that correct?"

"That's correct. Go on," the Sarge replied.

"Now, here is my trick question, did she say the third symbol represented dominion or was there more to her explanation?" Asiram asked.

John Lee looking a little confused whispered, "That there doctor said that the third symbol be power and dominion, not just dominion."

"Oh shit, Helga used to wear rings and necklaces that were cartouches. I used to ask her why she bought things that she didn't know the meaning of. She emphasized that she knew the full meaning of every piece of jewelry she owned. What I'm saying is that she owned a cartouche that represented the land of the dead, as well as one, that amplified eternal life. She also owned one that symbolized power and dominion. If we can find someone who speaks Chinese, then I might be able to tell you the location of the specifications for the Carbon Factor. I didn't listen to much of the conversation in the hospital, but now that I hear what was said in simple terms, the shit is coming back to me. Helga played us from the beginning and, I must say, to the end. She knew that I would fall in love with Zanthius and that, through hell or high water, I would protect him with my life. When she had sex with you, Zanthius, it was all about planting things on you, around you, and in your 'idiot spy' ass. You, my friend, didn't see it coming or going, but at least you were smart enough to catch it eventually.

"Helga played us to the pinnacle, and I must say, brilliantly. She knew that I would fall for you because I had never had a meaningful encounter with a man. She knew that you were a lonesome cowboy in search of something without a definition— your father, Ben Beckmire. She played us to the hilt. I mean come now, think about it. How did your mother realize that she needed to reach out to you and the Sarge? Zanthius, you had hit rock bottom and needed help to preserve your life. I'll bet you a dime makes a dollar that Helga calculated this and is orchestrating this symphony from her grave if she is truly dead. She often said to me, 'my finest work is being carefully created'."

"Honey, that's a lot of calculating. Are you sure that woman was capable of creating a symphony without an end?"

"That's the point. Can't you see it? If you had not gotten through all the phases of this process, then those seeking the mysterious Carbon Factor would still be chasing ghosts. That bitch wrote this play, turned it into a symphony and sold the rights to Lucifer. By the way, she often spoke of her association with Hades. I'm telling you, if someone translates what those Asian characters mean, then I will know exactly where the true information is. And, buddy, believe me, to extract it we might need the 5th fleet, the entire Marine Corps, the Army, Air Force, and the Coast Guard."

John Lee said, "Somebody better be trying to call Jong, right about now."

The Sarge began to think about all that Asiram had said and finally blurted out, "You know Baby Girl, you might be on to something." He picked up his phone, called Jong and said, "I need to see you as soon as possible. Don't dally getting here."

When Jong arrived at the room, he assigned the Sarge, he knocked hard on the door. There was no answer. After several elongated knocks on the door, Jong threw his hands in the air. The Sarge who was in Zanthius's room, heard the commotion and walked out into the hallway where he saw Jong standing in front of his room. He yelled to him, "What on earth are you doing down there?"

"This is your room? Is it not?"

"Oh, sorry, Jong, I am in the room you assigned to Zanthius and Asiram, my bad." As Jong walked towards the Sarge, the Sarge recognized that Jong was moving slowly as if something was hurting him. He asked, "What's going on my brother. You're moving a little slow there."

"Yeah, I guess I'm in need of rest. We have been on a whirlwind and my mind normally tells my body what it wants to do. However, my body is now telling my mind what it can't do."

"I feel bad for you and regardless of our tasks tomorrow, I'm sending you home."

"Good luck with that one. I'm not going anywhere until we all disperse and go our separate ways when this thing is over. What happened to me in the Nam could have been a lot worse. I am functioning, perhaps a little slow today, but I'm as good as anyone else. Perhaps too fast on the trigger, but I'm a part of this team and where you go, I go." The Sarge embraced him and said, "I love you, Man, and I know you love me. You have to admit something to me."

"What's that?"

"This has been an exciting roller coaster ride for us! Hasn't it?"

"Best damn ride I've been on in a long time and I'll admit one other thing, I wouldn't have missed this for anything. Why did you have me hustle down here?"

"Do you still speak and understand Chinese?"

"Of course, I do. Do you still speak English?"

"Okay, smartass. I need you to look at the pictures of Zanthius's inners and tell me if you can define what these characters or symbols mean." The two men walked into the room and Jong asked Zanthius, "How the hell are you feeling?"

"I'm much better now. Happy to be conscious and with the love of my life, who at some point in time this year, God willing, will be the mother of our child."

Jong spoke to the lovers, Jilkes and John Lee, and asked, "Which one of you are responsible for me losing my much needed sleep?" Jilkes pointed to John Lee, who pointed at him and everyone laughed.

The Sarge asked, "Can you tell what these characters or symbols mean?"

Jong replied, "Chinese is not my native tongue." He looked at the characters and studied them intensely. He smiled and then carefully looked at them intently. While poking fun of the others in his native tongue, he began to laugh. Jong continued to laugh until he became hysterical. The Sarge said, "We feel like laughing, as well. Can you enlighten us as to what that stuff means?"

"Happy New Year, Motherfuckers!"

The Sarge yelled, "What's wrong with you? This is a serious matter and one that might end this entire charade."

Jong, now laughing uncontrollably, blurted out again, "Happy New Year—Gong Hei Fard Choy, if you're in Hong Kong or Macau; or Happy New Year—Gong xi fa cai, if you speak Mandarin; and Happy New Year in New York, if you speak English."

At this point, Jong grabbed his side after laughing so hard. He said, "I have to leave now because I will probably laugh myself to death if I stay here. The funny thing about this is, I have always wanted to say to you guys, "Happy New Year,

Motherfuckers." Just leave off the motherfucker and those words say Happy New Year."

He laughed his way out of the room, and on his journey to his room he ran into Mallory who asked, "What's wrong with you?"

"Gong Hei Fard Choy," Jong answered which only accentuated his laughter.

As Mallory entered Zanthius's room, he reported, "I ran into Jong and I guess he said something to me in Chinese."

"Which one was it? Gong Hei Fard Choy or Gong xi fa cai?" the Sarge asked.

"I guess it was the first one. What does it mean?"

"Happy New Year."

## CHAPTER TWENTY

In the meantime, Asiram hearing the translation, was laughing her head off. In between the laughter, she was trying to decipher the relevance of his statements and the imaging that was prevalent on Zanthius's internals. She loudly exclaimed, "I know two places where the real Carbon Factor may be! Listen, if I am not mistaken, I think Helga's play that turned into a symphony, has been exposed. The first statement about land of the dead was just a tribute to the 'idiot spy' for surviving, against all odds. The second was intended to tell the 'idiot spy' that if he were still alive then eternal life was his, in a weird sort of a way. The third notion of power and dominion exposed all of those who were at fault, such as hundreds of mercs, Allen, Shari, Ariel, T-Rex, Scottie, the target, his son, as well as Walter. The assertion of Happy New Year was her way of saying, I think, 'if you got this far then you deserve the final outcome—possession of the Carbon Factor'.

"Now, these are just my assumptions but I stick by them. Please, humor me. I spent a lot of time with Helga, and we had many adversarial missions, but that did not stop us from being mates. Daddy-in-Law, if I had to make a calculated guess, I would say that in a world of options and hiding places, I would bet my farm on Asia and more specifically, two specific locations—Hong Kong and Tokyo."

"Why those two places?" Mallory asked.

"As I said, Helga and I had adversarial missions in both places but we found time to bond and have drinks with each other. We talked about death, a life full of love and sex, and the power that women have over men that they don't utilize. Zanthius survived each challenge, and Jong has defined the final piece. I bet my husband, that the full package is in one of those two places."

"You can't just randomly bet me without me knowing what's at stake."

"What's at stake is the end of this murdering train we have been on and the chance to live our lives in harmony and peace. Helga knew exactly what she was doing. She knew that people were on to her and that she had run out of options. Therefore, she screwed my 'idiot spy' husband and planted all kinds of high-tech shit in him without him knowing. For his sake, that had better be all she gave him, or his mother is really going to be pissed at me."

"Honey, I'm sick. Can you order me a cup of soup and some hot tea?"

"If you can say it and ask for it, then you can pick up the damn phone and call it in yourself. I think right now I'm feeling a little jealous, so you might want to do that yourself." The Sarge looked at Asiram and dropped his head. She knew that she was displaying emotions that should have been shared privately, if at all, but couldn't help the way she was feeling.

"You be sounding like me and this colored fellow and we ain't even married. Do you be wanting us to leave here and come back later after you done finish making up or out?" Everyone in the room began to laugh.

"No, your point is well taken," Asiram replied.

"Where you be taking my point?" John Lee inquired.

"I mean I understand what you're saying. I agree with you and I appreciate what you said."

The Sarge continued to focus on the meaning of all of the things that he had heard from the doctors, as well as Asiram. Finally, he announced, "I think we have a plan. I was thinking about letting that crooked-ass cousin of mine retrieve the card and the condom. But I don't trust him as far as I can see him, family or not. Therefore, unless he has those new jets bugged, we head out to your ranch Asiram and gather our families and head to Hong Kong. We follow your lead to Hong Kong and see if that leads us to somewhere in Japan. While Walter is extracting the card and the condom, we will be crossing another ocean. Can you guys find any holes in my thinking?"

"Daddy-in-Law, I'm just trying to figure out which one it is and why my attention is focused on those two places. I can't make a connection to either place that would allow me to make a choice. I mean if we go to Hong Kong or Tokyo, what are we looking for? I don't know what the next questions or part to this riddle are, and until I have something to look for, I don't know if the trips make any sense. I mean, where do we start looking?"

"I see what you mean, but if your analysis of signs as confirmed by the doctors and Jong, as well as your dealings with the lady, are correct, then she pitted you against the world, to save Zanthius. There has to be some common ground that we can begin to explore, I just need you to focus.

"In the meantime, I'll call Walter and tell him that there is no way in hell we can make the third mission happen today. I will attempt to buy us some precious time and allow Zanthius to consider every small detail of his relationship with Helga. Jilkes and John Lee, I need you two to go to your room, and get some sleep. That's an order."

## CHAPTER TWENTY-ONE

The Sarge and Mallory stopped by Jong's room and when he answered the door, he broke into laughter. The Sarge humored him for a few moments and asked, "What's the status of the new equipment and the pilots? Have you made a decision about who would best serve us?"

"I have chosen four that qualify. It looks as if we are going to have a white woman, an African American man, as well as, two white guys. According to the manufacturer, the woman set a new record for take-off in that equipment. She landed the damn thing perfectly on a runway that was 150 yards short of the regulations for that plane. She is tech savvy and apparently knows her way around that plane. The African American guy, her copilot, is as mechanical savvy as they come, and was a former fighter pilot over in the desert. They both qualify as captains-in-command. The female is somewhat of a risk taker, whereas the African American, goes strictly by the book. Only two of our current pilots qualify for operating the new equipment, and therefore, I hired an additional two pilots to take their roles, all former military."

"Can you give me a little more information on the risk taker? I mean we want to travel safely and I, for one, don't want a cowgirl up there flying my ass," Mallory stated.

"When I say risk taker, I mean if there is a problem with the equipment, it is she who I would want to have at the controls. I do not mean risk taker in the sense that she likes flying planes upside down, although she has. I mean, that in a pinch, she will figure it out and keep us safe, if at all possible."

"We may be out of here and back at the ranch by tomorrow. However, we might have to leave for Hong Kong, or Tokyo the next day. What's the protocol for making a trip like that? Is it the same as for Australia?" the Sarge asked.

"I think so, but why, are we going to Hong Kong and/or Tokyo?" Jong inquired.

"Happy New Year Motherfucker," the Sarge said and walked away. He yelled back to Jong, "I'm going to have a briefing tonight, so get some rest and place those pilots on alert. I need them rested and ready to book at the drop of a dime." The Sarge started to yell something, then turned around and walked back towards Jong and said, "I'm going to call the ranch in a few, but I need you to call as soon as possible and make sure that everyone there has a passport. If not, they need them to go the post office and apply for one. Tell Clyde I need his man at the post office to do this quietly without notifying anyone about it."

"Let's just say we must head to Hong Kong to set up a conference. That keeps us under the radar. Maybe we can use one of our charities as a front, but I need all our people in the same place. I'm hoping Asiram will come up with the common denominator so that we can figure this shit out and be done with it."

"Maybe I can work with Asiram and reconstruct memories of two of my favorite places. If you think that will help, let me know and I'll be right on it. Once I call the ranch, I will get a head count and make the appropriate reservations."

Mallory and the Sarge started walking back down the hall when Mallory said, "You know Asiram's calculations are a bit sketchy, if I must say so myself. She has the parts, the tools, but not the diagram, and that's what concerns me."

"Yeah, you're right. It's pretty damn superficial, but it makes sense to me, considering that the condom and the strip joint card, I believe, were just another test for Asiram and Zanthius. That Helga woman was either a brilliant strategist or a lucky lottery player. Why don't you pick one and let me know tonight? Catch you later."

In his room, the Sarge decided to call Walter and try to buy some time. When Walter answered the phone Ben said, "I have two options for you in terms of picking up that thing. Option number one is that we give you the details to retrieve the card and condom and you get it yourself. Option number two is that you wait until a key member of my team recovers from a brief stay in the hospital and then we go to work together again."

"How about option number three? You and the balance of your team go retrieve the merchandise and hand it over to me," Walter announced.

"That's not an option because I don't do missions without the full complement of my people. I guess you haven't learned a thing about us, have you? Your choice, but we are not going to entertain option number three."

"Did you secure the information that we spoke about?"

"It's here in my room. Do you want to stop by and pick it up?"

"I'm in the parking lot, in a white minivan. Can you bring the information to me in five minutes or so?"

"I'm on my way. What's so important about these disks, other than your compromising behavior?"

"Unless you really want to be involved in national security matters, I suggest you never mention that you had those things in your hands. Otherwise, an extractor will be extracting your ass, Cousin. See you in a few. I'm in the rear of this dive. Aren't you worried about bed bugs and shit? I'm afraid to come into that place."

"You know, Walter, sometimes it's nice to sleep where people without schemes or resources lay their heads, if only for a minute. It kind of gives you moral direction for the bad that you do, to support the good that you want to do, while trying to kill the ugly that hides behind plate glass windows and exploits the masses. You should try it sometime. It's a strong form of catharsis."

"Whatever, Cousin, see you in a few."

The Sarge called Chakes and Montomie, as well as Brown, and Bernstein, and asked them to provide backup for him because he had to leave the premises for a minute. Everyone agreed to meet in the lobby in five minutes.

As the Sarge walked down the steps, he was met by Brown, Bernstein, Chakes, and Montomie, who were waiting for him. The Sarge said, "Listen, I don't trust my cousin. I'm about to turn over these disks to him, and I just want to make sure that this guy doesn't do anything stupid. Brown and Bernstein, I would like you two to cover the front of the white minivan parked out back and Chakes and Montomie, cover the rear and both sides. I know what you're thinking. It's his family, and he doesn't trust him? My answer is clear. I only trust my true family, and four of them are with me now."

As the Sarge approached the minivan, Walter lowered the window and asked, "What's up with all this security?"

"Standard operating procedure, that's all. There are a lot of shady people hanging around here, so we try to make sure that with the sensitive information that I have, there isn't a chance that someone will rob me."

The Sarge entered the minivan and with a smirk said, "There were two disks in the box and we couldn't figure out which one compromised you, so we brought them both."

"Has anyone seen the disks?"

"Unless they can see into my pockets and discern the very nature of the information, then I would say absolutely not. You seem a bit anxious about this, Walter. Is there something else on the disks that you don't want me or my people to see?"

"Ben, I told you exactly what this was about. Insofar as the other information that might be on these disks, I have to treat it as a matter of national security. Therefore, since you know nothing, it keeps you and your people from being tortured."

"Good luck with that one. I didn't know we had relegated ourselves to threatening each other, have we? I mean, I don't know and certainly my people don't know what's on those disks and we could give a shit one way or the other. This, so far, has been a mutually agreeable relationship. We do your dirty work and stumble into untold millions of dollars for our charity work. However, let me be crystal clear to you, if you threaten me or mine, I will exercise that hit order I have on you and your family. Just think about this--we will pay for it, with your money. How ironic is that?"

"Why are we always threatening each other, Cousin? We come from the same fabric, although miles and years apart. I'm just telling you that a lot of the shit that you're doing has national security consequences and I'm only trying to protect you, as you serve the greater good of our country."

"Walter, horseshit! You got the disks! We'll need a few days to do the other work or you and yours can waltz into the place and secure the card and condom. If that mess is that important, I suggest you exercise that option and be done with it. I'm looking at a few days before we are at full strength again."

Walter remained silent for almost a minute when the Sarge asked, "Are you okay?"

"I'm fine, just trying to figure out the consequences of such a move."

"The only consequence I see is that a civil servant retrieves the directions to a product that could change the balance of power in this world—sort of a hero like, conclusion. If we secure it and decipher it, well who knows, we might get into the black-market business. Just kidding, Cousin."

"Do you have the necessary information with you for me to retrieve the products?"

"I not only don't have the information; I don't even know where the hell it is. That my Cousin, is why I am not going to try this without the full complement of my people. As far as I know, it is an intricate process, but I will gather all of the people involved to ascertain the facts about location, entry codes and passwords."

"I'll be back tomorrow afternoon. Have all the information ready for me by then. Do we have an agreement?"

"Indeed, we do. I will get it together and be prepared to give it to you tomorrow. Nice to see you, I'm out of here," Ben stated.

While walking back towards the entrance, the Sarge muttered to his guys, "What a fricking snake, and somehow I'm related to that bastard."

Chakes said, "Sarge, he had at least two people looking out for him. What's strange is that someone kept moving their gun sight so that I could see the reflection."

"Probably Mike, I'm okay with that because I think he realizes that he's in bed with a snake and doesn't want to go down with him. I'll check it out, I have his number."

"I saw another chicken hiding in the brush with a long gun. Not the kind of thing you would do unless that family bond isn't too strong. What are your thoughts on that, Brown?" Bernstein asked.

"Go screw yourself, Bernstein. He was my stepdad. He wasn't real family. The guy was an opportunist that married my mom and tried to kill me."

"Guys, please stay focused for a minute. I think both of your statements make sense to me. He is not real family. We have killed for him, and he has demanded all kinds of horseshit from us but has delivered on the trinkets. I think I'm really going to play my cousin. I need to see Jong immediately."

The group went directly to Jong's room and banged on his door. He answered and said, "I was told to get some rest. Why are you people banging on my door?"

"I have a tech question that I need to ask you. Is there any way you can remotely erase the material on those two data disks that you copied?"

"Come now, Sarge. That's against the law."

"What law, and in what country?" the Sarge asked.

"I knew you were concerned about the material, but I didn't know what to do with the information, so I decided to place a red flag on each disk."

"Okay, what's a red flag?" the Sarge inquired.

"I essentially encrypted his disk with a code, or sort of a password that won't allow him to open, access, or view any of the files unless you approve it first," Jong stated.

"When were you going to tell me about this?" the Sarge asked.

"That's really simple--when you asked. Listen, I didn't view any of the files other than the one that pops up amplifying a man being nailed by another man. I mean, I'm not the smartest cookie in the jar, but I do know that when someone is jerking your chains around and you have fallen into some extremely damaging information; you copy, encrypt, and wait for some ridiculous assignment, thus increasing your bargaining capability."

"You guys are the best. Everyone is concerned with options and not consequences. I love you people. Now, how about we erase those disks that he has. Is that possible?"

"I told you as soon as he tries to access the information without the password that I encrypted—boom, erased."

"Can you pull up the files on your machine so that we can review them?"

"Absolutely," Jong said.

"I'm going to schedule a briefing after I take a siesta. I suggest that you guys do the same. Thanks for watching my back."

## CHAPTER TWENTY-TWO

At the briefing, the Sarge said, "People you know how we operate. I don't keep secrets, and I share what intel that I have on the so called bad guys, as well as the good guys, who may be bad. I say that to indicate that we may have been played all along, but I will leave that to your analysis."

John Lee asked, "Where be Asiram, Larry and Zanthius? Don't you think they be needing to see this as well?"

"I'm not sure it's appropriate for Asiram."

"I be wanting to know why not. I be thinking if this here stuff be important." Jilkes looked at the Sarge and nodded in approval.

"Okay, Jong, let's take this thing to their room."

Ten minutes later, Mallory knocked on the door and a disheveled Asiram answered it and exclaimed, "Oh my; 'hell, hell, the gang's all here'. Give me a moment to change into something a little less revealing."

Jilkes yelled, "It's a matter of national security. Your attire is okay." Everyone laughed as Asiram shut the door.

A few minutes later she opened the door and said, "You people may have been the best in that Vietnam jungle, but here in the concrete jungle, your timing sucks. Come on in."

The Sarge said, "I think some of this material may be a bit too offensive for your viewing, Asiram. However, John Lee said that you, Zanthius and Larry are a part of the team. He wanted me to warn you if what you see is too disturbing, then go into the bathroom."

"First of all, I didn't sanction anyone to censor what I can see or can't, see. Second, who is the subject of what I'm about to see, and where is Larry?" Jilkes indicated that he would go and get Larry.

A few minutes later, the Sarge said, "This is about my cousin, Walter and how he may have been double dealing us from the start. We suspect that he has his hands into some pretty dirty shit and we don't have a clue as to what is on these disks, except that one part of it may be very disturbing."

"Can we get on with the production? I have work to do to bring my husband back to normal," Asiram announced.

Jong opened his laptop and stated, "I did nothing to this program to impact the way it opens, this is not my creation." He placed the data disk into the drive and immediately a video of Walter being nailed and kissed by Harold appeared. Asiram said, "I knew he was on the other side of the equation."

The group watched the three minute clip. Afterwards, Jong began to open other files that were apparently related to a drug business, a prostitution ring, illegal arms sales, and the selling of Iranian oil, while sanctions were in place against the regime. Harold and Walter were the minds behind many international schemes that endowed them with hundreds of millions of dollars.

Beckmire said, "Now, I know why Walter didn't hesitate to blow Harold's head off. He was afraid of him talking, as well as seizing the opportunity to inherit their empire, and funneling the illicit funds into his own personal accounts. My question is, why has he been so helpful to us?"

"Guys, I didn't mention this, but when me and Whitmore shot one of the mercs at the farm in Virginia, when we stumbled upon him, he said, 'Walter is not going to like what you've done. He is going to be unmerciful and exact his vengeance upon you.' I asked him, "Walter who? The guy replied, "Walter, Who-the-hell-do-you-think? He's the man in charge of this OP," Chakes replied.

"Now, that's some scary shit. So, your cousin is the ringleader of this shit? Just think about it. Every move we have made has been telegraphed. He shows up at OPs like the bank, the farm, lends a helping hand to assassinate his own people and lead us to victory, without a band playing. What a cunning son-of-a-bitch," Mallory stated.

Beckmire confessed, "He told me about his fall from grace and his interludes with Harold and how he wanted to seek some sort of forgiveness from me. I told him that I was not in the salvation business, and, therefore, could not provide solace for him or his soul."

Jong interrupted the Sarge and said, "Guys, you're not going to believe this, guess who was a part of his organization?"

"Don't play games, Jong. Who?" the Sarge asked.

"Give me a drum roll first. Helga Spengatsenburg, was on his payroll."

Asiram said, "You have got to be crazier than a fox, because this shit is really starting to come together. Guys, once in Paris I had an assignment to extract information from someone, while Helga had the assignment to terminate the same person. We made a deal, and I inadvertently, asked her, who the hell was her handler, and why does he or she always seem to pair us on the opposite sides of the street. You know what she said to me? Well, my husband's, ex-lover, said to me, you will not believe me if I told you. He is a civil servant—grade 15 or 16, but a helluva lover and as kinky as can be. I, to this day, don't understand that grade stuff, but it ties someone like him to our fate. I would really like to extract your cousin, Daddy-in-Law."

The Sarge looked at the group as he thought about his next comments and/or actions. After a moment of silence, he said, "I need a drink and a moment alone in the bathroom."

The Sarge walked over to the mini bar and took two bottles of cheap vodka. He poured the two bottles into a glass and said, "I have been hoodwinked and screwed without lubricants. A son that I didn't know existed in the real world shows up, his mother who totally dissed me, calls me to meet her for lunch." The Sarge looks around the room and says, "How about his, some people try to kill me. I meet a real-life spy, and my son, that I did not know I had, marries her. My cousin works for an agency that is full of spies and he's a raging homosexual, but under wraps. Mind you, I am not homophobic, but this guy makes us steal shit from a bank that reveals his pleasures. He then, kills his own partner, who by the way is nailing the shit out of him, and the data disks indicates that he is the ringleader of a drug, arms dealer, prostitution, oil smuggling ring, and who the hell knows what else. People I'm going to go and take a shower, alone damn it, and try not to think about this craziness, until much later. Adios."

As the Sarge walked out of the room, he never looked back. Mallory exited the room and said to the Sarge, "I think we should continue to figure out this business model and how we can work our way around it, especially since this guy has us wired and we don't even know how. Perhaps we should buy a shitload of those throw away phones to communicate with him."

The Sarge entered his room and called the main number to the ranch hoping that Carlos or one of his men would answer the phone. The Sarge said, "Carlos, this is Ben Beckmire. How are things out there?"

"Things are going good here, the neighbors are just fantastic. They continue to patrol and escort the ladies and us everywhere we go. We eat like crazy every day. I mean the food never stops coming and the children are having a wonderful time exploring the outdoors and learning about the animals. I would say that we are doing extremely well. How about you guys? When are you coming back this way?"

"We are trying to close out this business here, but we may have a long trip in store for us once we get back there. Is my wife anywhere around?"

"Let me fetch her."

A few minutes later, the Sarge said, "Hi, honey, how are you?"

"I'm doing fine, but you won't be once I see you again."

"Okay, I know I forgot to call you last night, but all is well with us. We literally spent the night in the hospital with Zanthius who became sick from digesting that capsule. I'll tell you the rest when I see you in a few days."

"Ben Beckmire, nothing can wait. What happened to Zanthius?"

"That capsule has been the bane of his existence, as well as ours. Once he swallowed the capsule, some kind of system kicked in, and basically wrote symbols on his internals. Please don't think I'm crazy, but his insides had Egyptian and Asian symbols written on them. I know this isn't making any sense to you, but I will show you the pictures once we get out of here. More important, is the fact, that my so-called cousin has been playing me from day one, and I can't discuss the matter over the phone. I hope everyone is having fun out there. I think we will wrap this phase of this mess up in a day or so and then we'll head back to Asiram's ranch. I miss you terribly and can't wait to see you, honey."

"I miss you as well, sweetheart. Keep those guys and girl safe and out of harm's way. Missuluvu."

CHAPTER TWENTY-THREE

Mallory and Jong purchased eight throw away phones for the Sarge. As the Sarge looked at them, he said, "I'm going to continue to use this phone as long as we are here and until I convince Walter to retrieve the card and condom, himself. If he is tracking me by this device, then I'll let him. Once he indicates that he's going to get the package, then I'll dump it, or tape it to a taxi, or something. Jong, did you find anything else useful on those disks?"

"It all points to Walter as the leader in all of these ventures. Additionally, Scottie and Allen were on his payroll. He runs a sophisticated outfit with levels of responsibility with no direct connection to him."

"So, if Helga worked for him then why didn't he know what she was doing and why was a hit placed on her? I need to get with Asiram and Zanthius, maybe they can shed some light on this mess."

###

Zanthius and Asiram walked into the room where the Sarge was and he stated, "I know we briefly discussed that Helga was on Walter's payroll."

Asiram replied, "I don't believe he could afford her."

"Scottie and Allen were also on his books according to the information on the disk," the Sarge said.

"How on earth could he afford to have those people on his payroll? I mean he is just a technician, of sorts. He is a field agent and not a guy with a lot of power and or access to that kind of money. I mean, how can he manifest that kind of power from behind his desk?"

"Well, according to the disk, he controlled a prostitution ring, sold weapons on the black market, a drug ring, and shipped oil out of Iran to China during the embargo and other places for a pretty profit. He was into money laundering.

"My cousin has played us like a fiddle. Knowing our every move, showing up at our missions, and quickly, without hesitation, killing his partner and lover. He has tracked us from the start and has never been more than a hundred yards from where we are. He is a mastermind with some peculiar proclivities. We essentially have been cleaning up his problems.

"I told him that we could not accomplish mission number three because Zanthius was hospitalized and that we don't do business without our full complement. I also told him that we needed a few more days and suggested that we give him the place, the codes, and the password so he can obtain the package. I was expecting to hear from him by now, especially since Jong initiated a virus that was password driven that he would never guess in a million years. If he attempts to open the disks that we gave him with the wrong password, all data will be erased before his eyes. We can always blame his dead partner Harold for setting up an elaborate protection process. What really bothers me is why would he put a hit out on Helga if she worked for him?" the Sarge inquired.

"Maybe Helga didn't want to see the world go to hell in a hand basket because someone was going to profit from the sale of a new dirty bomb. Whatever her reasons, she certainly wouldn't want to turn the disks over to Walter. Also, he wasn't prepared for the likes of the 'idiot spy', his father and his band of hitmen. I say that with a sense of reverence and admiration, of course. I don't know or care what her reasons were. I only care about getting it into the right hands, and as we now know, it ain't your cousin's hands. I'm concerned about him more than ever because we know how ruthless he can be. He's probably waiting for all this to end, and then he will send in the Marines to liquidate us," Asiram said.

"If you consider all that we have been through, I'm almost sure Helga didn't want us to be involved with the card and the condom. If they were that critical to the discovery, then why didn't Walter realize that when he had the 'idiot spy's? wallet. I mean, come on now, he is a spy and is trained to look for the unobvious. If you think about it, what you said, Asiram, about Helga developing stages of success or failure and detailing the consequences of each step, makes sense. Think about it--land of the dead, eternal life and power and dominion, and then the final awards ceremony of Happy New Year, relating to Asia. I think the card and the condom were meant for Walter to obtain and we should let him retrieve them and discover any hidden meaning in the hologram and the writing on the condom," the Sarge stated.

Much later, the Sarge gathered the group and said, "Jong, I need those planes torn apart and checked for any signs of explosives. I want our pilots to search them from head to toe and I want the manufacturer on site by tomorrow to go through them, according to the specs, and make sure that they're safe. If they say they can't accommodate us, then tell them their contract with the government will surely be terminated. I need those

things torn apart and put back together in two days. If they have
to use ten people, then authorize them to do so and we'll make
my cousin pay the bill."

Zanthius sat in the room evaluating the information he
heard and focusing on his brief encounter with Helga. Asiram
asked, "Are you feeling okay?"

"I'm still a little out of it, but I need a moment to myself."
He continued to stare blankly into the air, speak aloud, and then
whisper information, as if he were carrying on a two-way
conversation. He would ask a question and then answer the
question. He pointed to the door and said, "I gave you a condom
and a card, I hope you don't use them."

Zanthius then mumbled something else, and yelled, "The
key. I need some water. Honey, would you step out of the room
for a minute while I recreate in my mind a scenario that I am
sure you won't like and one that I don't want to have to pay some
unwanted price for?"

"I will not."

"Honey, I beg of you. Please trust me on this one."

"Eventually, you're going to have to tell me about it, so
buddy, you might as well put on your big man drawels and let it
flow because I ain't going nowhere."

"Pops, please reason with her. You know every time
Helga's name is mentioned, my dear wife gets a little crazy."

"Son, I'm not going to get in the middle of your marriage.
You knew this woman was stubborn when you married her, so
get used to it. I did."

Zanthius looked at Asiram and inquired, "What I'm about
to say happened prior to you, and, therefore, no harm, no foul.
Okay?"

"Zanthius, get on with the fable."

"I'm going to trust you on this one and I hope you don't let me down. Anyway, I entered the shower first, and made it hot and steamy. Helga came in and said, 'Marco Polo, have you ever been to Asia'. I said no. She said there is a hotel in Kowloon and a game that kids, as well as adults play, when they're in swimming pools called Marco Polo. We played it for a few minutes and when she tagged me, well, a certain act was momentarily performed and this went on for a while. Later, she told me the people at that hotel were very loyal and that you could trust them with your life, as well as, your keys. I dismissed all of that because I didn't want to play Marco Polo anymore, I wanted to play another game. Later, and I mean much later, she said, 'If you ever get to Asia, you should also go to the Miyako, or some hotel in Tokyo. I still have a bottle of Grand Marnier in my personal box there'.

"That's it! When are you going to get to the screwing part?"

Zanthius threw his hands into the air and Asiram exclaimed, "Just kidding, honey, but you had better never ask me to play Marco Polo!"

"I haven't been able to connect the dots on this one because I, like your wife, was waiting for some hot and sexy stuff to transpire," the Sarge said.

"You guys didn't get this? Asiram, you said you thought this thing was planned by her in stages. We survived the land of the dead, which led us to the life eternal stuff. We are in the power and dominion stage because we're the only ones who know what and where this thing may be. She was not only a brilliant strategist, but a cunning and untrustworthy person as well.

"There is someone at the Marco Polo Hotel in Kowloon who is holding a key for me or someone else. There is a private bar somewhere in Tokyo that has a secured bottle of Grand

Marnier and the exact location of the product. I'll bet my wife on that one. Now, that is the short, sweet, and end of the deal. The real problem is connecting the dots, so we know about such things as the who and the where and the obstacles we will face. Jong, do you have any family in either of those places?"

"I have family all over the world, including in this room. Why?

"If I'm not mistaken, the two places she named are gun free zones and we might need some assistance if everyone buys into my thinking. Pops, I am sure as shit, that the road ends there. Why would she give me a condom and a card to a strip joint in Russia and tell me that she hopes that I won't need to use them? Now, that's some crazy mess, but this lady was brilliant and tried to make things simple, complex, and intriguing all at the same time, but also dangerous. Asiram, when you looked at the card in the sunlight, what did you see?" Zanthius inquired.

"I saw the card and when rotated, I saw Helga."

"Was she holding anything in her hand or was there anything hanging around her neck?" Zanthius asked.

"I'm not sure. I have pictures of her on the card in both positions." Asiram began to look through her photo gallery and came upon the photo of the card from the Russian strip joint. She said, "Okay, here is the picture of the card as it is intended to be first viewed."

Everyone crowded around to see and make deductions. John Lee said, "I be wanting to look at this here card with Jilkes to try to figure out what we be seeing at every positioning of the card. You people be looking at it from different angles and be seeing different things. We'll just wait our turn, but I recommend that we each study one picture at a time and then we tell what we be seeing."

"That is great thinking, John Lee. Okay, me and my husband first, and then we'll pass it around," Asiram stated.

In the interim, Jong received a call from his pilot-in-command (PIC) who informed him that a crew of seven from the manufacturer had arrived and were literally tearing the planes apart. He was further informed that five more were on their way to restore what the others had torn apart, evaluated and provide final inspection of all mechanicals and were sanctioned to put the planes through a series of tests. Beckmire said, "Excellent work, my brother."

Asiram and Zanthius were huddling as if they were playing a game of *Family Feud*. They discussed the various details they saw but were unable to find anything significant until Zanthius looked at the belt Helga was wearing from Saddlebags, an expensive specialty store in Arizona, and made a mental note of what he saw. Everyone saw the first photo and failed to discern anything significant. The teams looked at the second photo in the hologram mode, and the image was considerably different. Zanthius said to Asiram, "Notice the position of the belt and the image it's portraying, that's the key." Asiram looked intently at it, then smiled at her husband and whispered, "You are a brilliant 'idiot spy', even if you don't want to be."

The Sarge said, "This is a team project and we can't evaluate anything if you people are going to talk during our investigation."

Jong's phone rang. It was his pilot-in-command who gave him some disturbing and mind-boggling news. The PIC indicated that both planes were laced with explosives and that his people found them and removed them before the manufacturer's people got there. The PIC told Jong that the explosives were placed in the nose and the tail of each plane. He also told Jong that the new copilot discovered them and defused both sets of explosives without incident.

As the group joined Asiram and Zanthius in looking at the card, the Sarge looked at Jong and inquired, "What's wrong, my brother?"

Jong hesitated about sharing what he had learned and said, "Perhaps I should speak to you in private."

The Sarge looked around the room and said, "I thought we were in a private situation."

"I just got a call from our pilot-in-command, who said that our new copilot discovered explosive devices in the nose and tail of each plane." Suddenly, there was a deadly quiet in the room as everyone reflected on what that discovery meant to each one of them. Jong continued his report, "It was the new African American pilot that made the discovery, and he surmised that the devices had been on the aircraft for some time. They were not a new addition based upon the sterile conditions of the environment. He also said it appeared to him that the explosives were a secondary issue and that there was a gyroscope configuration that could control the functions on each plane and depending upon the programming configuration; a midair collision could be the inevitable conclusion."

"Walter, controlled Scottie, the mercs, Helga and Allen and who knows who else. So, I'm assuming those products were not intended for us. However, if you sign those things over to us, and you know that you have live explosives on them, then I assume you intend to activate them with us on them. Any opinions on this matter?" the Sarge asked.

"There is no need to debate the intent of these findings. What is needed is to extract and reconnect the packages to the sender, just as we did with the SUVs. I say we get that shit and give them to their rightful owner," Jilkes said.

"I never agree with him, but this time I be believing that he be right and that be the course of action we take," John Lee stated.

Beckmire looked at Mallory and the two men smiled. Mallory said, "You remember that captain back in the Nam that we were going to frag, but didn't have to because someone else did it for us? Just saying, but he is your family although a distant relative."

"I really don't think we should do anything other than convince the person who controls those devices to accept the responsibility of retrieving the card and the condom. I am sure that Helga, from her grave, has a plan for whomever comes for that package," Zanthius said.

Asiram looked at the card and announced, "We have a lot of priorities that we must attend to. I recommend that we move forward to have the planes certified, and that we immediately focus on the card and the condom. I, like my husband, believe this is where our salvation rests."

"I agree totally," John Lee said.

"Jong, I, for one, would never fall asleep on a plane that someone had placed explosives on, even if removed. Can you call the company and tell them that we don't like the configuration of those two jets? We want to get new planes, but it must occur in the next two or three days. Do you think we will get some action from them, and what would be the cost of such a move? More importantly, are we leasing or outright buying the planes? Whatever deal is better for us, that is the deal we select to get rid of those two planes. Anyone have any questions or concerns about what I'm asking him to do? I mean do you agree or disagree. I think air travel is risky to begin with. I sure as hell don't want to fly on a plane that has been tampered with," Beckmire announced.

Jong looked at the Sarge and said, "I know you better than your wife and I know exactly what Mallory, John Lee, and Jilkes are thinking. I know everything because I am the person who makes shit happen in this group."

"Is this another one of your Happy New Year, Motherfuckers, moments?" Everyone broke into laughter.

"It is exactly that because I have been brokering a deal with those people ever since I realized those planes were in our possession, and the fact that your cousin has bad karma. The fundamental statement remains the same but I also don't want to pawn those things off to someone else and have them potentially blown out of the sky. I have been working on this for over four weeks. Guess what guys, and lady, I think we should unload those planes immediately, if all agree."

"You are truly amazing, Jong!" Mallory exclaimed.

"No, I'm actually better than that." The group broke into laughter.

The Sarge interjected, "I think we need to focus on this second picture and try to figure out what Helga was attempting to tell us. I personally don't see much difference in the two pictures other than the background and the reflections."

"Well, we be seeing the words '*Mi Ya Ko*' in the background that sounds like that there hotel in China," John Lee stated.

"The hotel is in Tokyo, nut," Jilkes said.

"Now, that is some interesting stuff, because we did not see that, but we saw part of a key in the first picture and a full key in the second picture in the shape of a belt buckle. Unless we're crazy, all clues lead to Hong Kong and Tokyo."

"Oh yeah, I see that. Look at this Sarge and then rotate the card. Now, you should see the key and the full belt buckle."

"Well, I'll be damned, that Helga was truly a spy with a lot of tricks. So, Mr. Better than Amazing, can you consummate that deal on the planes in the next few days and have them ready for us to move our families to Asia?"

Jong answered, "I'm working on it as we speak. But the matter at hand, is that you have to convince Walter, that more of us are sick and that he has to do the work himself or wait until we are whole again."

"Excellent point, Better than Amazing. Okay, I want Gladstone, McArthur, Brown, and Bernstein to not show their faces around this place until I give them the all clear sign, just in case that kingpin has us under surveillance. I also need Larry to get me the specific information on how to access his box; with passwords, numbers, keys, and everything else. In an hour, I will call Walter and tell him that my whole damn crew is sick with flu like symptoms and that we are definitely unable to do that work. I know he's probably becoming a little anxious, especially if he has tried to open those data disks and found out they're blank. I would give a hundred bucks to see his face. Oh, and Jong, if they can get those new planes to us, there is no way he can track us, unless he goes to the FAA and starts poking around. Besides, our old planes are registered to one of our shell companies.

"If they can get us the new equipment, that would be a lifesaver. I'm counting on you, Mr. Amazing! One more thing, I need Jilkes, John Lee, and Larry to go to the drug store and buy aspirin, Nyquil, and other cold medicines. I'm sure my crooked ass cousin has eyes on us. I want to make this ruse look as real as possible before I make that call. While you guys are with Larry, get him to write down an elaborate process for opening his box and obtaining the card and the condom. Jong, I don't know how many people are at the ranch, but make sure they all completed the passport process and are ready to leave on a moment's notice."

"Did you get good vibes from that senator?" Mallory asked.

"Frankly, I did.   Why are you asking?" Beckmire responded.

"Just wondering, since everyone that we have had contact with is either on the take or running some elaborate illegal enterprise while giving the false appearance of being a good civil servant."

"I don't disagree, but she also has presidential aspirations. Her background and affiliations would certainly be under worldwide scrutiny, don't you think?

"John Lee, what did you think of her?"

"I be feeling that she may have some history and there be a lot of questions, but I be thinking that woman is on the straight and narrow, but she needs oversight. She be a granny and she won't be leaving no snakes for that there baby to have to deal with. I'm thinking she be solid and honest to a point, but she ain't up in no stuff like yo cousin be. Now, he be a new kind of snake. He sheds his skin with both genders."

"How about you, Jilkes. What was your impression?"

"I'm with John Lee. That is who we need to get the final product to. Let her get it into the hands of the right people and expose those who wear rings that amplify their affiliations with Lucifer. She is where I would place my money, but then again, we thought your cousin was a straight arrow; didn't we?"

"It's a damn shame that you have to evaluate the moral fiber of the people who are charged with running our government. At every turn, we encountered deception, theft, double dealing; the selling of government information; and guys and girls moonlighting as mercs, drug barons and pimps. I think the government needs a new interviewing process. This one is broken," the Sarge surmised.

The guys came back from the apothecary with a ton of useless cough medicines and assorted pills that would not be used. If anyone was watching them, it was a masterful charade. The Sarge told Mallory that he was going to call Walter and tell him that the mission was being held in abeyance, due to illness. He asked John Lee and Jilkes whether Larry was able to write down the specific details necessary to retrieve the card and the condom. He was told that they had the information that Larry had written down.

As the Sarge prepared to dial Walter's number, his phone rang. To his amazement, it was Walter who asked, "How are your people doing? Do they have the flu or something?"

"I'm not sure but it seems like everyone is coming down with watery eyes, runny noses, and low to moderate fevers. I'm feeling a little in the pink, as well. What's going on?"

"I need your guys to complete this mission, but that seems impossible given the health issues. I am going to have my people retrieve the information, but what I can't figure out is the significance of the card from the Russian strip club and the condom with the writing on it. Do you or your people have any working theories on the relevance of the card and the condom?"

"Walter, your people had that stuff in their possession. Are you confirming that no one looked at or studied the card or the condom? As I recall, the card is a hologram and when rotated under the right light it displays the image of a young lady, who I assume is Helga. Now, the different positions manifested by rotating the card seems to be way above our pay grade. Your people, seemingly, should have completed due diligence on them before turning them over to us. Walter, I'm beginning to believe that you're trying to play us, beyond the scope of work that we agreed upon. On several occasions, you have asked me about briefcases and suitcases that contain money and whether or not we found them. Are you telling me that your agency is so disorganized that you can't keep up with money and/or do analysis of important information that is in your hands? I mean you had the pieces right in your possession and now you're asking me if we have any working theories about the relevance of these materials?"

The Sarge began to cough uncontrollably and Mallory was on his knees laughing his ass off. "I apologize, Walter, I know that sounded pretty gross, but I was unable to divert the phone fast enough. Therefore, you heard the brunt of me coughing up mucus. I think my team has caught a virus. Do you want me to give you the information where the subject matter is stored?"

"How long do you think you and your people will be down with this bug?"

"Walter, if I were a doctor, I would say at least four to five days, as long as we stay completely away from each other, a thing that's virtually impossible for my guys. They are falling ill one at a time, and it almost makes me think this is a planned event. You wouldn't have anything to do with releasing some kind of limited virus in the air to incapacitate us, would you?"

"Ben don't be stupid. Why would I want all of you people sick at the same time? What possible benefit would I derive from that? By the way, just humor me for a moment, did any of your people tamper with the data disks from Harold's safe deposit box?"

"How on earth could they do that? The disks were placed in Asiram's purse and were not touched until I gave them to you. Why do you ask?"

"I'm having problems accessing the information on them. Does she happen to use magnets for pain or anything?"

"Hold on, let me call and ask her." The Sarge placed a fictitious call to Asiram and loudly asked, "Daughter-in-Law, do you use magnets or did you have a magnet in your purse when you placed those data disks in it?" He pretended to have an intense conversation with her then returned to his conversation with Walter. "Walter, I'm afraid that the purse she carried had her magnetic bracelet in it that she uses to reduce the pain in her wrist due to an injury. Now, if the information was erased, I suggest you get the disk back to me, and let Jong look at them and see if he can reconstruct what was on them. You know, of course, that comes with a certain risk, but he's my brother, and he does not have loose lips. Your choice, but I think he can do that because that is what he does, recapture information for businesses."

"Ben, I don't think that I need that kind of exposure, and therefore, I'm recommending we just forget about those damn disks. When can you get the information to me about how to access the box where the card and the condom are?"

"Give me about ten minutes and I'll have the information for you. I will give you a call with the details. Does that work for you?"

"That's fine, but I do have one other question. As I looked at the ownership of those two new planes, I was intrigued by the composition of the companies that are listed on that manifest. Seems to me that you guys have a lot going on. It is hard to figure out who owns what, how much they have, and more importantly, who are the rightful owners of those companies.

Can you shed a little light on that matter? I'm simply curious as to why a group of Nam vets have such an intricate web of companies that, seemingly, only focus on giving away money to nonprofits."

"Walter, the only way to understand who we are is to believe in what we do. We do good work by making our limited resources available to needy people so they can help people help themselves. When you get to that point in your life where you want to help others, then you will understand the nature of our companies, our website, and the reasons for our privacy. I will call you back after I get the information. Catch you later."

The Sarge called Jong and once again asked him to make sure the pilots were legal and ready to depart in a couple of hours. He also inquired about the status of the new planes and was told that they were a work in progress. Jong informed the Sarge that a call would be made to him to confirm the timetable for delivery and pickup of the old/new planes that were rigged to explode. The Sarge decided to wait until Jong got back to him before he gave Walter any information relative to the location of the card and the condom. Everyone was pretty much rested and desirous of leaving their current digs for the comforts of the ranch.

Thirty minutes had passed when Jong called the Sarge and said, "The pilots are legal, the planes are fueled, provisions are aboard, and wheels can be up as soon as we arrive."

"Good work, Mr. Amazing. Do you have any idea how much cash we picked up from Harold's boxes?"

"I have no idea, but if I had to guess, I think it's in the neighborhood of $8 to $10 million. We never counted the money from the hotel in LA. What I will say, is that we have too much cash on hand, and when we get to the ranch, we have to begin a new banking process with the locals. I'm not worried about anyone getting greedy, but I do remember that we blew up a house, and fires and things like that do happen," Jong stated.

The Sarge reflected on what Jong was intimating. He asked him, "You have any suggestions on what we should do with it?"

"I'll get with Brown and Bernstein, and we'll develop a proposal that includes current costs, past obligations, and cash on hand. Then we'll figure out what our walk-around money needs to look like," responded Jong.

"Good idea and keep me posted," the Sarge said.

The Sarge must have talked Bernstein up because the next call he received was from him. Bernstein said, "Sarge, I need to call Yvett and the first thing she is going to ask me is when we're coming back. Frankly, I want out of this dive and so do the rest of the team. Can we at least stay somewhere a little cleaner than this place?"

"My brother, I too, want out of this place. I just spoke with Jong and the planes are being prepared for flight. The only thing I have to do is make a call to Walter and give him the details about the card and the condom and then we are out of here. Listen, one way or the other, we are out of here later tonight or early in the morning. I implore you to be patient because we don't want any issues with Walter until we are safe and can watch his world self-destruct. Any premature movements might alert him to the fact that we are on to him and that would put us all at risk. I'm of the belief that my cousin would kill his own mother to keep his other world secret. Just be patient and we will be out of here as soon as possible."

The Sarge placed a call to Walter and began the conversation with the thunderous sounds of coughing. He said,

"Please forgive me but I think I have now been infected as well. You have a pencil handy? I want to give you the information about that card and its companion."

"I do, give me a moment. You need to get that cough checked out by a doctor. You sound terrible."

The two men talked and the Sarge gave Walter the details relative to the items in question. Walter asked, "Do you expect any surprises when we attempt to retrieve the package?"

"What kind of surprises are you referring to?"

"I mean did you guys give the same information to anyone else, for let's say, a considerable sum of money?"

"Cousin, if I respond to that insult it might affect our relationship, so I'm going to pretend you just didn't accuse me of double dealing. As a matter of fact, your humor has the potential of getting you an ass whupping and I don't mean the kind you might enjoy. I mean the kind that includes broken bones and shit like that. Pick up your packages and turn them over to the senator. We're going to get some rest and try to beat this virus you infected us with. Catch you later."

The Sarge called Mallory and said, "Have the team meet me in the lobby in thirty minutes and be prepared to check out of this place. We're going back to the Yellow Brick Road, or some fricking place like that."

"I am sure the guys will be ready in five. See you in the lobby. I'll have Jong pay the bill and perhaps we should call Uber or a cab company and leave Walter's shit here. I'm sure they're bugged," Mallory stated.

"Good thinking. Call Jong first and have him coordinate our departure with Uber, Lyft, or cabs. Maybe we can call an ambulance service, and have it transport McArthur, Gladstone, Brown, and Bernstein to the airport and the rest of us leave from the back door of the hotel. It's a little thin, but I think that those watching us might bite on it.   Delay that Uber, Lyft, or cab request until we can get some ambulances to transport our sick comrades to the airport.   Have Jong contact the desk and tell them that we have some sick people that need transportation to the hospital."

Thirty minutes later, four ambulances with blinking lights arrived to transport the questionable sick. In the rear of the hotel, Ubers, Lyfts, and cabs were awaiting for the balance of the team.

Walter's people called him and informed him of the movements. He informed them to stand down and conclude the surveillance.   It wasn't obvious to him that he had been hoodwinked and hustled.

After the ambulances were loaded, the members of the team presented the drivers with an offer they couldn't or wouldn't refuse. They were rewarded handsomely. It turned out to be a win-win situation for everyone.

Much later, as the team boarded the planes, the Sarge, announced, "We're going to turn in those planes that were gifted to us because they had a devastating gift aboard them. Jong has been working with the company to replace them and we will know the status of that transaction once we arrive in the land of milk and honey. I will never be able to repay you people for your brotherhood and your diligence in keeping all of us safe. I will say this, just one time, I love you people with all of my heart, and I appreciate all of your sacrifices and pain in making sure that me and my family are safe and protected. I know we killed a lot of people, but I don't feel sorry for them because they would have terminated any one of us if they were as good as we are. We are not Musketeers with a slogan that goes, 'one for all, and all for one'. However, if you screw with any one of us, you will have to deal with the lethal repercussions of all of us. We don't miss. I love you guys and see you back at the ranch."

"I am not a guy and I did not hear a single word about my being a part of this team. Are you some sort of new sexist, Daddy-in-Law?" Asiram inquired.

"See guys, this is my new daughter-in-law, and she's the kind of woman that you really don't want to cross. Sweetheart, we are going to your ranch. My love, we blew up your farm. Baby Girl, we destroyed your home in Philly. Now, everyone here realizes how important you are. Perhaps I need to stop on the way and buy you a plaque or something that illustrates the fact that we would all be dead if it was not for your participation and guidance in these episodes that were created by my son, the 'idiot spy'.

"We all love you and appreciate all you have done. To prematurely illustrate our feelings for you, tentative designs for your new farm will be presented to you. What was to be a surprise, is your ownership of a certain senator's land that he won't be needing. So, on behalf of these old guys from the Vietnam era, we want to present you with a farm expansion plan that you will see once you are back at your ranch." She smiled with tears in her eyes and walked away.

## CHAPTER TWENTY-FOUR

As the planes ascended into the night sky, lit by a full moon, the weary occupants could not avoid its presence. Throughout each plane one could hear people saying, "Wow, look how bright the moon is, or look at the radiance of the moon, or la Bella Luna".

Meanwhile, deep in the bowels of Russia, there was another glow, but it was ominous and at a secret weapons development plant that was experimenting with the Carbon Factor. A cloud that resembled that of earlier nuclear explosions was visible, as well as deadly. The entire plant was decimated, and the loss of life was great.

In an attempt to exploit and explore other scientific combinations to increase the power of what they considered was the formula for the Carbon Factor, Russian scientists, inadvertently, created the master of all modern weapons. The explosion left a crater that was a half a mile deep and one and a half miles wide. Although the explosion was monitored by systems near and far, there was no indication of harmful radiation being emitted.

The world was curious to know about this disaster, but more interested in knowing the components of the product that created so much devastation. The common consensus among world leaders and scientists was obvious; how could they obtain and secure such a weapon and at what expense? The Carbon Factor, and anyone connected to it, had just been placed at the top of the food chain. However, all that the Russians had learned had been destroyed in the explosion and, therefore, they were back at square one. It would be years before anyone would discern the additional elements or compounds that were utilized and caused this massive loss of life.

## CHAPTER TWENTY-FIVE

An hour out from the ranch, the copilot entered the cabin and so informed Asiram. She thanked him and pulled out her cell phone to call Clyde when Zanthius stated, "Wait a minute honey. Let me get you one of the new phones that Mallory purchased."

"What's wrong with the phone I have?"

"There is probably nothing wrong with your phone but we're trying to figure out how Walter is always one step behind us. The phones that we have been using surely are a possible answer to that riddle."

"Wow, my husband, the 'idiot spy', is forever thinking and acting more and more like a spy. I'm proud of you, love."

The captain turned on the local news and suggested that the team listen to the developments out of Russia. The headlines were not surprising; "At a secret weapons development plant, deep in the bowels of the Russian interior, an explosion occurred that had the impact of a nuclear detonation but lacked the definition of an atomic bomb because there was no indication of radiation being emitted into the atmosphere." Everyone seemed nonchalant about the news except the 'idiot spy' who exclaimed, "The damn Russians tried to create that formula and look what it cost them!"

"What formula are you talking about?" Beckmire asked.

"I'm talking about the Carbon Factor. If I am correct, the price on our heads exponentially, went through the stratosphere.

I'll bet you a thousand dollars they tried to combine that mess with something else in hopes of trying to get a bigger bang and they got a blowout."

"Jesus, I pray to God you're wrong because that means we're all in for a long ride and a very dangerous one at that," Beckmire announced.

"Pops, no sign of radiation in the atmosphere. Come on now, you know they were playing around with that thing that I thought was a joke. It's real. We had better sharpen our defenses and security if we want to stay alive. I think once we get to the ranch, we should shower, shave, and be prepared to leave for Asia with every single member of our family in tow. I think we have to treat this new information as a warning and we have to adjust our behavior and movements to keep everyone safe."

Mallory looked at Zanthius and inquired, "What makes you so sure that what happened over there is connected to us?"

"At some of the sessions I participated in while in St. Moritz, that was the key aspect of the Carbon Factor. It was rumored that by itself it is just a large bomb that uses the hydrogen molecule and sucks up everything that is hydrogen based. However, supposedly, with the right amount of nuclear materials, you have a new super bomb. I think the Russians were testing different elements and stumbled upon an important ingredient that blew that place to hell. Look at the size of the destruction. That has to be at least a mile wide and a half mile deep. If it were nuclearized, the atmospheric monitors would have picked it up. I'm telling you, we had better get ready for Freddy because he surely is going to be on his way."

As the news became more relevant to the group, Mallory handed Asiram a new cell phone and asked her to call Clyde. A sleepy Clyde answered the phone and was told that the planes would be landing within the hour. He indicated that he would be there to pick them up. The atmosphere on the planes was solemn. Everyone began to self-reflect and confirm their commitment to seeing this thing through. Larry walked up to the Sarge and announced, "You know I can help in this matter. All you have to do is let me know if you need me. I'll be there for you, the guys, and Asiram. I can play a significant role if you like. Just think about it and let me know."

"I appreciate all that you have done. Lessons from the kind of work that we used to do might come in handy here since you are considered a sleeper or an enigma and people can't figure you out. Thanks for reminding me, and if your brother is correct, we are all going to have to step up and play a more decisive role in keeping each other safe."

The planes landed and were met by a bus load of women and children. The scene was gratifying and full of love. The action that caught everyone's attention was the reception that Bernstein received from Yvett. She jumped off the bus and skipped to the plane. When he hit the landing, she grabbed him, and kissed him with such power that he became weak in the legs. Bernstein did not have time to catch his breath because each kiss was more powerful than the last. The pressing of her body against his created a burning desire that was fulfilling, spiritual, but yet decadent. This man was going to be hers, and if he wanted her, every aspect of her body and soul would be his to love.

On the ride back to the ranch, Clyde gave them an update on what had been happening and the fact that they had started a school for the children. When they arrived at the ranch, the smell of fried chicken and burgers was in the air. The locals had come together in a hurry and threw together a feast fit for kings and queens. It would be a night of love making and celebration, but as the night transitioned into day, a world of uncertainty awaited the festive members of the Beckmire clan.

Immediately after the group left the airport, two new G650s landed in succession. As they pulled into the hangar, Beckmire's pilots drooled over them. A pilot from the first plane to land exited the aircraft and asked, "Hey guys, do you know where I can find a Mr. Jong?"

The pilot on the ground screamed, "Give me a moment and we'll get right back to you!"

Jong's pilot-in-command placed a call to him, but Jong had discarded that phone and neglected to give the pilot his new number. Fortunately, the pilot knew Clyde's number and placed a call to him. Clyde answered the phone and the pilot said, "Clyde, I need to speak to Mr. Jong."

"Hold on, he's right here. Jong, somebody be calling you on my phone."

Jong answered by asking, "Who's calling?"

"Mr. Jong, this is your pilot and we're standing here in front of two new G650s and sir, I must admit, I'm about to have an orgasm. They are absolutely beautiful. Oh, hold on, the guy from the factory needs to speak to you."

"Mr. Jong, we redirected these two planes from a company that couldn't make its payments. This was their maiden flight. I need you to come and sign some papers and give me authorization to take two of your current planes back with us. Is there any way we can consummate this deal tonight?"

"I'm on my way. Oy the way, were you able to make those specific modifications that I requested?"

"Sir, you will enjoy the way we did this thing. It's absolutely brilliant."

"Okay I'll be there within the hour. Please allow my pilots on board and discuss anything they need to know about any peculiarities with these new planes."

"Sir, your people are qualified to fly these aircraft, and as a matter of fact, they have the manuals and are questioning my people about certain things as we speak."

Jong walked over to the Sarge and said, "We have a deal and the products are in place."

"What the hell are you talking about, Jong?"

"Sarge, we have two new planes in the hangar and I need to go and sign some paperwork."

"You pulled that deal off?"

"The proof of my talent is in the hangar."

"They sent us two new planes?"

"Sarge, the proof is in the hangar."

"Listen up, everyone. Mr. Jong here, or should I say, Mr. Amazing, has brokered us a deal on two new G650s that are waiting on us at the airport. I think we should give him a hand and officially change his name to Mr. Amazing." The group loudly applauded Jong. He took his bows, smiled, and said, "Since you all know, and I know, that I am Mr. Amazing, I prefer that you refer to me, as Jong." He waltzed up to the Sarge and said, "I need another day to coordinate this new travel plan. First, please do not articulate it, except to the team members. Second, you need to assess whether there are any pressing needs at home for any of the guys."

"Are you trying to replace me, Mr. Jong? If so, I gladly prefer to be in my easy chair watching TV and some dumb shit like those three sisters and their daddy who went south on them and came out being another gender. Anyway, I like listening about their terrible lives with their messed-up husbands and lovers. Now, that's some interesting shit."

"No, Sarge, I'm just slightly more detail oriented than you are on certain matters. On deployment and execution, you are the best. But on matters of cars, planes, hotels, boats and shit; I'm Mr. Amazing."

"Okay, Mr. Amazing, keep it up because we're going to need a lot of innovation going forward. If my son, the 'idiot spy', is correct, we have just been taken off the endangered species list and placed on a new list where a full bounty is offered for our heads."

"Can you ask Clyde to see to it that our pilots have everything they need? I mean rotating dinners, nights off when they can drink, showers, real meals, and free time. We need them sharp as a tack and ready to fly when we need to bail out of any place that we may be," Jong said.

"Discreetly ask Mallory and McArthur to join us in the back for a moment," the Sarge said.

A few minutes later, in the back of the house, the Sarge said, "Mac, I'm going to need you to provide a front line role moving forward. That means I'm going to give you management responsibility on certain Far East matters. I don't know exactly what they are at this time, but I'm going to need you to be a surrogate for me, which places your head near the top of the food chain. You know it is at that place people take notice of you and figure out ways for your demise. I know it makes no sense to ask you to volunteer because I know you would curse me. What say you?"

"I say, stop smoking that stuff. It's messing up your brain. You know we do as you ask and never complain about our missions. I don't know why you keep acting like you're not in charge and like you're not Sergeant Beckmire. Get a grip and lead us out of this mess."

## CHAPTER TWENTY-SIX

The next day was full of activity. The Sarge, his team and a few others, maintained their exercise routine. Jong and the pilots performed a shakedown of the aircrafts. Ava, Courtney, and Monica orchestrated getting together what would be needed for the trip abroad. Zanthius and Asiram continued their daily dose of love making.

As the news about the Russian catastrophe began to be reported with more accuracy, rather than hyperbole, it became clear to many that this was the result of scientists attempting to expand the concept of the Carbon Factor, as opposed to defining it. The satellite images of the detonation made the destruction crystal clear. It was performed at either a weapon's depot or a secret development plant that was experimenting with an uncontrollable product.

The Sarge began to wonder why he hadn't heard a word from Walter and decided to give him a call. Walter answered by asking, "Where the hell are you people?"

"We're close by. Why? Have you been trying to track me or something?"

"Naw, nothing like that. I just missed talking with you last night. I tried to give you a call, but your phone was dead."

"I knocked the damn thing in the toilet by mistake. Got a new one and I'm sure the new number showed up on your phone. Anyway, did you get the products from the box?"

"That's our mission, in approximately two hours from now."

"It's a shame about what happened over in Russia, isn't it?"

"That depends on which side you support. I personally feel that they shouldn't be playing around with nuclear shit in secret places."

"So, are you saying it's okay for America to play around with shit in their secret places?"

"I'm just saying that you can't trust those people. They say one thing and do the opposite."

"Anyway, I just called to check on you to see if you picked up the package, so we can go home and live like normal human beings," Beckmire stated.

"See, Ben, that's what I like about you. You're so full of shit. You know damn well that all evidence leads to the Russians playing with the Carbon Factor formula," Walter replied.

"Walter, I'm not a spy and I don't know what the Carbon Factor actually does. If they have been playing with that stuff, why are you being so lackadaisical about retrieving the items? Is there a new problem that has taken its place in the land of mystery and hocus pocus? I'm just asking, because a lot of people died trying to obtain the products and you're having your morning tea before you try to secure this world changing technology. This doesn't add up to me, Cousin. Is there something else you haven't told me about that perhaps is compromising you or our government?"

"Ben, why don't we meet for brunch and I'll give you the skinny on what's going on?"

"No can do. I have plans with an old friend of mine that I just can't cancel. Why don't I call you tomorrow or you call me later after you've retrieved the package? I really want to know if that is the final straw in this adventure so my people and I can go back to our homes."

"Ben, people are focusing on what happened over in Russia. I will obtain the information today and will let you know as soon as we have figured out what it means. By the way, as for Asiram's neighbor, the senator, it was confirmed, he died from an overdose of Viagra and Cialis. It caused his bad heart to stop beating. I guess he wanted to make a point. I'm sure it won't matter to Asiram how he met his demise, considering the fact she now owns his property."

"My daughter-in-law is a very enterprising young woman. It became easy for her to get the property when the senator refused to pay property taxes because he was a sitting US Senator. How absurd! It's like the guy running for the presidency of the USA—he doesn't pay taxes because he's smart and I guess the rest of us are really stupid."

"Well, the senator lived a double or triple life was a politician who had a for sale sign painted on his chest. Apparently, this guy belonged to a lot of secret organizations and was being paid a helluva lot of money off the books. Why didn't he pay the taxes on his farm? Anyway, the story in the *Washington Post* was extremely damaging to his reputation. Listen, Ben, you beat my call by two minutes. I was planning to call you about a situation that we have in a volatile part of London that we need to attend to. It's a matter of national security for a lot of democratic countries in the region."

"Walter, we're sick, we're tired and we need a break from cleaning up someone else's mess. I told you when I last saw you, that we would need a few months off to heal our wounds and enjoy our peace. There is no way in hell we are going to find ourselves in London anytime soon. Don't ask and don't bring it up again, or I will hang up this damn phone on you."

"Okay, Ben, but while you're resting and enjoying your families, a lot of people are going to be mourning their dead based upon the chatter we're picking up and relaying to our counterparts at MI-6."

"Walter, we are not the world's secret police force, and for damn certain, we are not yours!"

"Ben, I know that. I appreciate all you have done for us in terms of removing certain negative forces from the planet. I probably have never thanked you for all that you and your people have done. Let me take this opportunity to just say thank you and say that you and yours are most appreciated. Oh, and by the way, Zanthius De Lombardo's mother has a lot of relatives in the Barcelona and the Valencia areas of Spain, if I'm not mistaken. That is one of the target areas, as well as, our own beloved Naval Academy. Is your son still at that institution? The plans of those evil doers expands to the very area where Jong is from. Talk to you later, Ben." Walter abruptly hung up the phone knowing that he had just left Beckmire with a lot to consider.

Beckmire decided to inform his group of the ominous information he had received. He called Mallory and asked him to convene the team for a briefing. He called Asiram, Zanthius, and Larry and told them that he was having a meeting and that he needed their input.

Thirty minutes later, the Sarge asked everyone to turn their cell phones off. He said, "Somehow, I am still of the belief that we are being tracked. For the life of me, I can't figure out how. Therefore, whenever we have these briefings, I implore you to turn off the phones."

"Now, guys and girl, I believe we must make some tough decisions. I will ask for your input on a few critical issues. The first one is about the Carbon Factor. I'm sure some of you think that the real journey begins in Hong Kong and transitions to Tokyo. I know we had planned to do this thing in three days or so and be done with it. However, I just got off the phone with that snake of a cousin of mine. He said they received chatter that evil doers are planning to bomb places in London, Barcelona, and Valencia, Spain, and the Naval Academy in Annapolis. I also hear things are about to jump off in your backyard, Jong. Now, my treacherous ass cousin knows the connection with my other child being at the Naval Academy. Zanthius, he's talking about where your mother's people are in both places in Spain, and Jong they know where your people live in Japan. The one thing we can't and will never do is split up our forces. As a team, we are formidable.

Now, I need to hear discussions from you people about how we can address the logistics. Any ideas? You know what, let me back up a minute, this ain't Vietnam and I ain't the Sarge in charge of this squad. You people have families and things to attend to. So, I'm backing my ass up and asking you, first and foremost, what are your individual needs as far as time and space?"

A silence grew in the room and Brown replied, "You know, Sarge, this adventure has been extremely taxing and dangerous. If I didn't know any better, I would say, this is Vietnam and you are the Sergeant Beckmire. I just think this whole thing is a dream and I haven't awakened from it. You ask a lot of us, and if you think about it, we ain't 21 years of age anymore. So, if you're going to treat us like we're twenty-one years of age, then I'm out of here. On the other hand, if you want us to plan this thing to the end, then get on with the briefing and stop smoking that crack shit; just saying."

"I be wanting to go home, but I ain't ready until they begin to build my new home. So, I ain't got no where's to go and neither does my black friend, cause his wife done gone off with the preacher. He be dumping her, soon as he sees my lawyer back home, so he ain't got nowhere to go either. I guess I'm stuck with his black ass some more," John Lee stated.

"Chakes, how about you and Montomie?" the Sarge asked.

"We're planning on going down to South Beach after this, open up a fancy bar and restaurant, but I guess we can wait awhile. Is that right, Bro?"

"You nailed it, dude. Do me a favor and ask the Sarge why he's pulling teeth when they're all healthy." Montomie stated.

"You ask him, he's standing right there," Chakes said.

"Whatever. Let's get on with it, please," Montomie said.

"McArthur and Gladstone, what about you people?"

"Sarge, first, that 'you people' shit has to go. Second, I told you last night to stop smoking that dope. We be good! Right, Stone?" McArthur said.

"You called it as I would say it, my brother. Where you go, I am going to be close behind you," Gladstone stated.

"Okay, Zanthius and Asiram, you people don't get to vote because it's your asses--the kisser and the extractor, that got us knee-deep into this quagmire."

"Mallory, what's your take?"

"Guys and girl, I'm feeling like I hit the damn lottery or something. I'm enjoying myself, finding myself, and realizing that sitting and playing house, is not what makes my blood boil—it's being with you fricking guys that make my life worth living. I'm ready to go fight Martians, or go to Venus, although that would require a lot of love making, I hope. Anyway, Sarge, you know I'm in."

"Jong, I know this has been difficult for you, but I must admit you have been a real trooper. I really want you to take one of the jets and go home and get some rest."

"Permission to speak freely, Sir?"

"Whatever! Say what you like."

"You must be smoking some foreign substance to tell me to go home and get some rest. Do I seem like I'm without a penis? Sorry, Ms. Asiram, but I have been insulted by a man that I would now only take a 'BB' pellet for. I used to say I would die for this man, but he has reduced my loyalty to pellets. Someone please tell him I will kick his ass if he ever offends me in such a low life manner again. I'm no low life animal, I'm Mr. Amazing, and tell him not to forget it."

The Sarge was standing before the team with tears flowing from his eyes and wondering how on earth, he deserved a group of dedicated friends like these.

"I guess somewhat out of order and not connected to the order I went in, Whitmore and Bernstein, what are your needs?"

"I guess I feel like the rest of the guys. Why do you continue to play like you're not in control of this situation? We need you to act like our commanding officer, and therefore, what you say goes and we're all over it. Keep us safe and keep us busy. This has been one helluva ride for me, and like the corporal, I am enjoying every minute of this adventure, thanks to the 'idiot spy' and his lady. By the way, where is Larry? He should be here." Whitmore said.

"Let me call him right now," the Sarge stated.

"Bernstein, what are your needs in terms of time?"

"Sarge, I'm in love with your niece. She said, whatever you ask me to do I had better do it because it's because of you that she has opened her eyes and her heart to trust another man. So, I'm yours to command. I like having my cake and eating it too, but I also like having the family that has saved my ass on so many occasions right before my eyes.

"This entire thing, Sarge, and I'm surprised you don't get it, is about love and respect. Each one of the people in this room loves you and respects you and would kill to protect you. We know this, but you seemingly have forgotten the fact that it works both ways. We have killed for you, and yours and will continue to do harm to those who think they can cause injury to any member of our group. You mess with one of us and you will reap the wrath of all of us. Stay with the motto and we'll all live to love another day," Bernstein answered.

Beckmire exclaimed, "Okay, you assholes, tell me what the hell I'm supposed to do? You all have other commitments, my family is under attack, and without you people I'm vulnerable. Tell me what you expect from me?"

"I expect the kind of leadership that you have always given us. Listen, you are Sergeant Ben Beckmire, stop whining, and tell us what we need to do. We're simple people, and you are our leader and will forever be until the day we die," Jilkes said.

Larry entered the room, looked at the Sarge and asked, "What's the deal? Did someone in here sign their death certificate?"

"No, Son, I am crying because I'm happy. They rarely see me cry like this."

"Sarge, now would be a good time to tell us the connection between you and Larry. I think the whole team is interested in knowing about the dynamics of your relationship," McArthur stated.

The Sarge was about to say something when Larry interrupted him and said, "Pops, I got this one. Okay people, you want to know how we came to be, and all that stuff, right? Let me give you the raw version of it and you can deduce for yourselves how he helped me and how we helped each other.

"My name is Larry Holland and I was known as Larry the Wanderer, on the streets. I used to sell drugs and hustle. I got busted and was sent to the precinct where the Sarge was on duty. He asked me to give up my dealer and I wouldn't. He literally begged me to give him up, while all of the time, this sly fox knew who he was. He tested my loyalty. Eventually, I was sent unexpectedly, to a prison where the cook raped me. That's right people, he raped me! He knocked me out cold and had his way with me. I swore from my cell that I would kill him before nightfall. Little did I know that the prisoners had a bartering program in play and someone had placed and won the bet for me. The cook broke the terms and conditions of that unwritten agreement, and therefore, I didn't get my vengeance because he was murdered before I had a chance to exact my revenge on him. I see the way you guys are looking at me, I see a lot of sympathy on your faces.

"Listen, the Sarge helped me get over it. We went on and did some real dastardly things. We reduced the drug smuggling into Philadelphia by eliminating the big dealers, not the corner minimum wage dudes. We were a team and we gave the dealers fair warnings, and when they didn't heed them, we put them in a permanent state of rest. So, I never did the Nam thing, but I certainly have earned my stripes. We were considered, *The Edge*. Are there any questions or further concerns about who I am, or what my qualifications are?"

After a long silence, John Lee acknowledged, "I know I be speaking for the rest of the team when I say, welcome to our tribe. I saw your work in DC and thought it was good. Shit happens, but we be one big family and it takes a big man to talk about the shit you talked about. I know I can trust you and so can the rest of the team. Welcome."

"I feel like this has been the best meeting I've ever had with you knuckleheads. You make me proud to know all of you. Now, let's get down to business. Okay, we have several issues--London, Kowloon, Tokyo, Spain, the Naval Academy. Those places are related to the mission that we are trying to conclude. How ironic, the new hot areas are connected to, areas we happen to have family. I'm beginning to wonder if one of these locations is the place we are to be murdered by my nefarious cousin."

"Now, that be a great question because I never liked that there fellow and always had suspicion about the way he looked at my minority friend," John Lee said.

"What the hell are you talking about, the way he looked at me?" Jilkes stridently retorted.

"I'm not the jealous type, but I be watching him scope your ass out."

"Country Boy stop the bullshit and stay focused. Everyone finds me fascinating including those who shouldn't. They can see that you be my woman," Jilkes said.

"Unless you want another ass whuppin, then I recommend that you stop calling me your woman. I be a man, you worm," John Lee professed.

"Whatever. It seems to me that if he knows we are on to him, it only makes sense that he would have to see to our demise. It would not be hard for him to achieve that mission with the explosives that were in those planes. Is he going to attempt to get the card and the condom today?"

Jilkes in a couple of hours," the Sarge replied.

"Pops, can I say something?" Zanthius asked.

"Of course, you can. What's on your mind, Son?"

"There is no way we can gain access to the Naval Academy, but we can find out from Walter who it is we should be looking out for. I mean a rumor about an event happening in Spain, Japan, or anywhere for that matter, is, just that--a rumor. I believe your cousin, and therefore my uncle, has a conclusive plan to eliminate us, especially, if he thinks that the card and the condom will direct him to the product. Think about it. Helga worked for him, so did Allen, as did Scottie, and so did that guy, T-Rex. And what did he do to poor Harold? Well, we all saw him summarily execute his partner without hesitation. I also hear that both of those gifted planes were loaded with explosives. This guy has used us to clean up his mess and now it looks as though it's time for us to be cleaned.

"Now, if you ask my opinion, we are the last links to his network and it's probably time for him to clean up all of his messes. I think once we decide on a plan of action, we deviate from it, and choose another option. We can't be in three places at the same time and, even if we could, it would spell ruin for the group, especially if we were split up. On the other hand, if we fail to do anything, a lot of innocent lives might be lost. The question is, will that be because we didn't act, or because we chose an alternative to the suggested plan?"

"Did Walter provide you with broad details, or specific information?" Asiram asked.

"He just mentioned the places and knew that we had family in each one. I need to call him and pretend that we are going to sign on to this mission and see what he says. Regardless, I'm hoping that when he retrieves the card and the condom, he will be sent on a wild goose chase, thus, giving us time to have a breather from his missions."

"I wonder if Mike is aware of his boss's activities, and if so, is he a part of them?" Mallory asked.

"He has been solid. I hate to think that he too, is a mercenary. The basic questions remain on the table, what are our options and where should we focus our attention?" the Sarge asked.

"I'm hoping that we get at least twenty-four to forty-eight hours of rest. This stuff is happening so fast, I sometimes lose focus and that ain't good. We all need to commit to a schedule of rest without interruption because I think we all are exhausted and ruffled," Chakes said.

The discussion lasted approximately two hours. There was no common consensus, but the overall conclusion was that people be given time to breathe away from the group. The Sarge made a unilateral decision and granted everyone thirty-six hours of liberty with the condition that no one would ever be alone.

## CHAPTER TWENTY-SEVEN

Thirty-six hours later and after liberty, Beckmire's main group assembled in front of the ranch at 0600 hours. Most looked rested, but a few of them looked as if they had been in the company of Venus de Milo because they had the after look of lust about them. They stretched and began a three-mile brisk run. On every television channel, the news about the devastation in Russia filled the screens, and the group secretly knew that the Carbon Factor was in play.

Zanthius slowed his pace and began to run alongside his father. He said between intakes of air, "I'm sure whoever retrieves the card and the condom will meet their maker. If Helga can have things written on my intestines, then I know she can have deadly toxins released from the card and the condom. I am also sure that between what Asiram recalls of Helga and what I remember of our discussions and time together, all points lead to Asia. Have you heard from Walter?" Zanthius inquired.

"I have not. I'm concerned about it because if he didn't attempt to retrieve the products then he definitely knows that we're not in town or near town. When we get back, I'm going to give him a call and ask him," Beckmire stated.

"Are you saying that in thirty-six hours you have not heard a word from your cousin? I find that hard to believe since he usually checks in twice a day. Doesn't he want to make sure he knows where you are? Perhaps the change of telephone numbers left him a little baffled. Anyway, I think you need to reach out to him on one of the throw-away phones. Let him try to figure out where we are. Knowing him, I am sure he already knows that we have flown the coop and are back at the ranch," Zanthius indicated.

"Son, why are you so sure that the Helga person gave the product its final resting place in Kowloon or Tokyo?"

"Pops, I feel there was a hidden message about the use of the card and the condom. Think about it--she gave me clues to figure out the rest and that's why I'm sure it ends in Asia," Zanthius replied.

"Let's drop back to Jong, Jilkes, and John Lee and see if everything and everyone is prepared to leave on a moment's notice," Beckmire stated.

The men slowed their pace until they were in line with Jong and his buddies. The Sarge said, "Is everyone ready to board those planes and head east?"

"Everyone has a passport and visa. Therefore, I do not see any problems other than the fact that we will have to be naked when we arrive. I have been in contact with some extended family members, and hypothetically, I have asked them if they can provide us with some throw-away devices that are heavenly clean," Jong said.

"What are the chances of us leaving under the cover of darkness and arriving there in the morning," the Sarge asked.

"If we leave by 2100 or 2200 hours, we should be there by sunrise. We will be bucking the headwinds. Before you ask me the next question, let me say that the pilots are legal, shared the same thirty-six-hour liberty that we did and have stocked the planes with all kinds of food stuff. We are good to go at your signal."

"Mr. Amazing, you're so valuable to this team."

"Well, I'll be a three-legged, short, overweight pig. How about me and my African American friend? Are we valuable too?" The Sarge stopped in his tracks and walked over to John Lee and kissed him on his cheeks. He then turned to Jilkes and did the same thing.

John Lee said, "That be a first. You never kissed me and my colored friend before."

"What's up with this African American and my colored friend shit?" Jilkes inquired.

"Oh, I just be thinking about voting for that Republican fellow who wants to build a wall and send all of the African Americans back to Africa."

"Anyway, knucklehead, tone it down or I'll have to give you another one of those ass whuppins."

"You always be ready to do violence to me. Why can't we all just get along?"

"Anyway, what's up, Sarge?" Jilkes asked.

"Zanthius is adamant that we can end this thing in Hong Kong and Tokyo. What's your take on it?"

"Listen, me and the old white racist believe in the 'idiot spy' and, trust his judgment when it's sanctioned by you. Is there some doubt about his credibility? We sure as hell don't doubt his calculations and his resolve. We follow you, and therefore, there can only be one master of this house—Sergeant Ben Beckmire."

"I know you guys are loyal. This is all new to me, you know this concrete jungle shit with people fighting not for their country or honor, but for payment. I am not sure about Hong Kong and Tokyo, but my son and his wife feel strong about it. I need input from everyone because we're all at risk, especially, if he is correct about what happened in Russia a few days ago. Just an inquiry, that's all."

"Well, I be believing that it makes sense to go over there where Jong's people be. That there woman Helga gave some real live directions if you be asking me. I mean that woman wrote on the 'idiot spy's' internal organs. Now, how, and when the hell, did she open him up and write that shit on his bowels? I believe over there in that there Hong Kong, we be finding some hardship and that there Carbon Factor. I really believe that," John Lee said.

"We can't protect the Naval Academy, be in Barcelona, and try to prevent the crazies from doing their thing in Jong's back yard, all at the same time. We are only 10 + 2, with a couple of new recruits. Even if we stretch it, we're only twenty at the max. What is our destiny, guys? I want everyone to think about their own personal commitments and then decide where we need to be. I wish I had an indication as to when my cousin is going to get the card and the condom, that would help immensely. Let's get back together in an hour. In the meantime, I'll reach out to him and see what he found."

"By the way, forget about the strategic nature of who should be available for consultation. You and they are all my family. We know we can't all ride on the same bird together. Mallory, can you have Clyde or one of his people buy us more of these throw-away phones with long distance roaming capability?"

"I'll take care of it. I think Monica wants to ride into town and do a little shopping. All I have is a credit card."

"Zanthius, give him a stack or two or whatever he wants? I don't want anyone using credit cards while we're in the field. By the way, I think everyone should have a stack or two at his or her disposal when we are traveling," Beckmire said.

## CHAPTER TWENTY-EIGHT

Walter considered his options relative to the annihilation of Beckmire, his clan and the retrieval of the card and the condom. He felt that his shenanigans would be overlooked if he were the one who presented the power changing information to the President himself. He recognized that politically, the senator was a good bet, but presenting the package to the President of the United States, would be incredible and historical.

As he looked at the information Beckmire had sent him, Walter felt that a small group would be able to complete this operation without any problems. He told Mike to pick four of their most trusted and to meet him at his place within the hour. Mike asked him if it was wise to recon at his place rather than just showing up and picking up the package. Walter indicated that he was in control of this matter and began to question Mike's loyalty. Mike said, "Chief, there are in excess of two hundred people who will never walk this earth again because they tried unsuccessfully to achieve what we six are about to attempt."

"This thing is under control. We don't need a brigade of people to pick up a card and a condom that should lead us to the information on the Carbon Factor. Listen, if you have some other pressing appointments, then by all means, please attend to them. I can handle this thing alone," Walter said.

"Walter, you're the boss and I do exactly what you say. I have never questioned your ethics or your decisions, but in this case, I feel that we should do a recon first and position the 5th Army around the place to make sure that we don't have any problems."

"Tell you what, Mike, I want you to find out exactly where Beckmire is, and what he's up to. I'm not feeling you on this assignment. Therefore, I am reassigning you to that task."

"Walter, I just think that we need more men. I am with you, 100 percent of the way."

"Then you will do exactly as I have requested. Find Beckmire! That is all, you're dismissed."

As Mike walked away, Walter began to wonder if Mike had information about any of his operations and, if so, how did he come by it? Walter yelled, "Mike, hold up a minute." As he approached Mike, he studied his expression and then asked, "Have you ever had a conversation with Scottie or Allen?"

"Why would they talk to me? I work for you, and they were your counterparts."

"Just wondering, that's all. One more thing, I heard that they worked for someone who was basically invisible. Have you heard anything to that effect?"

"Walter, I am a civil servant, and those two people worked for themselves, or someone who was way above my pay grade."

"The question remains, have you heard any rumblings about who they may have worked for?"

"Not at all. I thought the two were untouchable until they met up with Beckmire and his people. Why are you asking me questions about them?"

"Oh, I just heard some noise and wanted to know whether or not it was a little noise or a lot of noise. Okay, get me the details on Beckmire and report to me as soon as you find out."

As the two men parted, Walter said to himself, "No loose ends! I have got to place Mike on the hit list and maybe I can connect him to Beckmire's demise. I have placed my cousin on a kill list, had him eliminate everyone who worked for me, and now it's time to tie up the remaining loose ends. It's going to be difficult, but certainly not impossible to kill a healthy sitting United States Senator. My life would be easier if she were like that moron with a bad heart who lived next door to the extractor. He became too greedy and the brotherhood knew he was a liability. I've done worse things, so if I put my mind to it, I should be able to fix this issue and move on with my life without any connections to my past. Beckmire and the planes will be easy; Mike is a nobody. The senator will require planning, execution, and I have the right person in mind to do that work for me—Ben Beckmire. I think I need to have his wife and son killed, link it to the Senator, and let him plan her demise. I never really liked the bitch. She's powerful, but like most of us, greedy as well.

"A satchel full of unmarked and laundered bills will make any of those righteous asses buy into my program, and besides, that latest scandal will surely take her out of the running for the Oval Office. She'll need money for retirement. I need to think this one through. I have to make sure I get rid of the little dirt first, work my way up and out of this mess I've created. Not bad for a GS 16, or whatever the hell I am. This might be a great time to test Mike's loyalty, have him kill Dr. Courtney Beckmire and the 'idiot spy'. Then Sergeant Beckmire will seek revenge, kill the senator, once she's linked to the murder, and then I'll make Mike run into a retaining wall or something like that. Not a great plan, but a plan that has potential."

As Mike entered his office, he began to think about the circumstances and issues that Walter had raised. He too, had somewhat of a soliloquy. He said to himself, "all of a sudden, I get the feeling that Walter may be more than he portrays. Why on earth would he ask me about contractors, knowing full well that they don't talk to me? I heard that Scottie, T-Rex, Allen, and others spoke with him a lot, but they never talked to anyone else. They wouldn't know who I was if I slapped them. He's really becoming unglued. What's perplexing is, why must he know every move that Beckmire makes? Beckmire is doing an incredible amount of wet work for him, but apparently, he doesn't trust him, and shows up uninvited at the jobs. There is either a lot more to Beckmire that I don't know about, or Walter has his feet immersed in more shit than I can imagine. I never really trusted Walter but began to trust him less when his people began to take on Beckmire and his crew, especially since Walter had the inside scoop. What's his end game. Is it in the best interest of the agency, is the question I keep asking myself?"

Walter attempted to reach Beckmire on two different numbers but to no avail. His blood pressure began to rise because he knew that Beckmire was no longer in the area and was probably on his way to the outback. He knew that Mike wouldn't be able to find him and suddenly felt Mike was extremely expendable. He revisited his scenario of having Mike do the work on Zanthius and Courtney. It seemed like a perfect way to end his accounting problem. He intimated to himself that he needed a self-contained small unit that could accomplish the same goals without the huge payouts that he made in the past. He thought about the money he wasted on the senator from Virginia, who had the 'idiot spy' in his back yard but could not close the deal with the people that he provided him. He laughed about what he thought were the strengths of Beckmire and his group and found them to be lax in many ways. His problem viewed through distorted lens, was that he only saw parts of their operation and those parts were conveniently bastardized by his presence and that of his men. "How can those old guys be that efficient and deadly?" he thought to himself.

Meanwhile, halfway across the country, Beckmire placed a call to Walter. Walter responded, "This is Walter, who's calling?"

"Ben Beckmire, how are you?"

"I'm doing fine but a little concerned that I can't seem to reach out and touch you."

"That's because you have reached out too many times to touch me, and in some cases have compromised delicately planned events that we had agreed upon."

"Whatever! Where are you and what did I do to deserve a call from you, my dear cousin?"

"I'm calling about the packages; the card and the condom. Did you retrieve them and, if so, what are the relevant details?"

"Cousin, you are mighty anxious about me getting those packages. Why didn't you get them yourself if you were that concerned?"

Beckmire checked his watch, began to make strange noises, and abruptly hung up the phone. He was cognizant of the fact that Walter might have been trying to track him and wanted to delay answering the question. He called back on another phone and said, "Listen, Walter, I don't have a lot of time to deal with your BS. Did you get the packages? Yes or no?"

"Cousin, can't we be civil? You seem to be in a hurry or something. By the way, when are you going back home?"

"As soon as I am sure that we have terminated our relationship on the matter of certain products, I will then pay attention to the details of our tribe. Once again, did you get the packages?"

"Well, let me just say that I'm on my way to obtain them, and as soon as I have them, I will give you a call back. Is this number or the last one a good one to reach you?"

"Neither, Walter I will call you in a couple of hours and hopefully by then you have retrieved the packages and we can attend to our personal lives. Goodbye, Cousin." Beckmire hung up the phone quickly as he approached the three-minute mark on his watch.

## CHAPTER TWENTY-NINE

The Sarge and his entire entourage were preparing to make their way to the far east. At 1500 hours, Jong made the seat assignments on the planes and each plane was to leave in ten-minute intervals. The Sarge was looking for Carlos when Courtney said, "Check out the barn. For some reason, those two, love playing in the hay."

"Well, I'm not going to walk in on them, I'll catch him later. Honey, can you do me a favor and go into town? I need you to pick up at least fourteen throw away phones, and make sure they have international calling capabilities. I will ask Clyde to call ahead, but I need you to make sure that they are all internationally functional. Do you have any cash on you?"

"Not a problem, but while I'm gone, you had better not go peeking on your old girlfriend."

"Courtney, really? If you don't know that you are my one and only by now, then God help us all because we are going to need divine intervention."

"You don't seem to have any time for me lately." Beckmire froze in his steps and said, "I'll get Larry and Marisa to go into town. How about you and I go off to the other side of the barn and see what it's like to play in the hay?"

"I knew you wanted to be near that woman. Come here, man, and give me a kiss. I'll go to town because I want to pick up a few things that I need. Do you love me, Ben Beckmire?"

"I love you so much that I would consider taking a bullet for you!" Courtney flipped him the bird and walked out of the room. Beckmire ran into the foyer and yelled, "I love my wife so much that I would take a bullet for her."

Monica looked at Mallory and asked, "Well, would you do the same for me?"

"You know I would, baby."

## CHAPTER THIRTY

As expected, everyone wanted to fly on the new planes, so Jong paid attention to the seating assignments. The Beckmire clan had grown in numbers with the onset of kids, wives, and lovers. He placed Larry in charge of the older plane with his family, Rashida, and her child, along with several of Carlos's men on it. The two new planes had members of his brotherhood plus Ava, Carlos, Asiram, and Zanthius. It all worked out and for those who did not get to ride on the new planes, they were guaranteed first accommodations on them on their next adventure.

Jong reserved the fifth & sixth floors of the Marco Polo Hotel in Kowloon for his party and paid a premium to do so. He contacted members of his extended family and arranged to get transportation, surveillance, and some fire power for his friends.

Beckmire asked Jong if all was in order and he stated, "I'm Mr. Amazing, and I have this one under control. I have family members providing transportation and providing extra eyes for us, as well as, securing some basic bug repellant. Is there anything else we need to be concerned about and how long are we going to stay in Hong Kong?"

"I don't know, I have to figure that out, along with Zanthius, and Asiram, who were Helga's contact. There must be key words or symbols that will get us close to the prize, but I don't know what they are. Besides, I know the gang is going to want to shop and play here for a few days. However, I need the pilots legal and ready to go in a flash, if necessary."

"I agree. I also took the liberty of asking my first cousin to secure our planes and guard them while we are here. I told him I would get that loan shark off his back if he did this for us. So, I may need you and a few of the guys to do some local work for me."

"We support our own, brother. Whatever you need."

The plane rides to Hong Kong were uneventful and most of the members of the team took this time to get some needed rest. None of the pilots had ever flown into the Hong Kong International Airport, but it was the newest members of the team who said they had studied the approach and would take the lead.

The only female pilot and black copilot overtook the other jets and at exactly 1.15 hours out from the airport, began to calculate their approach and communicate with the tower. Approximately thirty minutes from the airport, the lights became visible and the city was aglow. On the right side of the airplane was Hong Kong, magnified by its high-rise buildings and its over-use of energy to illuminate the city. On the left side of the plane was Kowloon, a magnificent place with strange customs and the boat people who it is alleged, had never placed their feet upon land. Everyone was wide awake, thrilled by the sights and beauty of the original gateway to Asia. Larry said to Marisa, "I hope we have time to visit some of the places mentioned in *James Clavell's* books. I bet you don't remember the name of his first book?"

"Oh, Larry, that's an easy one. Whenever you make me mad, I think of that name for you, *King Rat.*

"Wow, that's pretty funny, although I would have thought you would have called me, *Shogun*."

"Come now, my wandering husband, *King Rat* is the title that I have given you."

"Anyway, I would like to travel to Victoria Falls and see exactly where a lot of his work took place."

"Honey, Victoria Falls is in Zimbabwe. You mean Victoria Peak."

"Thanks for the correction. I must have missed that part, but anyway, his books really gave me the inspiration to want to learn more about the culture and the history of this part of the world. I liked all of his books including *Gai-Jin, Shogun, The Nobel House,* and *Tai-Pan.* Those books stimulated so much interest in Asia in me. I have never been to Asia but through his books I felt as though I had been to each place he mentions. I accidently stumbled upon his book *King Rat*, which is about his internment in a prison camp, which is factual. I just hope we have enough time to do this, and if not, my present to you for being a wonderful wife and mother, will be to bring you and the kids back here for a vacation. And honey, if you guys venture out in Kowloon, please, do not take photos of the locals. They believe if you take their photo, you also take their soul. Therefore, that becomes a function of an immediate liability, or unexpected payment. Remind the others of this fact as well."

All three planes landed without a hitch. Marisa said to Larry, "You know there have been some dangerous moments when I have had to step up and end a life, I'm so happy to see my man make me proud. I love you so much, Larry. I don't think I spend enough time telling you, thanking you for the way you protect and provide for us. If we get a chance to have time tonight, I'm going to show you in an old fashion way how much you mean to me. Now, let's get ready to make this thing end."

Larry looked at Marisa and said, "Honey, you know we are rich and we can live anywhere and how we want. However, I want the simple life because it keeps me grounded and focused. Besides when we get back home, I'm going to buy us a new house as we begin the rebirth of our marriage. I thank you for being there, taking care of the twins, and I promise you I will pay more attention to you and your needs. I love you so much." As they kissed, one of the twins said to the other, "Mommy and Daddy are going to exercise today."

The group, on a staggered basis, entered and exited customs without a hitch until it came to John Lee. The customs agent asked John Lee, "What is the purpose of your visit?"

"I'm here to visit your country. Is that a problem?"

"So, where are you staying while you're visiting my country?"

"Ah, can I call that little fellow over there and ask him? He be making the reservations."

"Sir, you don't know where you're staying? How long are you staying?"

"Ah, I don't be knowing that either, but if you let me call my buddy Jong over here, he can answer all of your questions."

The customs agent called his supervisor and told him that the guy he was questioning didn't know where he was staying, or how long he would be staying. The supervisor asked two agents to escort him into the office. In the office, the supervisor looked at John Lee's passport and said, I see you were recently in Australia. What were you doing there?"

"We be on a spiritual trip to the outback."

"Where did you stay in the outback?"

"We be staying in the outback."

"Sir, I'm trying to make this easy for everyone. Where did you stay in the outback?"

"I told you, we stayed in the outback."

"What part of the outback, sir?"

"The part where there be strange animals, people who talk funny and some who are dark like my friend, Jilkes. Did I do something wrong?"

"Sir, we're trying to figure that one out. Who arranged your trip here?"

"That be Jong, that fellow over there looking at me like I be stupid, or something." The supervisor asked an agent to summon Jong. When Jong walked in, he was asked, "Do you know this person?"

"Sir, I have never seen that big white man in my life." John Lee looked at Jong, turned beet red and said, "This don't be my idea of a joke. These fellows have guns and are looking at me awful strange."

"Uncle, this is the best redneck friend that I have in the entire world. He is my brother, and the one I told you about from over there in the Nam."

"Well, you best be prepared to take a whuppin when I get out of here. These guys got me sweating up a storm in here, and you be playing a joke. I be joking too when I whup yo ass." Everyone broke into laughter and shook John Lee's hand.

As the group entered the vehicles, Jilkes could not control his emotions and continued to laugh. John Lee exclaimed, "I don't find a pig's ass worth of funny from that there business! Them there boys almost made me mess my pants. I gotta tell ya, I was afraid."

Jilkes stopped laughing after seeing John Lee's expression and proclaimed, "You ought to know I would kill everyone in that airport if they laid a hand on you." John Lee, feeling vulnerable, grabbed Jilkes, hugged him, and never said another word the entire trip to the hotel.

At the hotel, Jong could tell that John Lee was upset and went over to him and said, "If my little prank scared you, then please accept my apology. I never meant to put you in an uncomfortable situation but thought it would be entertaining. I'm sorry, big guy, it won't ever happen again."

John Lee said, "That situation reminded me of my first day in that boot camp where I didn't know no one, didn't have a clue as to what was being said, and asked of me. I felt lonely and scared in that there office and thought for a minute that the people I be loving dropped me off on the side of the road without saying goodbye."

"Damn, John Lee, I really feel like shit. It's not funny. I completely understand how you feel because those were my same thoughts when I arrived at boot camp. Can you ever forgive me for my insensitivity?"

"Oh, I'm not mad. I am simply happy you people didn't leave me in there with those funny looking people. You know we be friends until the end and the end will come pretty damn fast if you pull some shit like that on me again." The two men laughed, hugged, and shook hands.

As Asiram and Zanthius checked into their hotel room, Zanthius said, "Now, I have to figure out how to put the pieces of the puzzle together to find out why we're here. I'm sure this is the beginning of the end of this journey, but I don't know how to connect the pieces. Honey, when I face a problem of this magnitude, I usually need to have quiet and alone time. So, I'm going to fix myself a drink, and you and the rest of the team can scour the countryside while I try to figure out the missing pieces."

"Sweetheart, I know you're going to figure this thing out, I'm not even concerned. You have shown me that you're more than the 'idiot spy', much more. As a matter of fact, I think you are one of the smartest men I have ever known. I love you and I'm going to go and fetch the girls to see if they want to hang out for a little bit. Catch you later."

Zanthius fixed his first drink, then his second drink, and by his third drink he didn't have a clue as to where he was. He called Larry and said, "Bro, I'm in need of some fresh air. Can you take a walk with me?"

"Meet you in the lobby in ten minutes." Larry called the Sarge and reported, "Zanthius wants to take a walk and I'm going to go with him. Do you foresee a problem?"

"Let me call Jong and I'll get back with you."

The Sarge called Jong and asked him if it was safe for Larry and Zanthius to take a walk. Jong told him he had a team that would follow and sort of escort them and he would meet them in the lobby to tell them to keep an eye out. The Sarge called Larry, told him that Jong had some locals to escort them, and that he would meet them in the lobby.

Zanthius arrived in the lobby and saw Jong talking with two guys in their native tongue. He then saw Larry exit the elevator and walked towards him. Larry said, "The Sarge suggested that Jong provide us with an escort."

"How the hell did he know we were taking a walk?"

"Zanthius, he's our father! There are no secrets between him and I. If you have issues with communicating with him, then I suggest you have a private walk and talk with him.

However, realize that we are on foreign soil without any support. It made sense for me to tell him."

"I guess you're right.   I don't have any problem communicating with Pops."

As the two men walked towards Jong, a hotel employee walked over to them and said, "At the Marco Polo hotel, you put shoes outside door at night, I make them look new for the morning." Zanthius stared at him curiously and nodded. As they approached Jong, Zanthius announced, "I guess if you have some people available to escort us that will be okay."

"My people are not going to escort you, but they will be extremely near and if you decide to go in the wrong direction, they will suggest alternate routes. Kowloon is full of mystery, engulfed in ancient beliefs and surrounded by a rich history but, as in most large cities, there are those who would love to take advantage of foreigners. Just stay together and be mindful of your surroundings."

"Yes sir. It might help if we had our own protection," Zanthius stated.

"I know how you feel, but we haven't quite worked that one out yet. My people will be carrying but I don't recommend that you guys hit the streets with weapons."

As the two men began to walk and chat, Zanthius blurted out, "I kissed that woman and she passed a capsule to me. She slipped a card from a Russian strip joint, as well as a condom with writing on it, into my wallet. She said that she hoped I never had to use it. She asked me about playing Marco Polo as a child in the pool and here we are at the Marco Polo Hotel in Kowloon. What's the connection?"

"I don't know all of the details, but did she give you any other hints?"

"That's exactly why I wanted you to come with me so that you could ask me questions to help fill the void until I come up with suitable answers. However, those are the only clues she gave me. She often told me that I was the worst fricken spy that she had ever met, or something like that," Zanthius responded.

"I think if we're going to figure this thing out, you have to recall her statements in the same context that she issued them. I mean, did she say you were the worst fricking spy that she had ever met, or did she say you are the worst fucking 'idiot spy' that she had ever met. Other than screwing your brains out, did she have any proclivities that would remind you of any of the details of this saga?"

"You are absolutely correct. She didn't say I was the worst fucking spy that she had ever met, but that no wonder I was called the 'idiot spy'."

"Your sexual encounter with Helga, was it normal? Did you play games or did you just dive right into it?"

"Well, actually, I recall telling her that I was going to take a shower and that if she wanted to join me it would be okay. I cut the hot water on and created a steam bath and as she entered, she said, 'Marco' and as I recall, I didn't say anything. A few seconds later she again said, 'Marco' and I didn't respond again. A second or two later, she said, 'Marco' and I said 'Polo' and that is when she dropped to her knees and began to provide some magnificent fellatio.

"I distinctly remember her saying that if you say 'Marco' two times and 'Marco Polo' on the third occasion then you will receive some wonderful information. In the bed, as we were stimulating each other, she whispered, "I wish I had my shoes on so that I could feel like a real slut while you make love to me", or something to that effect. As I recall, she had a fetish for shoes, purses, belts, and expensive perfumes. I just can't figure out why I was so adamant about coming here to Hong Kong but it was based upon the information that we gathered from the doctors who diagnosed the writings on my inners."

"Zanthius, what did that guy say to us at the hotel as we were about to leave?" Larry asked.

"He said leave your shoes at the door and I will make them like new for the morning. Oh shit! Are you thinking what I'm thinking?"

"Brother, I believe that if you said 'Marco', 'Marco' and then 'Marco Polo', that might give you something that your wife can't give you."

With an ominous look on his face, Zanthius asked, "What's that, Larry?"

"You tell me, Zanthius. Anyway, I think the shoe man might be the key person as well, and that is something that Asiram can't give you--the key to the Carbon Factor."

"This is exactly why I wanted you to walk with me. Okay, let's head back but keep this between us. Look for the shoe man, and let's see if what we came up with is as thin as an eggshell or as solid as a gold bar."

CHAPTER THIRTY-ONE

At the senator from Virginia's funeral, the senator with aspirations of being the next President of the United States said to Walter, "What a shame about our colleague. I guess those young girls literally killed him."

"Yeah, he was mixing booze and those pills that redirect the blood from the large brain to the small dumb one. Great turn out for his departure, don't you think?"

"Stop the bullshit, Walter, where is the package? My bid for the Oval Office is tied to this thing, especially since that other bullshit is about to hit the papers."

"I'm going to pick it up as soon as I leave the repass. According to my people, it has the direct coordinates to where the formula for the Carbon Factor is. If that is so, your bid will be solidified by the morning and our futures will be, as well."

"Can you guarantee me success this time?"

"I most definitely can. I have the final pieces and that team that you met just want to rest and get out of this business. Too messy for them."

"That's a shame because they seem extremely efficient and effective. I would hate to be on their hit list. Anyway, please attend to that matter and help me get over this hurdle that those assholes on the other side are about to raise about me. By the way, my package was slightly underweight. Is there a problem?"

"As you know, we incurred a significant amount of expenses on this detail, and in some cases, the money disappeared. We have surveillance of a homeless looking guy picking up one case, but two others have gone completely off the grid. Your issue will be addressed and a premium will be added for our oversight. Enjoy the rest of this jerk's funeral, he really was a loose cannon, as well as, a double-dealing son-of-a-bitch. Catch you later."

Beckmire called Walter, but to his surprise, Walter did not answer. He then called Mallory and said, "I just called the triple dealing asshole of a cousin of mine and he did not answer the phone."

"Maybe he's on his way here to join us on this wild goose chase."

"Mallory, what's up? Why do you think it's a wild goose chase?"

"The clues are just too shallow to make any sense of them and I'm still leaning towards focusing on the card and the condom. I just have a gut feeling that the juice is in those two items. Sarge, don't get me wrong, my wife is going to enjoy the hell out of this place, and so am I. However, I just feel that this is a mirage."

"Just say that you're right. Don't you think we all could use this boondoggle and just relax and enjoy ourselves?"

"Sarge, you are not listening to me. I'm going to have some powerful sex and lots of funny foods. Plus, my wife is going to love me more, especially when I hook her up with one of those tailors and have her shit handmade with her name embroidered on the inside. Dude, I'm going to have a great time. Okay, back to your reality. The package is not here, I just feel it in my bones and this conversation is between you and me, and not available on HBO."

"You're a funny dude, Corporal. Give me some reasons to discount Zanthius and Asiram's ideas, and I will act upon them. You have to admit they came up with a theory when we had none."

"Sarge, I think their theory is good. However, perhaps we reacted a little too quickly without doing due diligence."

"Perhaps, for the first time in this adventure, we didn't have people shooting at us," the Sarge indicated.

"You may be absolutely correct, but as sick as this may sound, I miss being shot at and shooting back at people," Mallory lamented.

"Now, that is some real sick shit, but I must agree with you. It gets my blood boiling and I just love shooting the bad guys. This escapade has sharpened both of my pencils, the big one works well and the little one has been just outstanding, if I must say so, myself," the Sarge boasted.

"I know this is some crazy shit, but as I said the other day, this shit stimulates me and makes me feel alive again. I mean growing old and planting shit is cool; but dodging bullets, shooting bad guys, opening cases full of money, and buying new jets are beyond my wildest imagination. This is science fiction to me and I'm loving every minute of it. It's the down time that pisses me off. I wish they would send more people to erase," Mallory replied.

"Let's you and I go downstairs and have a drink because I need to talk to you about this shit some more. I'm having the time of my life. That may sound sick as shit, but the fact of the matter is, I have you guys at my side, a new son, Rashida, an old son, a new daughter-in-law, and my wife is packing a damn pistol. Now, that's some scary shit. Like you, these are some amazing times for me, and I can do it without that little blue pill. Now, check that shit out," the Sarge announced.

As the Sarge and Mallory entered the lounge, they were amazed by what appeared to be a large number of women that were there drinking. Deep in the back, in a corner, were John Lee and Jilkes with two outstanding looking Asian women. The Sarge said, "I don't think this is the atmosphere we want to be in. I'm going to call Courtney and see if she wants to have a drink, and if not, I'm going to my room. As a married man, this scene spells trouble to me."

"I'm going to call Monica, as well, to see if she would like to join me."

Brown, feeling lonely, as well as horny, walked into the lounge and saw the rich scenery and said to himself, "If I can't enjoy the company that's here, then I need to enroll in therapy." He saw Jilkes and John Lee and waved to them. John Lee got up from the table, walked to the bar and said, "We be needing you to come over to our table because we be outmatched."

"What do you mean, outmatched?" Brown inquired.

"There be three of them and two of us, and we need you to convince the one that speaks perfect English that we're legit."

"I only see two women at your table. Where is the third one?"

"Oh, she be right back. She had to go and powder her nose."

Brown followed John Lee back to the table, introduced himself to the ladies, and thought they were two beauties. As he was about to say something, Jilkes announced, "Here comes the one who speaks perfect English." Brown turned around to see who he was talking about and his heart fell to the floor.

As if in slow motion, he watched as a 5'10", drop dead gorgeous, Asian woman with long flowing black hair, walked towards the table as if she owned the entire province. Brown, although mesmerized, stood up and offered his seat and realized that they were eye to eye with each other. He introduced himself and the magic began immediately. She said in perfect English, "My name is Okema."

After a lot of trivial conversation, Brown inquired, "Where did you learn to speak English?"

"I studied at Cambridge and the London School of Economics."

"Oh my, what are you doing here?"

"I left London in a hurry because of a trifling man I thought I loved. I found out that he loved a few others, as well, and I decided to run away to save face."

"Ah, saving face is especially important in your culture. I must say, everything about you is so appealing to all of my senses that I'm not sure you have the time or want to listen to me express my admiration for you. Before you say anything, I want to say that when I turned around and saw you walking towards us, I became extremely anxious. These two blokes will tell you, I'm not the kind of guy who shows his hand, but I must say you are stunning."

"What is your name again?"

"Richard Brown and I am extremely pleased to meet you, Okema. What's your last name?"

"It's Okema Fugahiro and it's nice to meet you. What brings you and your friends to this part of the world?"

"A group of us are on a mission to retrieve some materials for a dear friend of ours."

John Lee looked at him and said, "You sure be a talker." As Brown began to join in the conversation, he realized that Okema seemed uninterested in a conference type discussion. He asked her, "Would you like to go to the bar and have a drink and let these guys enjoy themselves without us being a third wheel?"

"Why not? But let me make it perfectly clear, Mr. Brown, we are not out on a hunt. We sure don't want to get caught up in any craziness and we are all going to leave together. So, if you want to have a conversation with me then that's fine, but please demonstrate that you are a gentleman at all times."

"You have my word as a Boy Scout, that I will in no way embarrass you. As a matter of fact, you just might find me stimulating, which could lead you to request another encounter at a later date."

One hour and three glasses of champagne later, Okema was relaxed and breaking barriers by slightly, gently touching Brown's hands and arms. He recognized the intimacy but maintained his distance, continued to talk to her about investments and the organizations their charities contributed to. Okema found him attractive and ever so seductive but maintained her dignity and self-respect. As the bewitching hour approached, Brown concluded that he wanted to see her again, and stated abruptly that his intentions were to see her again and again. She slowly bowed her head and when she raised it, she threw her hair to the side, and said, "I like you, Mr. Brown. I find you quite attractive. Although it may, or may not have been your intent, I find myself attracted to you on several levels. If I feel this way in the morning, I will give you a call."

Brown suggested that he would get an Uber to give them a ride home. Okema said, "We have a driver, and he's probably pulling up out front as we speak. Will you be staying here tomorrow? If so and if I feel the same way minus the champagne in the morning, I will give you a call, if you like."

"I would like that very much. I do hope you understand that I'm no player but a guy who is looking for a relationship, or friendship that has the ability to stand the test of time. I am truly enamored by your intellect and your beauty. I feel the real you was on display tonight and that person has captivated all of my senses. Let me walk you to your vehicle." Okema touched his hand, smiled, and turned to walk away, but stopped and said, "I like you, Mr. Brown, please don't turn out to be a jerk."

CHAPTER THIRTY-TWO

Larry and Zanthius were putting the final touches on what they thought were the answers to obtaining the key factors that could end the cumbersome, dangerous, and deadly adventure of finding the Carbon Factor. Larry asked Zanthius, "Do you think that by chance we ran into the keeper of the key?"

"I used to believe in chance, but I now believe in people and spirits appearing at significant times. But this doesn't usually happen to me. While I was in the outback, I saw an image of a strange man, who presented me with a key. I know this is hard to believe, but when me and our father were in the outback a lot of strange shit happened."

"Zanthius, to me this all falls into place because I have listened to the Sarge talk about the strange and wonderful things that happened concerning his heritage. He is a true believer so, therefore, so am I. I must admit while I was there, I too, felt strange and wonderful things."

"Enough with the hocus pocus. I passionately believe that the shoe guy is the keeper of the key, but before I make contact, I want to make sure that we have things in the right sequence and everything else in order."

"I'm going to go to my room and make love to my wonderful wife. I suggest you run this by Asiram and see if we missed anything before, we present it to the Sarge. Goodnight my brother. It was great to take a walk with you and try to figure this mess out. Catch you later."

Larry entered his room and saw that the kids were sound asleep. Marisa was fully engulfed in a blanket and asleep as well. Larry said to himself, "I missed another opportunity," and entered the bathroom to take a shower.

When he came out, he rubbed the hotel lotion on his body and slid into bed. Marisa turned from her pretended state of sleep and began to rub his inner thigh. Larry in turn reached over, kissed her passionately on the lips, began to breathe slowly in her ear and tell her how much he loved her. As she peeled back the covers, she displayed her new bedroom attire, Larry knew that the deal was consummated. He kissed her. She kissed him, and they found pleasure by using all of their tools to stimulate and satisfy each other. He moaned as he was being suckled and she let out an occasional scream when he reached her magic spot. They both swam in a pool of lust, love, and stimulating sex.

Brown, John Lee, and Jilkes walked their newfound friends to their car and each said their good nights. Brown kissed Okema's hand, and said, "I so hope you call me because what I want from you will take more than a night to achieve. It's more like an eternity that I'm looking for. Good night."

Okema entered the car and watched and waited for her friends to, uncharacteristically, stop giving sloppy kisses to Jilkes and John Lee. When they finally finished trading juices, the two women entered the car and Okema said, "Wow, you guys must really like those two Yanks." Their response were simple laughter and embarrassment.

As the driver drove off, Okema thought to herself, "I liked that guy and he has aroused things in my body that I never knew existed. I have slept with men, but I have never not slept with a man and have the juices in the middle part of my body flow freely, anxiously and have multiple orgasms from conversation." As the car pulled approximately ¼ mile away from the hotel entrance, Okema shouted, "I left my credit card on the table. Drive back to the hotel."

At the hotel, Okema told her friends that she would talk to them later. She entered the hotel and hesitantly walked to the house phones, stared at them, and took a deep breath. She dialed Richard Brown's room. He answered, and Okema said, "I want to stay with you tonight, but I do not want to have a physical encounter. Can you handle that, and do I have your word that you will always be the gentleman that you spoke of earlier?"

"Please, come to my room. You will not regret a single moment for I will be the gentleman that I naturally am."

"I am putting my life and virtue in your hands, Mr. Brown, please honor me and my traditions."

Brown rushed into the bathroom and brushed his teeth, combed his hair, and changed hurriedly into pants and a shirt. Okema knocked on the door and he took a deep breath and said, "Just a minute." He looked around the room, felt that things were in order and opened the door and said, "I hope there isn't a problem."

"The only problem I have, Mr. Brown, is that I find myself attracted to you on many different levels. Therefore, I want to spend my time trying to figure out why and how you seduced me without ever laying a hand on me."

"Okema, if you allow me to speak freely and honestly, I will tell you who I am and all that there is to know about me. I saw you and my heart stopped communicating with my brain. You are a very touchy-feely person and you kept touching my hands, my arms, and on occasion, you touched my legs. Now, I am no superhuman being, but I do consider myself a sensitive human being and I must admit, I have had my fun. Yet, when I saw you, I lost all my cool and surrendered to your beauty first and then your intellect. I am honored and happy that you came back, and I offer you serenity and comfort, without compromise or jeopardy."

"Wow, if I were obtuse, I would fall for all of what you just said. However, I'm a smart girl. Now, Mr. Brown, what you said was extremely enticing and welcoming, but I wonder if I proposed a different scenario could you maintain the cool you talked about? Hi, Rich Brown, I'm Okema Fugahiro, nice to meet you. Do you have any champagne?"

"If I don't, then you can best believe that I will walk this country until I find a bottle suitable to your taste."

"That won't be necessary. Open your minibar and let's see what's in there." Brown opened the minibar and there were two bottles of fine champagne. He said, "I must be doing something right because I don't have to walk across this country to find you your desired drink."

He opened a bottle and poured each of them a glass of the wonderful drink. They toasted and began the arduous but surprisingly, meaningful task of getting to know each other. They talked for over three hours and as he began to yawn, so did she, and that is when they decided to share his bed but not the moment.

They entered the bed as friends and would wake up in the morning as friends. Okema thought about her need for pure sexual stimulation but realized that she knew truly little about her host. Brown wanted to have a sexual encounter with her but realized that if it happened, it might spoil the prospect of any future relationship. He commiserated with his larger brain and fell asleep.

During their sleeping encounter, there was a significant amount of innocent touching, but the two never met in the center to exchange animalistic vows. The future would be bright for Okema and Brown, if in fact, they wanted to trust each other totally. Trust would be the consummating factor that would present them with options for their future.

Larry and Marisa ended their second encounter of the night with a lot of noise. One of the twins woke up and asked, "Are you guys exercising again?" Larry looked at Marisa and they both broke into laughter.

Marisa replied, "No, honey, we were just having a conversation. I'm so sorry we woke you up. Why don't you go back to sleep?"

"I'm hungry and besides it's light outside and time to get up."

Later, as Larry was leaving the room for breakfast, he noticed shoes that had been shined and were placed at several of the doors. As he viewed this oddity, he chuckled to himself and thought, "the hypothesis discussed with Zanthius was not too thin, after all. Maybe my brother and I hit the big one last night."

Marisa called Rashida and invited her and her child to join them for breakfast. Entering the restaurant, Larry saw Zanthius and walked over to him and inquired, "Did you see what was in the hallway this morning?"

A half asleep Zanthius mumbled, "What?"

"I'm talking about the shoes that were shined last night and left at the door for their owners. Come on now. You had to have seen those boxes outside of each door."

"Larry, frankly, I didn't see a thing because I am still half asleep. I am only here because my wife, of a short time, made me get up and take her to breakfast."

"Anyway, I think our conversation was right on target. Asiram, may I borrow your husband for a few moments so that we can sort out why we're here in Hong Kong?"

"Sure, Larry. Zanthius, what do you want for breakfast?"

"I wouldn't mind having some pancakes, a couple of eggs, plus bacon and a large orange juice."

The two men walked towards the entrance to the restaurant and were met by Courtney, Monica, Mallory, and the Sarge. Larry said, "Good morning to you all and I need to speak with you, Pops, and you, Mallory."

Zanthius said, "Hey, people, top of the morning to you."

As the four men walked into the lobby, Larry said, "I need you, my brother, to focus for a minute and think with your big brain about your activities with Ms. Helga. Now, as I see it, that woman went through great lengths to give you all kinds of hints. You know she was a sick and desperate witch when she encoded your internals. Now, we have come this far and we are just tourists but that is not the reason that we are here. Helga left you clues, but I'm afraid that they are not enough. She left you a card from a Russian strip club and a condom with writing on it. She even went so far as to use those two things as the final clues, if in fact, you weren't dead, but was smart enough to figure out the other hints. I say all of that to ask you to focus on the latent meaning of every word that she said to you before the two of you had to bail out of that place in the Swiss Alps."

The Sarge exclaimed, "Wow, Larry, you didn't get much sleep last night, did you?"

"As a matter of fact, Sarge, I didn't get any. My wife was truly my Mona Lisa last night." Everyone blurted out something different, but all congratulated him on getting over his hiatus.

The Sarge said, "Zanthius, we think we know the name of the hotel in Tokyo, but before we move your mind there, let's revisit your brief interlude with Helga. We are here in Hong Kong because of a game that kids play in a pool--Marco Polo. Did she say anything else about the game or the name?"

"Guys, I'm hungry and my mind functions better after I eat and after I have had some coffee. Can we hold this in abeyance until I have accomplished both tasks?"

Larry looked at the Sarge and said, "I guess we can wait an hour or so until boyfriend here has selfishly accommodated his inner being."

"Not nice, Larry. Asiram woke me up and demanded that I take her to breakfast and then you show up, like Sherlock Holmes, asking me a hundred questions before I have eaten. I'm just hungry and my wife wants to eat breakfast with me this morning, that's all."

"Okay, Zanthius, I apologize because I had a wonderful night and I shouldn't let my eagerness impact your morning. Sorry, Bro."

When they entered the restaurant, the entire team, minus Brown, was there ordering food and having a rather loud gathering--a thing that is frowned upon in Hong Kong. Bernstein looked at Jilkes and asked, "Where is Brown?"

"Wasn't my turn to watch him."

"That's not how we roll." A silence fell over the group and Jilkes said, "Sorry, Bernstein, we were out pretty late last night but we did see him enter his room. I think I'll give him a call."

Jilkes and John Lee got up from the table, and as they turned around, a 5'10" Asian beauty floated into the restaurant as if she was Venus de Milo. Everyone looked and admired her beauty, including the children. Five steps behind her was the person of interest, Richard Brown, walking with a newfound swagger and with his head held high.

John Lee said, "Well, I'll be a pig's uncle! That there boy kept that girl all night long. I'll be damned."

Brown walked by the table with his new swagger and didn't acknowledge anyone until he got to the head of the table and said, "Courtney, I would like you to meet my friend, Okema. Okema, this is my mentor's wife, Courtney. Hey, people, this is Okema." He went down the line introducing her to everyone and when she got to John Lee and Jilkes she said, "Mums the word."

As they found a chair and squeezed in between people, Jilkes said, "Your boyfriend insisted that we go to your room and make sure that you were alright. You have a helluva way of making an entrance, and perhaps you can teach John Lee and I to walk with all of that swagger."

Brown held up a glass of water, saluted Bernstein and said to Okema, "These are all my best friends and board members of the charities that I told you about. That little Jewish fellow down there is my main man but I could say that about each one of these guys. I would take a bullet for any one of them, that is how much they mean to me, and me to them."

"Those are pretty powerful words, Mr. Brown, if that is an accurate statement. I personally don't know anyone who I would surrender my life for and I guess that is a sad testament about my relationships with my family and friends. Perhaps, over time, you can teach me the meaning of such dedication and friendship."

Ava asked, "So, Okema, how did you meet Richard Brown?"

Okema paused for a long moment, and answered, "I met him in the bar last night. Mr. Jilkes and Mr. John Lee were entertaining my associates and when I entered there was this magnificent specimen of a gentleman x-raying my very existence. To minimize the chatter, let me say, I left the hotel with my friends, but decided to go back, place my trust and life in his hands. We enjoyed some champagne, talked most of the night, and I joined him in his bed where he behaved as the consummate gentleman. So, in obeisance to his swagger and his head held high, all we did was sleep and talk."

"Now, that's my kind of girl. She cut right through the chase and into the freezer and never missed a beat. Where are you from, and where did you learn to speak such perfect English?" Ava stated.

"I am a graduate of Cambridge University, as well as the London School of Economics, and I have spent too much time in that part of the world. I have only been back in this area for a little over two weeks."

"Impressive," Ben Beckmire blurted out. "What do you do for a living?"

"To be honest, I am not doing anything at the moment. Just visiting my friends and trying to figure out my next move. I could say I run a large hedge fund, or that I'm a banker, or that I'm a teacher, but none of that would be true. Listen, I'm a Johnny come lately to this party and apparently the focus of some intrigue, rightfully so. You must realize I am nervous, as can be, especially wandering in this place after spending last night with a stranger. You guys with all of these kids, look like John Que America, and probably think that I'm some kind of night caller. My credentials are certified, but my career is on hold because I'm between that and a relationship with a man who jilted me. If it is alright with you guys, I would like to order something to eat."

Brown placed his arms around her and whispered, "You blew the air out of all of those tires; wonderfully done."

John Lee said, "Me and my buddy be wanting to meet up with your friends later and have a tour of this here town. Can you give them a call? My minority friend had the number but can't find the phone he stored it in."

"After I eat, I assure you I will get in touch with them and see if they are available."

Zanthius said to Asiram, "Now, she is one absolutely gorgeous woman, but no one is as gorgeous or smarter than my wife. I love you Asiram and always will. I'm so interested in putting this behind us, and having our baby, and doing nothing except teaching him or her to love and respect everyone."

Larry watched Zanthius take his last bite of food, and three swigs of his coffee. He walked over and said, "Okay, Bro, it's time. Can we have that discussion now?"

The Sarge looked at Zanthius and said, "The sooner the better." He looked at Mallory, then at Brown, and inquired, "Can we meet for a minute or two?"

In the lobby, the Sarge said to Brown, "Rich, I don't pretend to know what on earth you're doing, but I would like you to hold our group and our charities harmless in your dialogues with Okema. You're a grown man but you're also a part of an intricate organization. For all you know, she could be a spy. I mean, the fact that you, Jilkes, and John Lee, met three of the most exciting looking Asian women that I've ever seen, begs me to ask certain questions. All I'm saying is, minimize the information sharing until you're sure of who you're dealing with."

"Sarge, I told her what we do to help people, but I never told her where our funds come from. I just met her and I must admit I am intrigued by her aura, and, you have to admit, she is one sexy woman. I'll get a little more information about her, and I'll have Jong check her background. Perhaps, later you should give Walter a call and see if he can ascertain any information about her as well. Listen, guys, I might be horny as a toad, but I am not as dumb as a rock. I will keep my wits about me until I am certain that she is on the level."

"That's all we can ask you to do, my brother. I agree with you; damn she's fine," Mallory said.

Brown went back into the restaurant and found Okema on her telephone, speaking in her native tongue. Jong understood every word she said and later told Brown that she was asking her girlfriends about rendezvousing with Jilkes and John Lee. Brown relocated to where Bernstein and Yvett were sitting and once again introduced Okema to them.

###

Meanwhile, Larry, in the company of the Sarge and Mallory, was in the process of picking up where he left off with Zanthius and asked, "Can you recall the exact comments Helga made while you were in the shower with her? By the way, don't spare any details. We need to know all of the sordid intel."

"Well, I remember going in the shower first and Helga coming in and saying, "Marco". I didn't respond. She said once again, 'Marco' and once again I did not respond. On her third try she said, 'Marco' and I said Polo' and she said something to the effect that was the order that I should eventually speak those words."

"Okay, great. See how we got from middle America to Hong Kong. Now, somewhere between here and there she must have said something else to you about the location and the person she entrusted the key with," Larry inquired.

"Not really, all I remember is that she said you are in the right room and you will have to remember that number as well."

"What number, what room and where were you?"

"I was in Room 234, in St. Moritz."

"Damn, Bro, you have just answered the magical question. Mallory, will you go to the house phone and see if room 234 is vacant and available for immediate occupancy?" Larry then said, we're doing good here, Bro. I'm confident we will have the answer to the riddle before noon. I just need you to continue to focus with your little brain and let your big brain remember the small details."

Approximately ten minutes later, Mallory returned to the lobby with an extremely perplexed look on his face. The Sarge asked, "What's up with that look?"

"You're not going to believe this, but for the balance of the year, the room has been booked and paid for. I asked the clerk who was the lucky person and he told me he couldn't dispense that kind of confidential information. As I turned to leave, he said, 'There is a mystery that encompasses that room. If you present the correct information in the correct format then it is yours for the balance of the year'."

"Well, I'll be a banana eating jackass. Helga played you to the hilt, Zanthius. In my humble estimation, if you had failed at the card and the condom phase then she knew you would be dead and wouldn't know about Hong Kong or Tokyo. Even more interesting, is the fact that the card and the condom are a ruse to throw off someone. The question is who?" Larry queried.

"I'm guessing that I know the who. It's my cousin and I'll bet you one shrimp on that information. Helga worked for him, as well as Allen, Scottie, the senator from Virginia, and a whole lot of other people. I'm sure he's mixed in this soup as the major ingredient--salt," the Sarge said.

"Damn, Sarge, you're probably correct, but I want to stay with Zanthius for the moment. Okay, Zanthius, so I heard you say the following during the sex scene in the steamy shower; 'Marco—Marco—Marco Polo'. Is that correct, and are you sure it was in that order?"

"I am positive about the order."

"Okay, this is going good. Can you tell me about the room? Room 234, what did she say about that?"

"I recall her saying that number might mean something or be important to me in the future. At that point in time the small brain was thinking and the big brain was in a coma. However, there seems to be a part of my memory that focuses on the number 234. It was all a blur because I was half high and interested in getting my friend taken care of, if you know what I mean," Zanthius stated.

"If I'm not mistaken or hallucinating, I think we have solved the Kowloon part of this deal. Now, before you interrupt me, let me lay out my observations. We're here in Kowloon and at the Marco Polo Hotel. Helga mentioned the number 234 as an important number. We also know that Helga had a fetish for shoes. If I'm not mistaken, we need to focus on the boxes for shoes outside of the rooms. Mallory just told us that the room in question has been rented for a year and that there is an access code as well. Now, I'm guessing that the access code is Marco—Marco—Marco Polo and that the person who shines the shoes is the person with the key. I know it's pretty thin, but we're here in Kowloon and that is the best I have to offer. Does anyone else have any input on this issue?" Larry stated.

"You are incredible, Larry. I believe that you have figured this out, whereas most of us were too close to it, and I wasn't clearly focused because of my choice of which brain to use. My big brain heard it all, but my little brain got in the way of transmitting it to the big one. You have been able to put the pieces of the puzzle together, if your assumptions are correct," Zanthius stated.

"I'm not accepting any accolades until we have successfully entered the room and gained access to the key," Larry replied.

Back at the table, the ladies were planning a shopping trip and asked Okema for suggestions. Okema said, "If you don't mind my tagging along, after I go home and change, I can take you to places where they make really good quality and stylish clothing." Everyone encouraged her to come along.

As Brown walked Okema outside to catch a taxi, she whispered, "I hope you can handle me, Mr. Brown, without any expectation of hot and heavy sex."

"In time, all things become possible or impossible. I like what I see, hear, and I would like to continue learning things about you. See you back here in an hour or so?"

"Are you going to accompany us?" Okema inquired.

"If I'm not mistaken, it appears to me that the ladies want only you to go with them. I don't think they're interested in me hanging around," Brown stated.

"You're probably right.   I'll see you later, Mr. Brown. Okema paused, and then asked, "Do you want to come with me, now?"

"I would love to come with you, but I have some work to do before our meeting this afternoon."

Elsewhere, Jilkes asked John Lee, "Do you think last night was a little strange? Here we are having a beer and two great looking women show up and begin to talk to us. Are we that good or do you smell something fishy?"

"I be thinking the two we be with are cool, but that beauty with Brown is more than she pretends to be. Now, I be thinking that she be a spy or something like that."

"Wow, John Lee, I hadn't taken it to that level, but you may have a point. I did get a picture of her and I think I'll ask Jong for his input."

Within a matter of minutes, Brown entered the building and Jilkes asked, "You got a moment?"

"What's up guys?"

"John Lee and I were thinking about our encounter last night and feel that it was pretty much staged. What's your take on that?"

"Guys, this is why I love you. I was thinking to myself, "What on earth are lookers like those ladies doing in this hotel bar." I think Okema is with some government agency. One line of questioning that caught my attention was her inquiries about our foundations, as well as, the source of the funding. I never mentioned to her that we have private jets. But I must tell you this, I really would like to have a carnal affair with her."

"Let's interrupt Mallory and the Sarge and let them in on our assessment."

As the three men approached the Sarge and Mallory, the Sarge said, "Damn, boys, those are some catches. They're all good-looking ladies."

"We all agree on that. However, me and the guys are thinking that they might be more than fine specimens of females. John Lee and Jilkes think that our chance meeting with those ladies last night might have been staged. I am utilizing my big brain, and somewhat, agree with them. Let me make it clear--I so desperately want to do her, but for the good of the cause, I am being as transparent as possible. That woman slept in my bed with absolutely nothing on and I didn't touch anything. Now, that didn't stop me from looking at every aspect of her body. Oh, and she sleeps with her legs wide open. Go figure."

"Let's assume you guys are correct. How should we handle this? I mean do we let our extractioner closely examine those parts that you didn't touch or do we play the game and see how dangerous they are? I don't know because I was securely in bed with my wife and not out in the bar trying to help my small brain get a piece of anything," the Sarge stated.

"Now, Sarge, I take interception to that."

"Exception, Big Country," Jilkes announced.

"It don't matter how it came out. He knows what the hell I was saying. Anyways, if they be spies and secret types then I be interested because that girl sure could kiss. I want to play this here game because when she pressed her body up against mine, I thought it was the 4th of July."

"Okay, you horny toad, let's focus. Brown, how do you want to play this one? Actually, how do all three of you want to play this one?" the Sarge inquired.

"I just be wanting to play and play hard," John Lee said.

"I'm with Big Country. It was fun, stimulating, and for the most part innocent. Rich, you took a helluva chance taking that lady to your room without anyone knowing about it. You know we don't do solo unless we have an eye or an ear nearby."

"I know I broke protocol last night, but she showed up after we all went to our rooms."

"Okay, the problem is, did she get a chance to plant a bug? Mallory, can you call Mr. Amazing and ask him to meet us at Brown's room?"

Fifteen minutes later, Jong showed up and inquired, "What's going on?"

"We need to check out Casanova's room to see if his new *mi amor* left any listening devices in his room," the Sarge said.

"Wow, now that's scary. Why is there suspicion that she did that?"

"The story is too long to repeat, but I'm sure lover boy will tell you the wonderful details of his night with that beauty."

As they entered the room, in plain sight was a listening device near his phone with a note that said, "There are two others in here. Please do not remove them until we have had a chance to talk." Jong placed a finger to his lips indicating that silence was the order of the day and said, "Brown, get your wallet because you're paying for this day."

Once in the hallway and away from his room, Brown said, "Well, kiss my ass. Why would she inform me of them?"

John Lee said, "I be thinking that she wants out of this and wants you to be knowing up front that she be a spy, or something. Now, that there girl has redeemed my faith in spies. She told you that those bugs were crawling in your room and for you not to remove them. I think she be bit by a snake."

"What the hell do you mean, she was bit by a snake?"

"Sometimes I think you people be the dumbest pigs in my pig pen. That there girl likes you a helluva a lot and has put herself at risk."

No one spoke a word until the Sarge looked at Mallory and said, "Get our essential people together and let's take a walk outside. By the way, have Carlos meet us as well."

Thirty minutes later, the team assembled in the courtyard and was given the details about a breach in their security. They all had new phones, but no one had coordinated the distribution of the numbers. Zanthius said, "Everyone write down your throwaway phone numbers and I'll make a copy of them and distribute them to the team. How the hell could this have happened? If that's the case, then we need security."

Jong said, "I can take care of that. As a matter of fact, I have people already placed in the garment district where I'm sure Okema is going to take the ladies. I have access to weapons, but I really don't want us to get caught up in an international situation that may be an embarrassment to our government or leaves someone lingering in a prison. I think we all remember our training and can pretty much handle ourselves in a street fight. However, in today's world, everyone has a gun. We can't risk it here."

"Why would she leave me a note about the devices?"

"Boy, if you don't listen to me, I'm going to have my minority friend kick your ass. That there girl wants you to save her."

"My concern is greater than saving her. I want to know how the hell her people knew we are here, and what they know about the package," Brown said.

Zanthius said, "Pops, maybe she doesn't know why we're here and perhaps that is the reason for bugs. Maybe her people think we are some kind of gang or something and, therefore, are paying particular attention to us. Brown needs to have the conversation with her and discern the real deal. We could speculate for the next few months and still the real reason could escape us. Let Brown have the discussion, as she suggested, and then we can figure out what we're up against."

"The 'idiot spy' has spoken. All praise the 'idiot spy'," the Sarge said.

## CHAPTER THIRTY-THREE

Approximately an hour and a half later, Okema exited a cab, walked to where the house phones are located in the lobby and called Richard Brown. He answered and she said, "I'm in the lobby. Where is everyone?"

"I'll be right down."

In the lobby, Okema pondered what she would say to Brown but concluded that she would be completely up front with him. As he exited the elevator, she could tell that he had a concerned look on his face. She said, "Please walk with me! I need to tell you who I am and what I do for a living."

As they strolled out of the lobby, Okema said, "There are two men sitting in a white sedan and they are a part of my team. I work for a British intelligence agency and I am what you would consider a spy. Please don't speak but smile occasionally to indicate that you are interested in what I am saying. On the other side of the street, are two weird looking guys who are also a part of my team. They will follow us on foot. Now, your friend, Mr. Jong, has six people placed all around. They are watching my people watch you and your people. I am aware of why your group is here in Kowloon and we are here for the same reason-- the Carbon Factor. I need you to believe my next statement, and depending upon how you react to it, may determine how this thing ends. If there is such a thing as love at first sight, Mr. Brown, then I am in love with you. I prayed that you would break our agreement and attempt to have sex with me last night.

You, Mr. Brown, have stirred up emotions that I have never felt for a man, especially a man, that I know nothing about other than his service record and what he does for a living."

"Wait. Why did you leave that note in my room?"

"Because I wanted you to know who I am but, more importantly, that you use that information to conclude that I'm now playing both sides of the fence. You, Mr. Brown, disarmed me at first sight, seduced me without touching me and suckled every aspect of my body without moving a muscle. I had multiple orgasms talking to you in your room about charities and not about sex. I am not your dumb blonde, but I am your brilliant woman with natural black colored hair. I don't think my country has the wherewithal to handle the Carbon Factor."

"Why did you place those bugs in my room in the first place? I'm not the brains behind this group. You probably should have bugged the 'idiot spy'."

"The 'idiot spy's room is bugged as well, but the chatter from his place is always the same--sex. I selected you from the pictures we have of your group. I studied your face from various angles and somehow became fixated on you. I was totally surprised by your reaction to me in the bar, actions that left me anxious and confused. Yes, Mr. Brown, I am a spy, but I resigned effective the first of next month."

"Okay, I'm confused as hell. What exactly do you want from me?"

"You haven't been listening to me. Mr. Brown, I want to get to know you inside and out, but more important than that, I want you to want me and to love me. I know this all sounds crazy, but I have never conducted myself in the manner that I have in your company. I had multiple orgasms simply talking with you. Unless you're stupid, you should see that I have no control around you and I can't stop thinking about you. I know this is crazy, but I am telling you the truth, Mr. Brown. I know spies don't tell the truth, but I am being totally honest."

"What do you want from me? I'm asking you the question again. Do you think that I can help you obtain the Carbon Factor? I'm low on the food chain in this matter and I can't offer you anything. I'm a foot soldier, with no information, who follows orders and says without judgement or question; 'Yes sir'."

"I want you to give me a chance to prove to you that my feelings are beyond reproach, and that I would also like to begin a relationship with you if, in fact, we're compatible. In other words, Mr. Brown, I like you more than I have ever liked any human being. I am willing to risk my life and my freedom to show you how much I believe in the man I spoke with last night."

"Listen, the ladies are probably getting anxious to go on that junket you promised. Let's head back, reconnect later, and continue this discussion. I'm obliged to divulge this information to my team and they will have to sanction any further communications between us.

"On another note, I watched you sleep last night and you slept without clothes and with your legs, uncommonly, wide open. I studied your breasts, lips, ears, legs, and that area that makes men do crazy things. I thought also about having that view every night. I also thought about having intelligent discussions about economics and the world every night. Although you are ahead of me in the orgasm bracket, I so much wanted to place my lips in that incredibly special place of yours and give you pleasure beyond your wildest imagination. At one point during the night, I removed what little cover there was on your body and studied you like a puzzle. I have to tell you Okema, your breasts are so inviting, your love zone is well sculptured, and I would love to have you watch me as I pay particular attention to both. Nevertheless, that may not bode well in our current situation. Are my family and friends safe on this adventure with you? I must admit to you we are extremely lethal when dealing with those who would hurt our family."

"My people will be attending to the group when we go shopping, with the utmost concern for our safety. If you like, I can have more police presence in the area."

"I like that, but you didn't answer the question. Will they be safe from any nonsense from your people?"

"My people are of no consequence to your family. They will protect them, if necessary."

###

When Okema and Brown arrived back at the hotel, Courtney and the group were patiently waiting. Courtney looked at Brown and proclaimed, "I should have known that you were the holdup."

"We just went for a small walk. She promised me that you guys would be in good hands."

Courtney asked, "Can Ava and I speak with you for a second before we head out?" As the three huddled, Courtney inquired, "Will there be cover for us?"

"More cover than you can imagine. You'll have the British, locals, police and Jong's family, looking out for you," Brown announced.

Courtney looked at Ava and asked, "Do you still have that present I bought you?"

Ava opened her purse and said, "I don't go to the bathroom without it." She had her P380 pistol tucked deep in her purse.

"How did you get that into the country?"

"I smiled at the agent and he let me go. Just kidding, it was packed away in my bag and I literally forgot about it."

"How about you, Courtney? Did you forget about yours as well?"

"I never said I had one, did I?"

"Do you have one?"

"I do, but you can't tell the Sarge."

"You know, guys, you could place this entire mission in jeopardy. Please be careful and certain in your resolve if you have to use those things."

The group descended upon three shops in proximity; suits, pants, tops, jackets, and shirts were fitted and ordered. The ladies acted as if they had never seen a tailor before and were picking out fabric and being measured. It was a splendid outing for them, as they had a chance to shop somewhere other than the local Target.

Brown asked the Sarge to call a meeting because of the new revelations. After the group gathered, Brown reported, "I met the most beautiful woman I have ever seen and she turns out to be a spy. She has professed a desire to be with me and get to know me inside and out. She is also aware of the Carbon Factor and works for one of the British intelligence agencies.

"Now, I told her that I would have to divulge this information to you guys and she didn't blink an eye. I asked her over and over again 'what do you want from me'? I made it noticeably clear that I am a foot soldier and that I respond to orders without questioning the directive. I told her she should have bugged the 'idiot spy's' room. She said that it was bugged and that all they hear from that room are sounds of passion. I told her that our response to anyone who attempted to hurt a member of our family is lethal and over the top. I inquired about the trip the ladies went on, and was told that the local police, her people, and others, would be on patrol. She also indicated that her people, as well as Jong's associates, would be watching out for us, as well. Yes, she knows about your extended family, Jong.

"In some ways, I am confused as can be, but in other ways, I am excruciatingly excited by her as a woman. I do believe she is into me and she wants to find a way out. Okema stated that she resigned. Now, I don't know what to believe, but I am giving you my take on the situation, as well as, my biased impression of someone who I like an awful lot."

Looking at Zanthius, the Sarge said, "Damn, Son, you are the apple that didn't fall far from the tree. Zanthius, make sure that you do not disturb the bugs and go about your business as usual, but button up any discussions with Asiram about our mission. Brown, I suggest you as well leave the bugs just where they are. I see an opportunity here in the midst of a minor storm. Do you think you can convince her to have a private session with a couple of us?" the Sarge asked.

"I think that if she wants to continue with this escapade, she has no choice but to agree to that request. If she compromised me, for the sake of the family and with tears in my eyes, I would terminate her life."

"I don't think you be needing to kill that there woman because she is your lifeline. I know you think I don't know shit, but I be telling you this will all work out in our favor. She be having to be debriefed, and depending upon what she has to offer, we make her the deal that she really wants," John Lee stated.

"What is the deal she really wants, John Lee?" Brown asked.

"She be wanting to spend real and long time with you, my brother. I feel it in my bones. Those other two be kind of spies as well. They don't make decisions; they follow her orders. I knew that when they sat down, but I didn't think that I be liking my lady friend so soon. They be honest spies who we can convert."

"John Lee, how do you know so much about how they feel?"

"You have to know about pig farming before you can really understand them there women types. Now, I be a pig farmer and I know them there types, and that Okema was shivering around you as if she had the flu or something. She be more nervous than my dearly departed favorite pig. That woman be looking for salvation and she found it when you got up from that there chair and offered it to her. Boy, you did not see the look on her face. Jilkes, did you see how she looked at him?"

"I am not the soothsayer that John Lee is, but she was completely won over by the time she sat down. I saw her eyes roll, her demeanor change, and she locked her legs in a three way position. When a woman does that, she is completely out of her element and afraid of what may come next."

"My question is how can we use her and what is the cost of such a consideration? I mean, Zanthius, you married a spy after a few months and she hasn't killed you. How bad can Okema be, and how on earth did she connect us to the Carbon Factor? Brown, for your safety and ours, we need to have a briefing with her. Jong, how reliable are your people, and where is Larry?" the Sarge asked.

"Larry is the lone black man walking around the garment district looking homeless, but lethal. He's watching our people along with two of Carlos's men. I think they are well covered. Insofar as my people are concerned, they are the best crooks on the island, and connected to one of the most powerful gangs on this side of the world," Jong stated.

"Good to know and thanks for your connections over here in Asia, Mr. Amazing. Brown, I personally don't have any idea how you should handle your love life, but you know if she must go, you might be the one to do her. Do you have a problem with that?" the Sarge inquired.

"Sarge, it's a part of who we are and what we do. If you put one of us in jeopardy, then you have the collective to deal with. No problem whatsoever, but I must admit, it would probably be hard to do."

"Okay, we have to set up a meeting with her and you have to arrange it as soon as she gets back. Can you manage that, lover boy?"

"It's done my liege, anything else?"

"Actually, there is. John Lee and Jilkes, did you find anything out of the ordinary with the two women you were with, in terms of their questions?"

"I frankly didn't find anything out of order. I mean they came in, sat down and John Lee told the barkeep to bring them a bottle of champagne. The conversation began and there was never a word about what we do or why we are in Kowloon. Am I right, John Lee?"

"My favorite pig couldn't say it any better. Even if them there girls knew who we were, they never asked or said anything about who we be or why we be in Kowloon. That there champagne just took over all of us and we just laughed a lot. They asked us questions about working out and building muscles. I didn't see or hear no nonsense that would have put me on alert, even if I be wanting to take my little friend to my bed and do the nasty with her. Jilkes, you agree with that there assessment?"

"I absolutely concur with your analysis, my friend."

"I can't figure out what the hell she or they want from us. If they're British spies, why are they coming clean? They may want to cooperate on some short- term, or long-term basis, but we don't set those terms. I can't figure this out, but once again, love prevails. I trust John Lee's assessment of the situation and when he has a sour taste in his mouth, then I get concerned. Since we are together, have we put the pieces in place that will define our purpose here?" the Sarge stated.

Zanthius announced, "I think that Larry and I figured this thing out for this part of the adventure. I wish he were here to help me explain where we are. Larry reconstructed my bathroom and bedroom activities with Helga, and I think we have figured out why there is a card from a Russian strip joint and a condom with writing on it. Let me just say, I believe that whosoever seeks the card and the condom will meet with a terrible fate or will be left standing in the middle of the highway in the wrong lane. The card and the condom are a ruse. It is our conclusion that Helga realized that if I didn't get past the card and condom level then I was either dead or compromised. Therefore, her writings on my internals are the keys to where we should be and what we should be looking for. The concept of the Marco Polo water game and staying in the Marco Polo Hotel in Kowloon with the same name seems a little coincidental. Saying Marco, Marco and Marco Polo is probably the opening code to Room 234, by the way, that is the same room number that I had in St. Moritz. Also, Helga had a fetish for shoes. Larry and I deduced that the person who shines shoes at night is the holder of the key, but we first of all must gain access to Room 234. That's our story, in a nutshell, and I believe we're right in our assumptions."

"When did you and Larry discuss this hypothesis?" Mallory asked.

"I met him in the lobby and I wanted to take a walk, so we did. He started asking the right questions that made me remember the scene and we jointly figured out what I said to you. Listen, we know it's thin, but that is all we've got for the moment. First and foremost, when he gets back, I think he and I should go over our assumptions and make sure they are solid. Then we'll decide when to go to the front desk and play the game and see if we win."

"Why don't we just go now and see what happens?" Mallory asked.

"This may be a one-shot-shootout; meaning that we will probably get only one try to get it right. I think there is too much at stake to rush into this without giving it as much thought and consideration as possible. I kind of want this thing to end in a sense, I guess."

"What does that mean?" Mallory stridently asked.

"I don't know how to really say this but I'm just going to lay it out there. I met my father as a result of the Carbon Factor and met you guys as well. I reconnected with my mother which was a needed activity on my part. But, more salient and on par with that is, I met a spy, fell in love with her, married her, and we are now expecting a child. In addition, and equally as important, I find this entire affair revolutionary and exhilarating in the sense that I am having the time of my life and I have mixed emotions about wanting this adventure to end. I mean, the shooting of people and people shooting at us, has exorcised another dimension of my latent personality that is intrigued, motivated, and satisfied by the outcomes of this adventure. In plain and simple language, I'm having the time of my life and I'm having it with my brother, my father and a few of his good friends."

"Boy, I don't have a clue as to what the hell you just said. Can you say that in English?" John Lee asked.

"John Lee, the 'idiot spy' just told us how much he likes the fight that we're in," Jilkes announced.

"Well, why, the hell, didn't he just say that rather than using all of those foreign words?"

"I think you have just expressed the sentiments of every man in this room, including Carlos and his people. Yes, this is a dangerous activity and yes it potentially comes with a sad price if one of us were to get seriously injured or killed. I think, I speak for the rest of the guys as well, when I say, 'touché 'idiot spy', touché'. I will admit, I told the Sarge that this was not the right venue and that the card and the condom were the things to investigate. I will never again doubt the value of the joint analysis that you and Larry conducted. I am proud of you both," Mallory exalted.

## CHAPTER THIRTY-FOUR

The ladies returned from their shopping trip with loads of bags and boxes. Bernstein said to Yvett, "I sure hope you took advantage of that outing and purchased everything that you wanted."

"I didn't want to spend too much money on things, but I did find a few outfits that I liked. Courtney and Ava kept buying me things, but I felt uneasy about accepting their gifts. Besides, we might need that money for more important things," Yvett stated.

"Sweetheart, that is so touching and considerate, but I wanted you to have the time of your life spending my money because soon I want it to be our money. I think we certainly can afford to allow you to splurge and buy things that I will appreciate both night and day," Bernstein replied.

Courtney said, "Bernstein, we hooked her up and tried to tell her we were just buying clothes, and not twenty carat diamond rings. Ava and I took care of her, and most of the things she bought will be sent to the ranch."

Brown asked Courtney if Okema left after she dropped them off. He was informed that she had. As he turned to walk away Courtney advised, "I think she is interested in you, Mr. Brown. All she talked about was you and how kind and gentle you are."

"Courtney, this next question is important. Did she ever talk or ask about what we are doing in the Kowloon province or anything else related to our business?"

"She spent all of her time with me, Monica, Yvett, and Ava. You know we would have jumped on anything that sounded intrusive. Her questions were about, why a good-looking guy like you, didn't have a steady girlfriend. I told her that you preferred men on occasion and her little eyes became as big as golf balls."

"Did you really tell her that?"

"I most certainly did, but later I told her that I was only kidding, that you were a ladies' man who only selected the brightest and prettiest women to date. I also told her that for the past few months, you have been dateless. She smiled and asked about the things you liked, disliked and I just made stuff up as I went along. Catch you later, Mr. Brown, I'm sure your little Asian flower will show up soon."

"Courtney, between you and me, Okema is a spy who bugged my room as well as Zanthius and Asiram's room."

"Get the heck out of here. Are you trying to be funny?"

"I am not. She told me without me asking that she is a British spy and she knows a lot about our mission here in Asia. That's why I'm asking you about the conversation to make sure that she didn't use this trip to gather information about why we are here. If you think of anything that she said that might be useful to us, please let me know."

When the Sarge saw Courtney with more bags than she could physically manage he asked, "What on earth did you buy?"

"I bought everything that I didn't need or want, but I liked."

"Fair enough, did Rashida and Marisa go crazy as well?"

"Now, you know my girls know how to shop, and especially after I informed them that you mandated that they act as if there was no tomorrow."

"I never said anything like that, nor would I."

"Whatever! There is a store that Okema took us to that has a men's department, and they have some outfits that I think you would like. You know it's all custom-made and, therefore, I couldn't pick out anything other than fabric. Do you think I could convince you to go shopping with me and have a few suits made for you at my expense?"

"I'll go anywhere with you just to have some alone time together. I'm glad you ladies had a good shopping trip, and I have to say, you all deserved it."

"Brown told me about Okema and asked if she had said anything or inquired about the nature of our visit here. I told him that all the lady spoke of was him, and she never asked any questions that would catch my attention."

"Yeah, we're trying to figure out how to deal with that issue, because he seems to like her a lot. I think he's a little crazy for falling head over heels for her in just under twenty-four hours."

"Oh, I see. Then what the hell was it when we met? Didn't that, like happen in a matter of minutes, Mr. Ben Beckmire?"

"Honey."

Courtney threw up her hand and said, "If you want to talk to me, contact the hand and ask it how long it was before you were begging me to go out with you."

## CHAPTER THIRTY-FIVE

Normally, in a developing relationship, people feel out each other's likes, dislikes and try to figure out if they want to consider a second, third, or fourth encounter. In Brown's case, it had been a matter of twenty-four hours and he and Okema were in deep conversations about things that people usually reserve for months after dating. He flatly said, "There are things about how this happened that really makes me not trust you."

"I can see where you're going with that but remind yourself, at each juncture, I have been forthcoming. It was I who left you the note telling you that your room, as well as that of Zanthius and Asiram's, was bugged. Yes, I am a spy, but I will give everything up right now for a chance to have an open and honest relationship with you. Have you ever just talked with a woman and she had multiple orgasms? Has a woman ever invited you into her room and watch you sleep and dream of you? Well, Mr. Brown, I am no virgin but I have never felt the passion that I feel for you."

Okema continued, "I didn't know a damn thing about you other than what I saw in the pictures and what your purpose was in Kowloon. I need you to trust me like you trust that Mr. Beckmire and that Mr. Bernstein. I will trust you blindly. I can't really express my feelings but I know that what I have told you is the truth. I have never had a man impact me the way you have. You respected me and did not take advantage of me as you could have easily done. More importantly, you looked at me with love in your eyes instead of lust when we first met. I need you to trust me, Mr. Brown. I can get you through the ordeal related to the Carbon Factor before those nitwits from the North surmise how to open that door. You can tell your people that Helga played the East against the West but made the game fair. From what I hear about your 'idiot spy' and his uncanny ability to figure things out, I don't think they have a chance in hell, but I must admit, we Brits are also highly interested in securing the information and playing the super power role."

"Okema, I get sidetracked when you talk about our meeting because I was extremely disappointed when I found out you were a spy. Now, I know there was no way for me to know that other than by your open admission of the fact. When I turned around and saw you in the bar, everything that I have and everything that I am became yours. The other night in my bed, as I viewed every aspect of your body, I so much wanted to wake you with the pleasure of my mouth in a very strategic place. I watched you the entire night and when you moved, I freakishly tried to get a better view of that place that drives men wacky.

"There was a point when I had fantasized so much about you that I had envisioned we were already lovers and that my advance would be acceptable and unsurprising. I lost some perspective because to me, you are the most beautiful woman that I have ever met. The downside to that proposition is that, you turned out to be a spy who is interested in the same product that me and my family are. I don't believe that makes for a solid relationship on any level, and first and foremost, my family supersedes any love or emotional involvement. As a matter of fact, I was asked if you were deemed a compromising aspect to our mission, would I be able to carry out your termination. The fact of the matter is that I could."

"I'm sorry to hear that. I understand, and hopefully, you will attempt to find the good in me and not those aspects that would signal my demise. Mr. Brown, I am in way over my head. There are two solutions—I, or we, can assume a relationship which will mean that I must accelerate my resignation by two weeks, or we can deny our feelings and regret it for the rest of our lives. I know where I want to be in that equation. How about you?"

"I don't know you, but damn you make me think like a crazy person. What the hell do you want from me?" Brown asked again.

"Mr. Brown, I don't think you are daft, but I must have your hearing checked. I want something that is made up in fantasy land and storybooks. I want to love a man that I don't know, who captured me at first sight and avoided the temptation of seduction during our first night's encounter. That is what I want, Mr. Brown. That spy shit is easy. Either it is or it isn't, the million dollar question is the one that only you can answer. I don't like this business nor the seedy people who pretend to be something that they're not."

"Okema, I have to talk to my people in order to continue this encounter. Again, I am saddened by the fact that you're a spy. I'm happy about the fact that I adore what I have learned about you so far and I am enthralled with your looks and your sexuality. As you can imagine, I can't jeopardize our mission for the sake of my own personal gain."

As Zanthius scanned the English version of the local newspaper, he came across an article that caught his attention about the air quality in a large Chinese urban area. Seemingly, in order to breathe the air in those areas, it was necessary for citizens to wear protective masks around their mouths and noses. What struck him as curious was an article in the business section about the large purchases of coal from any country that would sell it to China. As the rest of the world was attempting to limit its footprint on the environment by reducing its use of carbon, China was buying enormous amounts of the product. At first, Zanthius shrugged off the notion that something was suspicious and continued to read the paper but was drawn to the article about carbon. As he read it again, he learned that their import of coal had increased by 35% in a single month with indications that their future purchases would climb to approximately 65% in the succeeding months. He wondered why when the rest of the world was trying not to use carbon, the Chinese increased their imports by staggering amounts. He stood up and whispered in Asiram's ear, "They're capturing the carbon market. They must have knowledge about how to harness the Carbon Factor!"

"What on earth are you talking about?"

"I'm talking about the Chinese government's increased purchases of coal. They increased their imports by 35% in a single month and it is estimated that the number will climb to 65% in the coming months. Honey, they are on to the Carbon Factor and I think we need to make our move and get out of this part of the world as soon as possible. We need to talk to my father because if I'm correct, this thing is about to hit the fan."

Later in the foyer of the hotel, Zanthius explained his epiphany to his father and Mallory. Mallory asked him, "What does the behavior of the Chinese have to do with us?"

"Mallory, they are amassing tremendous amounts of a coal, while the rest of the world is trying to reduce its footprint. If I am correct, they might be experimenting with harnessing the Carbon Factor. Why else would they increase their imports over the past and coming few months? I think they are probably watching us, like everyone else, and we don't even know it. If the British know that we are here, you can bet your last dollar that the Chinese damn sure know we're here as well, and our purpose for being here. I think we should try to access the room tonight with what I think is the code, and we need to get the hell out of here and go to Tokyo by morning. Guys, I just think this thing is going to get bigger than we can imagine. We are in a place where we only have our fists and a few knives for protection. That's not very comforting, if you ask me."

The Sarge studied his son, and thought, "how on earth did he get the title 'idiot spy'? This guy is always thinking ahead and rarely backwards. I think he might be on to something, but I will see how Mallory responds first."

The Sarge asked Mallory, "What are your thoughts about what he said?"

"Sarge, I hate to admit it, but I have come to listen to him when he talks. I think he might be on to something. Frankly, I too, think that we need to get out of this vacation mode, get the work done and get the hell out of here."

"See if you can reach Jong and have him put our planes on standby for immediate departure. Also, see if you can reach Larry and have him join us."

As Mallory walked away, the Sarge said to Zanthius, "I was thinking how thin your premise was about the Carbon Factor until my friend Mallory nodded in agreement about what you said. Son, I'm proud of you and wish the hell we had these moments much earlier in our lives. It would have been nice."

"Pops, you have to thank Larry also. By the way, have you called your cousin lately? I'm curious about what he found out about the coordinates and the other information on the condom and the card."

"I have not, and as a matter of fact, I think I will call him right now."

The Sarge pulled out one of his phones and called Walter. When Walter answered, the Sarge inquired, "How's it going? Did you find what you were looking for?"

"We held that operation in abeyance because more pressing issues came up that required my attention. We are scheduled to access the package in two days or so. How is it going over there in Asia?"

"How the hell, do you know that I'm in Asia?"

"Come now, Cousin, I am the damn government. It's my job to know where people are who we do business with."

"Oh, I see. So, you're spying on me?"

"I wouldn't call it that. I think you and yours are having a wonderful vacation over there buying a lot of clothes and stuff like that. When will you people be coming back this way? I have a critical assignment for you in Addis Ababa if you would consider it. We have a Russian captain who was once a spy for us being held by pirates, and we need to rescue him before they find out who he really is. If we get him first, it is a major coup for us and a huge bargaining chip in our attempt to continue détente with the Russians."

"Now, that is one bad part of the world and it has no apparent government structure in place, just a bunch of bandits that make their money from being modern day pirates. I'm sure my people don't want to enter a war zone without full military backup and that ain't likely to happen, so I don't think we would be good for that job."

"Cousin, I need you to think about it because that Addis Ababa opportunity, not the Carbon Factor, if successful, gives you a complete break from my agency and literally retires your group with full compensation and benefits."

"Walter, what the hell does that mean? That sounds like some more of your convenient untruths. I mean we don't have a lot of trust in what you say, especially when everything you do is counterfactual. There is no way in hell, we are going into Addis Ababa, and that is my final response."

The Sarge looked at his watch and then hung up the phone without saying goodbye. He knew he had approached the time frame that would allow Walter to know his exact location. He called Walter back from another throwaway phone and said, "Sorry, Couz, we were cut off."

"Not a problem, but please call me when you guys finish your vacation, nice to hear from you," Walter acknowledged.

The Sarge looked at Zanthius and said, "That son-of-a-bitch knows that we are here and I have no way of telling how. I guess that's the benefit of being a spy who sells drugs, runs prostitution rings, smuggles oil out of Iran, and sells government secrets. What a humanitarian."

"It looks like he's a perfect example of the Beckmire clan," Zanthius retorted.

"Watch it, dude! Don't make me give you a spanking."

"I guess I kind of missed that aspect of life. Mom never laid a hand on me and I thank her for that, but sometimes I knew that I was testing her resolve. Anyway, did he say anything about the card and the condom?"

"He said that other pressing business prevailed and that he would access the products in the next few days. You know something, that's a bunch of horseshit. A lot of people died, a lot of the money was spent, and the international importance of world domination is at stake! Why would he put it off another day or so? I have to ask myself, what would make me put it off, rather than go get something that is allegedly world changing? There is something wrong with this equation and I don't like it."

The Sarge called Walter back. When he answered, the Sarge said, "I thought this Carbon Factor was the most important thing to be developed in the modern world. Why is it taking you so long to retrieve the information that could lead America to its formula? Walter, once again I think you have played us. But remember, my friend, what goes around comes around."

"See, Cousin, you have got to stop believing in fantasy and instead make things happen. I had another pressing assignment and, therefore, I couldn't retrieve the information."

"Walter, it's supposed to be earth shattering technology, and you had other pressing issues? You know what, I'll catch you later."

The Sarge hung up the phone and said to Zanthius, "That guy has played us again and I don't know which game we're supposed to be playing--hockey, basketball or baseball?"

Mallory reappeared with Jong and Larry in tow. Jong said, "Less than ten minutes ago, my people here on the island told me they suspect there are Chinese operatives in the area that are paying particular attention to the shopping and movements of the team. I don't know exactly what that means, I'm just passing it on."

"Did Mallory ask you to place the pilots on standby?"

"Sarge, they are always on standby and the planes are always monitored by them. When are we leaving?"

"That depends on Larry and Zanthius and their theory about how to enter a certain room and obtain a particular key. I'll have them brief the team later, but I just wanted to know the status of the planes. Also, my cousin has an idea about where we are, and I am now becoming paranoid about his ability to keep up with us. Do you have any ideas as to how we can minimize his intrusive knowledge?"

"Let me think about it and get back to you later. I guess immediately, one thing we could do is take all the electronics we have, place them in a barrel and let them burn. That's one way, however, let me think about other possibilities."

"Great, Larry, you and Zanthius have come up with some interesting ideas about how to access Room 234 and obtain the key. I would like you guys to find a safe place and hash this thing out until you have considered all possible options. I would like to move on this thing within the next few hours. Is that a problem?" Zanthius looked at Larry who shrugged his shoulders and the two men walked off without further discourse.

In the restaurant, the two men discussed every angle of their hypothesis and decided they had come up with the best game in town. If any notion of success was in play, it was with their strategy.

Larry said, "I think you should go to the desk and tell them you want to move to Room 234 and see what they say. When they tell you that it has been rented for a year, you tell them that you're a part of the rental group and you have the code to enter. I'm hoping we are correct in our assumptions, and therefore, all you must do is repeat the code in the agreed upon manner. Let's go over it again."

Zanthius interrupted Larry and said, "Bro, we already did that. I know our response to that question. Let's just go to the front desk and try it."

"Okay, but I think we're leaving something out that I can't put my finger on. Let's just do this and be done with it."

As the two men started towards the desk, Larry watched as a woman strolled through the lobby with a bag full of shoes. He said to Zanthius, "Hold up a minute. I think there is an additional question about the shoes we have to ask."

"Perhaps you're right, but I think you're over playing this game. Let's walk to the front desk and inquire about the room and give our manufactured code and pray to the heavens that it's correct. If they act as if there is another part to this equation, then you can ask something about shoes, or whatever, but I can't see how shoes would be a big part of this equation," Zanthius stated.

Larry looked at him and said, "This is a one shot deal my brother. If we fail on the first try, there will be no further attempts. I suggest we take another look at what we have and do our due diligence, and besides, what's a few more minutes going to cost us?"

As Zanthius turned around to follow Larry, gunshots rang out from the exterior of the hotel. The two men instinctively dove to the floor and tried to assess where the sounds were coming from and who was the intended target. As they made their way to the window, they could see two men sprawled out in the street with at least four other men surrounding them with weapons drawn.

Larry whispered, "Those aren't any of our people and they sure don't look like Jong's family members. I wonder what's going on."

As a crowd began to swell around the scene, Larry and Zanthius made their way out of the hotel and tried to discern what had just happened and who the dead men were. One of Jong's people casually walked over to them and said, "Too much press, better you not be here."

Larry and Zanthius went back into the hotel and watched people filming the event on their phones from the window. Zanthius said, "You know what, we either get in with the code or we get in the old fashion way, what are your thoughts?

"I'm with you because everyone is distracted and they may have forgotten all essential aspects of entering Room 234. However, my only concern is, what if the shoe person is the key holder and we forcefully, breach that room? We then forfeit any chances of getting the key," Larry stated.

After briefly going over their plan, the two men approached the front desk. Zanthius said, "I would like to stay in Room 234, I hear it's available."

As the desk clerk pulled up the room manifest on her computer she said, "So sorry, but Room 234 is taken."

Zanthius looked at Larry and then explained to the clerk, "My friend suggested that I visit Kowloon, stay in the Marco Polo, sleep in Room 234, which has been reserved and paid for by her for a full year."

The desk clerk said, "So sorry, but the room taken, but I will get the manager and see if she can help you with an equally suitable room. Just a minute, please."

Five minutes later, a 5'6" Asian beauty with long flowing hair walked up behind Larry and Zanthius and said, "Hi, my name is Trinh, and I am the manager. How can I be of assistance to you gentlemen?"

Larry and Zanthius were distracted by her beauty, and Zanthius finally said, "We, or rather I, would like to stay in Room 234 that has been reserved for the balance of the year by a friend of mine."

"So sorry, sir, but that room is reserved and is off the books."

"There must be some way to show you that I belong in that room?"

"So sorry, sir, as I said before, Room 234 is not for rent. Have a nice day and I'm sure the desk clerk can accommodate you with another room. Thank you and goodbye."

As she started to walk away, Zanthius said, "Marco, Marco, Marco Polo." Trinh- stopped immediately in her tracks and said, "Please follow me and provide me with the second part of this puzzle." Zanthius looked at Larry and Larry looked at her shoes and asked, "What time shall I leave my shoes outside for cleaning?"

"You may leave your shoes at exactly 11:10 pm tomorrow night. The attendant will pick them up, provide service to them and you will be able to gain entrance to your new room, 234, at exactly midnight. Please be aware that we are precision oriented here and any departure from the timetable will forfeit entry and shoe service. Thank you and have a wonderful day."

As the two men celebrated by giving each other high fives, one of Jong's family members walked in the hotel, went straight to the lobby phones, and called Jong. After a brief conversation, he walked past Zanthius and Larry and told them to stay close tonight.

In the meantime, Jong placed a call to the Sarge who in turn called Mallory and requested that the team meet in the next half hour to discuss some new threats, as well as, new developments.

In the restaurant, people were discussing the fact that two men had been shot in the middle of the street outside of the hotel. Mallory noticed the abundance of ears nearby, ran his hand across his throat, and suggested that they meet outside by the pool.

As the group reconvened, Jong reported, "There was a shooting outside of the hotel a few minutes ago and the people slain were Chinese. More importantly, they worked for the Chinese diplomat who was in Los Angeles when we botched that drug deal. I don't know if this is a revenge trip, or if someone is collaborating with various groups to orchestrate our demise. From the weapons they carried, the purpose of their mission was to send a deadly message to us, but they were apparently handled by the British. Brown, where is your female acquaintance?"

"I have no idea."

"Also, apparently, a female shot the two suspects and was seen getting into an awaiting vehicle that drove off. My family detailed her looks, but one member said she was short and the other said she was tall, so not much of a description," Jong reflected.

The Sarge said, "If attempting to obtain the card and the condom, don't kill Walter's ass, I am personally going to blow his head off. I'll bet you a hundred bucks that the Chinese people in Los Angeles worked with my cousin. I bet you."

A stillness fell over the pool area and Jong said, "We have been compromised again, but I can't figure out how. The only way to figure this thing out is to magnetize everything and everyone once we get through customs and leave all communication devices in a barrel of water."

"Zanthius, have you and Larry figured out anything about that room yet?" the Sarge asked.

"As a matter of fact, we have. We expect to gain entrance tomorrow at midnight, and hopefully, pick up the final piece necessary to obtain the Carbon Factor formula."

"Can we accelerate the timetable because I want to get the hell out of here as soon as possible?"

Zanthius exclaimed, "No! The timetable dictated to us is precise and the information conveyed about it was stated with a sense of finality. Larry, what are your thoughts?"

"Zanthius, I'm completely supporting you on this one. That beautiful woman was precise and officious about the time. As a matter of fact, she said that they operated with precision and that the times are the times."

The Sarge said, "I feel naked sitting here in the hotel with only a butter knife as my weapon. I'm thinking that I would like to get the women and children out of here in a hurry. Anybody have any comments on that?"

"I be thinking that be a good idea because we know what we have to do and they be getting somewhat in the way if they stay! What be your thoughts my minority friend?" John Lee inquired.

"John Lee, I'm going to kick your ass if you keep playing that minority shit with me, but anyway, I like the way this cracker thinks and I agree with him."

"Sarge, no he didn't just call me a cracker. If he did, then I have to take his ass outside and beat the shit out of him again."

"John Lee, you are outside and the last time you tried to beat the shit out of him, well, he kicked the piss out of you. But he loves you like no man should love another man."

"Well, in that case I apologize to my friend, but he told that there girl I like, that I was a pig farmer."

"John Lee, in case you have forgotten, your favorite pig is buried in front of your now demolished home and in your backyard, there are nothing but pigs running around," Jilkes stated.

"I guess that do make me a pig farmer, but a friend wouldn't go and tell a potential mate that, would he?"

Zanthius yelled, "Guys, our backs are up against the wall and all we have to fight with are butter knives. Can you two lovers kiss and make up for the good of the order?"

The Sarge sat pensively trying to put all of the pieces together in his mind and said, "We took the head of the wrong snake. The real head is in Washington, D C. We need to get back there and handle him before he handles us. Brown, I think it is time that we had a sit down with your little friend and try to figure out what's going on with the Chinese. Zanthius believes that they and the Russians, are trying to buy up all the coal in the world, and he thinks that they too, are experimenting with carbon. I guess that's not our immediate concern, but it is something that we might have to deal with once we get to Tokyo. Zanthius, the woman that told you about the timetable, do you think she can be trusted not to tell the rest of the world that someone has come for the package?"

"Pops, we don't know that woman from silk, other than the fact she is incredibly attractive. She said what she had to say, gave us the timetable, and suggested that we should be on time. That's all I got from her. Larry, did you surmise anything different?"

"I got what you got and that was, don't be late and don't be early. That was the gist of her conversation."

"Mallory, what do you think about getting the women and children out of here?" the Sarge inquired.

"I like the idea, but I don't like separating anyone. I think we should stick together and take our chances rather than having them in one place and us in another and worrying about them the entire time." Brown's cell phone rang and it was Okema who said, "I called your room and when you did not answer I decided to call your cell phone. I'm in the lobby, are you free?"

"I'll be there in about five minutes."

He told the group that it was Okema and that she was in the lobby. Mallory asked, "Do you think all of us should talk with her or can you use the big brain to do our bidding?"

"After that grilling at breakfast, I'm not sure she feels like being the center of our discussions, but I will see."

"Why not probe her for further information about her intent and the intent of the people she works for? That is a simple conversation and it is divided into two simple parts," the Sarge said.

"Guys, I like her a lot, but I'm with the only real family that I know, and no one, and I do mean no one, will ever come between me and my real family."

"Now, that is what I like to hear and I think you should have the conversation with her by yourself," Mallory stated.

When Brown entered the lobby, he saw Okema staring out of the window. He walked up behind her and said, "I thought I wouldn't see you again, but here you are."

"Mr. Brown, I see once again you have forgotten our previous conversations. This time I need to speak to you and that Sergeant Beckmire, and any others who might make decisions about what I have to tell you. Where are they?"

"Everyone is out by the pool because we don't know what rooms you bugged."

As the two walked towards the pool area, Okema reached out and grabbed Brown's hand, and said, "I know it has been a supersonic trip so far with me trying to convince you of my intentions, but I need you to believe that whatever you felt when I walked into that bar, multiply it by infinity, and you will know where I stand, insofar, as my reactions to you."

The team saw Brown and Okema approaching holding hands. She greeted everyone and the Sarge said, "Guys, you all met her and if you want to stay for the conversation, you're welcome. If not, we will meet immediately after this if there is significant information to be shared." Most of the team left except John Lee, Jilkes, Mallory, and Jong.

Okema didn't waste any time and said, "I have been told that wherever you people go, you leave a trail of destruction and death. Today there was a shooting outside of the hotel and I'm sure you're aware of it. What you're not privy to, is that the shooters were planning to kill as many of you and your family members as possible. Yes, they were here to spray bullets to send a message that your heads are wanted on a stick because of some job you did in Los Angeles.

"The Chinese person involved in that détente/drug deal has placed a bounty on your heads in the amount of $1 million per body. The two men that I shot and killed today were here to collect. I say that you and your family members are in extreme danger. If I were you, I would leave Hong Kong in the next few hours."

The Sarge studied Okema's disposition and held his silence for more than a minute. He asked, "Are you truly interested in my brother, Mr. Brown, or are you playing him to play us?"

"Mr. Sergeant Beckmire, I have never had an orgasm from just talking to a man. In the presence of Mr. Brown, I had two and was approaching the third when my concentration was broken by Mr. Jilkes telling my friend that Mr. John Lee was a pig farmer, a thing by the way, that she is thrilled with. Mr. Brown also had me in his room where I slept with no clothes on in an attempt to gauge his true character. I am either unappealing to him or he is truly a magnificent gentleman; he never laid a hand on me. This is particularly important information for me to share because I want to have a permanent place in Mr. Brown's heart, and as such, I find myself protecting him from adversaries that he is not even aware of. At first sight, I wanted to run away with Mr. Brown, oh and by the way Mr. Jilkes and Mr. John Lee, my friends are considering being on the flight you take. We are used to men trying to seduce us rather than appreciate us. Mr. Brown was excitingly good at both. So much for that admiration society and on to matters that are life concerning.

"The Chinese influence is strong here. You must always be aware of their influence on the island. Those people you offended in Los Angeles owe money to the triad and they will stop at nothing to enforce their will. You must protect your children and your women and keep them close at all times because if they capture any of them, you will begin to receive packages with pieces of their anatomy enclosed. These people have no code of honor and they will come for you no matter where you are."

The Sarge looked at her with fire in his eyes, and asked, "How do I take the fight to them?"

"You are good people and they are unbelievably bad individuals who have made themselves ugly by placing an abundance of tattoos on their bodies. Mr. Sergeant Beckmire, taking the fight to them is truly a thing that I would not suggest. My thoughts are that you leave this area immediately and not look back until you are on familiar ground, and even then, I would keep a sharp lookout over those who are important to me."

"Just suppose we want to take them on, where would we find them and how do we get to the head of the snake?" Mallory asked.

"We monitor them because of their drug sales, prostitution rings, and money laundering. I, as a result of being involved in the shooting of two of them, will now have to watch my back. My agency wants me to leave Kowloon in the morning. You don't have the manpower or the skill set to take on these people."

"Just say that we're going on a suicide mission, and we want to send a message. Can you get us to the head of the snake and can you get us the firepower that we need to annihilate that crime family?"

"I can get you as much firepower as you can carry, but it is suicidal to take on the triad."

"Listen, if they were coming here to shoot our women and children, then we want to take the fight to them and show them our mettle. How soon can you get us weapons, transportation and addresses for the head of the gang?"

"Mr. Corporal Mallory, I can't directly be involved in this kind of suicidal mission where foreigners are killed trying to take on the triad."

"We didn't ask you to get involved. We asked you for weapons and directions. Can you assist and how soon?" the Sarge asked.

"I have to speak privately with Mr. Brown and make a few calls as well. Mr. Brown, are you free?"

"Okema, can you call me Richard or Rich and drop the Mr. Brown title?"

"This is a very formal country, Mr. Brown, and until we decide upon which direction we are headed, I must address you and the members of your group formally. Can you walk with me for a few minutes?"

Brown stood up and looked at the Sarge and inquired, "You have any orders for me on this one?"

"We already talked about this situation and I remain steadfast. If she crosses us, you will have to kill her and if she helps us, well, you might have to marry her. We all know that no one from the outside comes between us. Therefore, listen, learn, and decide what impacts us all. You have any input on that, Mallory?"

"Anything I say would simply be overkill. He knows where his bread is buttered."

Okema and Brown left the immediate area of the group and she said, "What they ask of me is not impossible but is definitely a career concluding move for me. I have gotten drawn into this problem, have gained a price on my head for killing two men today, and I am scheduled to leave the island first thing in the morning. I need to know if you think there is a possible future for us. I also realize this entire event has been moving at light speed and it is as confusing for me as, I assume, it is for you. Can you tell me what you want as an outcome between us?"

"This is all happening at warp speed, like you said. All I know is that you have been the one constant on my mind. I can't seem to shake the idea of you or your physical presence. I spent a night watching your voluptuous body calmly move about in my bed as if you were in your own. I saw you smile in your sleep and wondered if you were thinking of me. I mentally made passionate love to you in a most sensuous manner using everything that I have to bring you to unrealized heights and pleasure. You are my enigma, and my body and mind are trying to decode your very essence. I asked myself, "what would be my mindset once I had you and satisfied my ego, as well as, my desire? The answer keeps coming back that I could never completely, in the short term, master those feelings. I think of a relationship with you for the long run and that is where I want to be. The problem we have is that you are a spy, and spies lie for a living. Will I have to live with you each day knowing that you are the master of fabrication, or will I be able to trust the very words that come from your majestic lips?"

"I told you I will give up everything to be with you and I really don't even know you. My trust in you is what stimulates my erratic behavior and it's simply based upon a night that was filled with meaning, not sweet seductive nothings, but honesty and truth. You could have violated me last night and I wouldn't have said a word. I would have hated myself for making a mistake in judgement for thinking you were the person that my dreams had reminded me of and who I had waited for. These things are probably strange when it comes to people who do not share the same faith, but I tell you, Mr. Brown, I'm yours to command. I will be honest and faithful to you if you choose to give these feelings that we both have, an opportunity to mature and thrive."

"Listen, let's continue to discuss this and make sure that we have secure ways to reach each other. I don't think anything will be decided upon this evening, and I don't want to make hasty decisions that may leave me wondering if I made the right decision about someone who may become important to me for the rest of my life."

"Oh, so you feel that I am important?" Okema asked.

"I have said that from the start in ways, of course, that don't compromise me or appear to be a come on for some short-term gains. Yes, you have become, in such a short period of time someone who could occupy my time, space, and heart. I want to be sure before I throw a curve ball that we're playing the same game," Brown indicated.

As the two started back towards the members of the group, Okema said, "I think your people should forget about an offensive move against the triad. They are too many and they are way too ruthless for urban dwellers like you guys."

"You might be underestimating our team. We have seen some rough times and lots of death."

"What are you guys, morticians or something?"

"No, we were once considered, the 'killing machine' in Nam. We were so good that the enemy placed a bounty on our heads. We have cleaned up drug empires, and within the last four months we have probably put to rest approximately two hundred mercs, if not more."

"Wait a minute, is that the same Sergeant Beckmire from Vietnam?"

"The one and only and Corporal Mallory is his sidekick. When someone comes for one of us, we play an enormously powerful and unforgiving termination game. Their problem was that they were going to, indiscriminately shoot up the restaurant while our kids were in there, a thing that we will not or cannot forget. The triad has accomplished getting our attention, especially since they want to send body parts back to us. Let's just say we will shoot everyone remotely related to the triad if a single child is touched, and I mean that literally," Brown announced.

"When you do that dastardly deed, how do you plan on escaping?"

"There may be no escape, but there will be mass casualties and mayhem! That you can count on, my love."

"Oh, I see. Now, I'm important and your love. You keep promoting me. When will I become your everything?"

"When the moon is full, your body is ripe and our minds are clear. Let's tell these guys about your reservations."

Okema spent ten minutes telling the members of the group how ruthless and treacherous the triad is. She cautioned the team about attempting to take them on.

Mallory said, "The events of earlier today were to send a message to our family. We have kids with us and let me tell you this; muff with our children and we will find a way to erase that part of the island where you exist."

"Okema, our children are sacred. Our family is all that we have to celebrate these days, since my son kissed a woman and swallowed a capsule. The members of our group are what I consider extremely lethal, precise and beyond the notion of sadistic. As a point of reference, John Lee gutted a woman from that place that men do stupid things over, up to the base of her brain and then cut her heart out and took a bite out of it. Death is nothing new to us! We're good at what we do and that is eliminating threats against us. When you mention our children, well, all bets are off, and the deal just went nuclear.

"Can you give us any intel about where the head of the snake lives and where his people congregate? If you assist us with that, then we may lighten our load on Brown about a relationship with you and perhaps even champion your cause. We have long recognized that he needs the touch and understanding of a real woman. My sage agrees that you might be the one. Can you tell us where those who would harm our children reside?" the Sarge asked.

"What are you going to fight them with, sticks and stones?" Okema sarcastically inquired.

"If necessary unless you can help us obtain the proper tools to eliminate a problem that the British have here on the island. Listen, we know that China is now officially in control of the island, but you have significant interests here that you want to protect. We can lighten that burden since this triad interferes with a lot of good work that is done here. Give us the details and some weapons and we will make your life here easy, and in doing so, the Chinese government may benefit as well," the Sarge responded.

"I need to take a walk with my consort and discuss a few things before I play my hand, Mr. Sergeant Beckmire. Give me ten minutes."

At the opposite end of the pool and far away from listening ears, Okema said to Brown, "I don't want you to be involved in this event. This will surely spell ruin for your people."

"Are you crazy!? Didn't you hear anything that I said? That's my family and I will die for any one of them."

"Please, don't take offense, I want to make sure that you know I will be left alone if you and your people take on the triad." Okema looked at Brown and uttered, "I will take the first bullet for you, and if I die, then it was meant to be." Okema stared at Brown and said, "I will have my friends deliver weapons to you in two hours and I will also have my people on the periphery to secure your retreat. You must be successful. I will not tolerate failure, Mr. Brown, and therefore, you had better make sure that the plan is solid."

"Okema, why not join me in planning it?"

"Mr. Brown, I am supposed to be on a plane heading to London in the morning, unless you propose to me. Okay, I'm just kidding, but I must be on that plane heading to London, or I will have other issues that you and your group can't help with."

Okema met with the group and began her conversation by begging them to leave the country and regroup in a place they control. She told them that the triad family they were about to take on numbered in the hundreds and were even feared by the police. The Sarge asked, "Hypothetically, if we left this area and went home, would we have to look over our shoulders each day for these guys?"

"They have signed a pledge to terminate your lives and everyone near and dear to you, so yes. They would come to America for you, but there you could set the stage and the place. Here, if things go bad for you, they will capture and butcher each one of you and won't stop until you're all dead, including the women and children."

"Seems to me we have two choices--face them here or wait for them back home. Either way, I don't find any comfort in knowing that they will hurt our women and children and butcher us, as you say. Mallory, what say you?"

"If we get the right equipment, enough intel and exit routes, then I say we take it to them here and show them that they just threatened the wrong people. If the plan is clear, solid, and we have input from the guys, then I say we make Hong Kong a little safer for its citizens. Jilkes and John Lee, what say you?"

Jilkes looked at John Lee and nodded his head. John Lee replied, "My best friend and I don't want anybody hunting us, so we say, let's take it to them there fellows in their own back yard and hang a few of them with shit cut off for public display. I be thinking, if we get enough of them here, they might not want to come across the water for another ass whuppin."

Okema asked, "Are you people insane or are you that good at this kind of work?" The Sarge looked at his people and exclaimed, "We have done some insane shit, but I like to think that we are just that good, even as old as we are!"

Okema received a telephone call from her associate who told her that the boss of the triad wanted to see her head on his desk before morning. Okema, excused herself and engaged in a conversation in her native tongue that no one understood. In essence, her associate told her to leave for the airport immediately and to not go back to her place.

She expressed the gist of the conversation to the group and John Lee stated, "Well, I guess you be going back with us once we have cleaned out the toilet. They be wanting your head, our heads, the women's, and the children's heads. They just be wanting heads, so why we be sitting here? We should go and take their heads tonight."

Jilkes looked at him and agreed, "You are absolutely correct. We need to move on these mothers before they cause us to drop a nuclear weapon on this place."

Okema's phone rang again and it was her associate who said, "I have their central location and the man himself is there having his women wash his fat ass. I need your new friends to meet me at the back of the hotel in ten minutes to unload this stolen cache of weapons and ammunition, all new and untraceable." Okema looked at the Sarge and announced, "Your weapons will be here in ten minutes. Can you have your people meet us at the back of the hotel?"

"Brown, call the guys and have them meet us in the lobby."

At the back of the hotel, the team received weapons neatly packed in boxes with ammo. Bernstein said, "I guess you hit a home run my brother, looks like enough firepower."

"The Sarge is going to brief us shortly on the fall out of that mission in Los Angeles. Seems like that boy is not fairing too well in prison. His cell mate told him, 'this could be easy or this could be hard and he chose hard', which means he got beat up and the rest is history," Brown replied.

As the group received a plethora of weapons and ammunition, they noticed that the two women in the van were the same two that Jilkes and John Lee talked to in the lounge. Somara, John Lee's friend said, "I like pig farming. If you want me to come and visit some time, let me know. Here is my card with my private cell number. Please be careful and call me as soon as this thing is over. I will be near to provide an exit strategy, if necessary."

"Well, I'll be looking to see your pretty face again and I got to tell you, I be thinking about you all the time and missing having that there drink with you. Do you think we can do that drinking thing again real soon?"

"You tell me when and where, and I will be there. How about your friend, is he going to speak to my girlfriend?" Somara asked.

"He be silly and not sure that she like him and all that."

"She adores him and wants to see him again. Maybe when this is over, we can all have a drink and talk about pig farming."

After unloading the weapons, the team received the coordinates to where the head of the triad was, along with the location of several of his family members. The Sarge said, "These people have promised a most gruesome death for all of us, our wives, lovers and more importantly, the children. In upstate New York we gave quarters, there will be no quarters given in this situation. I want this thing to be extremely loud, bloody, and gruesome, so that it sends a message. Jong, I want our women and children on planes and out of here within the next two hours. Do you see a problem with that?"

"The pilots are legal and the planes are ready. I can make assignments in ten minutes and we will be out of here."

"Great! People, this mission is going to be problematic because we don't know shit about Hong Kong. We are walking into the enemy's house with loaded weapons and he is an ignoble son-of-a-bitch who wants the head of Brown's new friend on his desk before morning, not to mention everyone in our family. Now, I know you guys are gentlemen and don't like people who would cut a woman's head off just because he has the power to authorize it. I say we cut his head off and stake it to his bedroom door. This fight can't be avoided, as it will come to us sooner or later. I don't want to wait until later to have this fight. I want to get this shit over with, in a hurry, save on fuel costs and be done with it one way or the other. What say you?" All team members raised their hands which indicated the mission was a go.

###

Bernstein and Brown were placed on front security and Carlos and two of his men were in charge of the rear entrance access. The women were given thirty minutes to gather their belongings and to board transports to the airport. Mallory explained, "Sarge, I have to escort my wife to the airport or she will worry her head off."

"Mallory, we're all going to the airport to see our love ones off safely and then we're going to deal with that vermin. You ought to know that Courtney doesn't listen to me and the only way to convince her that this is necessary, is to place her and Ava in charge of the group. I figure we head to the airport with a weapons vehicle that is near but not on airport property, and when the plane is safely in the air, we come back and get dressed for the dance. From now on we will always have a weapon on us. I think we should keep Jong neutral so that if the shit goes south, he can find a way to buy our freedom. What say you?"

"I say we go with your gut feeling. The only thing that makes me happy about this deal, is that I get to see my wife off safely. I don't have a good feeling about this one, but you know we never have a good feeling because we have to worry about everybody else."

"Have you heard any remarks from John Lee or Jilkes?"

"Funny you should ask. I was thinking that I need their full buy-in because those two guys have the uncanny ability to sniff out disaster. Do you think we should ask them for their input?"

"I would consider that bad karma, a thing that we should try to avoid."

"Bad karma. Have you become, an Asian?"

## CHAPTER THIRTY-SIX

At the airport, those with love ones and children bid them farewell. Marisa asked Larry, "Are you coming with me?"

"I will do whatever you want me to do because I love you more than you can imagine."

"Although, I would love for you to come with us, I want you to stay with your father and make sure that every living member of our group gets on those other planes in the next twenty-four hours, Larry. Don't mess this up or I will not speak to you ever again. Make sure the people we consider family, and who defend us, are protected by your stealth capabilities. More importantly, if you come home with a scratch, I'm going to personally kick your ass. I love you and this entire adventure has made me realize what a helluva man I married. I'm proud of you Larry Holland. I know you will find a way out of this place and come back to me and the twins. Now, kiss me and the kids and tell them you love them and that you will see them real soon."

Courtney watching and listening to their conversation walked over and said, "Son, when she finishes kicking your ass, I'm going to jump in and put a real hurting on you if you don't come back safe and sound with all of those guys in tow. I love you, Larry. Make us proud again."

Courtney then walked over to Beckmire and asked, "Why does Asiram get to stay and the rest of us have to leave?"

"Sweetheart, Asiram has some unique talents that probably do not align with the oath and codes you swore to abide by. She is why we are here, sweetheart, and I need her intel to figure out where we head next. I know it sounds simple, but this is a complex operation. Your safety and that of the children are of utmost importance to me. Just humor me for a bit longer and this thing will be over and done with. I love you and can't wait to make more love to you. I will see you soon."

The plane roared into the night sky. The team began to focus on their life or death situation in a foreign land that depended on information from a person that they didn't know. As they examined the weapons, Brown said, "Sarge, randomly pick a round out of that tub and hand it to me." The Sarge handed him a .45 caliber round and he loaded it into his weapon that had a suppression device on it. He turned and fired the weapon at the wall and to his surprise, a huge hole resulted. The Sarge inquired, "Can you give us an explanation for your actions?"

"Our benefactor is a spy. I'm still not sure of her motivations and I wanted to make sure that we wouldn't be shooting blanks." Okema walked over to Brown and kissed him on the lips and said, "The 'idiot spy' has nothing on you. I would have done the same thing, but I need you to trust me on this one because there is no room for error."

Okema began the briefing by stating that the boss of the triad lived above his very elegant whore house. She explained that it gave him an unlimited supply of newly forced and converted sex slaves. She reported that he lived on the third floor and his legal family lived on the fourth with separate elevators and exits.

Somara said, "I procured some vests and masks for you guys, especially for my friend. Please use them since a lot of this action will probably take place at close range."

Okema announced, "The atmosphere outside of the club, will probably be relaxed because they have a sense of invincibility. They incorrectly think that no one would ever attempt to compromise their domain, especially, not a bunch of Vietnam era players. On occasion, we pull raids in the area just to make sure that the fire safety codes are in place. We never go after them in their own houses. Now, this is an excellent opportunity to break their backs and have them rethink their business model. If this gets really gory, it will make the investigation process more intense and bring in people from the mainland to oversee and provide management and official statements. I recommend that me, Somara and Yeshida provide long range cover from three varying points of reference.

"Once the attack begins at the boss's house, an alarm will go off and people will come out of the woodwork like cockroaches. Those are the ones that we will take care of. Inside the place, there will be heavily armed security. If you make the scene bloody enough it might make the authorities think another triad was involved and make them believe this was a gang fight." Okema laid out a map of the area and showed them where they would be strategically located and what exits they should take if all went wrong.

###

At midnight, the group entered vans provided by Okema and headed for the red-light district. They drove to an alleyway across from the Red Dragon, the headquarters of the triad.

Once at the location, the Sarge decided to have Zanthius and Larry drive the vehicles, after everyone else got out of them. Larry looked around the area and said to Zanthius, "I don't like the looks of those windows facing that joint. It's as though they're a part of the security for the club."

Zanthius looked at them and agreed with Larry who said, "We should inform the Sarge that there may be a threat to our people entering the building from across the street."

Asiram looked up at the windows and said, "That is a lookout post and we need to eliminate it."

When the Sarge walked over to where Larry was, he asked, "What's all the chatter about?" Asiram pointed to the windows as someone flicked a cigarette out of one. Okema admitted, "That was not in our intelligence reports. How do you want to handle it?"

"Larry, I need you, your brother, Carlos and two of his men with you and Asiram covering the retreat. I need that place secured prior to us entering the club. We do not know who the friendlies are, but I suggest that you go in blasting and ask questions later. Do you think you'll need any of my main strike team to assist?"

"I think we can handle this one, Sarge. However, in case this thing is bigger than we think, you guys need to be on standby and be ready to roll. This may be where their little army lives," Larry stated.

"Okay, but don't take on more than you can handle. Two people should always be firing while the others are loading their weapons; continuous fire will disorient them. You guys have ten minutes to breach and secure that place."

"Okema, are there any other details that you may have forgotten?"

"Just one, Mr. Sergeant Beckmire, and that is we need ten minutes to get to our posts."

"Well, that one we can plan for. Be there in ten, and if you guys want to fly to the States, then you can join us on our planes. On my mark---4---3---2---1---mark!" Watches were synchronized. The game was about to begin. Okema and the ladies disappeared into the night blending in with the locals and reached their independent locations, secured their positions, and assembled their weapons.

Zanthius checked his watch and pointed to Larry and counted silently with his fingers from five to one. The two men stumbled into the building as if they were drunks and met no resistance. As they ascended the steps, they could hear chatter and loud music playing. The noise gave them cover. When they entered a room on the second floor, they found men smoking marijuana with weapons plainly in sight. Larry instinctively began to spray the room with gunfire and Zanthius joined in. A total of nine men and three women were slaughtered in less than a minute. The two discarded their magazines and loaded fresh ones into their weapons and chambered a round. On the third floor, the two men were joined by two of Carlos's men who were given the assignment of checking out the other rooms on that floor. As Zanthius opened a door, Larry began to spray the room, and, once again, Zanthius joined the party late. As they made their way to the fourth floor, it was obvious that a fight had started outside of the Red Dragon, and it fortuitously gave the Sarge and his band of merry men an opportunity to enter the building without fanfare. John Lee, Jilkes, Montomie, and

McArthur headed for the entrance and elevator that the boss of the triad used. As they approached the entrance, a guard had left his post to take a leak. Jilkes grabbed him by the neck and John Lee ran his blade through the guys heart. Jilkes exclaimed, "Are you trying to kill me? I felt that blade against my vest."

"I just be trying to make sure he be dead. I would never hurt you. I love you!"

Meanwhile, Larry, Zanthius, and two of Carlos's men entered the room that had a complete view of the Red Dragon. It was occupied by eight men. Larry took out four and Zanthius terminated the other four.

Zanthius asked, "Do you think this is like a video game?"

"In video games, you get to play it as many times as you like. These people will never enjoy their weed again," Larry confirmed.

"That's pretty cold, Larry. How do you justify this when you sleep?"

"Zanthius, they threatened my children and vowed to hurt them. It's easy, my brother, it's easy."

"I guess you have a point there, but I still find it hard to reconcile."

"Any one of these guys would take Asiram and turn her into a freak, with a skill set that you probably wouldn't understand. What would be your reaction?"

"I see where you're going with this."

From the fourth floor window, Larry and Zanthius could see a lot of movement on the street and people being shot from a distance. From afar, Okema, Somara, and Yeshida were filling the streets with dead bodies of members of the triad. Larry saw a van drive down the narrow street and ten people got out of it. He and Zanthius began to take heavy fire. The three ladies refocused their attention. They lent a hand to conclude the onslaught.

It was dark inside the Red Dragon, but it was not difficult to discern where the opposition was hiding. Like cockroaches in the night, the triad members kept the Sarge and his men pinned down with random fire. In the rear of the building, John Lee, Jilkes, McArthur, and Montomie heard the motor of the elevator running and were surprised, when the door opened, to find the boss of the triad hiding behind two of his henchmen. Jilkes summarily executed the guards and John Lee placed his weapon to the head of the triad and marched him to the front of the building where Jong was positioned. Jong told him to tell his men to stop firing and drop their weapons. He told Jong to go fuck himself and that's when John Lee pulled his blade out and severed the man's right ear.

John Lee said to Jong, "Direct him to tell them to give up." Again, the triad boss uttered some guttural words and John Lee drove the knife slowly into his leg, close to his private parts. The man instinctively started yelling to his men to lower their weapons and to leave the club. He yelled his instructions twice and the gunfire subsided. Fourteen men dropped their weapons. Jong told them to cut the damn lights on, and when they did the Sarge, prematurely, stood up and was knocked back down by a gunshot. The team turned a surrender into a massacre, killing all fourteen men.

Jong and Mallory attended to the Sarge who was unconscious and bleeding. Mallory called Larry and told him and Zanthius to drive the vans to the front of the building. Jong called Okema and reported a man was down and they would pick her group up last. Okema told him that they would hold their positions until the van left the area and that the third van should pick them up. Brown asked, "What should we do with this guy that's bleeding all over the place?"

Jong replied, "He's the person who threatened to kill our kids and butcher our women. What do you want to do with him?" Brown looked at Bernstein shrugged his shoulders and fired two rounds into the man's head.

Jong said, "We need his head cut off of his body!"

John Lee announced, "I be taking care of that little detail!"

As Zanthius was driving the van, he inquired, "Who got hit and will they be alright?"

"It's your father, Zanthius. We can't seem to locate the wound, but we had to get the hell out of that place."

"Where the hell is the nearest hospital?" A groggy Beckmire mumbled, "I'm not going to no damn hospital. Boy that hurts like hell. Is everyone okay and accounted for?"

"We're all here except for the three ladies who gave us covering fire. Larry should be getting them in a minute or two. I have to take that vest off you and find out where you're bleeding," Mallory stated.

As Mallory struggled to get the vest off, he saw a small fragment of a round that was protruding from the Sarge's side. He said, "This doesn't count as a wound, this is nothing."

"Nothing my ass. I have to thank Okema and her friends for getting us these vests. I'm damn happy I had it on. Okay, did we get all of the bad guys and what happened to the head of the snake?" the Sarge asked.

"Brown executed him without saying a word, and John Lee decapitated his ass," Mallory indicated.

"My question is, are we done with these guys or did we leave someone alive that can come back to haunt us?" the Sarge inquired.

"I guess we'll have to wait to see what Okema has to say about that. I think she called the police because there are a lot of blinking lights heading down the road," Mallory said.

"Wow, this wound hurts like hell. Okay, let's get our people and try to conclude this activity by tomorrow and get the hell out of here. Zanthius, I want you and Larry to go over the details of gaining access to that room and getting that key. If we're successful, I want to be on our planes heading for Tokyo at 0200 hours. Mallory, I think we might need to keep our eyes open tonight in case we didn't kill all of the cockroaches and they try to return the favor."

"Do you want to have a professional take a look at that wound?"

"Naw, the bullet just broke skin. It hit the vest. Maybe we should start using these things as a matter of protocol. What say you?"

"I say we should use every available tool that will keep us safe."

"Who do you have in mind for the first watch?"

"I want to use Jilkes, John Lee, Chakes, and Gladstone and rotate them out with Brown, Bernstein, McArthur, and Montomie, unless you have other options you want to explore," Mallory indicated.

"Mallory, that's fine. As soon as we get back, let's check with Okema and her people to find out if they were compromised and if they need to stay with us tonight," the Sarge stated.

## CHAPTER THIRTY-SEVEN

At the hotel, the group placed most of the illicit weapons in the van that Larry was driving, but they each kept a pistol and two magazines. Mallory looked at Okema and said, "We can't thank you enough for the help you provided us tonight. I'm not sure how that translates to your security here, but I assume that the people who wanted us are aware of your involvement. It would be good business if you and your crew took up residency here at the hotel."

Okema looked at her challenge, and asked, "Mr. Brown, is it possible that you and I can reside together without any compromising behavior on our part?"

"We did it before, so, I guess we can do it again. Besides, I need the time to talk to you about my feelings and where I would like to go from here."

While they were adoringly looking at each other, Somara and Yeshida were deeply engaged in conversation with Jilkes and John Lee. Everyone appeared to be happy. Okema said, "Somara and Yeshida, I need to talk with you for a moment to discuss our security issues."

As the three women huddled, Okema said, "I don't think it's smart to go back to our places because we don't know if we have been compromised. I recommend we stay here at the hotel and leave directly from here for the airport in the morning."

Somara said, "I have been invited to Tokyo by Mr. John Lee, and Yeshida has been invited by Mr. Jilkes. We believe that we are going to be hunted by those associated with the triad, and our, and your best bet, is to stay with this group. In addition, we're going to resign from the agency, and if invited, take up life in America."

"You barely know these blokes, and you're leaving the agency and going on a junket with them?"

"You didn't know Mr. Brown, but yet you spent the night with him."

"Nothing happened; we talked, slept and that was all, no physical connecting."

"We are not passing judgement but letting you know that we like those Americans. We're willing to take a chance and travel with them." Okema looked at them and inquired, "Why don't you spend the night with them and hold to your traditions and beliefs by telling them that you want to learn about them before you experience the carnal aspects of getting to know them."

"We will, if you pledge to do the same thing," Somara stated.

###

Meanwhile Brown asked Mallory if he could reassign his watch to someone else so that he could spend time with Okema, discussing what's next. Mallory suggested that he invite her on his watch and that way they could multitask. John Lee and Jilkes had already told Yeshida and Somara that they had watch duty and they were welcome to hang with them.

At 0300 hours, Chakes woke up and decided to get dressed and get himself a cup of coffee. Gladstone asked, "Where the hell are you going?"

"I'm going to get me some coffee and call my wife and tell her I love her. I had a terrible nightmare and I think I need to get me some coffee to stay awake for the next few hours."

"Hold on, I'll go with you."

The two men prepared to leave the room and Gladstone said, "Hey, grab your piece and at least two mags. You never know what we'll walk into."

"At this hour, most people are asleep, but if you insist, I'll grab my weapon."

"Tell me about your dream and stop that bullshit about you're going to call your wife. I know that you and Kim are on the outs because of your little play with Melinda. Dude stop trying to play me and don't let her play you either. She may act like an angel, but an angel, she's not."

"How do you know so much about my relationship with my wife. I hope you didn't cross that line!"

"I should slap the life out of you for even suggesting that. If you don't know, I would kill for your dumb ass. Listen, you played, she played, but she played harder than you. Your wife screwed everybody that entered your house to do work--from the cable guy, to the painters, to the electrician, the plumber and she was having a ménage a trois with the fucking guys who cut your grass. Dude, do you really think that your wife wanted you to use condoms because she didn't want to get pregnant? If you bought that one, then you'll buy anything."

"How do you know so much about my wife and my house?"

"You remember that day I was supposed to pick you up and we were supposed to go into town for that early ball game, but you had some other business to take care of? I drove past your place and watched the grass cutters come out of your house, go into the garage, and kiss your wife. I said to myself, 'That woman is screwing the help'. I drove by a week later and saw the plumber push Kim up against the wall and bang the shit out of her. You had secret cameras installed; I know you saw the same shit.

"That menopause shit drives a woman crazy and your wife is a prime example. I gave the cable guy an option that he couldn't refuse and he told me that she was good at what she did on her knees. I tried to keep all of this from you, but you kept passing it off like nothing was happening. Your lack of attention to detail almost got us derailed, and I kept asking myself why are you in denial? I tried to protect you but failed as a friend because I didn't know how to tell you that your wife was getting banged."

"I want to get back to town and kill that bitch."

"Now, that's why I didn't tell you. I knew that would be your response. Listen, you got it on tape. I'm glad that you followed my advice about not letting her know about your various accounts and not letting her have access to your funds. If I were you, I would take $1 million in cash and give it to her. She is afflicted and you need to cut your losses."

"I have one question for you, and it won't make a difference. Did you sleep with my wife?" Gladstone looked afar and then back at Chakes and growled, "Don't speak to me for the rest of the week. You have once again insulted me by thinking such a thought. No woman, especially no nefarious woman, should ever come between the brotherhood and bond that we have. I mean it--don't speak to me for a week."

Chakes and Gladstone were returning to the hotel when Somara asked John Lee, "Those are your guys, right?"

"They be our buddies, but I be wondering who that is following them on the other side of the street?"

"Look at Gladstone's hand. He's directing us. Let's get out of the truck and make a show of strength and see what happens."

As John Lee, Jilkes, Yeshida, and Somara exited the van with weapons in the ready position, the two individuals on the other side of the street turned and walked away. John Lee asked, "Where you boys be coming from?"

"We went to get coffee and picked up those two. I think they were going to try to mug us or some silly shit like that," Gladstone said.

"They don't be looking like the mugging type to me, but you guys should have told someone that you were going out to look for a party."

"You're right, John Lee, but my man here has some problems back home that he and I needed to discuss."

"Yeah, we be understanding them kind of problems because my man has the same kind of thing going on, but he be fine Chakes. However, you know boy, we don't be doing stupid. We let stupid try to do us and then we be smarter."

"You know, John Lee, you are one smart pig farmer. I love you people and thanks for watching our backs. Do you think Mallory or the Sarge need to know about our midnight walk?"

"I didn't know you guys went for a walk. I just be thinking you out watching over all of us. See you at rotation time."

Yeshida looked at Jilkes and asked, "Mr. Jilkes, do you have a family in America?"

"I guess you could say that. I have a wife who is interested in someone else, who by the way is interested in corrupting, not only her soul, but my bank account."

"That does not sound particularly good. What will you do about that situation if I can be so bold to ask?"

"It has been over in feelings for a long time and I guess we just haven't made the decision to formally conclude it. What about you, are you married?"

"Oh no, Mr. Jilkes. I am from a place where my parents pick my job, my house, and my husband. I will not allow myself to be bartered and traded. I am what you might call, a revolutionary. I don't want marriage, I want happiness."

"Wow, that sounds complicated. I mean the part where your parents pick everything for you. Are they happy with your choice of career?"

"They think I'm a secretary in a government agency."

"I wonder what they would think if they saw you in action, and even more so, if they saw you with a black man?"

"Mr. Jilkes, my choices have been mine and they have been few. They would not approve of any man that they did not pick. To be more specific, they would probably turn their backs on me, I would be an outcast, especially, if they knew that I liked a black man."

"You like a black man?"

"Yes, Mr. Jilkes, I like you. I want to stay in touch with you. If your Mr. Sergeant Beckmire was telling the truth, then maybe I could be somewhere near you, but not intrude or corrupt, as you say."

"Are you always this trusting and blinded by emotions?"

"Mr. Jilkes, I am trusting what you have said to me, and by how you have treated me. I'm blinded by a simple matter, and that is, I don't know you and you don't know me, but in the scheme of life, it could be a perfect segue to a lasting friendship. I don't want marriage, as I said, I want happiness. You made me laugh, smile, and relax. My world is full of no laughs, few smiles, and never relaxation. My world is full of commands and demands, as well as expectations. As I shared, I want to smile, laugh, relax, and I think that we can do that with each other. However, it is bad karma to intrude or have an interlude with another's claim."

"You're so funny, and I adore you. In the past forty eight hours we have laughed, smiled, relaxed and taken lives. I'm not sure that is the recipe for a good relationship."

"A good relationship, Mr. Jilkes, begins with a smile, a laugh, and then relaxation. The fact that we, preemptively, terminated lives that would have taken ours, is a sign of a strategic alignment. We both care about those who do good in the world."

"You know, you guys are going to be hunted like we are. I think that you should come to America with us, or with me. The one thing I promise you, is that I will never abandon you and I will always make sure that you have enough money to leave whenever you want. When I return, I plan on announcing the termination of my marriage. Therefore, if you like and if you trust me, we can head south, buy some land, build a house, and then decide if you want to stay. What do you think?"

"Mr. Jilkes, if you will have me and respect me, then I would like to walk down that path with you. It makes me incredibly happy. So, now I can say I smiled, I laughed, I relaxed, and I was made happy. In my world, and please do not ask me for further clarification, you have taken care of one of my 'Hs'. There are three, but you must not ask me about them as it is perceived as bad karma. It is only after I have accomplished the other two that I can freely discuss the importance of reaching that most important goal in life."

"Sounds like we're going to have fun trying to relate to the different cultural aspects. I look forward to understanding more of your culture and customs."

"How did you happen to develop such a strong bond with the team? How did you all come together?"

"We were all drafted and served in Vietnam under the command of Sergeant Beckmire and Corporal Mallory. John

Lee and I did not hit it off at first, one day we got into a fight over his insensitive use of the 'N' word. After that little episode, we became the best of friends. The rest of the guys are like brothers, and I do mean brothers, because everyone of us would take a bullet for each other. We were sent on a lot of one-way missions, and on each occasion, we were able to inflict heavy casualties on the enemy and return safely.

"We were called the 'bow people' because our weapon of choice was the bow and arrow. This reunion is the result of someone trying to kill the Sarge, his wife, and his son's mother. It has snowballed into a big production with a lot of drama, danger, introspection, international intrigue, mystics, and mysticism in the outback, and finally, here we are in Kowloon, and this is where I have met a person of interest to me."

"Wow, Mr. Jilkes, and who might that person be?" Yeshida lowered her head as if bowing and raised it with a smile when Jilkes cuddled her hand and answered, "That person would be you."

Meanwhile, John Lee and Somara were having an intense discussion about farming, with a focus on pigs. He told her where he lived and how he had built houses for the people who worked his land and how they take care of his farm. Somara asked him about his relationship with Mr. Jilkes, and he spent a half hour telling her what a great and decent human being he is and how much he loved the man. Somara shifted gears because she did not want to waste time and said, "You know in the morning, Okema, Yeshida, and I are supposed to be on a flight leaving for the United Kingdom. I think I'm going to miss you when that plane leaves."

"Well, all you have to do is invite me over and I can come anytime. Hell, I ain't got nothing else to do. Now, what would be better is if you came on over to where I be staying and let me show you around, and we kind of get to know each other. You ain't got no husband or nothing like that, do you?"

"I am a single butterfly, Mr. John Lee. Do you have a wife or something like that?"

"Naw, I had one, but them there bad guys killed her and hung her from the upstairs railing in my old house."

"I am so sorry to make light of that. Please accept my apologies."

"No needin for you to apologize. You didn't kill her or my favorite pig."

"I feel sorry for your loss, especially under the circumstances she died."

"Well, she be in heaven now, and I be trying to figure out what to do next, once we be done finished this here work."

"Mr. John Lee, are you afraid of me?"

"Now, what on earth would make you ask a thing like that? I'm not afraid of you, but you gotta know that I don't know any Asian women. You be the first one that I see that I like."

"Mr. John Lee, do you like me? And are you sure, or is it something else you would like to get from me?"

"Now, that there seems like a loaded question, because any way I answer it, it's going to sound strange to you. Now, I be liking you, and I be liking that other thing as well, but I ain't crazy enough to try to get one without the other. So, I just be trying to play it cool, and wait until you decide what road you want to take."

"I guess, Mr. John Lee, that is a sign of respect. What would happen if we were to find ourselves in close quarters--would you attempt to take advantage of me?"

"Now, why on earth would I try to get something that is not mine or it ain't been offered to me? That there be the coward's way to act, and I ain't no coward. I just be a guy who likes you, but ain't going to ask you for nothing or try nothing with you."

"Mr. John Lee, I would like to kiss you again, is that permissible?"

"Well, I want to kiss you too, so I guess it be permissible."

On the other side of the hotel, Brown said to Okema, "So, where are we in our search for an identity? You're a beautiful, sexy woman, and I am an alright looking guy who adores you. You are a spy who will suddenly be on every illicit group's hit list. You can't stay here and, going back to London is not going to offer you much protection either. Now, if you come with me, the world changes even more because everyone in the world seems as though they want us dead. But I want you to come with me, so, what do you want to do?"

"Mr. Brown, if I have to tell you one more time what I would like to do, I may have to reconsider my notion of you, as a highly intelligent person. I want to be with you, but I am not ready for sex, and enslavement yet. I have had two wonderful moments of intense pleasure just from talking with you. Come now! Do you think I do not want to know more about you, and, especially, graduate to a full relationship where sex between you and me is not seen as a conquest but more like the evolution of two interested people? If you will not take me with you, then at least, tell me you will be in London to see me to continue our adventure."

"Okema, my reaction to you is the same each time. I can't get over your beauty and it is bewitching to me. You can't stay here. You'll be hunted down in London and I can't think of a safer haven than in America, with me. Let's make it happen and figure things out as we move forward."

Okema looked at Brown and said, "You will find honor in this decision, as well as contentment, Mr. Brown." She reached over and kissed him on the edge of his mouth and whispered, "You will not be sorry, Mr. Brown."

## CHAPTER THIRTY-EIGHT

In the morning, the Sarge complained about how sore he was but refused to seek professional attention. Mallory looked at the wound and said, "I think we need to head to the hospital because that wound looks as though it's infected."

"I'll be alright."

"No, you won't! Jong call Jilkes and John Lee and tell them that the Sarge has to get to the hospital, right now."

At the hospital, the four men were met by Brown and Okema who secured one entrance and Yeshida and Somara who provided security for the other entrance. Jong listened to the dialogue between the receptionist and Mallory and felt that something was awry. After obtaining intake information from the Sarge, the receptionist made a call from her cell phone and spoke in her native tongue. Jong realized that she made a call to a triad member and indicated to him that an American was there with a gunshot wound. Jong looked at Mallory and John Lee and announced, "We need a doctor. We have to get out of here, now!"

"What's wrong?"

"That receptionist made a call on her cell phone and told someone she has an American here with a gunshot wound. We need to get some supplies, collect a doctor, and take that woman to find out who she called."

"Jilkes, John Lee, go and find me a doctor. Make sure he has a bag with bandages and stuff to treat the Sarge's wound. Come on people, we have been compromised." John Lee started down the hallway and saw a man reading a chart and asked, "Are you a doctor?"

"No, I'm an automotive engineer."

"Okay smartass, this is a real gun and I'll blow your head off if you don't come with me."

John Lee took him into the waiting room where Jong and Jilkes were extracting information from the receptionist. The Sarge looked a little out of it and Mallory said, "We need to have him looked at here, and not on the go."

The doctor, who said he was an automotive engineer, looked at the wound and reported, "He has an infection that should clear up in a couple of days. I can give him a shot and some medicine and that should do the job. I don't want anyone hurt in this hospital. If you promise me that, I will treat him, and you can be on your way in five minutes."

Okema called Somara and exclaimed, "Four guys wearing long coats just drove up here in a hurry! What's your status?"

"We have six weird looking people wearing long coats approaching as well. I think we can handle this, but call Mr. Jilkes and Mr. John Lee. Tell them we have company and that we may need their help at the east entrance."

Jilkes got the call and said, "John Lee, the ladies need our help. People are showing up here with long coats and guns underneath. Mallory, do you need us to stay with you and Jong, or you got this? Why don't you barricade yourselves in a room?"

"Go, we got this, and hurry back, damn it."

Jilkes and John Lee ran through the lobby and John Lee said, "Well, I'll be damned, which way is east?"

"Follow me, Big Country. You can't know everything." As they rapidly walked through the lobby, Jilkes saw Brown who motioned them to the other entrance. As they approached the entrance where the ladies were, John Lee and Jilkes installed silencers on their weapons and the die was cast. As the individuals in long coats started towards the door, the two men followed by the two ladies began to methodically eliminate the threat. As they stepped over the carnage, Jilkes told Yeshida and Somara to get the vehicles and meet them in front in two minutes. Brown and Okema assassinated the four individuals at their end and made their way to the lobby.

The Sarge received his shot and two bottles of pills and was told to never come back. The Sarge told him that he would send the hospital a donation for its troubles.

In the vans, everyone was accounted for as they made their way back to the hotel. They were met by the rest of the team who had no idea what had just transpired minutes ago.

Mallory said, "Those of you who did not make the trip to the hospital will do first duty, starting now. I don't believe this thing is over. We must last until midnight to make sure that Larry and Zanthius get access to that room and then gentlemen, we're out of here."

"How is the Sarge doing?" Whitmore asked.

"Mr. Stubborn Ass got an infection, and therefore, has to be cared for. He'll be alright, but we had a little incident at the hospital and had to leave ten plus dead. Okay, Jilkes, I need you to make us safe and assign people to do security."

After Jilkes made the assignments, Yeshida said to him, "You and Mr. John Lee were extremely courageous and conclusive in your approach to dealing with those gang members. Both of you walked through the door fixated on the targets and began to fire without worrying about any consequences. Are you two always so brazen, focused, and suicidal?"

"I don't agree with how you described us, but our safety and the safety of the team depends on decisive interactions with our foes. No time to call for détente in the middle of a gunfight, the goal is to walk away from it alive. We have done that many times, and we always seem to come out of it alive. I guess the enemy was confused when the two of us showed up and placed life ending rounds into their heads. It's old school for us."

"Mr. Jilkes, how do you explain that old school premise?"

"Old school is the way we did it back in the day. And, back in the day, that is how we did it. You got that?"

"I don't think so, but you must promise to explain to me in detail these metaphors, that you use, that are new to me. I am tired and need to take a nap. Would it be alright if I got a little sleep while you and the others keep watch?"

"Absolutely, but I need you to stay very close to me so that I can watch over both of us."

"I like that idea, Mr. Jilkes."

At 1700 hours, the teams rotated in and out of the security details. Jilkes woke Yeshida up and told her that their duty was over and it was time for some real sleep.

She inquired, "Does that mean I can take a shower and get into a real bed?"

"That's exactly what it means. Do you want to check with the front desk and see if they have any rooms for you and the other ladies?"

Yeshida dropped her head and responded, "I was hoping that I could stay with you without having to obligate myself. I think my friends have come to some understanding that will allow them to stay with Mr. Brown and Mr. John Lee without the expectation of a physical union. I want to stay with you, but I do not think that I am prepared to engage in a casual physical undertaking. Will that be a thing that we can accomplish, Mr. Jilkes?"

"My only intent is to secure you and sleep. I am not of the mindset to engage or attempt to involve you in a meaningless situation. The event that I would like requires a meeting of the minds, and an examination of a potential future. I am interested in you as a woman, but I am not ready to embark on a sexual escapade solely for the sake of enjoyment. Everything is good. We should be able to continue this relationship without rushing into a situation that leaves you or me examining our actions."

## CHAPTER THIRTY-NINE

At exactly 2100 hours, Zanthius and Larry met in the lobby to review their strategy to gain access to Room 234. Jong and Whitmore were assigned close-up security, while Gladstone, and Chakes, as well as, Montomie, and McArthur, were lookouts for the outside area of the hotel. After much discussion, they agreed that the strategy they had developed was the only practical one they could employ to access the room and acquire the alleged key to the Carbon Factor.

At 2345 hours, they positioned themselves near the reception desk and watched the minutes tick off their cell phones. At 2350 hours, Zanthius announced, "I'll be right back, I have to drain some water."

"You wait ten minutes before the time to gain access to the room to realize that you have to take a piss! What's wrong with your timing mechanism?" Larry motioned to Jong and Whitmore to watch the restroom. At 2356 hours, Zanthius left the restroom and headed for the front desk. At 2358 hours, Larry asked the receptionist, "We would like to stay in Room 234, is it available?"

The receptionist replied, "Let me check and see." After twenty or so seconds, she said that the room had a passcode attached to it. Do you know the code?"

At exactly 2359:30 hours, Zanthius said, "Marco, Marco, Marco Polo." The receptionist handed him the key and said,

"You must have shoes outside the door no later than 0010 hours past midnight."

Zanthius took the key and said to Larry, "Come on, let's get up there and place the shoes outside the door. I hope there is no code necessary for the person collecting the shoes."

At exactly 0004 hours past midnight, Zanthius placed shoes in the bin outside of his door.

At exactly, 0010 past, a key on a chain was placed in the bin. Larry opened the door and found the item with a note that read, "your next task will be void of any drama, get it into the right hands and not those who are a certain ring type, like the cult in Washington, DC".

The two men high fived each other and Larry said, "The plan was a little thin at first, but after constant questioning to the void, we were able to pull this puppy out of the water. I never thought I would ever have the chance to use my Kepner Tregoe problem solving skills."

Zanthius called their father and said, "We should be on our way to the airport. I have the key."

The Sarge looked at Mallory and said, "Those two new aged types pulled it off. They have the key, so call our guys and tell them we are out of here in thirty. So much for your HBO, you, and me comment. They live differently than we do. They look at all the dots, not just the connecting ones."

"Whatever! I'm glad to be wrong, but anyway, you know we may have picked up three new passengers."

"Love is a trip, ain't it? You remember when you met Monica and the associated drama? Well, my friend, this is like the love plane--if you don't fall in love on these adventures, then love is not for you."

###

Room 234 was dusty and probably had not been entered since Helga had stayed in it. It was obvious that the hotel honored its confidentiality agreement with her and left things exactly as she had. Zanthius looked about the room and said to Larry, "This seems so virtual to me. As I look around this room, it reminds me of being in her room in Switzerland, where I killed a man. This woman had intercontinental habits and this seems like déjà vu to me." He walked towards the closet, saw three huge cases, and said to Larry, "I wonder what the hell is in these cases."

Larry walked towards the closet and said, "Let's not start opening things that may have her signature on them. After all, she was a spy."

"I'm not sure you saw any of the cases used by the mercs, but these cases mirror them. Call Pops and tell him about our discovery and see what he says."

Larry called the Sarge and told him that they had discovered three large cases that looked like the same ones that the mercs used to house their money. The Sarge told Larry that he would contact Jong and have him come up and sweep the place and make sure that the cases were not rigged.

Ten minutes later Jong, John Lee, and Jilkes were at the door. Jong said, "Damn this place is dusty. Where are the cases?"

"They're in the closet," Larry said.

As Jong looked at the cases, and after ten or so minutes, he said, "This one doesn't appear to be rigged, but I'm not sure about this broken lock." As he examined it closer and noticed that dust was all over it, he said, "I think it's safe, so I'm going to open it." He positioned the case right side up and flipped it open. Everyone in the room was amazed at what was in the suitcase.

John Lee exclaimed, "Now, that there stuff be better than cash money!" The suitcase was full of bearer bonds and stock certificates. It contained stacks and stacks of FB, Amazon, TSLA, TWX, Google, and BABA certificates. As they opened the other two suitcases, their enthusiasm was minimized, those suitcases contained only cash.

Mallory instructed Jong to carefully empty the suitcases and make sure there were no hidden explosive or tracking devices attached to the money. He called the Sarge and gave him all the details.

The Sarge said, "We want to conclude this shit smoothly without any issues. Tell them to wrap up things and be ready to leave the Marco Polo Hotel in a hurry."

At the airport, with all present and accounted for, Jong made seating adjustments to accommodate their three new associates. When Okema, Somara, and Yeshida saw the planes, Okema asked Brown, "Are you guys the owners of these planes?"

"These are the newest additions to the fleet and we have a smaller one. Our trip out here was the maiden voyage of these planes and they handled extremely well."

"How is it possible to own jets as expensive as these are?"

"We have a tremendous portfolio and our investments, as well as our recent adventures, have been accidental income generating events."

As the two jets roared into the morning sky, everyone sat back and took a deep breath. The close to four hour flight would result in much needed rest for the group.

## CHAPTER FORTY

The co-captain of each plane, came on the intercom systems and indicated that they were approximately one hour from landing in Tokyo, Japan. They suggested that all metal objects be placed in the newly created compartments. He also informed Jong that they would not be legal until late in the afternoon because of FAA regulations. Jong suggested that they make sure there was tight security on the planes, as well as have them refueled and ready to go, in case things got out of hand.

Jong looked at Brown and asked, "May I have a private word with you?"

"What's on your mind?"

"Will your new friend, Jilkes', and John Lee's, need additional accommodations, or will they be occupying the same space as you guys?"

"Believe it or not, these relationships are as platonic as can be, with the deep hope of developing into something more sustaining for the three of us. The current arrangements are fine because nothing is going to happen while we are here."

At the Miyako Hotel, everyone was still a little tired from all the action and the flight. It was agreed that there would not be any sightseeing by individuals or groups unless sanctioned by the Sarge. Therefore, most of the group tried to catch-up on missed sleep, but everyone knew that was impossible.

Jong booked dinner reservations for twenty-two at 1830 hours and was able to acquire a private room. At dinner, Zanthius explained how he and Larry decoded the mixed messages from Helga and were certain that once they had their discussions at the bar, the fruits of this deadly adventure would be realized.

The Sarge tapped on his glass with his knife, and after getting everyone's attention, he said, "I want to salute my two sons for figuring out the essence of this outing, as well as providing security for us and eliminating threats in Hong Kong and other places. There is no way I can thank you guys enough for coming to my rescue. As you all know, this has been a very profitable adventure. I might add, as a result of the tenacity of my two sons, our coffers are further enriched by staggering amounts of money. I have no idea about the value of the bearer bonds and stock certificates, but I suspect they are each at the $10,000 level. However, I can count out pure cash and that is an astounding $6 million in newfound money. Let's give the 'idiot spy' and his brother a rousing round of applause."

Everyone was having a wonderful time, including Brown, John Lee and Jilkes, who by accident, hit home runs in landing the three Asian beauties. At 1945 hours, the Sarge asked Mallory to huddle with him. He said, "Our pilots are almost legal, but not quite. I want to pick this shit up and head for the airport and be out of here in a flash. Get Jong's attention and get him over here."

When Jong joined the discussion, he said, "I am Mr. Amazing, and I know exactly what you're going to say to me. You want me to tell the pilots to have the planes ready to leave within the hour, right?"

"Mr. Amazing, you're absolutely wrong. I want them to be ready to leave in two hours because if the information about the Carbon Factor is here, and there is a bottle of Grand Marnier available, I want to make a toast to Helga and drink that bottle dry."

"Well, hell, I was close enough to maintain my title. Sounds like a plan to me."

"Mallory, I want everyone with a knife, a stick, or a broken beer bottle, in case something jumps off."

The group assembled outside of the bar and entered in mass. The bar was dimly lit and had a seating capacity of ten. The tables in the back of the bar were small and designed for two to four people. Larry and Zanthius occupied the center space of the bar. When the bartender inquired about their preference, Jong announced, "Ichigo-Ichiel." The translation meant, "for this time only or essentially, here today and gone tomorrow." In keeping with Japanese traditions where almost everything is done with a ceremonial twist; *kodawari* was the process employed to make the preparation of cocktails unique.

Jong said to the bartender, "Some of my guests may want tradition, but others simply want the bottle in the box that the key my friend has, opens."

Looking as elegant as small bank vaults that were for rent, there were rows of locked boxes housing spirits that guests purchased by the bottle and stored. Upon their return to the hotel, they could drink freely from them and return them to their storage bin when finished.

Zanthius presented the bartender with the key and as the bartender looked at it, he said, "A special friend of mine once controlled this key. Is she resting well?"

Zanthius looked at him and replied, "Yes, she is resting well and comfortably."

The bartender then asked, "What is the vault that you seek?"

Zanthius paused for a moment and confidently said, "The vault number is 234."

The bartender went to the shelf and pulled down ten glasses. Larry advised him that he would need at least twenty two, since Carlos and his men volunteered to secure the perimeter and would be invited in to drink. He proceeded to the box, opened it, and pulled out a full liter of Grand Marnier. He placed the bottle in front of Zanthius and announced, "I would like to add another glass to this toast in the name of my resting friend." The bartender retrieved himself a glass, uncapped the bottle and poured an ounce into each glass and said, "To a wonderful and mysterious woman who has been good to me and my family."

Everyone joined in the tribute to Helga and downed the drinks. The bartender looked at Asiram and said, "She spoke highly of you and left a special package for you or the bearer of the key." He opened his shirt, removed a key that was resting around his neck and opened another box that contained an envelope with a 5 USB data disk. He handed them to Zanthius and said, "My duties and pledge to Helga are completed, except for one thing, I was told to give this to you, young lady, if you were lucky enough to show up." He reached in another box and handed her a sealed envelope.

The Sarge looked at Jong and nodded his head twice. Jong made the call to the pilot-in-command and told him to have those damn birds ready to fly in forty-five minutes. Jong thanked the bartender and told Jilkes, John Lee, and Chakes to leave him a tip. The three men pulled from their fanny packs, $10,000 each, and left the money on the bar. The bartender smiled, bowed, and thanked the group for dropping by.

At the airport Asiram said to Zanthius and Larry, "That was like a funeral repass--drinks, salutes and goodbyes. I am saddened when I think of her and it has been awhile, but tonight the bartender and his passion for tradition actually caused me to shed a tear for her. You know, we had orders to do each other, but we found a way to employ détente and help each other on critical missions. We had totally different modes of operation. She would screw a snake, but I would just cut its head off."

She looked at Zanthius, who said, "For the thousandth time, now, honey, I wasn't in love with you, barely knew you, and you were late showing up for the party. Not my fault but look at us now--married and expecting parents."

Larry said, "This is where I find a seat and get some sleep, because you two are going to keep this up for a while. Good job, my brother, the 'idiot spy'. Good work, not bad at all!"

The jets roared into the night sky and Mallory said to the Sarge, "I like this kind of job when we don't have to conclude someone's life. It's refreshing, don't you think?"

"It's more than refreshing. It is also honorable for guys like us that trade in death."

Jong accessed one of the USB data disks and said to the Sarge, "Wow, this is some powerful shit, if it's correct. I mean I don't fully understand it, but I think in the hands of the right people this shit could make a difference. We should go on high-alert and do what is not expected of us, like picking that airport that is a hundred miles away, and have Clyde bring us as much artillery as he can carry. I'm saying this because I believe this game has really gotten above our pay grade. Some really nasty people are going to be gunning for us, including a certain member of your family. We have got to cut that umbilical cord and be done with this mess and your cousin. He is a major threat because he knows where we live and our habits."

Mallory stared at the Sarge and asked, "You got a plan, and is there anywhere we can send the women and children to be safe? I have to agree with Mr. Amazing. We have gone through hell to get this far. We thought that was Hades. I now believe we were just at the gate."

"I was thinking when we toasted Helga, that Asiram is a spy, Okema, Somara and Yeshida are all spies, and I'm wondering if we have been played or are being played?" the Sarge replied.

"Sarge, you forgot to include the 'idiot spy' in that group," Mallory reminded him.

"I would bet my life on him. Jong have the pilots divert to that other airport and call Clyde and ask him to meet us. I just want to sleep and think of my wife. Good night, gentlemen."

As Mallory and Jong were about to make their way back to their seats, the Sarge yelled, "Wait a minute, guys! Jong can you erase and copy parts of each disk and store them on a separate one?"

"Why do you want to do that, Sarge?"

"I think that if this game has gotten beyond our pay grade, then we need to improvise and develop an insurance policy. When we land, and if we must face a whole new level of negotiations, I prefer to have a couple of aces in the hole. Instead of the formula being on five disks, we add in number six, and make it ours to command. I'm becoming extremely paranoid after listening to Mr. Amazing. Jong, can you copy segments to a disk and then erase them off the originals?"

"I'm sure I can do that, and I must admit it makes sense to me. We need security and this is the best way to gain it. I have one more ominous question--who the hell do we turn this shit over to, and get it out of our hands?" Jong asked.

"That is an excellent question and I will leave that one to Larry, Zanthius, and Asiram, who are, what I consider, new age thinkers, and are aware of the propitious, the inadequate, and the grievous politicians. Let them have a go at it," the Sarge stated.

Jong went back to his seat and began to try to figure out what was significant and what was trivial in terms of trying to guess what to delete and not delete. McArthur watching him attempt to add reason to his decision inquired, "Why not randomly pick a section and send it to your fob? You certainly haven't illustrated any scientific knowledge since I have known you, so make it simple for yourself and hard for them. Randomize the deletions and be done with it."

"That's a great idea because I can't figure this shit out."

The captain dimmed the lights, and for the rest of the trip there was only loud snoring with John Lee and Jilkes leading the chorus. Jilkes's phone rang but he did not hear it or feel it vibrate. It was Mike, trying to call him to alert him of a situation.

CHAPTER FORTY-ONE

One hour out from their destination, the copilot came out of the cabin, woke Jong up, and told him that they were about to begin their descent. Jong stirred and asked, "Are we going to the other airport?"

"Yes, sir!"

"I'll call our man on the ground and see if he can accommodate us with a ride."

Jong placed a call to Clyde and there was no answer. He stumbled up to where the Sarge was sitting and reported, "I called our man on the ground and there was no answer. You want to call Courtney and check the temperature of the place?"

A sleepy Sarge answered, "Okay, let me use your phone." He called Courtney and there was no answer. He then woke Mallory up and asked him to call Monica. Again, no answer. He woke up everyone on the plane that had someone at the ranch and asked them to make calls and there was no answer. He thought for a moment and said to Mallory, "I bet you my right eye, my cousin is holding our people hostage. I bet you!"

"Cousin or not, if he mistreats a single person or even looks twice at Monica, I will gut him like John Lee did Scottie, except from his penis to his brain!" Mallory exclaimed.

"Get in line, my brother. Life as he knows it has now been concluded if he is responsible for this. I'm going to dial his number and see what happens."

The Sarge paused for a moment, took a few deep breaths, dialed Walter's number and there was no answer. He said to Mallory, "Perhaps I was wrong about him on this one."

Approximately thirty seconds later, his phone rang and Walter said, "Sorry, I didn't get to you on the first ring, but I was busy rounding up things. I knew you would eventually call me when there was no answer from the rest of your group. Just let me say this before you start issuing threats to me, everyone is in great shape and they are, shall we say, safe for now.

"I hear you may have finally retrieved the real Carbon Factor. I want to be the first one to congratulate you and your team on a job well done. I suspect we have a couple ways of resolving this issue, and as I look at it, they are simple. The hard way--where you and your guys attempt to storm the ranch and find everyone dead from a massive explosion, because we have rigged the house with a tremendous amount of C-4; probably enough to blow up the entire town. Oh, and by the way, we have placed radio controlled explosive vests on the children to really make a statement. Now, that is the hard way. The easy way is for you and your people to land and bring me the package without any fanfare. We will call it a day. You guys can sit back and enjoy yourselves until our government needs you on another assignment. So, in my estimation, the choice is yours. You can call me back on Courtney's phone in the next twenty minutes to let me know what game you want to play. Bye now! Oh, and yes, we do have people at the airport to greet you and your team."

The Sarge yelled, "Fuck! They're holding our families hostage." Everyone woke up and Zanthius yelled, "What are you talking about?"

"My fucking cousin is holding our people hostage until he gets the package."

"Pops, if he gets the package, we're all certainly dead."

"I know, Son, I know. Damn, how could I have missed this one?"

As Larry looked at the sullen faces and expressions, his mind began to kick into overdrive. He said, "No one knows about me. I'm an enigma. Is there any way once the planes land that I can slip out of the belly of this thing without being noticed? Maybe land without lights?"

"Where are you going with this, Larry?"

"Dad, if I can get off this thing, then I can do a lot of damage by myself. They don't know me and will probably have one thing on their minds; the data disks."

Mallory said, "You know Sarge they never interacted with Carlos or his people either. Perhaps they will be our saving grace."

The Sarge stared into space and Zanthius emphasized, "I like my chances when my brother is involved. I think if we can control the ILS system, then we can find a way to slow this thing down and let him bail out of here."

"What the hell is, 'ILS'?"

"At small airports, like this one, the pilot can control the lights on approach and takeoff. The pilot, in essence, controls the runway."

"Is there any way we can communicate with the other plane that has most of Carlos's people on it?"

"Dad use your cell phone," Zanthius said.

"Oh yeah, I guess I forgot about that instrument."

Jilkes after hearing all of the chatter, looked at his cell phone and noticed that he had missed a call. He opened up his messages and there was someone yelling "it's Mike, and it's a set up—it's a set up"; and then a smacking sound and thud, as if something or someone hit the ground.

The Sarge called the other plane and told Bernstein that he wanted to speak to Carlos. When Carlos got on the phone, the Sarge said, "I need you and one of your men to jump from the plane once it slows down. My cousin is holding our families as hostages."

"What are you saying, Mr. Beckmire?"

"Just what I said. My wife, grandbabies, and everyone else is being held captive by my cousin Walter. He has indicated that he rigged the place with C-4 and has placed suicide vests on the children." As the Sarge was about to say something else, Okema yelled, "They certainly don't know about the three of us!"

The Sarge turned around and said, "You are absolutely correct and they can't imagine the hurt that you three beauties can put on their asses. Okay, Carlos, I need you and one of your people to jump out of that thing when it reaches the end of the runway and makes the turn around to come to the terminal. In the cabin, the pilot will show you how to access a panel, and you will find small weapons and lots of ammo. Load up, my brother, and follow the directions of my son Larry, is that understood?"

"I saw his work and I think he knows what he's doing. We will support him 100%."

Beckmire said, "Okema, Yeshida and Somara will be there as well, there is a lot at stake and I don't want a soul hurt. If they hurt a single person on the ranch, you guys go in with weapons blazing, but try to minimize the collateral damage."

Jong instructed the pilots to set their course for the original airport and gave them specific instructions about what they were to do once the planes landed. Everyone was on board with the plan as it seemed like the best alternative to complete surrender.

On the approach to the airport, the captain called the tower and said that there was an apparent problem with the ILS and they needed to engage it and then disengage it. The captain thought that the control tower was under Walter's influence as well. He also knew that the controller would know how to respond to this statement, if in fact, they were in charge of the runways. The controller said, "We weren't expecting any flights tonight, and therefore, we have technicians testing the efficacy of the system under a controlled environment. I will call them and inform them that planes are in route and we need to abort testing and resume control of our ground systems."

"Excellent idea, since we are low on fuel and there are two planes in formation."

Walter's men in the tower asked, "What the hell is an ILS? Why the hell do they need to control it?"

The controller replied, "It is the system that illuminates the runways and allows pilots to see where they are landing, otherwise, they could run off the runway and create a problem for everyone."

"If this is a trick, I will blow your damn head off! You hear me?"

"Sir call your boss and ask him about the ILS. You can't safely land a plane in the dark with just the lights from the planes."

The two planes lined up and were on final approach to the airport. Larry said, "Listen, people. Once the plane begins to turn around, we have approximately one minute to hit the ground before they have to close the door. Check your gear and make sure you have no loose straps that could possibly snag you."

###

When the first plane landed, the designated group jumped out of the plane. It began to make its turn and the group had less than ten minutes to disappear before the lights of the second plane would illuminate them.

Unfortunately, when Okema jumped and rolled over, her vest got caught on one of the pop up lights. Larry saw it happen and yelled, "Don't move. The second plane is landing and it will expose you. Don't move!"

The captain of the second plane saw her lying on the runway, momentarily shut down its lights, and made a diversionary turn to avoid running over her. As the plane turned around, Larry knew that she was in direct line of the engine blast and didn't want to leave her exposed to the reverse thrust of the engine. He maneuvered himself to where she was and shielded her body from possible burns. As the second plane began to disappear, Larry instructed the group to follow him. At the edge of the airport, they began to make their way towards the long-term parking lot. Once there, they spotted a minivan and decided to commandeer it for their purposes.

###

Larry, who was driving, thought Clyde had been compromised and decided to drive to the property where Scottie attempted to breach the ranch. From a distance, he could see that the ranch was dark and concluded that Walter probably had men stationed there as well. In the interim, Larry had turned off the vehicle lights and was pretty much driving by the light of the full moon. Approximately one mile from the ranch, Carlos said, "Larry, this might be a good point for us to start our trek. Any closer and the sound of the engine might alert those at the ranch that we're coming."

Larry slowed the vehicle down and agreed, "You're probably right. This will give us enough time to determine the numbers at this ranch."

"My question is, how the hell did they get here? There were no large planes at the airport, unless they used the airport a hundred miles away and drove here. Okay, all we have are pistols and we're not sure about the number of people in their force, so, I suggest that we hit them, capture their weapons, vests, and move forward, any comments?"

I think we should proceed in two teams. My lady friends, and you and your man Carlos. They do not know the terrain, and I am going to move really fast, and I need to know that east, and west are covered. We have three sets of communication devices, and that is what we'll use." Larry looked at Okema, and said, "You, Carlos, and I will do the communicating. Let's do this, but I want you guys to give me a ten minute window, and then turn up the heat. I am going to cover two miles of territory, at a relaxed pace, in less than fourteen minutes. I will wait for you people to position yourselves in twenty minutes on my mark. I have no idea what we are facing, and Okema, you, and the other ladies, make sure you don't hurt the good guys-- you met all of them in Kowloon."

Larry purposely knew that he had underestimated his ability to reach the ranch and exceeded his timetable by two minutes. There was no active movement at the ranch, but his intuition told him that all was not well. Approximately a quarter of a mile from the ranch he began to scour the area for night noises and movements. It was apparent to him that he was not alone. His first indication was the smell of some horrendous cologne, and the second was the smell of cigarette smoke in the air. He knew the drill and decided to follow the smell of smoke. Unsurprisingly, it led him to two men who were leisurely resting in chairs on the deck of the house.

As he slithered near their position he decided to wait and give the rest of the team a chance to cover his back. Carlos's man stepped on a huge twig that made a loud echoing sound which alerted the two men. Larry cocked his weapon, seized the moment, and concluded their lives. He quickly descended upon their position, gathered one of their weapons and entered the house, where to his surprise, he found Clyde bound and gagged. Clyde saw Larry and moved his head to the left. Larry opened the door that led to the kitchen and found four of Walter's guys drinking and watching television. Larry watched as they reached for their weapons. He pulled the trigger on the weapon he had confiscated, but it did not fire. Luckily for him, Okema and her ladies provided covering fire and saved Larry from a miserable death. Larry checked the weapon and realized that it was made in Russia and he didn't know how to operate it. He looked at Okema, bowed, and said, "My wife will cherish you and your friends forever; as will I."

"You would have done the same for us, Mr. Larry Holland."

"Can we dispense with the Mr. Larry Holland mess?"

"Soon, Mr. Holland, but not yet, we are still bound by tradition."

Larry bowed again and said, "Collect their earpieces and follow me to Asiram's ranch. Where is Carlos?"

"Mr. Holland there were people camped out in the woods and Mr. Carlos and his man made the decision to veer from our current campaign and terminate that potential threat. They are rearming themselves and should be here within the next few minutes."

"We need to move towards the ranch, but first of all I need to free Clyde. Perhaps, he can give us an idea of the strength of this strike force."

Once free, Clyde told the group how the strangers appeared and caught his group off guard. He told them that he was visiting when two guys showed up with guns in their hands, and before he knew it, there were six of them. Clyde then added, "I don't have a clue as to how many are over at Ms. Asiram's place, but at least you got these bastards. I mean we thought the problem was over and had begun to live like normal ranchers, and bam, here they gather like flies on poop."

"Clyde, this is going to get messy and I need you to watch our backs."

"No, sir. That ain't going to happen! My wife is over there and I be damned if I am going to sit back in some safe place while Lord knows what is happening to her. No sir, I am going with you, or by myself."

"Okay, Clyde, but I need you to do exactly as I say and don't try to improvise. Do I have your word on that?"

"I can live with following orders, but I ain't going to stay behind. So, we best be getting on and determine a plan of attack."

When the small group entered Asiram's property they stumbled upon two locals. One of the guys said, "You had better know the owner's name or we gonna shoot you to hell."

Clyde asked, "Bernie, is that you?"

"Hell, yeah, and we got two of them tied to a tree over there and another one was tied up by somebody else."

"Do you know how many of them are at the ranch?"

"Hell, there has to be twenty-five to thirty-five of those little sons-a-bitches with their fancy weapons and black outfits. A lot of them be speaking some kind of foreign language, but they all be soldiers of some kind."

"Where are the two you have tied to a tree? By the way, I am Larry and this is Okema, Somara, and Yeshida and we have Carlos and his man making their way to the ranch as we speak. Can you take me to your hostages?"

The two men that Bernie and his friend captured were hog tied to a tree so tight they were having difficulty breathing.

Larry said, "I'm going to ask you a few questions and hopefully you will answer me truthfully. Before I begin, I have to show you my resolve in this matter so that you'll understand how important it is to me and my friends that you answer honestly.

Larry unsheathed a blade that he captured from one of his victims and dug it deep into the shoulder of one of the captives and then stabbed the other guy in the leg. Bernie yelled, "Have you lost your damn mind? You can't just stab people without asking them a question."

"If the sight of their blood bothers you, turn your head." The three women never flinched and knew it was an effective manner of interrogation, with the promise of life at the end. Larry peeled the tape back and said to the first guy, "How many are in your group? Have any of the hostages been hurt?"

"You stab me and then ask me a question, are you fucking crazy? I have nothing to say to your dumb ass." Larry looked at him, pulled out his pistol with the silencer, and summarily put a bullet in his head. Everyone looked aghast but said nothing. Larry said to the other guy, "So, what's your story? Are you going to give me information or do I waste another bullet?"

"There are thirty-five of us and most are well-trained and ruthless. I have no intel on casualties because I was stationed out here."

"What's your access code and password?"

"Genehenry 322."

"Is Gene your name?"

"Yes, sir, it is."

"How often do you check in?"

"When in doubt immediately. When in need, on the half hour. When in trouble, X-ray unplugged, is announced."

"Wow, so if I called in with that information right now, I would get a response based upon the circumstances?"

"Yes, sir, that is correct. I would just like to ask one question sir. Is there any amount of information that I can give that will allow me to get back to my family?"

"Why didn't you think about that before you considered the amount of money you would make?"

"This was supposed to be a training exercise and the trainees were paired with veterans. It became suspiciously clear to me that this was something other than a training exercise when we were issued live rounds of ammunition and some of the men spoke another language. It became abundantly clear to me that this was something other than the proposed training when we were told to give up our cell phones and were scanned. We were offered a shitload of money, with the proviso that we do what we're told, and we treat this mission as top secret."

Okema asked Larry if she could have a word with him. She said, "Mr. Larry Holland, we are not accustomed to your methods, but do believe that this one has merit and honor. We petition you to spare his existence."

"I have no intention of hurting this one further, but we must secure him and attend to his superficial wound. Wouldn't want him coming up behind us and hurting someone, now would we?"

CHAPTER FORTY-TWO

At the ranch, Walter welcomed the Sarge and the group and thanked Asiram for sharing her wonderful ranch with him and his men.

He said, "Cousin, this is bigger than God or country and even family. As a matter of fact, this is bigger than my own family. I realize that you are a sentimental human being and would hate to see anything happen to those wonderful grandbabies of yours, or for that matter, any of the other children that are here. So, now that you know that I'm babayega, as well as the dark angel, let's make this simple. You have something that I want and need. I have a whole lot of people that you love and adore. Now, on behalf of the government of the United States of America, I demand that you turn over all collected information relative to the Carbon Factor, and for consideration, I will not harm nor execute any member of this group. If in fact, you do not turn over said property to the government of the United States of America, I will arbitrarily and expeditiously begin to execute the children first by detonating the suicide vests that they are locked into. Now, before you say anything and threaten me with hell, shall I give you a little demonstration of my resolve?"

The Sarge looked around the room with tears in his eyes. He pleaded, "Walter, I will do whatever you like, but please take those things off the children. Please, I beg you, as well as the people who watch over us from our native land."

"Stop it, they're all dead, my Cousin. Dreamtime is full of poor people with good intentions. Where is the information that I want?"

Beckmire yelled, "Jong, give the man what we seized." Jong handed over the disks to Walter who asked, "Okay, Jong, did you attempt to access the information? Tell the truth."

"In all honesty, I did, but it requires codes and an understanding of scientific gibberish."

Walter looked around the room and said, "There seems to be some people missing from the group, Cousin. Where are Ms. De Lombardo's people?"

"They took commercial flights back to Barcelona. They are all family men, and this plan was put into play before we left the States."

Walter took the data disks from Jong and gave them to one of his people who immediately opened a laptop and opened each disk. After two minutes on each disk the man said to Walter, "This makes sense and I think we have what you want. My problem is that I need a couple of days to analyze each disk to make sure there are no gaps in the data, but unless these guys are nuclear scientists, they wouldn't understand it. This stuff is precise and direct. I must say there is some convincing information on these disks."

Walter asked, "Are you sure they haven't been tampered with?"

"Looking at the tracks in the data platform, the numbers are sequential, which leads me to believe that they didn't have time to mess with them."

Walter smiled at him and said, "Good job." In front of everyone, he fired a single bullet into the guy's head and said, "Can't take the chance of you having a photographic memory, now can I?"

The Sarge knew they were running out of time, and therefore, began to plead with Walter to release the women and children. He attempted to reach him from every possible angle including family, Dreamtime and Walkabout, and finally decided to let everyone know that Walter liked being loved by men, but it all fell on deaf ears.

Walter said, "Cousin, I understand everything that you're saying and I'm truly sorry but I have to do what is necessary to protect our government, even if it includes doing dastardly deeds to people I love and respect. This is not my call; I'm only following orders. The person with their hand on the trigger is the only one who matters. I have no say in this decision at all. Listen, when you see me on Dreamtime, you can try to kick my ass and tell the elders what a poor soul I am. By the way, I would not try to leave this building because it is wired to the max and will make what we did to Asiram's farm in Virginia look like a small barn fire. Those are radio-controlled collars on the vests the children are wearing. You have roughly ten minutes to say your goodbyes. Also, any movement towards the doors will immediately activate the devices. On behalf of our government, I thank all of you for the marvelous work that you assisted us with. Thank you and goodbye!"

"At least give me the name of the person holding the trigger so that I can curse him to hell and beyond, especially, if he's willing to kill innocent children and women."

Walter turned around, started to say something, and then continued towards the door. As he opened the door he said, "Cousin, if you must know who has his or her finger on the trigger then I will accommodate your last request, but first you have to guess." Walter looked at his watch and announced, "Sorry, no time for the guessing game. The person holding the detonator, is the next president of the United States of America."

"The senator?" Beckmire asked.

"None other. Nice to have known you, Cousin." The Sarge stood up and made a move towards Walter and was shot twice by his men. As the Sarge hit the floor and began to lose consciousness, he whispered, "In hell, Walter, I will avenge my friends and family."

Jong was the first person to free himself from the wire-ties. He reached under his boot, retrieved a razor blade, and began to cut the others free.

Mallory and Courtney were the first to reach the Sarge. Courtney said, "I love you so much, Ben Beckmire, and if I'm to die, I am happy to die with you but not while you're unconscious. I need you to wake your ass up. I need to dig these bullets out of you and do it without anesthesia."

John Lee, Brown, Jilkes and Bernstein began to cut the vests off the children when Zanthius yelled, "Place the vests in the fireplace." Whitmore, Montomie, Chakes, Gladstone, and McArthur began to stack the vests in the fireplace. Jong screamed, "People, we're out of time!"

CHAPTER FORTY-THREE

Okema said, "I hear the sounds of motorcars being started and driven away."

Mike, who was the other person, tied to a tree and bleeding from the head announced, "If that's the case, then they have placed their ordnances and they are prepared to blow that place sky high."

Larry looked at him and asked, "What are you talking about?"

"This supposedly, abundantly clear but unclear training mission, used live ammo and a shit load of ordnances, including suicide vests that would fit children and in addition, enough C-4 to obliterate a small town. When I deduced that this was all a setup, I called Jilkes and tried to warn him but someone hit me in the head and when I woke up, I was tied to this tree."

Larry exclaimed, "My family is in there along with everyone else that I love. We have to get to the ranch house now."

Okema said to Mike, "I'm going to leave you bound, but I will return to free you."

###

Without having any knowledge of the timetable for what was about to happen at the ranch, Larry began to run towards the lights of the ranch at full speed with multiple weapons. Clyde made a call to the few people who were on watch that night and said, "That body moving through the grass at a fast pace is a friendly, do not fire at him."

As the rest of the group ran far behind Larry, there was a brightness that filled the night sky and a monstrous explosion. It was the ranch house being blown to smithereens with ostensibly, all its occupants inside. The blast blew Larry backwards and the concussion knocked him out.

When Larry minimally regained his senses he asked, "What happened, did something blow up? I remember the sky becoming colorfully bright and that is the last thing I remember."

Okema stared at him with tears streaming down her face and responded, "Mr. Larry Holland, the lights and sounds that you saw and heard were from the place that you were heading. Although it sounded atomic, it lacked the chemical base."

It took Larry a couple of minutes to realize what had happened and what Okema was saying.

After regaining a modicum of his senses, Larry screamed, cursed, and pounded the ground and repeatedly stated, "My wife, kids and everyone that I love are in there." Over and over, Larry shouted the same thing. He stood up and attempted to take off at a fast pace but collapsed after a few seconds. As he stared up at the night stars with his eyes filled with tears, he rolled over and began to crawl towards the remnants of what was Asiram's ranch. He wobbled along without any notion of what had just happened.

It was catastrophic, evil, and Larry called for vengeance against all who participated in this pusillanimous act. A new war had just been declared, confirmed, and the real cacodemon had sworn allegiance to Lucifer with the promise that no quarter would be given to, or considered for anyone who had a hand in the disaster, or remotely knew about it. Larry Holland, aka Larry the Wanderer, parted with his God and swore allegiance to the King of the Dark Side, the Serpent, the Devil, Diablo, and the many other descriptions of the fallen angel. Larry would become the fury, the beast, the wrath, and the vengeance.

the end

also in the 'idiot spy' series

book 1: *hell, hell, the gang's all here!*

This story features an unlikely protagonist, Zanthius De Lombardo—a womanizing, self-absorbed, inconsiderate screwup. After a failed marriage and a suicidal bout with alcoholism, he becomes the HR director for a government-run energy company. He expects nothing more than watercooler gossip and an occasional office romance. Instead, Zanthius discovers that the business trip he is sent on is a one-way journey, and that the company is a front for a consortium of off-book assassins and spies.

Zanthius is caught up in a world of international espionage as governments race to acquire the secret formula for a powerful, cheap dirty bomb. Zanthius's once lackluster life is suddenly filled with spies, unscrupulous politicians, terrorists, secret societies, mercenaries, and the threat of death. His mother reveals information about his father, who, along with eleven of his friends, comes to his rescue. Little by little, the 'idiot spy' becomes the man he is meant to be. But is it enough to save the world?

book 2: *conjured and distorted truths*

In book 2, confrontations continue at every turn emanating from Zanthius swallowing a capsule that allegedly contained information about a dirty bomb. The group is hunted by mercs, double-crossed by a family member, and a loved one is dastardly dispatched of. Their leader sanctions an unspeakable and horrific death for a nemesis. The group's Virginia hideout is obliterated. They venture to a ranch in the Midwest where they root out carpetbaggers preying on ranchers. They begin to prepare for imminent attacks!

The group encounters low-level government employees who freely operate clandestine programs, without checks and balances. They interrupt a so-called détente meeting about an island in the Pacific, but it is actually a drug deal. They recover millions of dollars in payments intended for mercs. The capsule is retrieved and surrendered to devious government officials. Inadvertently, important property is returned to Zanthius that is fundamental to locating the formula.

Available at Amazon and BarnesandNoble.com